BRIGHT
MESSENGERS

GENTRY LEE

BRIGHT
MESSENGERS

BANTAM BOOKS

New York Toronto
London Sydney Auckland

BRIGHT MESSENGERS

A Bantam Spectra Book/June 1995

SPECTRA and the portrayal of a boxed "s" are trademarks of
Bantam Books, a division of Bantam Doubleday Dell
Publishing Group, Inc.

Library of Congress Cataloging-in-Publication Data

Lee, Gentry.
  Bright messengers / Gentry Lee.
    p. cm
  ISBN 0-553-09006-2
  I. Title.
PS3562.E3523B75 1995
813'.54—dc20   95–977
                                                           CIP

Published simultaneously in the United States and Canada

Bantam Books are published by Bantam Books, a division of Bantam
Doubleday Dell Publishing Group, Inc. Its trademark, consisting of the
words "Bantam Books" and the portrayal of a rooster, is Registered in
U.S. Patent and Trademark Office and in other countries. Marca Regis-
trada. Bantam Books, 1540 Broadway, New York, New York 10036.

PRINTED IN THE UNITED STATES OF AMERICA

BVG 10 9 8 7 6 5 4 3 2 1

*To Stacey, my wife
and my best friend*

ACKNOWLEDGMENTS

I would like to thank all those people who offered me support and encouragement during the writing of this novel, especially my wife, Stacey, and my editor, Jennifer Hershey, both of whom listened patiently to me on hundreds of occasions. I would also like to thank Stacey and my seven sons—Cooper, Austin, Robert, Patrick, Michael, Travis, and Hunter—for filling my life with love, joy, and richness, thereby making it easier for me to find the self-discipline necessary to immerse myself in the world of my imagination.

Jennifer Hershey has played a major role in shaping this novel. Her outstanding insights have undoubtedly improved the quality of the book. Also, her unwavering belief in *Bright Messengers* has helped me over more than one tough hurdle.

Thanks also go to Janis Dworkis, an enthusiastic friend whose comments on drafts of the novel were very much appreciated, and to Arlene Jacobs, with whom I discussed some of the medical issues associated with the birth of Maria.

My final thanks go to my mentor and friend, Arthur C. Clarke, whose generosity made it possible for me to begin a writing career rather late in my life.

INTRODUCTION

When I finished reading *Bright Messengers*, I felt like an aviation instructor who had just sent a pupil up into the sky on his first solo flight, and then watched, openmouthed, as he performed a series of dazzling aerobatics. Congratulations, Gentry: I find it hard to believe that it's less than a decade since we started exploring space together.

Could it really only be eight years ago that my agent, the late Scott Meredith, insisted that I meet Gentry Lee? With a full roster of projects, I was hardly eager to be introduced to a new potential collaborator. But then Scott began reeling off credentials: Gentry worked at the Jet Propulsion Laboratory, and he was the chief engineer on Project Galileo. Before that, he was director of science analysis and mission planning for the Mars Viking landers. Because he was so passionate to educate the public about what was going on in space, he formed a television production company with Carl Sagan, and the result was *Cosmos*.

This was a man I had to meet. Gentry boarded a plane for Sri Lanka, and the rest is history. The fruits of our collaboration are the three sequels to *Rendezvous with Rama: Rama II, The Garden of Rama,* and *Rama Revealed*.

During the writing of the final volume, *Rama Revealed*, published in 1994, Gentry created so many fascinating characters and situations that it became clear that we had a whole new universe on our hands that begged further exploration. But I had neither the time nor the energy to help Gentry explore it. So I was more than happy to say "It's all yours." Herewith the result, which I assure you is 99.999 percent Gentry. (I was able to pick a few minor nits.)

Even those unfamiliar with the *Rama* Quartet can fully enjoy *Bright Messengers*, though reading the earlier books will certainly give an added dimension. Perhaps Gentry's most remarkable feat has been to achieve what Somerset Maugham once said was the hardest task in literature—creating a person who is almost wholly good. He has even succeeded in making so devout an agnostic as myself slightly more tolerant of such unalloyed sanctity.

And I hope you will be as anxious as I am to discover what happens in the next volume, *Double Full Moon Night.*

ARTHUR C. CLARKE
Colombo, Sri Lanka
October 20, 1994

THE
GREAT CHAOS

1

The barely audible sound of the watch alarm woke Beatrice instantly. She rose in the predawn dark, slipping quietly out of her sleeping bag on the cot in the back corner of the large tent. Beatrice exhaled, saw her breath in the cold air, and shivered slightly. She rubbed her hands together and pressed them against the soft cotton of the long underwear that doubled as her pajamas.

Beatrice reached under the cot and retrieved the blue robe of her order, as well as the blue headpiece with the small white stripe. A brush and a hairpin were wrapped inside the folded robe. After pulling the brush through her long blond hair several times, Beatrice wrapped her hair in a bun and pinned it tightly against her head. She finished dressing in less than a minute and tiptoed past her sleeping colleagues.

Once outside, Sister Beatrice walked quickly toward the outdoor chapel forty meters away, at the far end of the small island. Across the water was Hyde Park and the large tent city operated by Beatrice and the other priests and priestesses of the Order of St. Michael. The little island in the Serpentine was their private haven.

Beatrice knelt to pray in front of a crucifix and a smaller, wooden carving of a young man being consumed by a great fire both behind and above him. "Dear God," she said as she did each morning, "help me today to do Thy work, to share with others Thy unconditional and ever-lasting love. In the name of St. Michael, who gave us the insight to understand Thy plan."

She crossed herself and moved a few meters to the right of the chapel. On a patch of worn grass Sister Beatrice sat down in the lotus position. In front of her, in the distance, she could see some light reflecting off the tops of a few of the buildings of the city of London. Her breathing became deep and regular. She closed her eyes. As her meditation began Beatrice had a momentary vision of snow piled high in front of her childhood home in Minnesota.

At 0440 the tiny watch alarm sounded again, reminding Sister Beatrice that it was time to end her meditation. She stood up, stretched, and pressed one of the many buttons that encircled her computer watch. Her schedule for the day, February 22, 2141, appeared on the face of the watch. *George Birthington's washday,* she thought with a smile, recalling a humorous junior-high-school incident. She scanned her activities for the next seventeen hours. There was a meeting with London city officials on the Kensington Gardens expansion at 0830, a fund-raiser at 1400 in Esher, a talk at the Wimbledon training site before dinner. . . .

Beatrice noticed the blinking light in the lower right corner of the display. It indicated that she had received a Priority B message during the night. *At least it wasn't Priority A,* she said to herself, remembering two weeks previous when she had been awakened at midnight to deal with a woman resident who had tried to kill her husband.

Beatrice activated the message display on her watch. The Priority B was terse. "Physical conflict between two young men, one Pakistani and one Irish, the Dell sector, 2225 last night. Both injured, one seriously. Hearing scheduled 1100. Sister Beatrice presiding."

I hope this wasn't another racial incident, Beatrice thought with a sigh. She walked across the pontoon bridge that connected the Serpentine to the rest of the park. She wondered why suffering never seemed to increase people's tolerance, as she thought it should. Beatrice remembered one of St. Michael's sermons about fear and prejudice. "Being afraid brings out our worst instincts," he had said. "It's then we should remind ourselves that we're little better than the monkeys, not little lower than the angels."

Each morning, after her meditation, Sister Beatrice walked briskly around the fenced domain in Hyde Park that now housed seven thousand homeless people. The tent community in the center of London had first been established in a small portion of the park almost two years previously. Granting a religious order the right to operate such a community had been an act of desperation by the city. By the late winter of 2139, London, like many of the great cities of the world, had become completely overwhelmed by the consequences of the worldwide depression known as the Great Chaos. Thousands of homeless and unemployed were wandering the streets, creating social instability, spreading communicable diseases, and wreaking havoc on what remained of the economic structure. The cost of providing food, clothing, and shelter to these multitudes was beyond the capability of a city whose tax base had been severely reduced by the economic crisis.

At that time the Order of St. Michael of Siena, a splinter Catholic sect loosely connected with the church in Rome, whose adherents followed the tenets of the young prophet martyred in late June of 2138, approached the officials of London with a proposal to manage a community for the homeless at virtually no cost to the city. All that the Michaelites asked was that the city provide a reasonable location and protection from the bureaucratic inertia of local government. At first the city had laughed at the plan. Eventually, however, under pressure from the city's economic leaders to do something about the alarming number of people loitering on the streets every day and night, the officials reluctantly permitted the Michaelites to establish a small tent city in the center of Hyde Park.

What was initially viewed by the city as both a daring and dangerous experiment was successful beyond everyone's expectations. The sect members, whose ordination vows pledged their lives to the service of their fellow humans, demonstrated both an unbounded energy and an uncommon sense of commitment. After some initial difficulties, the community became organized and produced outstanding results. Not only were many of the formerly homeless fed, clothed, sheltered, and kept off the streets of London, but also the positive attitude of the Michaelites, all working without any pay, fostered a spirit of hope in the homeless city that helped to dispel the miasma of desperation.

In the early months of the endeavor the Michaelites created an on-site employment agency to find work for the residents. Although at first most of the positions were menial and temporary, the jobs restored the self-esteem of many of the individuals living in Hyde Park. The employment agency soon expanded its efforts, cajoling nearby retailers into offering full-time positions to those residents with outstanding temporary work portfolios.

Sister Beatrice had been one of the half-dozen wide-eyed Michaelites who had had the temerity to propose the tent community to the city of London two years earlier. She had subsequently thrown all her energies into its organization, development, and management. It had been Beatrice who had originally suggested the idea for the Children's Sector, as well as many of the other innovations that had been instrumental in the tent city's success. When money had been needed for facilities and expansion, Beatrice had spearheaded the effort to obtain revenue by organizing support groups among the women of the London metropolitan area.

Now, in the cold darkness of the February morning, as she took her daily walk around the perimeter of the tent community, the twenty-four-year-old, blue-eyed Beatrice was acutely aware of the challenges still facing their endeavor. At a knoll on Buck Hill Walk, which bisected the Children's Sector on the western side of the park, Beatrice stopped and looked across an array of a dozen large tents that stretched across a broad field next to the water. *We have over a thousand children on the waiting list,* Beatrice reminded herself, *and nowhere to put them. Most of them are still wandering the streets, sleeping on cardboard in the cold.* She gazed across the pond into Kensington Gardens. Sister Beatrice could clearly envision the alterations necessary to change the region into the new Children's Village. *All we need is the space,* she thought.

When she reached the northeast corner of Hyde Park, near Marble Arch, Beatrice bounded down a long set of steps into a lighted area below the surface. Before this part of the park had been turned over to the Michaelites, what was now their community infirmary had been an underground parking garage.

"Good morning, Sister Beatrice," a doctor in a blue robe said as she walked into the reception room of the facility. He glanced at his watch. "Right on time, as always," he said with a smile.

"How's it going, Brother Bryan?" Beatrice said.

"Not too bad," he replied. "We had a quiet night after the fracas."

He handed her two sheets of computer output. "The Pakistani youth is in stable condition," he said. "The knife cut deeply into his intestines. We transferred him to London Hospital after we stopped the bleeding."

"And the other man?" Beatrice asked.

"Nothing serious," Brother Bryan replied. "The usual lacerations and contusions." He laughed at his own medical jargon. "Cuts and bruises," he said. "We kept him overnight for observation."

Sister Beatrice read the two sheets quickly before looking again at the doctor. "No new cases of tuberculosis?" she asked.

"Nope," Brother Bryan replied. "That's nine days in a row. . . . We're keeping our fingers crossed. It looks as if that intensive screening you ordered is finally paying off."

At the cost of discharging over a hundred and fifty residents, Beatrice recalled grimly. *Most of whom had not yet shown any overt symptoms of the disease.*

"The epidemic in the city shows no sign of abatement," Beatrice now said. "We talked with the London Medical Council again just two days ago. This particular strain is resistant to all the normal medications. The damp and cold only make it worse. We must continue to quarantine all the new residents until their test results are complete and certified."

Beatrice said good-bye to the doctor and walked down a long hallway toward the children's ward. She opened the door quietly. The large room was dark. A dozen beds were on either side of the central aisle.

Beatrice smiled when she heard the girl's voice call her softly in the dark. "You're awake early again today, Elise," she said, taking the nine-year-old's hand.

The little girl smiled. "I've been waiting for you, Sister Beatrice," she said. "There's something I want to ask you."

"What is it?" Beatrice said.

"Are you sure that my face will be okay after the chicken pox goes away?"

"Of course, Elise," Beatrice said. "I had a terrible case of chicken pox when I was five. I had sores all over my face. . . . Now look," she said. She shone the small flashlight from her pocket directly on her face.

"All right," Elise said eventually, "I guess I'll believe you." She reached up and gave Sister Beatrice a hug.

"One more thing," the girl asked a moment later as Beatrice started to leave. "Will you be singing at vespers tonight?"

"Yes," Beatrice answered after a moment's thought.

"Darn," Elise said, shaking her head. "I won't get to hear you, then. They aren't letting me out of here until tomorrow."

After leaving the infirmary, Sister Beatrice walked in a southeasterly direction, along the fence beside Broad Walk. On the other side of the tall fence, in the area of the park nearest to Mayfair, some early risers were exercising on the path known as Lovers' Walk. It was one of the few sections of the park still open to all residents of London.

When she reached Serpentine Road, Beatrice checked her watch and began to walk more quickly. She entered a small fog bank that was hanging close to the ground. Beatrice loved the way the eerie, quiet whiteness of the early-morning fog transformed Hyde Park into an alien place, where trees and statues loomed and disappeared, like ghosts, as she moved along the path.

Ahead of her, on the right, hugging the lower branches of a large tree, Sister Beatrice noticed a strange geometrical pattern in the fog. From a distance, this ring of light looked like a giant doughnut. Its empty center hole was the size of a large person.

Curious, Beatrice slowed her pace, her eyes remaining glued to the peculiar pattern. When she drew closer, and one of the park lights was directly behind the large tree, each of the two thick concentric rings of the doughnut of light became clearly visible. The rings consisted of thousands of remarkable tiny white particles, like droplets, each of which appeared to be sparkling with its own light as it danced slowly about within the confines of the inner and outer rings.

So what can this be? the puzzled Beatrice thought. The unusual bright torus in the fog began to drift in her direction. She took two steps off the pathway, toward the particles dancing and shimmering in the morning fog. The motion of the ring of light abruptly ceased, and for a few moments hung suspended in the air in front of her. Beatrice, temporarily mesmerized by the dancing particles inside the pattern, gathered her courage and stepped closer. Instantly there was a burst of light so bright that she was forced to close her eyes for a fraction of a second.

When Sister Beatrice reopened her eyes, the fog around her was completely normal. She could see no bright patches, and nothing that even remotely resembled a doughnut of sparkling, dancing particles. In her mind's eye Beatrice could still picture the instant she had closed her eyes. It had seemed as if each of the thousands of individual particles in the strange torus had suddenly exploded with light.

Sister Beatrice cast a sweeping glance around the park. She saw nothing out of the ordinary. After a few seconds she resumed her brisk walk toward the pontoon bridge that led to the Michaelite living quarters. Long before she reached the large bathhouse that was adjacent to their sleeping tent, Beatrice was already wondering if perhaps her active imagination had, by itself, conjured up the bright pattern in the fog.

2

"Every night, just before I go to bed," Vivien said from the next shower stall, "I tell myself that I am going to set my alarm and make the early walk with you. I *know* it would be healthy for me. But the same thing always happens. I snuggle into my warm bag and think about how cold and dark it will be at four-forty in the morning. . . ."

"Don't worry about it," Beatrice said above the sound of the running water. "As I've told you many times since we started working together, you really aren't expected to accompany me until after six o'clock. And given your nature, even that represents considerable sacrifice."

"It sure as hell does," Vivien replied, stepping out of her stall and grabbing a pair of towels from the stack. She dried her short hair vigorously. The two women were temporarily alone in the bathhouse. "You know," Vivien said a few seconds later, "in my old life there were times when I didn't even go to bed until after six in the morning. . . . At least not to sleep."

"Don't remind me," Sister Beatrice said, accepting with thanks the towel Vivien extended to her. She smiled warmly at her assistant. "Sometimes I find it incomprehensible that you ever decided to join our order."

Sister Vivien laughed. "To me, it's *still* absolutely mind-boggling. Each morning, when I put on my blue robe and that funny little headpiece, I ask myself, 'Is this really me? Or some other person, not connected in any way to the Victoria Edgeworth raised at Woodrich Manor in Essex?'"

Vivien walked over to the only mirror in the bathroom, just outside the shower area. Beatrice was still drying her hair with the towel when her reflection appeared in the mirror beside Vivien's. Beatrice's pale white body contrasted sharply with the rich copper tone of Vivien's skin. "Hey," Vivien said teasingly, "you look great. If you ever tire of this religious crap, you could do fine."

Sister Beatrice blushed slightly and moved away from the mirror. She was about to say something to Vivien about the bright formation in the fog when the outside door opened and two other Michaelite priestesses came into the bathroom. Beatrice decided to wait for another opportunity.

Vivien picked up a clean pair of long underwear from the bin marked MEDIUM, and a fresh blue robe from an adjacent bin. "I hope I didn't offend you, B," Vivien said as she rejoined her friend. "Sometimes I just can't stand being so damn reverent all the time."

"You're not expected to be perfect," Beatrice said, pulling her own clean robe over her head. She turned and looked seriously at Vivien. "But you *are* expected to remember who and what you are . . . and to set an example for others."

"Uh-oh," Sister Vivien replied, trying to defuse the reproach with humor. "I guess being a priestess of the Order of St. Michael means I can no longer admire the natural beauty of God's creations."

Despite herself, Beatrice smiled and shook her head. "Sometimes, my friend, you are incorrigible."

"Then you've forgiven me?" Vivien asked. Without waiting for a reply, she skipped back over to the mirror to adjust her headpiece. "I wonder," she said out loud, "how my Jamaican mother would wear this hat. The last time I saw her, at Christmas, she said that the robe was fine, but that the hat would have to go. . . ."

The two women walked together across the pontoon bridge into the main park. They were headed for the tent city headquarters located in what had formerly been a police station before the park was turned over to the Michaelites.

"There was a brawl last night over by the Dell," Beatrice said, her mind now completely focused on her duties for the day. "I'm in charge of the hearing, which is set for eleven o'clock this morning. . . . I'm going to stop by the imaging lab now. Why don't you check with Brother Timothy and make sure my presentation for the Kensington Gardens expansion has been properly prepared. . . . I'll meet you at breakfast in fifteen minutes."

Sister Beatrice approached a drab building set back off the pathway. She pulled a tiny, square identification card from its pocket on the back of her computer watch and inserted it into the reader just above the doorknob. The door opened and she entered a large room filled with computers, video monitors, and other electronic equipment. Sister Melissa greeted her and led Beatrice to a small viewing booth.

"Portions of the incident took place within the view of cameras number 407 and 408," Melissa said. "I've queued up the edited sequence for you. . . . Brother Thomas, from security, has studied it carefully and will narrate."

An older man, with a Scottish accent, joined Beatrice in the booth. "The first pictures," he said, pointing at the video monitor, "were taken at 2205. At that time Mr. Bhutto was sitting beside the waterfall at the Dell, talking to Miss Macmillan. You can see the two of them on the screen now. Bhutto is twenty-three and lives in Family Tent B-19 south of the Reservoir. He has been a model resident for six months, with an exceptional volunteer record and some solid work credits. Macmillan, twenty-one, occupies a cot in Tent F-6, restricted to maiden ladies, just north of the Bandstand. She is a recent arrival."

Although there was no audio track, Sister Beatrice could tell from the body language of the two young people that their conversation was friendly. The couple did not touch in the initial segment; however, a few of Miss Macmillan's gestures and expressions were definitely flirtatious.

"There was no significant change in their behavior," Brother Thomas said, "until ten minutes later, when they began to kiss."

The images for the second segment were fuzzy and indistinct. Nevertheless, once she was accustomed to the poorer quality of the picture, Beatrice had no difficulty following the action. When Mr. Bhutto leaned over and tentatively brushed his lips against Miss Macmillan's, the young lady reached up, put her right hand behind Mr. Bhutto's head, and pulled him toward her. They were kissing passionately when the videotape ended.

"One of the imaging components was failing," Sister Melissa explained. "By the time of the next segment, the system had automatically switched to the backup element."

The images that now appeared on the screen were indeed much sharper. The segment, which began three minutes later, showed the couple first kissing while standing up, and then walking into a secluded area a few meters away from the waterfall. When the segment was completed, the final frame was left frozen on the video monitor.

"This will be our last good picture of Mr. Bhutto and Miss Macmillan together," Brother Thomas said. "By the time the camera scans this particular region again, they will be mostly out of sight, over behind that group of trees. . . . Is there anything that you would like to see again?"

"No, not yet," Beatrice answered. "Please continue."

"The sequence will now switch to the other camera. We will see Mr. Malone and his friends, who are just beyond the grove north of the Dell. The time is six minutes later. . . . By the way, Sister Melissa has searched the complete video database with Malone's identification number and has found two additional segments, both last week, that show him conversing briefly with Miss Macmillan in the cafeteria. In the interests of time, we have not included those segments in this edited sequence."

A burly Irish youth, wearing a jacket as red as his cheeks, could be seen on the monitor. He was approaching the pool of water below the waterfall along a wooded pathway. Malone and his two companions, one on either side, were laughing heartily.

"The light in that area is not good," Brother Thomas's narration continued, "so we have enhanced these frames considerably. . . . Notice the dark object sticking out of the pocket of Malone's trousers. That is the handle of the knife that will later be used as a weapon in the fight between the two men."

The monitor was momentarily blank. "Allan Malone is nineteen, originally from Londonderry," Brother Thomas said. "He was arrested once as a juvenile for assault. He and his mother and two younger sisters live in one of the new family tents along Rotten Row, just north of the football pitch."

There was a cough beside her. Beatrice glanced over at Brother Thomas. From his red eyes she guessed that the man had been up all night preparing for this briefing. "Now watch what happens when Malone first sees Bhutto and Macmillan," he said.

As the three young men rounded a corner in the path, their attention was drawn to a scene off to their left. The cocky smile on Malone's face quickly vanished. A moment later his features tightened and his eyes narrowed. Then, again, the screen went blank.

"Unfortunately," Brother Thomas said, "we do not have any more video until a minute and twenty seconds later. . . . Because so much is happening, Sister Melissa has prepared the entire final segment in slow motion."

On the left side of the video picture, Bhutto and Malone were engaged in a furious fistfight. The Irishman's two companions were standing nearby, shouting encouragement to their friend. On the right, a disheveled Miss Macmillan, her skirt and blouse awry, was hastily slipping on her coat. When she was mostly dressed, she ran out of the picture.

The fight continued for another thirty seconds. Each man swung often and wildly, hitting his adversary only occasionally. Neither man had a definite advantage. After Bhutto landed a solid punch on Malone's left temple, the Irish youth pulled the knife out of his pocket and slashed at his opponent's stomach.

The camera recorded the burst of blood from the wound. Mr. Bhutto grabbed his stomach, now swimming in red, and collapsed on the ground. Allan Malone and his two friends hesitated a moment, then turned and ran away.

When the video sequence was finished, Sister Beatrice sat silently in the booth for several seconds. "Is there anything else you need?" Sister Melissa asked.

"No, I don't think so," Beatrice replied, taking the videocube Melissa extended to her. "You both have done your usual thorough job. Thanks very much."

She stood up to leave with a heavy heart. While making a quick mental list of everything she still needed to do before the hearing, Beatrice wondered if it would ever be possible for human beings to live with one another in harmony. Not for a moment did she think again about the unusual experience she had had during her walk in the predawn fog.

Even though it was not yet six-thirty, a queue had already developed in the cafeteria. Because of the cold weather, the residents waited inside, standing in winding ranks like those found in large amusement parks. The blue-robed Michaelites had their own separate line, which was much shorter, but the two lines merged at the entrance to the huge food service area.

Vivien handed Beatrice a tray when they entered the serving line. A large black woman was immediately behind Vivien. She and her two sons, both teenagers, were joking with each other as they made their juice selections. "You see," the woman said to her older boy in a lilting West Indies accent several seconds later, "you *can* be black and be one of the Michael folks. Look at this lady."

Sister Vivien turned on cue and smiled. The older boy stared at her with some surprise. "You're even pretty," he said abruptly. "Why would you want to be some kind of nun?"

The woman lightly cuffed her son. Vivien's eyes sparkled as she tossed her head sideways in her characteristic manner. "Young man," she said with a flourish, "it is a great honor for me to serve God and all of mankind."

The boy looked embarrassed. "Umm, umm," the black woman now said, changing the subject, "look at all the breads."

Spread out on a rectangular table across from them, each variety carefully marked and explained, were eight different kinds of bread. Bread was the primary element of all the meals in the tent city. The wheat from which it was made was raised in the bioengineering green-houses in Kent that were managed by the order. Each kind of wheat was genetically engineered to provide specific amounts of critical vitamins and bulk fiber.

Two young Michaelites, a man and a woman, were on the other side of the table, slicing new loaves of bread and helping to serve the residents. The black woman and her two sons hesitated in front of the profusion of choices.

"You're new here?" Sister Vivien inquired of the black woman after she and her family had filled their plates.

"Yes," the woman answered. "We were staying in an abandoned warehouse, down by the river, when the notices went out last week about the openings. . . . We'd been on the waiting list for almost two months and I was just about ready to give up. It's a shame you had to discharge all those sick folks, but it surely was lucky for us."

Beatrice leaned forward and looked down the line at the woman. "How long did your processing take?" she asked.

"Better part of three days," the woman replied. "The boys ached and moaned about being cooped up in those two tents down beside the water, but I told them it would be worth it. . . . When the docs finally told us that we had been cleared to become residents, I let out a whoop of joy."

The final serving area, after the juices, the breads, and the some-what meager selection of fresh fruits and vegetables, contained all the cereals, both hot and cold. Pitchers of coffee and tea were always set on the long wooden tables where everyone ate. Beatrice took a bowl of boiled rice, into which she blended a mixture of exotic spices. Vivien eventually chose some oatmeal.

"What I would really like this morning," she said quietly to Be-atrice, "are a couple of boiled eggs and a piece of sausage."

"Eating meat is not necessary for your health," Sister Beatrice lec-tured, "and represents an inefficient allocation of global resources. Twelve hundred people can be fed with the amount of grain necessary to sustain and fatten a pig that can only feed one hundred."

"But sausage tastes so good. . . ." Vivien said, her voice trailing off as Beatrice's stern eyes met hers.

Beatrice sat down and began to eat her breakfast in great gulps. Vivien, meanwhile, poured herself a cup of coffee and watched her companion. "What's the matter, B?" she asked after a few seconds. "You seem tense and preoccupied. . . ."

"The presentation needs more work before the meeting," Beatrice said grumpily. "We only have an hour to fix it. Then we have that damn hearing at 1100, so your personal training will be interrupted again. Brother Hugo only assigned the hearing to me because he hates making unpopular decisions. . . . This afternoon I must suck up to all those rich ladies in Esher. . . . There's never enough time to do everything. . . ."

The touch of Vivien's hand on hers stopped Beatrice. "Hey," Vivien said. "Lighten up. Aren't you the one who told me that we can't really do God's work unless we're free from stress?"

Beatrice stopped chewing and looked at her friend. "I guess I am pushing too hard again," she said. "This morning, near the end of my walk, I even had a hallucination. For a moment I thought—"

Sister Beatrice interrupted herself, took a deep breath, and counted slowly to ten. "Thanks, Vivien," she said, squeezing the hands wrapped around hers in the middle of the table.

H alf an hour after breakfast, Sister
Vivien slid her identification card
into the reader, retrieved it a mo-
ment later, and joined Beatrice in the kiosk beside the entrance gate on
Exhibition Road. Brother Martin handed them their cards and returned
the small presentation cylinder to Beatrice.

The two women, wearing blue shawls over their shoulders, passed
through the security area on the Serpentine Bridge. As they were walking
Beatrice slipped the cylinder into one of the pockets of her robe.

"I thought you sent the revised presentation over by televideo,"
Vivien commented.

"I did," Beatrice said. "This is my backup—in case anything went
wrong."

They passed a line of cold, mostly bedraggled people waiting to
apply for admission to the tent city. Several Michaelites were scattered
up and down the line, talking to the people and giving them encouragement. Sister Beatrice stopped briefly to discuss something with one of the
priests.

A few minutes later Beatrice and Vivien crossed Kensington Road into Knightsbridge. A shivering beggar boy, no more than ten years old, approached them on the sidewalk with both his hands outstretched. Beatrice bent down to his level. "What's your name?" she asked softly.

"Wills," the boy answered at length.

"That's a lovely name," Sister Beatrice said. "Now, Wills, if you'll come with us down the road a little, to that café on the corner of Prince Consort Road, we'll see to it that you have some breakfast. But we have no money to give you."

The lad looked nervously around him. "Just a little spare change, mum, if you please?" he said.

Beatrice shook her head firmly, patted the boy on the head, and proceeded down the sidewalk. "It infuriates me the way some people use their children," she said to Vivien. "I bet that boy's father or mother or some other adult relative is lurking in an alcove nearby. . . . The boy won't get to keep anything he manages to scrounge. . . . Just another reminder of why our Children's Village is so important."

They turned left before they reached the Victoria and Albert Museum and walked past a row of apartments. "To Let" and "Drastically Reduced" signs were everywhere. There was very little traffic.

On Brompton Road there were a few cars. It was light now, but the heavy overcast gave a gray tinge to the morning. Half of the stores and shops along the street were empty, victims of the relentless economic depression. In some of the entrances to the abandoned shops, street people had built elaborate cardboard homes. Shopping carts and large trash bags containing their belongings leaned against the empty shop windows.

"We have seven thousand people in Hyde Park," Beatrice said to Vivien. "Another ten thousand are housed in shelters scattered around the city. But the *Times* estimates the total number of homeless in London alone is more than a hundred and twenty thousand. And the number continues to grow—"

"Where are we going?" Vivien asked suddenly when Beatrice turned right onto Beauchamp Place.

"To the new administration building on Walton Street," Sister Beatrice answered. "The meeting was moved there because of the press attendance—" Beatrice stopped. Vivien was no longer beside her.

Vivien was standing several meters behind Beatrice. "This is too weird," she said, shaking her head. Vivien crossed herself and looked up at the heavy clouds above her. "Are you doing this, God," she asked, "to help me make my decision? Or is the wily Sister Beatrice responsible for returning me to the scene of my crimes?"

Beatrice looked at her assistant with a furrowed brow. "It was just over a year ago that we met for the first time," Vivien reminded her, "not fifty meters from this spot. . . . One of my johns was walking me back to the escort bureau. You and Brother Madison were on your knees on this very sidewalk, wrapping blankets around some poor unfortunate wino who had passed out and was freezing to death."

"That was *here*?" Beatrice asked, glancing around her. "I don't seem to remember the exact place."

"We crossed the street to avoid you," Vivien continued, becoming more animated. "I pulled my mink jacket closer around my shoulders. My john, one of those heartless Arabs with lots of money but no other redeeming virtues, actually laughed out loud when the wino slipped out of your arms and fell back to the sidewalk. . . . I watched you bend down and strain to pick the man up again. For just an instant our eyes met. . . . I'll never forget it. I remember feeling absolutely worthless."

Beatrice retraced her steps to stand beside her friend. "I cried that night when I returned to my fancy apartment in Mayfair," Vivien said reflectively. "I didn't know why I was crying, but I couldn't stop." She shook her head. "It was almost four months later when I approached you after your speech at the Marlborough School."

"I'm glad you did," Beatrice said after a short silence.

The two women hugged in the middle of the sidewalk, turning the heads of the passersby. "Come on," Beatrice then said. "We have a presentation to make."

"You were terrific," Vivien said as soon as Beatrice and she had reached Beauchamp Place on their return to Hyde Park. "I can't believe how well you handled everything, including the press. You never cease to amaze me."

"Thanks, Vivien," Sister Beatrice said. "I thought it went very well. But I'm upset with myself for being curt with Ms. Shields near the end of the meeting. That was totally unnecessary."

"But she deserved it," Vivien protested, nearly running to keep up with Beatrice. "The woman's a pompous asshole. If she could, she would have all the homeless thrown into the Thames and forgotten."

"So would many of these people, I'm afraid," Beatrice said. "And they'd probably throw us in with them. They only put up with us because we have a cheap, acceptable solution to an impossible problem."

"Were you surprised that they delayed the actual decision until later this afternoon?" Sister Vivien then asked.

"Not really," Beatrice replied. "Mr. Clarke promised that approval would come this morning, but it was obvious from the questions asked by Ms. Shields and her cohorts that there is still considerable opposition to the expansion. Especially since we won't apologize for admitting so many minority residents. . . . The council needs the closed meeting this afternoon to at least give the impression of deliberation."

The two women passed a yard where a group of schoolchildren
dressed in uniform were playing. "Those are the lucky ones," Beatrice
said emphatically, "and they don't even realize it. I can't wait until we
have decent play facilities for our children."

"So you still think your proposal will be approved?"

"Yes," Sister Beatrice said. "A lot of what was going on in the meeting was nothing more than political posturing. That always happens when
the press is present. Each one of the council members wants to be on
record as having expressed concern about some aspect of the proposal—
in case it turns out to be a disaster. None of them *wants* to give up public
access to Kensington Gardens, but they realize, under the circumstances, that they have no choice. The homeless numbers are simply
overwhelming."

They had reached Brompton Road. Beatrice turned left, continuing
at her rapid pace. "Can we stop for something to drink?" Vivien asked.

Beatrice checked her watch. "No," she said. "We barely have
enough time to prepare for the eleven o'clock hearing."

Sister Vivien scampered up beside her. "B," she said, in between
breaths, "why do you think the reporters asked all those personal questions at the end?"

Beatrice shrugged. "They always do that. Especially the ones from
television. They believe personalities are more interesting than issues or
ideas. . . . By not answering questions about myself, I try to keep the
press focused on our order, and what we are trying to achieve. But it
doesn't always work."

"I can certainly understand," Vivien said, "why they would be interested in you. You are definitely unusual. There are not many women
your age who could have made that presentation to the council this morning."

"It did go well, didn't it?" Sister Beatrice said with a smile. "I had
such a great feeling once I was into the presentation."

They walked along in silence. "Sometimes I wonder," Beatrice said
at length, "what my life would have been like if I had not joined the
order. Would I still be singing? Or might I have decided on some other
career? Maybe I could have been successful in training, or public relations, or even politics. . . . I definitely enjoy speaking in front of
groups. . . ."

Beatrice stopped abruptly. Sister Vivien did not see the troubled
expression on her sponsor's face.

"I think you could have accomplished almost anything, B," Vivien
said. "You have so many talents."

Vivien felt Beatrice's hand on her arm. "I appreciate your compliments, Vivien, I really do," Sister Beatrice said. She started to walk slowly. "But they are as inappropriate as the swollen pride I was just feeling. I had almost convinced myself that I was solely responsible for the Kensington Gardens expansion. That kind of overweening pride is a sin, Vivien, and I need you to help me guard against it. You must remind me when I seem unduly proud that my victories are God's victories, and that I can achieve nothing without His guidance. Otherwise, my use in His service will rapidly diminish."

Sister Vivien didn't know what to say. "I'll try, Beatrice," she managed to reply, "but it'll be hard. I still think you're really special."

4

B rother Darren was waiting for them when Beatrice and Vivien returned to their headquarters in Hyde Park. Darren was the clerk assigned to the eleven o'clock hearing, responsible for organizing all the meeting details. He was agitated.

"I thought you'd never get back," he said, hurriedly pulling the two women into a small office. "We have a big problem."

"Why?" Beatrice asked. "What's going on?"

"The fight last night has mushroomed into a cause célèbre," Brother Darren said excitedly. "Our entire Irish community is in an uproar. In their statements Mr. Malone and his companions said that Mr. Bhutto was in the act of raping Miss Macmillan, and that they only did what was necessary to protect her."

"And what did Miss Macmillan say?" Beatrice asked.

"She was vague about what she and Mr. Bhutto were doing when the fight began," Darren replied, "but there is no suggestion of any sexual assault. Mr. Bhutto's statement, on the other hand, is full of details. He stated that his 'intimate kisses' with Miss Macmillan were interrupted when Mr. Malone, without any provocation, seized him from behind and began striking him in the head. He contends that he only fought back to defend himself. The stories couldn't be more different. The young lady is unfortunately caught in the middle. That's why Brother Hugo—"

Darren stopped himself and looked down at the floor.

"Continue, Brother Darren," Beatrice said impatiently. "You were saying something about Brother Hugo."

"I'm sorry, Sister Beatrice," the young man said. "I know this hearing is completely under your jurisdiction. But when everything started happening this morning and you didn't return my page, I panicked. I needed to talk to someone."

"And what exactly did Brother Hugo say?" Beatrice asked.

"He said that it was your case, but that because of all the hoopla, plus the fact that Bhutto is still in the hospital, a postponement might be indicated."

Beatrice thought for a moment. "And is Miss Macmillan in seclusion, as I requested when we first met this morning?"

"Yes," Darren replied. "She is in one of those tiny private rooms down in the infirmary."

"Thank you, Brother Darren," Beatrice said. "Please carry on with the arrangements for the hearing."

"So there's to be no postponement?"

"Only if I decide in the next thirty-five minutes that one is indicated," Beatrice said with a smile.

Beatrice turned to Vivien as soon as Darren left the room. "I'm going to need your help with this," she said, grabbing both their shawls. "We must hurry. . . . I'll explain what I can on the way."

"I know you're nervous, Fiona, and that the start of the hearing is only half an hour away," Sister Beatrice said to the young woman in a soothing voice, "but I thought it would be easier for you if I asked some of the more difficult questions in private. I would prefer not to embarrass you in front of the others. . . . As I said earlier, we have received dramatically different statements from Mr. Bhutto and Mr. Malone. As the presiding official for the hearing, it is my duty to try to discover what really happened last night."

Fiona Macmillan was obviously uncomfortable. She was sitting on the side of a small bed, looking down at the floor most of the time. When she did glance up, her eyes kept darting around the tiny hospital room. She didn't seem to be listening to what Beatrice was saying.

"I've never been in any kind of trouble before, Sister," Fiona said after Beatrice prompted her to speak. "Until I came to London, I'd lived my whole life in Ayrshire, not far from the sea, with my parents and my brothers. My dad told me I'd have a better chance of finding a job in a big city. All the shops back home have closed, so there's no work for a girl."

"You're not in any trouble, Fiona," Sister Beatrice said. "I just want to ask you a few questions about your statement."

Fear appeared in Fiona's blue eyes. "I told the truth, Sister," she said, fidgeting nervously. "I swear I did." She glanced back and forth from Vivien to Beatrice. "Could you tell me, please," she said, "is Raza all right?"

"He's recovering fine," Beatrice said. "Fiona," she added after a brief pause, "we know that you told the truth. But you may have omitted some things. For example, you did not say exactly what you and Mr. Bhutto were doing at the moment that you were discovered by Mr. Malone and his associates."

"Exactly what we were doing?" Fiona repeated, as if she hadn't understood the question.

"Yes," Beatrice said at length. "Were you kissing," she continued slowly, "or were you maybe petting, or having intercourse . . . ? I'm sorry to ask you these explicit questions, Fiona, but I assure you the information is important."

The red-haired girl again stared silently at the floor. "Sister," Fiona suddenly said entreatingly, looking up at Beatrice, "I've been cooped up in here all morning. Could I please have a cigarette?"

Beatrice was momentarily taken aback. Before she could say anything, Vivien handed the young woman a cigarette and a lighter that she had pulled out of the pocket of her blue robe. Then Vivien walked over behind Fiona and opened the only window in the room.

"Thanks," the Scottish girl said, inhaling deeply and blowing the smoke toward the window. She smiled at Beatrice and Vivien. "You really want *all* the details, Sister?" Fiona said, now clearly more relaxed.

Beatrice nodded.

"All right," Fiona said, looking down again. "I guess I can do it." She took another drag from her cigarette. "Well," she began after a long pause, "we *were* kissing and petting, but we weren't having sex, at least not yet."

Fiona smiled nervously. "Raza was already big as a horse. I could feel him against my leg while he was kissing me on the ground. . . . Are these the kind of details you want?"

Sister Vivien encouraged her. "You're doing great, Fiona," she said. "Please continue."

"I had just started to slip my pants off," the Scottish girl said, "when Allan grabbed Raza from behind and hit him in the face. I screamed—"

"Had Mr. Bhutto forced himself upon you in any way?" Beatrice interrupted.

"No, Sister," Fiona replied. "Not at all. . . . It was even my idea to go over behind the trees. You know, there's so many people in this place—don't get me wrong, I really love it here—I thought we'd have a better chance to be alone."

"You've been very helpful, Fiona," Beatrice said after another short silence. "I think we have enough information now. . . . With your permission, either Vivien or I will summarize at the hearing what you have just told us. We don't want you to have to go through all this again. . . . I have only one more question. Could you clarify for me how you knew Allan Malone? Was he a friend of yours?"

"Oh, no," Fiona answered. "I barely knew him. He had tried to flirt with me a couple of times in the cafeteria, but I never gave him any encouragement."

"Thanks again, Fiona," Vivien said, gathering up the pair of shawls that Beatrice and she had draped over a chair. "We'll see you at the hearing in twenty minutes."

Vivien had to break into a trot several times to keep up with Beatrice as they walked back to the community headquarters.

"Did you believe her?" Beatrice asked at one point.

"Absolutely," said Vivien.

"So did I," Beatrice said, stopping for a second. "She strikes me as a straightforward country girl. . . . I must admit that I'm relieved. This hearing is not going to be as difficult as I had feared."

Beatrice smiled for the first time in over an hour. "Uh," said Vivien quickly, "about the cigarettes . . ."

"I know," said Beatrice, starting to walk again. "You've never really quit. I don't like it, but I guess I'll have to accept it. And I expect you to be discreet."

"Always," said Vivien, touching the cigarettes in her pocket.

When they reached the community headquarters, Beatrice stopped and glanced at her watch. "I'm going to stop by the imaging lab and pick up some extra evidence," she said to Vivien. "Just in case I need it. Will you please check with Brother Darren and make certain everything is ready for the hearing?"

Vivien nodded and Beatrice dashed off toward the lab. By the time Vivien arrived at the room where the hearing was going to be held, a large group of people had already gathered. They were milling around in the corridors. Brother Darren was scurrying about, looking very nervous. He relaxed considerably when Vivien showed up and started helping him with the crowd.

Beatrice arrived just minutes before the hearing began. Vivien explained to her that the Malone family had requested an extra allocation of seats for friends who wanted to provide moral support for Allan. After making certain that Raza Bhutto's family and friends were properly represented, Beatrice granted the request by the Malones.

"For those of you who are unfamiliar with one of these hearings," Sister Beatrice said to start the proceedings, "let me explain briefly what will happen here today. Whenever an incident occurs in our community that is considered to be unacceptable by our order, we convene a hearing to investigate it. We encourage everyone who took part in the incident to offer testimony. What we are trying to determine is the truth, nothing more or less.

"Based on what is learned at the hearing, the presiding priest or priestess may take no action. He or she may, however, issue reprimands, or even define constructive penalties for those deemed responsible for the unacceptable actions or activities. In the unusual instance where a resident has done something diametrically opposed to the purposes and objectives of the community, the offending resident may be summarily discharged as a result of one of these hearings. Sometimes, in the most serious cases, this discharge is made with prejudice, and both the individual and the evidence in the case are turned over to the London police."

Beatrice glanced around the room. "Following the opening prayer," she then continued, "we will listen to the statements by the participants. I remind you that each witness has sworn to tell the truth. Since Mr. Raza Bhutto is not strong enough to attend this hearing, he will participate by televideo. He has asked permission for his father to read his statement, and I have agreed.

"When all the statements are finished, we will watch together an edited video sequence showing whatever information relevant to this incident was recorded by the community cameras. I may ask additional questions of the participants, both before and after the video. At the end of the official hearing, each of the principals will be allowed to have one person say something on his or her behalf. Then I will retire with Brother Husayn and Sister Alexis, who are sitting here beside me, to discuss what we have seen and heard. Ordinarily judgments are rendered in fifteen minutes or less. . . ."

The hearing went smoothly. None of the statements was significantly changed from what had been received the night before. Early in the hearing, Beatrice summarized what Fiona had told them in the infirmary, having the young lady verify, with a simple no, that Raza Bhutto had not at any time sexually assaulted her.

After the videos incriminating Allan Malone were shown, Mrs. Malone made a long, passionate plea for clemency for her son. She pointed out repeatedly that the young man was both British and a Catholic, and had not been involved in any other unacceptable activity during his four months in the community. Mrs. Malone promised that she would keep a close watch on her son and she begged Sister Beatrice and the other two Michaelites to allow Allan to remain in Hyde Park.

The decision was reached quickly. When Beatrice returned to the room and announced that Mr. Allan Malone was going to be discharged from the community, with prejudice, his mother started to cry.

"Dear Ms. Malone," Beatrice said in closing the hearing, "I offer you my sympathy. Although I have no children myself, I can well imagine how painful it must be for a mother to face being separated from one of her children."

She paused for a few seconds. "Nevertheless, Ms. Malone, I believe that some of the comments you made during the hearing, especially those that suggested a British Catholic might be due a different kind of consideration than a resident with a foreign background, must not go unchallenged.

"Our order is trying to change the way people think and act. St. Michael taught that each and every human being is equal in the eyes of God. It does not matter, he said, what higher power an individual worships, or even if he or she does not believe anything at all. Every one of us is an integral part of God's plan, whether we know it or not. And we are all, St. Michael said, single cells in one giant, connected organism that makes up the entire human race.

"The day will come, St. Michael taught, when each of us, each cell in that giant organism, will understand its interdependence on all the other individual cells. That is what our entire order is about, Ms. Malone. We are trying to prepare humanity for that glorious day when there will be harmony among us, and the final evolution will be complete."

5

They barely made it to the train. Beatrice and Vivien walked out the Westbourne Gate only ten minutes before departure time. They hurried through the streets of London toward Paddington Station, slowing only when Beatrice was ready for another bite of her cucumber sandwich. The two Michaelite women had not been in their seats for more than thirty seconds when the train started to pull away from the platform.

"That was close," Beatrice said.

"You cannot eat like that," Vivien scolded. "It's not good for you."

"What choice did I have?" Beatrice replied. "I couldn't very well tell Brother Hugo that I didn't have time to talk to the mayor of Manchester."

"Yes, you could have," Vivien said. She shook her head. "B, it's probably not my place, but if you don't learn to say no, you're going to be an old woman before you're thirty. Look at you, it's only one-thirty in the afternoon and you're already exhausted."

"You're right, Vivien," Sister Beatrice said after a few seconds. "I am tired. It's been a hectic day. . . . I know I should slow down. But I worry that if I don't do things myself—"

"Then they won't be done right," Vivien said, finishing the sentence. "I've heard that argument before." She took Beatrice's hand in hers. "Why don't you try to sleep?" she said softly. "We have forty minutes until we reach Esher."

They rode in silence for several minutes. London's economic decay was evident from the window of the train. Most of the industrial buildings near Paddington had been abandoned and were boarded up. Those that were still occupied by businesses were in dire need of paint and repair. Makeshift shacks had been constructed by the urban homeless on many of the vacant lots. On one small school playing field two dozen scruffy people stood idly in a circle around a fire built from trash.

Vivien turned on the entertainment console in her foldout table. She sorted quickly through the menus, and then selected a video of a current pop singer, a strange-looking boy who had painted his face three different colors. He sang a loud, pulsating song calling for all the world's old people to get out of the way of the "new wave."

The train had reached cruising speed before Beatrice fell asleep. Vivien finished watching the news on her tiny console and then stood up. She walked forward through the train until she found the smoking coach. Sitting down in an empty seat against the window, Vivien smoked her cigarette slowly, pensively, without looking around.

Meanwhile Beatrice was dreaming. She could hear her father calling her. "Kristin, wake up, darling," he said.

She opened her eyes slowly. Her father was standing in the doorway, dressed in a blue suit. He was so tall. "Good morning, Daddy," she said with a smile.

Her father crossed the room and kissed her on the forehead. "It's snowing again, Princess," he said. "Make sure you dress for the weather." Her father's eyes were bright and loving. He smelled like the forest.

In the dream she put on her blue robe and headpiece and climbed down the long staircase in the center of her house. Her mother and father were already eating breakfast in the nook. They did not notice her clothing. Her mother smiled pleasantly and went into the kitchen.

"Kristin," her father said, glancing up from his newspaper, "you know we are very proud of you. Your grades are excellent. Your mother and I only want you to be happy."

His face was serious. Beatrice felt a burst of anxiety. "But we do not understand why you aren't singing anymore. Mr. Herbert called again last night. He said that a voice like yours only comes along once in a century.

He said that the senior play was specifically selected to showcase your talents. . . ."

Yes, Father, she thought in the dream. *I will do what you ask. I will be your princess again.*

The snowflakes were large and wet. They landed on her cheeks and mouth as she stood under the streetlight at the bus stop. She was wearing a ski parka over her blue robe. Howie came up beside her just as the big orange bus, marked EDINA PUBLIC SCHOOLS in large black letters, turned onto their street.

"Hi there, Kristin," he said shyly. Howie was a year younger than she. He had had a crush on her since grade school. "You were sure great last night," he said. "Everybody said so, even my mom and my dad."

"Thanks, Howie," the girl in the dream said.

The school bus stopped and Beatrice climbed up the steps. St. Michael, wearing his blue robe, was driving. He smiled warmly at her with his calm, magnificent blue eyes. "Good morning," he said. "Are you ready for another busy day?"

She was confused. Beatrice turned around, but Howie was no longer behind her. The bus was full of young people, both men and women, all in blue robes. *"Ky-ri-e Elei-son,"* they were singing. "Take a seat," Michael said gently. "We have much to accomplish."

Beatrice sat next to a window in the front. The glass was frosted over, but after she rubbed it she could see the snow falling outside. It was not dark anymore. At the next stop, Ms. Shields boarded the bus, wearing her blue robe.

Michael was touching her forearm. "I must go now," he said. He moved away from her, down the first step toward the door, and put on a jacket.

"No, don't," Beatrice said, feeling an unknown terror.

He smiled. "You'll be all right," he said. "Just remember everything we have discussed." The bus door opened and he walked out into the snow.

The driver's seat was empty, but the motor was still running. Beatrice moved over to the aisle and looked back into the bus. Her father and mother, now wearing blue robes also, were sitting directly behind her. Most of the rest of the passengers were children.

The steering wheel was huge. Her arms could not fit all the way around it. Beatrice took a deep breath and put the bus in a driving gear. The singing began again behind her. *"Ky-ri-e Elei-son, Ky-ri-e Elei-son."* She relaxed somewhat, and joined in the singing.

Ice began to form on the windshield. Each time she cleaned it with the wipers, the ice returned. Beatrice leaned over so that she could see through a clear spot in the glass. The spot was becoming smaller and smaller. Suddenly she saw, through the thick snow, two cars completely stopped in the middle of the road in front of her. She panicked, hitting the brakes hard. The bus yanked sideways and began to skid. It was rolling over.

"No," Sister Beatrice shouted vehemently. "No." She shook her head and opened her eyes. In the twilight zone between waking and sleeping she was momentarily disoriented.

Where am I? she thought, glancing around the almost empty coach. A businessman in his forties, across the aisle, was looking at her curiously. Beatrice managed a pleasant smile, took a deep breath, and gazed out at the English countryside.

"We think that what you are doing is wonderful," Ms. Washburn said. She moved her husband's golf bag and shoes around so that Vivien could place the charts in the trunk without bending them. "I was just saying to Brad this morning that what you have accomplished in Hyde Park is truly extraordinary."

The car was large and comfortable. Beatrice sat beside Ms. Washburn in the front seat. Vivien sat alone in the back. "Well," the woman said as she pulled out of Esher station, "how was the train ride?"

"All right," Beatrice said pleasantly. "It was not crowded at all."

"It hardly ever is anymore," Ms. Washburn said. "Brad is worried that service is going to be cut back again, what with the deficits and all. We'll be practically marooned out here then."

Sister Vivien stared out the car window as Beatrice and Ms. Washburn discussed the agenda for the meeting. The tony suburb of Esher looked mostly unaffected by the worst depression in modern history. Only a discerning eye could tell that the gardens were not perfect anymore, that the trees were no longer properly trimmed, and that the cars were now, on average, several years older than they had been a decade earlier. Here and there a foreclosure sign had been posted on one of the sprawling estates beneath the tall trees, but the lettering on the signs was small and unobtrusive.

They pulled into a driveway and approached a three-car garage. "Another topic that is on everyone's mind—because we see so much about it on television—" Ms. Washburn was saying, "is security. The pictures from the American cities are really frightening. I know it's a little out of your bailiwick, but it would help if somewhere in your talk today you would remind the ladies that in England we don't have heavily armed youth gangs who might band with the homeless to take over whole suburbs. . . ."

The sun had come out. By two-thirty the temperature was a comparatively pleasant twelve degrees Celsius. Beatrice and Ms. Washburn decided that the group of thirty or so women, mostly in their fifties and sixties, would be less crowded if Beatrice gave her presentation out on the back lawn.

Vivien set the charts up on the easel. After Sister Beatrice explained both the current status of the Hyde Park community and the prospects for expansion, she raised the financial issues. "We are requesting two different kinds of funds from our loyal supporters," she said. "In the first category are what we call sustaining revenues. These are the monies required to administer and operate the Hyde Park complex and our five other smaller homeless sites scattered around the greater London area. Since we have been fortunate in the last six months, both in obtaining new sources of revenue and in achieving greater operating efficiency, our request for sustaining revenues from each group is twenty-three percent less than it was six months ago."

Beatrice nodded to Vivien to flip to the next chart. "To achieve the Kensington Gardens expansion, however, assuming the city grants us permission to use the space, we need just under one million pounds of new money. We have set a goal of raising half that money from totally new sources. That is a very tough target, but we believe we can accomplish it by offering inducements—we might name the children's school after a benefactor, for example. The other half of this new money we hope to raise from our faithful friends from the past. Scaling strictly on the basis of past contributions, the total we are requesting from your group is shown here."

Beatrice paused, her eyes searching out the eyes of every member of the audience. "I can see you doing the arithmetic," she continued, her voice rising slightly in pitch. "Yes, we are asking for thirty-one percent more than you contributed six months ago. . . . That's a lot of money, I agree. But please spend a moment thinking about what will be achieved with that money. Together we will be creating a special haven for poor, downtrodden children, most of whom have never known what it is like to be free from want. They will have a home where they will be fed, clothed, sheltered, and loved. They will have a place where they can grow and learn, where their dreams can soar, where their imaginations can create. . . ."

When Beatrice was finished, she smiled briefly at the Esher ladies, and then knelt on the grass with her hands clasped together in prayer.

"Dear God," she said, "help us all to understand how interconnected we are, one to another. Help us also to remember what it was like to be an innocent child, and to rejoice that we have an opportunity to free some of today's children from the desperation of abject poverty. Bless the charity and love in the hearts of all those gathered here. Bless our work in Thy name as we recall the words of Thy son Jesus: 'Inasmuch as ye have done it unto the least of these, my brethren, ye have done it unto me.' In St. Michael's name. Amen."

"Have you known her long?" the white-haired woman standing next to Vivien asked.

"I've been her assistant for a little over four months," Vivien replied after she finished chewing the cake in her mouth. It was delicious.

"She seems so young," a woman on the other side said. "I bet she's not even thirty yet."

Vivien sipped her tea and made no comment. "What made you decide to become a nun?" the first lady asked. "Or should I refer to you as a priestess?"

"We are priestesses," Vivien said. "Actually I am still a novice. I have not yet been ordained. . . . And I joined because I wanted to do something for others."

"You don't sound like an American," the second lady said. "Where are you from?"

"From Essex," Vivien replied with a smile. "My father is an English country gentleman. My mother is Jamaican."

"Hmm," the lady remarked. "That's an interesting combination."

Across the room, Beatrice was surrounded and being peppered with questions. Vivien decided to go to her rescue. She stopped by the table, prepared a cup of tea for Beatrice, and picked up a pair of scones.

"Excuse me, ladies," Vivien said, moving through the crowd. "Sister Beatrice also needs some refreshment."

"Thanks," Beatrice said gratefully, immediately taking a long sip from the teacup Vivien had brought her.

"I'm sorry, Sister Beatrice," Ms. Washburn apologized from beside her guest, "I hadn't realized. . . ."

"It's all right, Ms. Washburn," Beatrice said.

"But our problem is altogether different from America's," a stern-looking lady said, continuing the conversation that Vivien's arrival had interrupted. "Everyone there is either rich or poor. Because they have such a small middle class and very few government-provided services, the disparities are more obvious. Plus, even with their new laws, it's still absurdly easy for any idiot to obtain a gun."

"Did you see Reginald Townsend on the telly last night?" a Ms. Blake said excitedly. "He did an interview with that black gang leader in

Ohio, the fellow who calls himself Six-Six-Six. The man kept waving his machine gun around during the whole interview. It was terrifying."

"And how about that house he's living in with his girlfriend," another woman said. "It's bigger than mine."

"Reginald asked him about that," Ms. Blake said. "The man said that he and his gang moved into the houses in the area after the previous residents 'vacated their premises.' Mr. Six-Six-Six became very angry when Reginald showed those videos taken the night Shaker Heights was overrun last month."

"What bothered me was that he showed no concern at all for the people thrown out of their homes," a woman offered.

Ms. Blake's tone was scornful. " 'Why should I worry about them?' he said to Reginald. 'They're rich white folks. They'll go live with other rich white folks.' "

She glanced around at the other women. "Maybe the Germans have the right idea," Ms. Blake continued. "They're not even trying to provide for the foreign workers who can't or won't find jobs. They're just loading them up and shipping them home to Turkey or Egypt or wherever they came from. . . . We would never do that here, of course. We English are too civilized."

"Ladies," Beatrice said, taking advantage of the brief lull in the conversation, "as we were discussing earlier, human beings are an extraordinarily complex species, capable of all kinds of behavior. Aggression and hostility are always present wherever there are individuals who have been regularly denied basic sustenance. In his Easter sermon at Lake Bolsena, St. Michael said that the final evolution could not take place until food, love, shelter, clothing, health care, and education were available to everyone. That's what we are trying to do."

"Sister," Ms. Blake said sharply, "I admire your work very much. But I must admit that I find you and your associates ridiculously naive at times. Thugs like that Six-Six-Six would not listen to your gibberish for even a second. . . . My husband and I contribute to your effort not because we believe that we are part of God's grand plan, or the final evolution, or whatever it is you call it, but because we don't want our neighborhoods invaded by armies of desperate people led by armed hoodlums."

All eyes were fixed on Sister Beatrice to see how she would respond to Ms. Blake's outburst. Even Ms. Washburn was momentarily speechless.

Beatrice moved over closer to Ms. Blake. "Thank you for sharing your feelings," she said, her clear blue eyes unblinkingly staring at the older woman. "I understand how easy it is, especially in these distressing times, to temporarily lose faith, both in God and in humanity."

She reached out and touched Ms. Blake lightly on the forearm. "My faith cannot restore yours," Beatrice said. "Only you can do that. . . . I would, however, like to extend to you, and to your husband as well, a personal invitation to spend part of a day with me in Hyde Park. You could see firsthand not only what we do, but how we do it. . . . I believe that your opinions about our naïveté might be altered by the experience. And there is a chance, I believe, that some of your faith in God and humanity might be restored."

"I bet that Esher group will come through with the money," Vivien said to Beatrice during the train ride to Wimbledon. "And do you know why? Not because of your slick presentation and prayer, both of which were carefully designed to loosen their purse strings—"

"I was expressing my true feelings," Beatrice interrupted, placing her Coca-Cola container on the table in front of her. "I hope you're not suggesting that I deliberately . . ."

"Of course not, B," Vivien replied. "I know, perhaps better than anybody, that what the Esher ladies heard and saw was the genuine article. . . . That's what is so amazing to me. I couldn't imagine doing such a gig. I would laugh out loud at my own hypocrisy. But you really believe all that shit."

"And you don't?" Beatrice said. "And you have less than ten days before you must make your final commitment?"

"Oh, I believe too," Vivien said lightly. "But in my own way . . . I guess I'm basically a cynic at heart." She paused briefly. "Let me put it this way," Sister Vivien continued. "I believe in what the Order of St. Michael is doing more than I have ever believed in anything in my life."

"I'll accept that for the moment," Beatrice said. "Anyway, you were saying. . . ."

"Yes," said Vivien, "about the Esher ladies . . . What really impressed them was your response to that Blake woman. You could see it in their eyes. You were loving, and fair, but tough at the same time."

"I hope she does spend some time at the community," Beatrice said. "I feel sorry for her. It must be awful to live in such fear."

"No way," Vivien said. "She won't come. . . . And she only said what a lot of the others were thinking."

The two women were silent for a while. Then Sister Beatrice leaned over and touched Vivien's hand. "Now's probably as good a time as any," Beatrice said, "to talk about your ordination."

Vivien looked at her sponsor with a frown. "Is this a scheduled activity?" she asked. "I don't recall seeing '1630 to 1700, talk to Vivien about ordination on Wimbledon train' on your personal calendar this morning."

Beatrice smiled. "No," she said. "Actually I just thought about it. But *do* you have any questions I could help with?"

"A few hundred," Vivien said with a shrug, "but I'm not sure talking about them will help."

"By the way," Beatrice said, "you might like to know that last week I turned in a positive recommendation for you. Your only remaining requirement for ordination is your personal testimony. Once that is fulfilled, the choice will be completely yours."

Vivien's face showed both pleasure and surprise. "So you *do* think I'd be a decent priestess? Even though I'm ornery, and opinionated, and not exactly what anyone would call a religious character?"

"We need independent thinkers in the order. We are still growing fast and want people who are willing to ask tough questions." Beatrice's smile expanded. "Of course, I would be less than honest if I did not admit that your devotion and humility, to name a couple of attributes, could be significantly improved."

Vivien laughed. "Hey, even I would agree with that."

They were distracted by the automatic announcement that the train was nearing Wimbledon Station. "Thanks, B," Vivien said as she was gathering up their things. "For your confidence in me as well as your friendship."

Beatrice gave her a brief hug.

6

"So remind me again what we're doing here," Vivien said, struggling as usual to keep up with Beatrice's pace. They were approaching the large Michaelite compound in Wimbledon. The sun had set and the February air was becoming cold again.

"One of my best friends in the order, Brother Terry, is now in charge of this training program. We were both with St. Michael in Italy . . . although I think that Terry didn't join until after the pope had sent Michael to the monastery. . . . Anyway, Terry asked me if I would come down and talk to the trainees."

The Wimbledon training complex was located where the All-England Tennis Club had once stood. To many in Great Britain, and the entire tennis world for that matter, one of the most devastating consequences of the Great Chaos had been the disappearance of the annual fortnight of world championship tennis at Wimbledon. Economics simply precluded its continuation. Spectators could not even afford to buy the tickets, let alone fly from America or Australia to watch the matches. The last championship at Wimbledon was played in late June and early July of

2137, one year before the nuclear bomb in Rome killed St. Michael and many of his followers. The All-England Club itself folded at Christmas in 2137 and the grounds stood empty until the late summer of 2139, when a major funding campaign by the Michaelites raised the money for the purchase of the property.

The Order of St. Michael had made a lot of changes. The enclosed center court, however, an architectural masterpiece dating to the early years of the twenty-first century, had been left intact. It was there that Sister Beatrice was going to address all four thousand of the trainees, recruits from throughout the British Isles.

"We will have dinner with the recruits," Beatrice told Vivien as they passed through the gates, "just after my speech. I want to visit briefly with Brother Terry now, in case he has any last-minute requests."

Over a hundred men and women, about half in their early twenties, were lined up in ranks on a large field to their left. They were doing calisthenics, as if they were a huge sports team.

Vivien reached out and touched Beatrice, who was still in front of her, on the left shoulder. "Before we go in," Vivien said, "can we talk about this personal testimony thing for a minute . . . ? Am I supposed to do anything other than stand up and talk about who I was before, and why I joined the order in the first place?"

"That's all," Beatrice said.

"Then couldn't I do it here, in front of the trainees, instead of back in Hyde Park? I don't know why, but I think I'd be more comfortable talking to recruits I won't see every day instead of . . . you know, some of the brothers and sisters in our community are so pious, they make me nervous. . . ."

Beatrice stopped walking and looked over at Vivien. "I think that would be all right," she said at length. "Yes, I'll talk to Brother Terry about it."

"The sister I'm about to introduce to you," Brother Terry said to the assembled trainees, "is devoted, caring, deeply talented, and absolutely indefatigable. . . . Recently Sister Beatrice has been leading our effort to expand our Hyde Park community in downtown London. Brothers and Sisters, it gives me great personal pleasure to introduce one of my role models to you this evening. It is an extra delight that I have been chosen to tell you, and her, that the city of London late this afternoon announced approval of our Kensington Gardens expansion."

There was no applause. The order did not prohibit it, but clapping was frowned on at religious functions. A smiling Beatrice approached the microphone at center court and gazed out at a sea of eager faces.

"Thank you, Brother Terry," she began, "both for inviting me here today to share a few minutes with all these wonderful new recruits, and for informing me of the success of our expansion project. I pray that God will guide us in this new endeavor, and that we will be able to reduce significantly the pain and suffering experienced by the two thousand more people who will eventually live in our expanded community.

"What I would like to do this evening," Beatrice said after a brief pause, "is offer some insight into the greatest undertaking of your lives, an undertaking which, if followed through to commitment and ordination, will irrevocably alter your entire perspective of yourself, your fellow men and women, and even the planet on which you live. . . . You are embarking on a great journey with God as your helmsman. All humanity, not just those wearing the blue robe of our order, are passengers on this voyage. Your task, should you decide to accept God's call, is to dedicate your life to serving the other passengers, to distribute to them the resources and love they need so that their minds and hearts can clearly see God's plan for all of us.

"These lofty objectives may not always be apparent as you proceed through the day-to-day activities in your six weeks of training here. You may sometimes wonder just how the Bible studies, meditation exercises, lessons in religious history, culture, and foreign language, group discussions, physical activities, and all the therapy sessions contribute to your preparation. Believe me, nothing in the curriculum has been included without a specific purpose. What is done here is modeled, as are all our training programs, on the preparations for ordination suggested by St. Michael himself in the months before his death.

"Those of you who successfully graduate from this program will be temporarily classified as novices in the order. You will be given both a specific assignment and an individual sponsor for the remainder of your tenure as a novice. Between sixteen and twenty weeks after you leave here, you must make a commitment decision. If you decide not to become ordained, you will come back to Wimbledon, claim your possessions, and return to what we call 'outside life' with our blessing. If you do choose ordination, and have both fulfilled the prerequisite requirements and received the recommendation of your sponsor, then you will be admitted as a priest or priestess to the Order of St. Michael.

"Your ordination vows are very simple. You swear an oath to God that you will dedicate your life to the service of mankind. You also promise to God a life of chastity and poverty. It was St. Michael himself who established these two promises as cornerstones of our order. When one of his early disciples asked him why he was so adamant about these two vows, Michael replied, 'Nearly every human I have met has an overwhelming passion for either sex or material possessions or both. To give them both up, forever, requires a painful sacrifice. It is impossible to subdue one's selfishness, and truly achieve the oath of dedication, without enormous self-discipline. Willingly accepting chastity and poverty indicates that the new priest or priestess understands the demands of the life that he or she has chosen.'

"On the day that you are ordained, all of your possessions become the property of the order, to be used in whatever way best serves our objectives. . . ."

Vivien was no longer listening to Sister Beatrice's speech. It had seemed simple enough, half an hour earlier when she had suggested the idea, to perform her personal testimony here. Now, as the time when Vivien would speak was fast approaching, she was having difficulty controlling her nerves. What was she going to say? Should she admit, in front of everyone, that after all this time she still had doubts about her ability to make the required commitment?

". . . I am often asked by people," Beatrice was saying, "why it is necessary for members of the order to have a new name, one that is different from the one by which they have been known all their lives. That policy also derives its origin from St. Michael himself. He believed that the achievement of a life of dedication to others required a total rebirth. What better way to symbolize that personal renaissance than with a new name . . . ?"

Vivien had heard Beatrice speak often enough to know that she was nearly finished. She began to panic. Vivien had still not organized what she was going to say.

Suddenly Beatrice was looking at her. Vivien had not even heard her name. She walked forward slowly, tentatively, into the brighter lights in the center of the open arena.

Vivien had thought of some witty opening lines, but as she fingered the microphone she could not remember them. She glanced around for help. Beatrice was smiling at her and making small nodding movements with her head.

"Hello," Vivien said finally, the echo from the mike making her even more jittery. "I'm Sister Vivien . . . and I would like to make my personal testimony."

She froze. She couldn't think of anything else to say. Vivien felt as if she were going to faint. She grabbed the microphone again out of sheer desperation. "I'm really scared," she said, "so it may take me a few minutes to get going."

Vivien backed up and took a deep breath. "I'm twenty-nine years old," she heard herself say a few moments later. "I lived in Essex with my parents and younger brother until seven years ago, when I moved to London." Again she paused. "My father was a banker, and also managed the family estate. He had been a confirmed bachelor until he met my mother, when he was almost forty, during a weekend outing in London."

It was becoming easier. Vivien looked over at Beatrice and imagined that she was having a private conversation with her sponsor. "My mother was a cabaret singer from Jamaica almost twenty years younger than my father. She was also black, as you probably guessed from the color of my skin.

"I had a wonderful childhood, although I'll admit that at the time I did not realize how fortunate I was. My parents loved my brother and me, and they adored each other. They indulged us, especially me. I can't recall ever wanting something that they didn't provide for me.

"Looking back," Vivien said, "I see that I was a very selfish young woman, completely wrapped up in my own life. I went to the university at Essex, but I didn't really work very hard at my studies. By that time I had discovered men and, probably more importantly, they had discovered me. As you might imagine, I was something of an exotic item in Essex."

Vivien didn't like the way the last phrase sounded, but she tried to forget it and continued. "When I came to London after university, I went to work for one of those temporary services agencies. I did secretarial work, bookkeeping, and odd jobs, usually working no more than three or four days a week by my own choice. That was back before the Crash, when jobs were plentiful.

"I loved London, particularly the nightlife. I went out often, drank too much, experimented with drugs and sex, and ran my credit accounts up to the maximum by buying clothes and jewelry. When the depression hit London hard, I couldn't pay my bills. Collectors started bugging me. I probably should have asked my parents for help, but I was too proud. A girlfriend of mine, who was also having money trouble, introduced me to a woman who ran an escort service."

Vivien backed briefly away from the microphone and gathered her thoughts. "I lived the next three years of my life as a high-class prostitute, although I certainly didn't think of myself in those terms at the time. The money was good, the hours easy, the bill collectors were paid off. But I was depressed most of the time.

"I started therapy, I went down to stay with my parents more often, I tried going to church. . . . Nothing made me feel worthwhile. That was when I began to think about joining the order. Still, I hesitated for four months, reading everything I could about St. Michael and attending seminars and other public functions of the order. During that time I also continued to work for the escort service and enjoy the life of the London playgirl.

"Why did I finally decide to join? That's not an easy question for me to answer. There were many reasons, I'm certain, but the one that stands out in my mind is that I had a desperate need to be at peace with myself. I thought perhaps that by performing service for others, the gaping hole inside me would be filled.

"I now like myself, and I feel that my life has some meaning. Nevertheless, as I stand here before you, I have not yet been able to make the lifetime commitment to the order. Why not? I don't know for sure. I'm afraid of making a mistake, I know that. . . . But I could make a mistake either way. No matter what I decide, however, I can tell you that my experience with the brethren of St. Michael, to use Sister Beatrice's well-chosen words, has irrevocably altered my life."

Vivien's passage to the storehouse where the household goods and personal effects were kept was temporarily blocked. Brother Andrew didn't see her. Vivien was standing off to the side, out of the light, and he was busy directing the pair of trainees who were moving the cars.

"Two more ought to do it," Brother Andrew said to the young man in jeans climbing out of the car that had just been left among the jumble of automobiles temporarily filling the lane between the headquarters and the storehouses. To Vivien's right, over a hundred cars were parked in close ranks, side by side, nose to rear, on a large open field. Another car pulled out of one of the lines and jerked to a halt in the lane not far from Vivien.

"I'm sorry, Sister," a lanky girl said when she opened the driver's door. "I didn't know you were there."

Brother Andrew heard the girl's comment, noticed Vivien, and came over beside her. He introduced himself. "Thanks for your personal testimony this evening," he said. "It reminded me of my last days as a novice. I, too, had a hard time with my final commitment."

He turned around as another car entered the lane. "Careful," Brother Andrew shouted at the young recruit who was driving. The car, a luxurious new sedan, narrowly missed hitting one of the other automobiles. "That one will bring thirty thousand pounds," he said to Vivien.

"Is there another way to Storehouse Eleven?" Vivien asked, not wanting to wander through the maze of cars.

"Yes," said Brother Andrew. "But if you'll wait another minute or two, I'll drive you over. It's really quite a walk."

Vivien glanced at her watch. The train departed from Wimbledon Station at 1920. She had roughly half an hour before she was to meet Beatrice at Brother Timothy's office.

"That's the one," Brother Andrew was shouting. "Pull it out over here, next to the green coupe."

A black Japanese sedan, four or five years old, wound through the array of cars, finally emerging and stopping about twenty meters from Brother Andrew and Vivien. "That's the pair," Andrew said to the young man. "Now, would you and Sister Edith please put all these cars back where they were . . . more or less."

Brother Andrew motioned for Vivien to join him in the sedan. "Both these owners were ordained today," he explained when they were together in the car. "One in Leeds and one in York. We'll have them cleaned up and on the lot by noon tomorrow."

He turned down a dark alley between two tall structures. "I never dreamed when I joined the order," Brother Andrew said with a sharp laugh, "that I'd end up as a car salesman. . . . God sure works in mysterious ways."

Vivien thanked him for the ride and climbed out of the car. Storehouse 11 had originally been a pair of outlying tennis courts. The Order of St. Michael had simply put a roof over the top of the courts and rearranged the ground space.

She placed her identification badge in the card reader and then, when prompted, entered the six-digit code that Brother Terry had given her. Vivien heard the door lock click. She opened the door and went inside the dark storehouse. Running her finger along the wall, she found the light switch.

When her eyes had adjusted to the lights, Vivien searched the walls and ceiling for the coordinate identifiers that Brother Terry had given her. As she walked in the direction of her belongings, the video surveillance cameras followed her.

The room was well organized. Furniture and containers had been placed in every conceivable spot, yet there were regular aisles among the pieces and the layout was easy to follow. Bedrooms, living rooms, and kitchen appliances were mixed up and scattered throughout the huge storehouse, arranged by owner rather than by type of furniture. Fancy Oriental furnishings, including some magnificent hand-carved teak, were juxtaposed with everyday plastic desks and tables from the discount store.

Vivien saw her bed first, over against a wall. Actually, what she recognized from the distance was her bedspread, a gift from her parents when she first moved to London. Her pace quickened the final thirty meters as she approached her bed. Vivien sat down upon it, bounced lightly a couple of times, and looked around her. On the right was her chest of drawers, to the left her armoire, both marked in duplicate with the same code identifying her bed.

A thousand memories swam in Vivien's mind when she opened the armoire. Her dresses were neatly placed on hangers, each carefully identified, and looked as if they had just come back from the cleaners. As she touched each outfit Vivien remembered a time she had worn it, and often even the store at which she had purchased the item. She found her red dress, the one her friend Olivia said made her look "sexier than Cleopatra," pulled it out of the armoire, and held it in front of her while she looked in the mirror. The contrast between the sleek, low-cut dress and the blue robe she was wearing made Vivien laugh. She considered for a moment putting on the dress, just to see if it still fit, but she decided that it wouldn't be a good idea.

She walked over and sat in one of the black-and-white living-room chairs. Vivien looked around at the objects that had adorned her apartment. A feeling of sadness began to grow inside her. The feeling strengthened when she stood up and moved slowly around the area, touching each piece of furniture with her hands and fingers.

At length Vivien returned to the armoire and opened its drawers. Her jewelry had been carefully bagged, two or three individual pieces per bag, and marked with the same code that was on her furniture. She pulled out the deep blue Brazilian aquamarine pendant and matching earrings that her boyfriend Ernest had given her on her twenty-fifth birthday. Again Vivien looked at her reflection in the mirror, this time holding the dangling earrings beside her ears with her thumbs and index fingers.

In another small bag she found her gold cigarette lighter with the flowing script *V* engraved on the back. How she had loved that lighter! She flicked it a few times, as much out of habit as to prove to herself that it still worked. Vivien remembered clearly the American businessman who had bought the lighter for her. They had spent a long weekend together in Brighton, during the early days of her escort work. Cliff had told her that she was too classy a woman to use disposable lighters. They had had a good time together those three days. He had treated her like a queen. Vivien had been both delighted and astonished when Cliff had given her a three-hundred-pound tip.

The memories, vivid pictures flooding into her mind one after another, were overpowering her. Vivien felt as if she were alone in a small boat, surrounded by an endless sea. Turning her back on her furniture, she crossed the storehouse floor to the door. She stood just outside in the cold, dark air, with the door ajar, and lit a cigarette with her favorite lighter.

The memories had followed her outside. Vivien could not escape them. How could she possibly give up everything she had known, she asked herself, for the uncertain life of a Michaelite priestess? There would be no more fancy dresses, no more beach vacations in Brighton, no more beautiful jewelry, not tomorrow, not next week, not ever. And yet, and yet . . .

She inhaled deeply and watched a set of smoke rings rise slowly in the damp night air. They drifted up near the large electric light on the corner of the roof of the storehouse. As the smoke rings began to break up Vivien noticed an unusual bright cloud hovering near the light on the roof. Puzzled, she walked over to the corner of the building so that she would have a better view.

What was hanging near the edge of the roof was a collection of sparkling white particles, almost like a small cloud of mist, but far more prominent and distinct. Each individual particle, as it gently whirled and eddied inside the collection, was reflecting the light from the bulb on the storehouse. And although Vivien's smoke rings had already dissipated and been carried away by the light wind, this peculiar bright cloud did not move, as if it were somehow affixed to the edge of the building.

Without taking her eyes off the cloud, Vivien moved to a position where the light was directly behind the particles. From this coign of vantage she could see the entire pattern very well. Vivien was fascinated by the way each particle appeared to be dancing along its own particular path, yet the overall outline of the cloud maintained the same structure.

A sudden chill ran down Vivien's spine when she recognized the shape of the cloud. Although the collection of particles did not have the sharp edges of a solid object, there was an unmistakable resemblance between this cloud of sparkling particles and the tiny ceramic angel that her family placed each year at the top of their Christmas tree.

Vivien's natural cynicism rushed to her protection. "All right," she said out loud, surprised by the unsteadiness in her voice, "what's this all about?"

The cloud moved ever so slightly toward her, still retaining its general shape. A burst of fear caused Vivien to step quickly backward. An instant later there was a blinding flash of light. When she opened her eyes again the bright particles were gone.

She stood transfixed, her heart still beating at a frantic pace. Sister Vivien stared for several seconds at the empty area where the cloud had been. *What did I see?* she asked herself, struggling already to keep a clear image in her mind.

She walked slowly back to the storehouse. Despite the fact that Vivien did not believe in miracles, or epiphanies, or even a personal God who cared about the life of each individual person, she was convinced that what had occurred was directly connected to the decision she was trying to make. When she stopped at the entrance to the storehouse and closed her eyes, the cloud in her memory now looked exactly like the ceramic angel of her childhood.

Vivien walked purposefully through the storehouse. When she reached her possessions, she dropped down on her knees and pressed her forehead against the bedspread on her bed. "Dear, dear God," she said. "Thank you for sending me that sign. Or whatever it was . . . I know now that I will request ordination. But, God, I still don't know if I can live my whole life, forever, and not want things."

She paused for a moment. "Can you help me with that, God?" she continued. "Can you teach me somehow, day by day, that serving and loving are enough, and that I don't need *things* to make me feel good? I hope so, because without a lot of help I don't think I can do it."

7

Vivien stared out the window of the train, thinking about what she was going to say to Beatrice. She had definitely decided that she wanted to be ordained, the sooner the better. Vivien had also decided not to tell Beatrice, at least not now, about the cloud of particles shaped like an angel. She didn't want her friend and sponsor to think that a decision as important as her ordination was being influenced by the unusual apparition.

On the seat opposite, Sister Beatrice was deeply engrossed in what she was reading. When she was finished, she asked Vivien if she would like to share a soft drink.

"Not yet," said Vivien nervously. "Maybe later."

Beatrice noticed that Vivien's brow was furrowed. "What's wrong?" she said. "Are you upset about something?"

Vivien shook her head and took a deep breath. " 'The time has come,' " she said, "the Walrus said . . ."

"And which cabbages and kings do you want to discuss," Beatrice said, puzzled but enjoying the literary game.

"I want to be ordained tonight," Vivien said hurriedly. "At vespers, if possible . . ."

Beatrice was momentarily silent. "Goodness, Vivien," she said at length, "this is certainly sudden. . . . Are you sure?"

"Yes," said Vivien. She leaned forward and smiled again. "At least as sure as I'm ever likely to be. . . . I won't say that I'm not afraid, B. I still worry that I'll screw up or that I won't be able to tolerate the lifestyle or that—"

"Did you pray for guidance?" Beatrice interrupted softly.

Vivien nodded. "I knew you would ask me that. . . . Yes, I did. I really prayed, too, I didn't just go through the motions. When I was out by the storehouse, after looking at all my stuff, I asked God to help me through the uncertainty I was feeling."

"That's good," Beatrice said. "God is the only source of strength we can always count on."

"But can we do it tonight?" Vivien persisted. "I really don't even want to wait until tomorrow morning. I'm sure I wouldn't sleep a wink."

Beatrice reached across and touched her hand. "I can arrange for it to happen tonight," she said. "During vespers."

"Thank you," Vivien replied.

At the headquarters in Hyde Park everyone was talking about the approval of the expansion into Kensington Gardens. Many members of the order offered Beatrice their congratulations. She accepted their plaudits gracefully, reminding them that she was not responsible for anything, that she had simply been God's agent in dealing with the London city officials. Sister Chintha, a Sri Lankan who ran the preschool for the community, was uncharacteristically emotional. "Oh, Sister Beatrice," she said, "I had been praying that our proposal would succeed. This will make such a difference to the kids. Now we will be able to do things properly."

Beatrice was a little surprised that Brother Hugo was not present. But she didn't think about his absence for long. She walked down the hall to the office that she shared with five other priestesses. "Are you still in charge of the program for vespers tonight?" she asked Sister Emily.

"Yes," said Emily. "What's up?"

Beatrice smiled. "Vivien is ready to be ordained," she said.

"That's wonderful," Sister Emily said, crossing the small room to hug her colleague. "You must be very happy."

"I am," Beatrice replied. "Vivien has a lot to offer our order."

"When do you want to do it?" Emily asked.

"After the sermonette, I think would be best," Beatrice said. "Just before we start the singing."

The nightly services began at 2100 and lasted only half an hour. Like all the other religious activities in the Hyde Park community, attendance was voluntary. It was no accident that on the two nights of the week when Beatrice sang, the attendance at the vespers service was always twenty percent above normal. On this particular February evening, just under a thousand residents, along with almost all the hundred and fifty priests and priestesses who managed the community, came to the large tent in the northern part of the park.

Brother Diego, a former actor and an excellent speaker, gave the sermonette for the night. His topic was "The Nature of Man," and he quoted liberally from the famous notebooks that St. Michael had kept in the last months of his life. Brother Diego's twelve-minute lecture discussed man's relationship to the primates, the mechanisms involved in evolution itself, and what St. Michael had believed would be the next important evolutionary step in man's continuing spiritual growth.

Vivien was sitting in the front row of folding chairs, next to Sister Beatrice. When Vivien kept squirming nervously, Beatrice reached over and held her hand.

Following Brother Diego's closing prayer, Beatrice mounted the rostrum and addressed the audience. "Before we sing tonight," she said, "I have the incomparable pleasure of performing the ordination ceremony for my own novice, Sister Vivien. . . . Will you all please stand and welcome her into the order?"

There was some scattered applause among a few of the residents, but it died out quickly. Beatrice and Vivien stood sideways to the crowd, facing each other. "Sister Vivien," Beatrice said, "have you voluntarily come forward to be ordained into the Order of St. Michael, whose purpose is serving mankind according to God's plan?"

"I have, Sister Beatrice," Vivien said with a quivering voice.

"And have you read and studied the writings of St. Michael, especially those that pertain to the duties and responsibilities of the priests and priestesses of this order?"

"I have, Sister Beatrice."

"Do you swear in God's name, Sister Vivien, that you will never again, as long as you live, engage in sexual activities of any kind, with or without anyone else, nor will you ever again claim as your own possession any object, item, or piece of property, regardless of its size or value, excepting only the amulet that symbolizes your ordination?"

"I swear, Sister Beatrice."

Beatrice reached into one of the pockets of her blue robe and pulled out a necklace made of ordinary dark twine. She held it aloft so that everyone could see. At the bottom of the necklace was a wooden carving the size of a large coin. On the carving a young man wearing a robe was standing with his eyes raised and his arms outstretched. Behind and above him were the flames representing the nuclear fire that ended St. Michael's life abruptly.

Without saying anything else, Beatrice put the necklace around Vivien's neck and affixed the clasp. Then she hugged her and whispered "Congratulations" in Vivien's ear.

At the rear of the tent Sister Laura entered a code word into the computer system and the sounds of an organ playing "Holy, Holy, Holy" were distributed to the speakers scattered throughout the tent. Vivien stepped down from the rostrum, smiling and clutching the amulet in her right hand. As she returned to her seat the clear image of a cloud shaped like a ceramic angel was uppermost in her mind.

During the two hymns sung by the whole congregation, Beatrice noticed that Brother Hugo had entered the tent, near the rear, and that someone was accompanying him. She could not see the other person at first because of the people standing between them. After the second hymn was completed, however, Beatrice saw the white stripes on the man's blue robe. *It's the bishop*, she thought quickly. *What's he doing here?*

The audience was waiting, in great anticipation, for Beatrice to sing. She began with an updated version of what had once been a fourteenth-century monastic song of praise. "Morning has broken, like the first morning. . . ." she sang to the accompaniment of several synthesized instruments.

When she was finished with the first song, Beatrice rested for only a moment before nodding her head at Sister Laura. The sound of the solitary keyboard hushed the audience. "A-ve Ma-ri-i-a," sang Beatrice in a voice so clear, so perfect, that everyone was immediately spellbound. As the song continued, the sound of Beatrice's beautiful voice provoked a deep and highly personal emotional experience in nearly everyone in the audience. She had a rare gift. To hear her sing left one feeling enriched and glad to be alive.

In the front row Beatrice's song brought immediate tears to Vivien's eyes. It also catalyzed in her an overpowering sense of love, for God, for mankind, and for herself. "Thank you, God," she whispered, "for giving me this moment."

None of the audience, most of whom had closed their eyes while Beatrice was singing, stirred for at least ten seconds after she had completed the song.

Outside the tent, the other members of the order waited patiently in line to give Vivien the traditional hug of welcome. Beatrice stood off to the side, trying to be as insignificant as possible. Still, there was a steady stream of residents in her direction, each telling her how much they had enjoyed her singing. She responded with a polite "Thank you" to the praise, but she did not encourage any additional conversation.

Brother Hugo and the bishop were standing in line waiting to greet Vivien. Hugo caught Beatrice's eye and motioned for her to join them.

"Quite a day for you," the bishop said to Beatrice after they exchanged pleasantries. "God must be very pleased with your work."

"Thank you, Brother Wallace," Beatrice replied. "We are honored that you are with us this evening. . . . Have you come to help us rejoice?"

"No," he said, patting Sister Beatrice affectionately on the shoulder. "Actually, the primary reason I came was to see you, to bring you a special message from Siena."

"What is it about?" Beatrice asked.

"I don't know myself," Brother Wallace replied. "But it must be important. It has been closed with the archbishop's seal and is marked for personal delivery into your hands. It's not very often that the electronic mail is bypassed."

"Sister Cecelia was just explaining to me last week," Beatrice said, "how easy it would be for a hacker to invade our message structure. I guess a sealed personal letter is the only way to ensure privacy."

The three of them had reached the front of the line. Brother Hugo hugged Vivien first, in his stiff and somewhat formal way. Hugo was an experienced, capable, cautious administrator, but personal warmth had never been one of his major attributes. After Brother Wallace released her, Vivien flashed a radiant smile. "Hey, that was great," she said in her mischievous tone. "I've never been hugged by a bishop before."

Beatrice was glad to see that Vivien was again her normal self. They embraced for a long time. "Thanks, B," Vivien whispered in her ear. "You know I never would have made it without you."

It was only after Beatrice left Vivien's side that she began to wonder in earnest about the content of her message from Siena. The Archbishop of Siena was the titular head of the Order of St. Michael. Although he was not really an archbishop in the official Catholic hierarchy (the whole relationship between the Order of St. Michael and the Roman Catholic

Church would be in a state of flux and confusion for the next fifty years), he was the supreme authority for all the priests and priestesses of the order, a large group who now numbered almost three hundred thousand worldwide.

Beatrice had only even heard of one sealed message from Siena before. The head priest in the Birmingham region had received such a notice following an investigation by the order's Conduct Council. In the message the Birmingham supervisor had been told to defrock half a dozen of his staff for having used their positions in the order to engage in profiteering.

As she crossed the park toward the offices Beatrice was making a mental list of all the reasons she might be receiving a message from the archbishop. Beatrice was the primary supervisor of forty-five priests and priestesses. Could something have been happening in her group?

It was not necessary for her to wait long to find out the contents of the message. The bishop handed Beatrice the envelope as soon as she reached the headquarters complex. "I'm certain you will want to open it in private," Brother Wallace said.

Her pulse was racing wildly when Beatrice broke the seal on the envelope. Her eyes darted across the page.

Dear Sister Beatrice,

Your outstanding service to God and the order continues to draw praise from everyone. We are delighted to add our official recognition of your devotion and dedication. You have been selected to become the first Bishop of Mars. Please come to Siena at your earliest convenience to discuss this unusual and challenging assignment.

Beatrice read the words again in disbelief. *What?* she was thinking. *Is this really possible? I'm to be the Bishop of where?*

When Beatrice opened the small office door and walked out into the community room, fifteen pairs of eyes, including the bishop's, followed her every step. "I'll be back in a minute," she said, rushing out the door, "and I'll explain everything."

She ran excitedly across the park, over the pontoon bridge, and into the tent where she slept every night. "Sister Teresa," Beatrice said. "Has anyone seen Sister Teresa?"

"She went to the bathhouse a couple of minutes ago," one of the other priestesses said.

Sister Teresa was Beatrice's main source of astronomical information. Teresa had been a physics student at Oxford before she had decided to join the order.

Beatrice accosted Sister Teresa on the path between the sleeping tent and the bathhouse. "Sister Teresa," she said, grabbing her by both shoulders. "Where is Mars?"

Teresa looked at Beatrice as if she had lost her mind. "Where is Mars?" she repeated. "Well, it's the fourth major planet orbiting the sun, it's between us and Jupiter—"

"No, you don't understand," Beatrice interrupted. "I mean where is it *now*, up there, in the sky?"

Teresa recognized the intensity in Beatrice's expression. Without saying anything, she led her down to the end of the island, near the outdoor chapel. They looked up together. "That's Mars, there," Sister Teresa said. "The brightest one, just coming out from behind that fluffy cloud."

"Thank you, Sister Teresa," Beatrice said. "Thank you very much."

Beatrice dropped to her knees and raised her clasped hands toward the tiny light in the night sky. "Dear God," she prayed. "I entrust my life to Thee completely. If it be Thy will that I do Thy service on Mars, let me do it in the very best way possible. In St. Michael's name. Amen."

J ohann Eberhardt took a breath on
his left side a few meters before
he reached the wall. He pulled
through the water with one last motion of his long arms and then exe-
cuted a flip turn. Relaxing his body only briefly before beginning his
powerful stroke again, Johann headed back toward the opposite end of
the twenty-five-meter pool.

Acht und neunzig, Johann said to himself, increasing the tempo as he
neared the end of his early-morning workout. There were three others in
the pool now. As usual, Johann had been the first one in the water when
he had started swimming thirty-five minutes earlier, shortly after the facility's computer-regulated doors had allowed him early access because of
his special pass.

Johann felt a surge of competitive adrenaline as he sped past a
swimmer in an adjoining lane. *What was that Italian's name?* he thought
fleetingly, suddenly remembering one of his best races. *Bianchi, wasn't it?*
Johann had overtaken the Italian swimmer in the final two laps of a four-
hundred-meter race during a dual meet between Germany and Italy.

When he touched the wall at the end of his workout, Johann

bobbed up and down in the water until his breathing became more regular. He recorded his elapsed time in his memory and set the automatic lane clock to zero. Then he climbed out of the water, grabbed a towel, and headed toward the locker room.

A Turkish man had been watching Johann from poolside. The young man was wearing a bathing suit, but had not yet been in the water. *"Sie sind Johann Eberhardt, nicht war?"* the man said as Johann passed him. The Turk had to crane his neck and look up at the towering Johann, who was at least twenty-five centimeters taller.

"Ja," Johann replied, stopping but continuing to dry himself. "Why do you ask?"

"I am a friend of Bakir's," the young Turk said. He glanced around quickly. "May I talk to you in private?"

Johann hesitated but eventually allowed the man to follow him into the empty locker room. Bakir Demirel had been an engineering colleague of Johann's for over three years. Both were registered with Guntzel and Stern, the leading technical employment agency in Germany. By chance, they had worked together on each of their last three assignments. Their skills were complementary. Johann was a superb systems engineer. His strength was in understanding how all the different parts of a complex engineering system worked together. Bakir's talent was more focused. He was an expert in the fields of software engineering and robotics.

Inside the locker room, the stranger immediately crossed to the shower stall and turned on two of the jets. Johann looked at him quizzically. "You never know who might be listening," the Turk said with a smile and a shrug.

"Now, what's this all about?" Johann asked in an impatient tone.

"Bakir received a contract termination notice from the city of Berlin yesterday," the man said.

"There must be some mistake," Johann said. "Bakir's contract was written after mine, and I still have three months to go. We haven't even finished upgrading the distribution system for Wedding and Moabit."

"The termination was almost certainly politically motivated," the Turk said. "It is common knowledge that Herr Farckenbeck has higher aspirations. What better way for him to establish his German patriotism than to summarily dismiss all the high-paid foreign workers in the Berlin Water Department?"

"But the contracts have penalty clauses," Johann said.

"Even better for Herr Direktor. This way he proves he is willing to sacrifice for the good of the fatherland." The man stared directly at Johann and his smile vanished. "But I did not come here at six o'clock in the morning to talk to you about labor practices in Germany. I came to ask a favor on Bakir's behalf. He is your friend, isn't he?"

Johann nodded. "As I assume you know," the Turk continued, "under the Foreign Workers Act passed two months ago, all non-Germans who do not have gainful employment are subject to immediate deportation. Technically speaking, following the interpretation of the law handed down by the courts last week, even those like Bakir, who are registered with employment agencies and have long work histories, can be deported between assignments. Although Bakir and his family have lived—"

"But that's absurd," Johann interrupted. "Surely someone like Bakir is an exception. The law was written to permit deportation of those foreigners who cannot support themselves and have therefore become a burden to the nation. Bakir has lived here all his life and is a successful engineer. He even has property and a savings account."

"Which could be confiscated," the Turk said with a wry smile. "Don't get me wrong, I am not implying that the Freisinger government is motivated by profit, at least not yet. But what I said is correct. Bakir *could* be detained as early as today, before Guntzel and Stern even begin to look for another position for him. . . . That's why I have come to you."

Johann was puzzled. "What does this have to do with *me?*"

"I'm coming to that," the man said. "You have met Bakir's wife, Sylvie, and his daughter, Anna, have you not?"

"Yes," said Johann. "I had dinner at their home a few nights before Christmas."

"Bakir believes," the man said slowly, "that it would be smart for him to stay on the move until he has secured another job. . . . But he is concerned about the security of his family while he is away from home. He sent me to ask if Sylvie and Anna could stay at your apartment for a week or so. That way his absence would not be so noticeable."

Johann did not know what to say. His immediate thoughts were about how Eva might react. He quickly reminded himself, however, that it was, after all, his apartment, and it did have an extra bedroom and bathroom. He pictured Bakir in his mind. *He has always been a good colleague and friend,* Johann said to himself. *I would like to help him.*

The request was simple enough. Yet a feeling Johann did not understand was holding him back. He fidgeted uncomfortably.

The stranger continued to stare at him. "All right," Johann said, when the protracted silence had become awkward, "I guess I can do it."

"Thank you," said the man, grabbing Johann's hand and shaking it vigorously. "Thank you very much." He glanced at his watch. "They will meet you in the Tiergarten, next to the Goethe statue, at exactly seven o'clock this morning."

Before Johann could reply the man had disappeared.

It was snowing outside. Johann wrapped his scarf tighter around his neck. He was wearing only a thick sweatshirt over his T-shirt and jeans.

He headed in the direction of the Tiergarten, the huge park that was an oasis in the center of Berlin. Since the indoor pool was on the banks of the Spree, not far from Friedrichstrasse, the walk to the Tiergarten was not far.

Johann was having second thoughts about keeping Bakir's wife and child in his apartment. Questions had been pouring into his mind ever since the strange Turk had abruptly departed from the natatorium. *Why me?* an inner voice kept saying. *I really know Bakir only from work. I have never been involved in any way in his personal life.*

Johann remembered the night of his visit to Bakir's apartment in Kreuzburg. He had met many people that evening, most of them Turkish, all of them supposedly friends of Bakir's. *Why is he not asking one of them for help?* Johann asked himself.

By the time he reached Unter den Linden and turned in the direction of the Tiergarten, Johann had convinced himself that Bakir must be a political activist. Perhaps he was even one of the leaders of the opposition to the Foreign Workers Act. Work stoppages and nonviolent demonstrations had been occurring periodically ever since the German legislature, bowing to the will of the Freisinger government, had passed the new law. *Bakir would not have been fired otherwise,* Johann told himself. *He's too good an engineer.*

Johann stopped for several seconds in front of the Brandenburg Gate. To his left, on land that had been part of the Tiergarten until early in the twenty-first century, a series of museums dedicated to the study of German history stretched out in a row almost as far as Leipziger Platz. The first and oldest structure, which Johann had twice visited as a child, was the Berlin Wall Memorial Museum. Farther down the street was the controversial Third Reich Museum that had recently been the target of so many protests.

Johann crossed into the interior of the park behind the row of museums. It was snowing more heavily now. The occasional small meadows beside the path were completely covered in white. Here and there rabbit tracks broke the perfect quilt of snow. The heavy clouds had delayed the light of morning, but the scattered park lamps provided enough illumination for Johann to see.

Every hundred meters along the path a huge VERBOTEN sign, placed on the top of a thick post just above a pair of the ubiquitous scanning cameras, reminded those who were enjoying the Tiergarten that sleeping in the park, during the day or night, with or without a tent or a sleeping bag, was a felony offense punishable by a minimum fine of five hundred marks and/or thirty days in jail.

A rabbit scurried across the path and Johann gave chase. He was no match for the little creature, but he did manage to get his sneakers wet in the snow. As Johann was catching his breath he noticed that he was standing next to a tall, electrified fence protecting the back of the Museum of the Third Reich. Johann was staring idly at the building through the trees and the falling snow, thinking about his girlfriend Eva and her job at the museum, when he heard a sharp voice behind him.

"Was tun Sie hier?" a man said, appearing out of the trees. He was wearing the steel-gray uniform of the National Security Police (NSP).

"I was walking along the path," Johann replied easily, "and I decided to chase a rabbit—"

"Your identity card, please," the policeman interrupted, extending his hand. As he drew close Johann could tell that the policeman, like most of the members of the NSP, was very young, twenty years old at most.

Johann reached into the small pouch around his waist and handed the policeman his identity card. The youth seemed unusually nervous, as if he were new to his job, or perhaps intimidated by Johann's size. The policeman was holding a portable computer, equipped with a small screen, into which he inserted Johann's card. Nothing happened. The surprised officer repeated the action, but the monitor remained blank.

"Your card must be a fake," the policeman announced imperiously. He pulled the nightstick from his belt. "You must come with me."

Johann smiled. "Perhaps you forgot to switch on the power," he said in a sarcastic tone.

A few moments later the angry and embarrassed policeman was reading information about Johann from the monitor in his hand. The personal data had been transmitted from the main database at NSP headquarters.

"What is your date of birth?" he said, wiping the monitor free of snow and holding it so that Johann could not see what was written on the screen.

"November eleventh, 2111," Johann replied.

"What is your occupation?"

"Systems engineer. I currently have a position with the Berlin Water Department."

The policeman was still not satisfied. "Where do you live?" he asked.

"Number twenty-eight, Schumannstrasse, Apartment F," answered Johann in an irritated tone. "Look," he continued, "I am obviously not a vagrant, and I have broken no laws as far as I know. If you continue to question me for no reason, I will be compelled to file a complaint with your organization. . . . My cousin Ludwig, who is one of your local captains, has repeatedly assured me that the NSP does not harass loyal German citizens."

The look on the policman's face changed dramatically. He immediately became apologetic and obeisant.

"I'm sorry, *Mein Herr*," he said, stammering slightly. "I had no idea that Ludwig Eberhardt was your cousin. He is my squadron leader's supervisor. . . ."

He seemed to temporarily lose his train of thought. "I was just doing my job," he said at length. "There are reports that activists may try to disrupt the grand opening of the museum tonight. We are on alert to stop anyone in this area of the park."

Johann held out his hand. "My card, if you please," he said curtly. "I must be on my way."

"*Natürlich*," the policeman replied with a wide smile.

The National Security Police had been created only four years earlier, just after the election of the Freisinger government. The original purpose for this new, national police force had been the reestablishment of border controls to protect Germany from the steadily increasing flow of immigrants, mostly Africans and Middle Easterners, who were pouring into Southern Europe from the Mediterranean regions. Although the concept of national frontiers had been supposedly abolished a hundred and twenty years earlier, when the European Federation had its political birth, Germany's unilateral declaration of its intention to patrol its borders had never been convincingly opposed by any of the other federation members. The system that had been set in place was very effective. Within two years the movement of unwanted foreigners into Germany had slowed to a trickle.

The scope and sphere of influence of the National Security Police had then quickly expanded. Inside Germany, as the economic depression accompanying the Great Chaos continued to deepen and more laws were passed to restrict the activities of non-Germans, it was only natural that the new security officers assist the local police authorities in their dealings with the sizable Turkish and Egyptian communities. In fact, as time passed the local police gradually abandoned all responsibility for the implementation of the laws governing foreigners, leaving their enforcement entirely in the hands of the zealous and fiercely nationalistic NSP.

Meanwhile other smaller nations, Austria, Hungary, and Slovenia among them, decided that a set of similar border protection procedures should be established in their countries. They contracted with the German NSP, not simply to set up the initial system, but also to provide continuing oversight and key management personnel during the implementation phase. As a result, the NSP and their steel-gray uniforms became symbols of the domestic turmoil that was occurring throughout Europe.

For those Europeans beleaguered and alienated by the cruel realities of the worst depression in modern history, it was easy to blame their own disenfranchisement on the large number of foreign workers present on their soil. To them, Herr Freisinger and the NSP were heroes, striving to return Europe to the prosperity it had once enjoyed. To those alarmed by the resurgence of nationalism and racism embodied in the policies of the German government, the uncontrolled actions of the NSP were startling reminders of earlier days in European history, when rights of ethnic minorities had often been completely ignored.

The encounter with the security policeman had alarmed Johann. Now more aware of the possible ramifications of helping his friend Bakir, he toyed with the idea of not showing up for the appointment at all. After a short inner debate, however, his sense of honor compelled him to be standing next to the statue of Goethe at seven o'clock.

Bakir, his wife, and his daughter emerged from the snowy bushes one minute after the appointed time. Sylvie was wearing a scarf over her head and was carrying both their three-year-old child, securely wrapped in blankets, and a small suitcase. After they exchanged greetings, Johann's Turkish colleague began thanking him profusely for his assistance.

Johann interrupted him. "I'm sorry, Bakir," he said slowly, "but I cannot agree to this arrangement. . . . I have been thinking about it carefully for the last hour, and I do not see how it is possible. To begin with, my apartment building has many regulations to guarantee our security. Only my identity card and Eva's open any of the doors. To obtain permission for Sylvie's card to be accepted by the locks requires another application, and personal approval by the building manager."

"Sylvie and Anna will not leave your apartment," Bakir said earnestly, "until I have found a job. They will stay in their room, if you prefer, and will not interfere with you and Eva in any way. Please, Johann, you are our only hope."

"But what about all your family and friends in Kreuzburg?" Johann said, a little surprised at the tone in his voice. "Surely it makes more sense for your family to be with people they know."

Bakir put a hand on Johann's shoulder. "I cannot explain everything to you now," he said. "There just isn't time. . . . But I have reason to believe that I have been wrongfully targeted for deportation by the NSP. If I can avoid arrest for a few days or a week, I will be working again. My job will then protect me while I try to clear my name. Meanwhile, if the

gray shirts seize Sylvie and Anna, I will be forced to surrender. . . . It's
very confusing, I know. But please trust me. I have always been honest
and straightforward with you."

Johann listened to his friend's entreaty with mixed emotions. He
wanted to help, but he kept thinking about dealing with Eva and the
possibility that he might be breaking the law. Out of the corner of his eye
Johann saw someone approaching. For a moment he thought it might be
the security policeman and he felt a surge of inner fear.

"I'm sorry, Bakir, I just can't do it," Johann said hurriedly as a man
walking his dog passed on the path behind them. "I could give you some
money, if that would help."

Johann saw the disappointment in Bakir's eyes. The Turkish man
stepped back and put his arm around his wife. "We are not asking you for
money," he said tersely. "All we need is time." He heaved a sigh. "All
right," he said. "I understand. I had thought that you might. . . ."

His voice trailed off as he turned to console his wife. Her eyes had
filled with tears. "What will we do now?" she lamented. "What will we
do now?"

Johann was miserable. He said good-bye awkwardly and turned his
back on Bakir and his family. For fifty meters Johann watched his footsteps in the snow, becoming increasingly aware of his feelings of guilt.
When he was again standing underneath one of the VERBOTEN signs, Johann spun around and looked back toward Goethe's statue. Bakir was no
longer there.

Johann shook his head and chastised himself. While he was thinking
about how easy it would have been for him to help Bakir, he noticed that
no snow was falling on the ground a meter or so to his right. Puzzled, he
glanced up at the light on the top of the sign. What he saw, suspended in
the air just to the right of the lamp, was a double helix of sparkling
particles, each a tiny droplet of white. Snowflakes were falling on top of
this bright helical pattern, but then disappearing, as if they were somehow instantly vaporized.

The double helix, about a meter long and thirty centimeters wide,
was twisting slowly around an imaginary axis. The individual particles
making up the two strands of the helix were brightly reflecting the light
from the top of the sign. Although these particles were moving freely,
both up and down, and from side to side, the overall shape of the double
helix remained intact.

Johann could not accept what he was seeing. He closed his eyes,
rubbed them once, and then reopened them. The strange bright particles
were still there. The only change that had occurred was in the orientation
of the helix. It had continued to twist slowly around. Again Johann
looked above the formation. He carefully watched several individual

snowflakes descend until they reached the top of the helical pattern, at which point they abruptly disappeared.

Johann's engineering mind began to ask questions, attempting to find a rational explanation for the phenomenon he was observing. A second or two later the double helix made a slight move in his direction. Johann jumped up, thrust his open right hand into the pattern, and closed it around some of the particles.

Suddenly there was an explosion of light in the pattern. A moment later the double helix had vanished altogether. Johann recalled feeling a strange warmth on his hand during the instant of his jump. As he held his right fist tightly closed he thought he could feel something inside. Slowly, carefully, he opened his fist directly under the light. Scattered around his hand, apparently stuck to his skin by the force of the impact, were exactly eleven tiny white spheres no more than a millimeter in radius.

After studying the objects for about a minute, and noticing that they were pure white and featureless except for a single narrow band of red around each particle, Johann used his identity card to scrape each of the little white balls into a special pocket of his waist pouch. During his walk home, he resisted the temptation to look at the tiny particles again, telling himself that he would analyze the spheres in detail after he reached his apartment.

9

J ohann burst into his apartment with uncharacteristic élan. "Eva, Eva," he shouted immediately. "Where are you? The most extraordinary thing has happened!"

"I'm in the bedroom, darling," was the reply.

Johann hurried through the living room and into the master bedroom of the apartment. Eva was lying naked on the bed. Candles burning on the two end tables were the only lights in the room. A violin concerto by Mozart was playing softly on the stereo system.

Hardly looking at Eva, Johann switched on the overhead light as soon as he entered the room. Then he unfastened the pouch around his waist and placed it on the bed. "Something amazing has happened to me," he said excitedly. "I still have difficulty believing it. . . ."

Slowly Johann began to realize that Eva had been planning an altogether different kind of encounter upon his return. He glanced back and forth between Eva and the candles. Her face registered both her displeasure and her disappointment.

"Uh," he said awkwardly. "I'm sorry . . . I didn't expect . . ."

"No, you didn't," Eva said in a resigned tone, pulling on her panties and then slipping a small shirt over her head. "So what else is new? Sometimes I think it's hopeless for me to try to inject any romance into this relationship. You're about as romantic as a toilet."

"I'm sorry, Eva," Johann repeated, sitting down beside her on the bed. "I really am. I *do* appreciate your efforts. . . . But something remarkable has happened to me. While I was in the Tiergarten this morning . . ."

Eva watched Johann curiously as he told the story. She was surprised by his unusual excitement and animation. When Johann described how he leaped up and snared some of the bright particles, he literally bounded off the bed.

"There are eleven of them altogether," he said. "And they are really minuscule, maybe not even a millimeter across. As far as I could tell in the park, they are perfect round beads, pure white except for one narrow band of red around each sphere."

With a dramatic flourish, Johann unzipped the special pocket in his waist pouch and switched on the bedside light. "Look," he said, stretching the pocket open as wide as he could and holding it so that Eva could see inside. "Aren't they incredible?"

Eva leaned over and stared inside the small pocket. She saw nothing. "Is this some kind of elaborate joke?" she said, starting to smile. "Goodness, Johann, you were really great. . . . You had me believing—"

"What are you talking about?" Johann said with alarm. Reading Eva's facial expression, he moved the waist pouch to the other side of the light and bent over it himself. He turned the pocket into several different orientations so that the light penetrated every nook. There were no longer any beads inside.

"But that's impossible," he said. "I scraped them in there myself, one by one, and then zipped the pocket."

"Maybe they're magical beads," Eva said lightly, "that can open zippers or move through walls. Maybe—"

"This isn't funny," Johann interrupted her. "I tell you that I myself placed those beads in that pocket and then zipped it. There's no way they could have escaped."

He looked in the pocket one more time and then sat down again on the bed. Johann shook his head. "What could possibly have happened to them?" he said.

Eva put her arm around him and began stroking his back. "It was a great story, Johann," she said, "the best you have ever told. It reminded me of your imagination and enthusiasm during our early courtship. . . ."

Johann turned toward her to say something. As he did, Eva kissed him on the lips, softly at first but then more insistently. Johann really wasn't in the mood for sex. Nevertheless, recalling how upset Eva always became when he didn't respond to her advances, he decided to go along.

They were in the middle of intercourse when the phone rang.

"Let it go," Eva said. "The machine will answer it."

But Johann was already distracted. *Could it be Bakir?* he wondered guiltily. *Asking me to reconsider?*

He heard his mother's voice on the communications machine. Johann disengaged himself from Eva and activated the receiving port of the videophone. His mother's wrinkled visage appeared on the large television screen on the bedroom wall.

"I'm here, Mother," Johann said. "I was in the shower. That's why I'm not using the video transmitter."

"It's your loss," Eva said quietly, jumping down from the bed and heading for the bathroom.

"What was that?" Frau Eberhardt asked.

"That was Eva," Johann replied. "She said to tell you hello."

"Oh, hello, Eva," Frau Eberhardt said. She seemed momentarily confused and did not say anything for several seconds.

"What is it, Mother?" Johann asked. "If this is just a social call, why don't I call you back tonight? I'm running late for work."

"No, I'd like to talk now," his mother said. She lowered her voice and had a conspiratorial look on her face. "It's your father, Johann," she said. "He has been terribly depressed all week. He was talking this morning about how much more he is worth dead than alive. He pulled out all the insurance policies again."

"What do you want me to do, Ma?" Johann asked.

"Could you come see us sometime this weekend?" his mother said. "Please, Johann, I have something urgent to discuss with you and you know how much your visits cheer up your father."

"I don't know, Ma. . . . Eva's grand opening is this weekend and we have several social functions to attend." Johann took a deep breath as he watched his mother's pained reaction to what he was saying. "Look, I'll do what I can. I can't say anything definite now, but I'll call you from work later. . . . Good-bye, Ma."

"Good-bye, Johann . . . Your father would really appreciate it."

He switched off the phone. "Shit," Johann muttered as he headed for the bathroom.

It was not a pleasant breakfast. Eva did not have the slightest interest in what may or may not have happened to the little white spheres Johann swore he had placed in the pocket of his waist pouch. On the other hand, she was very interested in, and angered by, the fact that Johann was considering going to Potsdam for at least a part of the weekend.

"You are almost thirty years old," Eva said, making no attempt to disguise her feelings. "When are you going to tell your mother that you have a right to a life of your own?"

He looked at Eva across the small kitchen table. Johann didn't want to argue with her, at least not this morning when he was late for work and still unsettled by what had happened in the Tiergarten. He tried to stifle his emotions as he took another bite of his roll.

"Aren't you going to say anything?" Eva asked querulously.

When Johann still didn't respond, her eyes flashed. "So you *are* going to visit them. . . . I suppose it doesn't matter that this is the most important exhibit of your fiancée's career. . . . Or that we have been planning this weekend since before Christmas . . . Or that everyone who counts in Berlin will be attending the opening . . ."

Eva pushed back the chair and stood up. She leaned across the table toward Johann. "No, of course not," she said bitterly. "I don't count at all when Mama calls. 'Oh, Johann, please come see us, your father and I can't live without you.' "

Johann glanced up at her. "That's unfair," he said. "My parents are going through difficult times and I'm their only child. They need my support."

"Bullshit," Eva said. "The only reassurance your mother wants is that you'll come running every time she pulls your chain. It never fails. Every time we plan something special, there's a new crisis with your parents. Can't you see it? Remember last month, when we were going skiing at Mittenwald? On Thursday afternoon she fell and injured her hip. Do you think that was just a coincidence? And wasn't her recovery amazing? Why, by Saturday afternoon she was able—"

"Stop it, Eva. Stop it!" Johann said in a loud voice. He paused a few seconds before continuing in a more subdued tone. "I don't want to do this right now. Too much has happened this morning. . . . And you know how much it upsets me when you criticize my mother."

There was an uneasy quiet as Eva cleared her dishes from the table. Johann tried to finish his roll and coffee.

"Perhaps you would be kind enough to inform me," Eva said after about a minute had passed, "just what rights I *do* have as your fiancée. I understand that I am not supposed to criticize your mother," she said, her voice rising, "but can I at least expect you to honor engagements that we have made together? And do I have the right to bring up occasionally the

question of when we are going to be married? As far as I can tell, the only
right that I have is to fuck you, and then only if you're in the mood and it
fits into your schedule."

Johann jumped up from the table and grabbed Eva by the arm. He
stood there, holding her, trembling from the powerful emotions he was
feeling. She said nothing more until his rage subsided. "Well," she said at
length, forcing a smile and removing her arm from his grasp, "at least you
finally showed you care about something other than those stupid beads.
It's nice to know that I'm living with a human being and not a robot."

Without saying anything else, Johann left Eva in the kitchen and
went into the bedroom. He was very upset. He hated emotional confron-
tations of any kind, especially with Eva. Johann already knew that he
would be going to Potsdam that afternoon, after work, to see his parents.
He also knew that he didn't want to tell Eva now. Johann would tell her
on the phone later. Yes, that would be the best way to handle it.

He walked into the bathroom and looked at his face in the mirror.
What a morning, he thought with a sigh. Johann splashed water on his face
and thought briefly about Bakir and his family. *Now what could have happened to those damn beads?* he wondered a moment later.

Johann stared out the window as the train raced beside the Grünewald.
The snow had stopped by noon, but almost ten centimeters had fallen
throughout the Berlin area. The Grünewald was a winter wonderland in
the twilight. Many people were walking around on skis. Children were
busy building snowmen and riding down small hills on sleds and tobog-
gans.

Johann's eyes were open, but he didn't see any of the winter scenes
unfolding outside the train. His mind was occupied by a thousand other
thoughts. He drifted into memory, into what seemed like another lifetime. *How did it happen,* Johann asked himself with difficulty, *that my
relationship with my parents inverted so rapidly? When did I become the parent,
and they the children?*

He recalled the moment when he had moved his belongings into
the spartan dormitory room in Berlin that he had shared for a year with
that whale of a boy from Kiel. His parents had both carefully inspected
the room before they left to return to Potsdam. His mother's eyes had
been full of tears when she had hugged him good-bye. Just before his
father had left, Herr Eberhardt had handed Johann a thick bundle of
marks, "for spending money" he had said with a laugh.

That was a different era, Johann thought, *when everyone thought prosperity was a birthright. And that it would last forever.*

He remembered being awakened by the videophone early in the

morning, a few years later, when he had his own apartment close to the university, and seeing his mother's worried face. "Have you heard the news this morning?" she had asked.

"No," Johann had replied. "I was up late studying for my exams. What's going on?"

"The stock market is crashing," his mother had said. "Your father is in an absolute panic. He has been sitting at his terminal since one o'clock this morning, but he has not been able to sell a single share. . . ."

The crash of the worldwide stock market in 2134 marked the beginning of a global economic crisis of unprecedented dimensions. Half of the Eberhardt family's assets were wiped out during the six weeks that the market was in free fall. What remained was reduced to insignificance by the failure of the Potsdam banks in 2135 and 2136. Nobody had predicted that the depression that would be called the Great Chaos would be so long and so deep.

Johann had finished his degree in systems engineering without being aware how tenuous his parents' financial position had become. Although he'd had to borrow money for his university expenses during his last two years, Johann was truly shocked during the winter of 2137 when he learned from his mother that the Potsdam accounting firm of Sprengel and Eberhardt was permanently closing its doors. The young man had rushed home from Mainz, where he was working at the time, to see if he could help in any way. But Maximilian Eberhardt, a rotund man in his late fifties, convinced his son that everything would be fine. He had plenty of contacts, he told Johann, who would send freelance bookkeeping and consulting work his way.

It was not to be. When Johann visited home just before he began his two-year assignment with the Berlin Water Department in the early summer of 2139, he learned that his parents were already behind in paying their bills. By selling some furniture, Johann's mother's jewelry, and the family silver and china, enough cash was generated to pay the bills and to enable the Eberhardts to survive for another year. By that time, however, Herr Eberhardt could no longer find any work at all. Johann started sending money each month to help pay for food and other essentials. Meanwhile his father, who had once been a hearty and gregarious man, withdrew from the world and became a disconsolate recluse.

Johann was certain that the "something urgent" his mother wanted to discuss with him was financial in nature. *They just drift from crisis to crisis*, Johann thought. *Without any overall plan.* In his mind's eye he imagined his mother and father being tossed about in a small boat on a stormy ocean. *But where will all this end?*

He had suggested once, and had nearly been thrown out of the house, that they could sell the family home. Even with the severe deflation that had occurred in the real-estate market, their house, a magnificently renovated old home on Kiezstrasse which the Eberhardts owned outright, would sell for over two hundred thousand marks. "If you are frugal," Johann had said to his mother, "the money will last for five years or so."

"Johann Eberhardt," his mother had replied with uncharacteristic vehemence, "don't you ever, ever mention selling this house again. Your father would rather die first. This house has been in his family since 1990, when his great-great-grandfather returned to Potsdam from the Ruhr. . . ."

The train had temporarily stopped only a few kilometers from Potsdam station. A recorded announcement told the passengers there would be a delay of several minutes. *Another by-product of this depression,* Johann said to himself. *Probably some software or equipment that has been improperly maintained.*

To pass the time, Johann switched on the television news in the arm of his seat. In process was a feature report on a group of tent cities that had been established in London to rehabilitate and house the homeless. Most of the feature, which included interviews with some of the members of the Order of St. Michael who operated the large Hyde Park community, as well as some of the residents, was focused on what the German reporter called the "surprising success" of the endeavor. At the conclusion of the story the studio commentator remarked that all the proposals by the Michaelites to create similar enclaves for the homeless in Germany had been turned down by the authorities.

The next item on the news showed a scene that afternoon at the Berlin Hauptbahnhof, where, according to the commentator, several hundred Turks, including women and children, were being forcibly loaded on a train to Istanbul. The camera panned slowly around the sorrowful faces as the voice droned on, carefully explaining that the train would not be overcrowded, that all the passengers would be well fed, and that each of them would be given five hundred marks in Turkish currency upon disembarkation in Istanbul.

Despite himself, Johann searched the crowd for any sign of Bakir and his family. As he was watching the screen he felt a strong surge of guilt, far stronger than any he had experienced that morning. *But what can I do?* he asked himself at length. *I have enough troubles of my own.*

10

Johann stood under the tall, bare tree directly across from his boyhood home, holding the bottle of white wine in his right hand. It was already dark and cold, yet he wasn't in a hurry to step up to the door. He was looking at the second-floor window, above and to the right of the baroque decoration that was over the door. Almost every morning of his youth he had opened it, first thing, and stuck his head outside to check the weather.

The house had grown smaller with the passing years. As a child, he had thought it was huge. There had even been two extra bedrooms, empty most of the time, in which Johann had been able to play whenever he chose. In one of those rooms a light was now on. Several months earlier his parents, at Johann's suggestion, had taken in a boarder, a quiet little man from Würzburg, who paid them a modest rent.

Despite the cold, some children were playing soccer down at the end of the street. Johann gazed in their direction, watched them running after the ball, and heard their eager cries. The scene was one he knew well. Fifteen or twenty years ago, the boy in the red hat, standing nearly a head taller than his companions, would have been Johann.

As he stood there Johann suddenly remembered a conversation he had had with Eva in the early days of their romance. She had been complaining that her father had never paid much attention to her when she was growing up, that he had only been interested in her brother. She had interrupted her complaint to ask Johann a question. "You know," she had said, "I don't think I have ever heard you talk about anything bad that happened to you when you were young. Did you have a perfect childhood?"

It was nearly perfect, Johann thought, summoning his courage to approach the door. *I raced home every day after school, eager to see my mother and tell her about my day. The two of us greeted my father with broad smiles when he came home from work.* He paused and took a deep breath. *There was certainly nothing to prepare me for this.*

His mother answered the door and gave Johann a huge hug. He handed her the wine. "Max," she shouted excitedly, "it's Johann. . . . And he's brought a cold bottle of Piesporter with him."

Johann's father, dressed in a rumpled shirt, blue slacks, and slippers, appeared in the atrium a few seconds later. "How are you, son?" he said with a slight smile. "It's great to see you again."

His father did not hug him. The Eberhardt men never embraced. In fact, they hardly ever showed any kind of emotion.

"I'm watching the news," Max Eberhardt said to Johann. "Would you like to join me?"

"He can talk to you after dinner," Frau Eberhardt said. "I want him now. . . . Come, Johann, let's go in the kitchen. I want you to tell me about everything in your life."

For just a moment, as Johann crossed the dining room behind his mother and smelled the enticing aroma of *Kartoffelsuppe,* he thought about telling his mother about the double helix in the Tiergarten, Bakir, and even the sorry state of his relationship with Eva. But Johann realized that such a conversation was impossible. He had never talked with his mother about what he was really thinking and feeling. And it was too late to start now.

Frau Eberhardt still cooked by hand, despite the automated equipment surrounding her in the kitchen. When they were in front of the stove, she took a small spoonful of soup from the huge pot and brought it over for Johann to taste.

"Umm, delicious as usual," Johann said.

"I bet your Eva can't make a pot of soup like this," his mother said.

"No, Ma," Johann answered. "Really good potato soup cannot be made by machines."

Frau Eberhardt basked in his praise. For a few moments she gazed at her son, silently stirring the pot. "Thank you for coming, Johann," she said. "Your father and I cherish your visits."

Johann looked over his shoulder and moved closer to his mother. "You said you had something 'urgent' to discuss with me," he said in a low voice. "Why don't we get it out of the way now so we can relax the rest of the evening?"

His mother grimaced. "I had hoped we might wait," she said. "At least until after we had had a pleasant dinner."

"Didn't you want to discuss it with me alone?" Johann said. "As we usually do?"

Frau Eberhardt handed Johann the large wooden spoon. "Keep stirring," she said. "I'll be back in a minute."

When she returned she was carrying an envelope. "Everything is in here," she said, "although I guess you only need to read the last document."

She pulled out a letter and gave it to Johann. It was printed on the stationery of the tax collection office of the state of Brandenburg. Johann returned the spoon to his mother and began to read.

The letter said that since the property taxes on the house were now three years overdue, and since past promises to pay them had never been kept, the state had reluctantly decided it had no choice except to seize the property, sell it at auction, and take the property taxes out of the proceeds. Any money remaining, after the payment of the delinquent taxes, plus the cost of the auction and some processing fees, would be given to the current owners of the house. The letter was signed by Herr Wilhelm Drommer, Tax Collector, and dated February 20, 2141.

"Can you believe that?" Frau Eberhardt said nervously. "Herr Drommer and your father were friends at the university."

"Mother," Johann said, after reading the letter a second time and starting to recover from the shock, "why didn't you say something about this before?"

"It's ridiculous," his mother said, stirring the soup and not looking at Johann. "We aren't the only ones who are delinquent. Frau Hirsch told me that the Muellers haven't paid their taxes since George died two years ago." She suddenly started to cry. "Oh, Johann, what are we going to do? This will absolutely kill your father."

Johann moved over beside his mother. Tears were running down her cheeks. "How much will it take, Ma?" Johann said quietly. "How much must we pay?"

"The clerk at the collector's office says we must pay at least six months' worth of taxes in the next two weeks. And we must also agree to regular monthly payments for the rest."

Johann turned his mother so that she was facing him. "How much is it, Ma?" he repeated.

"Over seven thousand marks," she said, new tears spilling out of her eyes. She buried her face in Johann's chest.

He mechanically stroked his mother's back as he thought about what she had told him. *Over seven thousand marks*, he said slowly to himself. In two weeks. *How in the hell am I going to raise that kind of money?*

Only for a few seconds did Johann consider not helping his parents and letting the house be sold to pay the taxes. During those seconds he was filled with anger and resentment. But he did not allow those emotions to continue. *That would be the wrong reaction*, he told himself. *My proper response is to help my parents.*

Max Eberhardt smacked his lips as he finished the last of the chocolate cake. "Well, Johann," he said, "I must admit that there are many reasons why I enjoy your visits. . . . Your mother never cooks like this for just the two of us."

Johann acknowledged his father's comment with a smile but did not say anything. He was still thinking about the seven thousand marks. The dinner conversation had been polite and circumspect. Johann and his parents had discussed the weather, sports, Eva, Johann's current job and future prospects, and the activities of a few of his childhood chums who had stayed in Potsdam. Never once had they mentioned either his father's unemployment or the problem with the house. His mother had been especially interested in Johann's job, and had been visibly relieved when he had informed them that Guntzel and Stern had already received a pair of firm offers for his services after his current contract was finished.

"Now," his father said, rising from his chair, "I think I have the perfect conclusion for this outstanding evening. Will you join me in the family room, Johann? I believe last summer's production of *Siegfried* at Bayreuth is finally available on the system."

Max Eberhardt's only real passion in life was the operas of Richard Wagner. He knew the stories and music for all of the operas, and often whistled one of the tunes while working or taking his morning walk. As a boy, Johann had been told repeatedly that Richard Wagner was the greatest German genius of all time, surpassing Beethoven, Bach, Bismarck, Frederick the Great, Martin Luther, Goethe, Mozart, and the others usually accorded a place in the German pantheon.

"And why exactly was Wagner so great?" his father had often asked rhetorically, even if Johann showed no interest. "Because he alone captured the essence of the German spirit. No true German can watch the Ring Cycle without being stirred to the bottom of his soul."

Whenever Johann visited his parents and one of the pay television systems was accessed, he always inserted his own identity card so that the charges would go on his account. The *Siegfried* they were preparing to watch had won universal praise and was still comparatively expensive as home entertainment. His mother thanked Johann quietly while the program was beginning, before she slipped out to prepare the dishes for the robot washer.

The giant screen, a hundred centimeters square, nearly filled the wall of the family room. As the music swelled, the camera zoomed into a cave where the dwarf Mime, the young hero Siegfried's caretaker since birth, was working to forge a new sword for his ward. The adventure had begun. For four hours the fearless Siegfried, the quintessential German hero, would overcome treachery, monsters, and even the gods on a pre-destined path to glory whose ultimate payoff would be a passionate liaison with the demigod Brunhild, the most beautiful woman in either heaven or earth.

Once the opera had begun, Johann watched his father more than the program on the television screen. Johann was familiar with the story. He had seen *Siegfried* three times in his life, twice during the family's annual summer pilgrimage to Bayreuth, and had probably discussed it with his father on a dozen other occasions. It was easy for him to follow the story simply by listening to the leitmotifs in the magnificent music.

He was fascinated by his father's complete absorption in the opera. He, Johann, was not able to forget for even a few minutes all the issues that were troubling him. Yet there was his father across the room, the nominal owner of a house about to be sold because of unpaid taxes, a man no longer able to support himself, totally immersed in a mythological musical story. *How can he turn the rest of the world off so completely?* Johann wondered enviously. But as he thought about his father he knew the answer. *Because otherwise he could not go on living.*

Frau Eberhardt brought them huge steins of beer just after the second act began. She then stayed for her favorite part, where Siegfried slays the giant Fafner, who is in the guise of a dragon, with his enchanted sword. Soon thereafter Johann, exhausted from his long and emotional day, fell asleep on the couch, waking only during Siegfried's final triumph with Brunhild. Max Eberhardt's attention had obviously never wandered from the screen. Now, as Johann watched him from across the room, his father seemed far away from Potsdam and Germany. He was the warrior Siegfried, high on a mountaintop overlooking the earth, experiencing the joy of being in love with one of the most desirable females ever created.

Johann saw true emotion on his father's face for one of the few times in his life.

Johann slept in the extra-long bed that his parents had bought when he was only fourteen. By that age his height had already reached two meters. But he did not sleep well in his adolescent bed. Throughout the night he was plagued by disturbing dreams.

The longest dream began with Johann in his office at the Berlin Water Department. Bakir and he were reviewing the design for a system that would more efficiently monitor and control the city's water purification plant. The proposed system did not require any human involvement at all unless a specific set of parameters were outside defined tolerance levels and the built-in fault analysis capabilities could not isolate and correct the problem in a reasonable amount of time. In the dream Bakir told him that the system had already been validated during three years of usage in Brussels, where it had a mean time between failures of seven months and had substantially reduced that city's labor costs.

Bakir said that five full-time positions in the Berlin Water Department would no longer be necessary once the new system was installed. Then the dream scene shifted abruptly. Johann was swimming four hundred meters in an important race. Although he was leading with only a single lap to go, through his goggles he could see the swimmers on both sides slowly but steadily catching him. His arms began to feel leaden as two competitors passed him in the last ten meters of the race.

When he pulled himself out of the pool, Eva was waiting on the deck. "Come," she said, "we must hurry." Eva was naked, which embarrassed Johann, but none of the other swimmers or coaches seemed to notice. She was already walking swiftly toward the locker room. Johann had to hurry to keep up with her.

Eva talked the entire time that Johann was dressing, but nothing that she said made any sense to him in the dream. It was as if she were talking gibberish. A commotion on the opposite side of the locker room disturbed them. Johann recognized the singer who had played Brunhild in *Siegfried*. She was dressed in a bizarre bikini made of armor, and was posing for the dozen or so men who were admiring her obvious attributes. One of the men, holding a dozen roses in the front row, was his father. As Johann and Eva came closer he noticed a forlorn, ragged figure standing in an alcove just off to the right. His mother was watching the adoration of Brunhild with tears in her eyes.

Johann wanted to comfort his mother, but Eva pulled him out the door behind her. "We don't have time for this foolishness," she said in the dream.

They rode together on the subway. Eva was now dressed. "Where are we going?" Johann asked.

"You'll see," she replied.

They disembarked at the Berlin Hauptbahnhof just as a train entered on the opposite side of the platform. The electronic voice in the station announced that the Istanbul Express would leave in five minutes. Johann glanced to his left and saw a long procession of Turks filing down the stairs to the platform. The women all had their heads covered in the traditional manner. Accompanying the Turks were a dozen NSP officers, headed by the young man who had accosted Johann in the park that morning. All were carrying nightsticks.

Bakir, Sylvie, and Anna were in the middle of the procession. They came over to greet Johann. "So you have changed your mind?" Bakir asked with a warm smile.

Johann turned to Eva, who was regarding him with scorn. "Move along," the policeman said in a loud voice. When Johann turned back to his friend, Bakir had disappeared. A few moments later Johann saw him on the far side of the platform, standing with his family in front of one of the train doors that had just opened. The NSP officers ordered the Turks, who were arranged in orderly lines in front of each of the doors, to board the train. They refused. The Turkish women in Johann's dream began to wail in unison. The sound was terrible.

"Come on," Eva said to him. "This is why we are here." She dragged him toward the recalcitrant Turks.

The platform was suddenly teeming with hundreds of different Germans, a cross section of the people that Johann encountered daily on the streets of Berlin. On a raised stage in the middle of the platform, Johann's cousin Ludwig, looking sharp in his gray uniform with the captain's insignia prominent on both shoulders, stepped up to a microphone. When Chancellor Freisinger, who was standing beside Ludwig, nodded his head, Johann's cousin began to speak.

"On the count of three," he said, "you should all move forward and push."

Eva yanked on Johann. "We must move over here," she said, "to be in a better position."

"One," said Ludwig. The moiling crowd pressed toward the Turks. Since he was taller than everyone else, Johann could see the terror in Bakir's eyes from far away. His friend was resisting the pushing.

"Two," said Ludwig.

Johann looked up at the top of his dream screen and saw a double helix of sparkling particles shining just underneath the station lights. As he watched, the particles formed into the pattern of a gun pointed at one of the long lines of Turks.

"No," shouted Johann. "No," he yelled again, freeing his arm from Eva.

The dream scene faded and Johann realized that he was actually in his bed in Potsdam. For a long time the images from his dream stayed fresh in his mind. It was several minutes before his heart rate returned to normal. He glanced over at the digital clock beside his bed. It was four-thirty.

Johann remained awake the rest of the night. At the first sign of light, he went over to his window, opened it, and stuck his head outside to check the weather.

11

Max Eberhardt was dressed in his overcoat, with a scarf wrapped around his neck and a driving cap upon his head. "Are you sure you don't want to go with me?" he said to Johann. "It's a beautiful morning for a walk."

"Thank you anyway," Johann said, shaking his head. "I think I'll stay here and talk with Mother."

"He goes out every morning after breakfast," Frau Eberhardt said after they had closed the front door.

"Does he ever look for a job anymore?" Johann asked.

"Sometimes," she lied, "but it's no use. The few bookkeeping jobs that are available are taken by the Turks and the Egyptians. Your father says they work at half price or less. . . . He hopes the situation will change with this new law."

The boarder, dressed in a simple suit and tie, walked down the stairs. He greeted Johann and his mother. "Would you like some fresh coffee, Herr Heinrich?" she asked.

"No, thank you kindly, Frau Eberhardt," the man said. "I had some coffee and rolls in my room." He smiled at his landlady. "I'll be gone for the weekend," he said. "I'm visiting a friend up in Lübeck."

"Your father doesn't like Herr Heinrich," Johann's mother said a few minutes later, when they were sitting together at the table in the nook adjoining the kitchen. "Max thinks that he is gay . . . and you know your father's opinion on that subject. From my point of view, however," she added, "Herr Heinrich is a perfect tenant. He stays to himself and is very neat. The only time we even know he is there is when he plays his music too loud."

"What does he do?" Johann asked.

"His current contract is with Kirsch Electronics. I think he told me that he repairs the robots that build automobiles and airplanes. . . . Something like that." Frau Eberhardt smiled wistfully. "I have suggested to your father that he might take some kind of a technical training course. There's a new school along the Havel, just on the other side of the Lange Bridge, that claims most of their graduates find positions in less than three months. But Max just scoffs at the idea. He says that he is too old to learn something new."

Frau Eberhardt refilled Johann's coffee cup and offered him another roll. "So have you and Eva set a date?" she asked.

"No, Mother," Johann answered. "Lately it seems that we're both so busy we don't have much time to talk. She has been working hard to prepare for the museum opening."

His mother leaned across the table and touched Johann's hand. "I know that you wanted to be with her this weekend," she said. "We really appreciate your taking the time to visit."

There was a long silence as Johann tried to decide exactly how to phrase what he was going to say. "Mother," he said at length, "you should have told me a long time ago about this tax problem with the house. You can't wait until these things get out of control."

She realized that she was being reprimanded. "I didn't want to bother you, Johann," his mother said defensively. "I thought maybe we would find some way to work it out."

"How, Mother?" Johann said, frustration showing in his voice. "How could you possibly have worked it out? Real-estate taxes must be paid with money. And you and I both know—"

He stopped. Johann could see that his mother was very uncomfortable. "What does Father think about this situation?" he said after a long pause.

"He doesn't take it seriously," Frau Eberhardt said. "Whenever I bring up the subject, which is not often, your father quickly dismisses it and reminds me of all his friends in the state government." She looked

out the window. "Sometimes, Johann, I think your father has lost touch
with reality."

Neither of them said anything for a full minute. "Mother," Johann
then said, "I want to help you, but I don't have seven thousand marks.
My portion of the savings account that Eva and I have earmarked for our
honeymoon is barely half the amount that is needed. . . . And you know
how difficult it is to borrow money at this time."

"I thought about calling my brother Hermann, and asking for his
help," Frau Eberhardt said after another long silence. "But Max would
never forgive me if I did."

"Did you hear what I said to you?" Johann interrupted. "I don't
have seven thousand marks."

"Yes, Johann," she said, "I heard." Frau Eberhardt turned away and
gazed out the window. "I hate it that we have put you in this position,"
she said softly. "I just don't know what else to do. . . . You have been
so generous since your father and I started having problems."

There must be some way, Johann was thinking. The pain in his
mother's eyes was obvious. He remembered two years earlier, when his
parents had raised some money by selling possessions. There had been
some items that his father had refused to sell.

"What's left in the attic?" Johann suddenly asked his mother.

She shrugged. "Nothing much," Frau Eberhardt said. "Really old
family stuff with no meaning to anyone except your father. I can't believe
that there's anything worth more than a couple of hundred marks."

Johann stood up. "I'm going to take a look," he said.

"All right," his mother said wanly. "I guess under the circumstances
it can't hurt. . . . But don't tell your father if you decide to take anything."

Johann was afraid that the creaky old ladder was not going to hold his
weight. He stopped on each step, holding the bag his mother had given
him in his right hand, and waited to see if the ladder was going to collapse. Frau Eberhardt stood in the hallway with both hands steadying the
ladder. She had an anxious expression on her face.

The entrance to the attic was a small rectangular panel in the ceiling
almost four meters above the floor. Despite his height, Johann could not
push the panel with any force until he was on the next-to-last step of the
ladder. When he did finally apply some pressure to it, the panel wouldn't
budge.

"How long has it been since anyone has been up here?" Johann
asked his mother.

"Not since that last sale," she said. "Be careful, Johann, I wouldn't want you to fall."

Johann moved up to the top step, carefully balanced himself in a crouched position, and pushed the panel very hard. It finally gave way. Dust and debris fell on his head and shoulders. After waiting several seconds for the dust to clear, he removed the panel and placed it to the side on the attic floor. Then, using his arms, he lifted himself up and crawled into the attic.

"I'll call you when I'm ready to come down," he shouted to his mother.

"All right," she said. "But don't be longer than forty-five minutes."

The only place in the attic where Johann could stand up completely was along the beam that cut the room in half. On either side of the beam the ceiling sloped sharply downward. There were not as many objects and packing boxes as Johann had expected to find, based on his childhood memories. However, he had not seen the attic for at least seven years, and many of the items sold two years earlier had been taken from the room.

Johann covered his mouth with a cloth to keep from inhaling the ubiquitous dust. Off to his left he could see an odd collection of objects, including two old mirrors, some discarded paintings of no merit, and a few smaller pieces of furniture. It did not take him long to determine that there was nothing in that jumbled mess that could be sold for any significant amount of money.

Against the opposite wall, under the only window in the attic, ten or fifteen boxes were stacked in piles of two and three. Johann found a sturdy crossbeam and crawled in that direction.

The first group of boxes contained photographs and video records, some carefully organized and labeled, and some scattered randomly around the interior of the boxes. The two boxes at the bottom of the stack were the most interesting. Inside them were old family photograph albums, a couple dating back to the first decade of the twentieth century. Johann flipped through these quickly, stopping only occasionally to look at an especially unusual photo.

Plaques, citations, degrees, awards, and trophies filled the second group of boxes. Johann found his great-grandfather Eberhardt's laminated medical degree as well as a plaque, with his great-grandmother Frieda's name inscribed upon it, announcing that her novel *Der Blau Stuhl* had won the Thomas Mann literary award for the year 2082. In the bottom of the same box Johann found a handsome wooden board, onto which was glued a paper document, written in script German, dated July 20, 1763. The document announced the appointment of Karl W. Eberhardt to a civil service position under Frederick the Great. Johann put the board into the bag his mother had given him.

The last set of boxes contained journals that had been kept by various members of the Eberhardt family. All of them had been carefully arranged and cataloged by his literary great-grandmother Frieda in 2115, just three years before she died of a stroke. Johann remembered her only vaguely, but her talents were a legend in the family. Whenever any Eberhardt displayed a streak of creativity or brilliance, Frieda's genes were always given the credit.

Two entire boxes were filled with Frieda's journals, a few handwritten, but most of them printed on paper. Assorted storage media, reflecting the changes in word-processing technology around the turn of the twenty-second century, were also labeled and cross-referenced to the printed pages. Johann read scattered tidbits of Frieda's journals before deciding that perhaps this material might be worth something. He had just started putting her journals into the bag when he noticed some unusual annotations on the master table of contents his great-grandmother had created when she was cataloging all the family journals.

Around the name Helga Weber Eberhardt, 1922–1979, Frieda had made a thick black circle. Five of Helga's journals were listed, the first one covering the time period 1938–1941. Johann's great-grandmother had drawn a fancy arrow pointing to this journal, and had written in the margin, in French, *"absolument extraordinaire."*

Curious, Johann dug through the remaining boxes until he found Helga's five journals, neatly wrapped in clear plastic and bound together by thick rubber bands. He opened the top volume and began to read. The first entry was dated 28 June 1938.

"Ich heisse Helga Weber und ich bin sechzehn Jahre alt. Ich vohne in Wilmersdorf, auf 38 Bayerische Strasse, mit meinen Eltern, mein Bruder Peter, und unser Hund Fritz."

At first, Johann could not understand what his great-grandmother Frieda had found so *extraordinaire* about this journal written by a sixteen-year-old girl. There was little of interest in the early entries, and Helga had no particular literary aptitude. Most of the events recorded were mundane and banal. A walk in the park with her dog Fritz highlighted the first weekend in August for Helga. Johann was about to put the boring journal aside when he read Helga's entry for August 8, 1938.

"From this day forward," Helga wrote, "I will be a new person. My life has been forever changed. This afternoon Katrina took me as her guest to a meeting of the League of German Girls. It was sensational. Tonight, after my preliminary training, I was accepted as a new member of the group. I cannot believe how much I have already learned about everything, but especially about what the awful Jews and communists are trying to do to our country. I will be forever thankful to Katrina for opening my eyes. Heil Hitler!"

Johann could not put the journal down. Helga described in detail her training sessions, the enthusiasm and patriotism of her friends, even the stylish new Hitler Youth uniform that she wore at every opportunity. What absolutely amazed Johann was how quickly the apparently ordinary teenage girl was transformed into a loyal and devoted Nazi, willing even to report her brother for actions considered not entirely satisfactory by the Third Reich. In the first five weeks of the journal, there was but one reference to anything political. By the beginning of October, however, when Helga celebrated Hitler's triumph in taking over the Sudetenland without firing a shot, she was writing about nothing but her activities associated with the League of German Girls.

In mid-October Helga and Katrina began attending Nazi rallies with Katrina's older brother Otto, a rising star in the *Sturmabteilung* (SA). From Helga's descriptions, it was obvious to Johann both that Helga had a schoolgirl crush on Otto, and that the young man was broadening her political horizons considerably. Helga apparently never questioned anything that Otto told her, or any of the propaganda that she heard at the rallies, for her journal entries during the last half of October read as if they had been lifted verbatim from Nazi literature. At the conclusion of one such entry, after a particularly vitriolic attack on the Jews, Helga wrote, "I will not be content until all Germany is *Judenfrei*! Heil Hitler!"

On the night of November 9, the famed Kristallnacht after which there was no doubt that Hitler's intention was to utterly eradicate the Jews, Helga defied her parents and joined Katrina and Otto in an orgy of terror and destruction that lasted until noon the next day. When she returned home, completely exhausted, the first thing she did was write in her journal.

"Last night and this morning were the most satisfying hours of my life," she wrote. "We have finally taught those Jewish bastards a lesson they won't forget. We have revenged the brutal murder of Herr vom Rath in Paris. We have burned their synagogues, looted their shops, invaded and destroyed their homes, and terrified their women and children. Otto even strangled one old Jew in Darmstadtstrasse when the fool tried to resist. It was a glorious night for everyone loyal to the Reich. Heil Hitler!"

Johann's fascination with Helga and her journal had turned to revulsion by the time he read her comments about Kristallnacht. He was also deeply distressed that one of his direct ancestors had been such a fervent supporter of the anti-Jewish policies of Adolf Hitler. Nevertheless, remembering a conversation that he had had with Eva about the Third Reich Museum needing more source material from the time period, he suspected that what he was reading was worth a lot of money. Glancing quickly at his watch, he put all of Helga's journals in the bag and crawled back to the center of the attic. He was down the ladder ten minutes before his father returned from his walk.

J ohann disembarked from the S-Bahn at Bellevue. The station was uncrowded, typical for a winter Saturday morning. In the middle of the station, beside the kiosks selling prepared meals, snacks, entertainment, and electronic newspapers and magazines, a small group had gathered to listen to a trio of blue-robed Michaelites, two with guitars, who were singing folk songs. Moving among the crowd were another three or four members of the sect. They were handing out leaflets and collecting money in large cans.

Johann instinctively made a wide arc around the group as he headed for the stairs to the surface. The first time he heard his name called he did not respond. However, when the familiar feminine voice said "Johann" again, much louder, he turned around, puzzled, and looked in the direction from which the voice was coming.

A tall young woman, wearing the characteristic blue robe with the blue-and-white headpiece, was rapidly approaching him. "Hello, Johann," she said with a pleasant smile.

For a brief moment Johann could not integrate the well-known voice and smile with the clothes of the Order of St. Michael. "Heike?" he said at length. "Is that you?"

The young woman laughed easily. "Of course," she said. "Who else could it be?"

Now that Heike was standing right next to him, Johann was embarrassed. "I'm sorry," he said awkwardly. "I didn't expect to see you dressed like this."

"We're not some kind of fanatic cult," Heike said, teasing him slightly, "despite what you might have heard."

"But I thought you were teaching in Staaken," Johann said, still off balance. "When did you . . . ?" He didn't complete his sentence.

"Early last summer," Heike said. "Right after the school year finished. I was feeling unfulfilled, and frustrated because I wasn't doing anything to help with all the problems this economic crisis has caused." She laughed again. "Actually I signed up for the training orientation almost as a joke, after a night of overindulgence. . . . But the more I saw, the more I liked. And the better I felt."

"And Klaus?" Johann asked. "What happened to him?"

"We separated for good when I went away to Freiburg for the six weeks of training," Heike said. "He's fine. . . . We're still friends. He told me last week that he's now engaged to a ballet dancer." Heike put her hand on Johann's arm. "But that's enough about me. How's life treating you? Have you been at home visiting your parents?"

Heike Schmidt had been Johann's closest friend during his last two years of school in Potsdam. Although there had been some mutual attraction that went beyond friendship, for a variety of reasons the pair had remained simply friends, like a close brother and sister. Heike and Johann had been able to talk about everything during those two critical years of adolescence. Now, as he looked at her, and remembered how close they had been, he longed for a companion with whom he could share his innermost feelings without worrying about her reaction.

After a brief chat, Johann invited Heike to lunch. She declined the invitation, explaining that she could only take a short break from her fund-raising activities. "We use every cent for food and other basic essentials, Johann," she said. "This afternoon we will take all the money we receive here to the supermarket in Tempelhof, where our volume buying earns us a huge discount. Then, tonight and tomorrow, we will distribute what we have purchased at our large center in Kreuzburg. . . . Early Monday morning I will return to Mariendorf, where five days a week I manage a day-care center for the children of people who are trying to find work."

Johann was more impressed by the tone of Heike's voice, and her general demeanor, than by what she was saying. She seemed completely content with her life. "By the way," Heike said a moment later, "you might mention to your father that the order has established support groups for the unemployed all over Germany. I know there's a chapter in Potsdam, for Greta Ulbricht's father goes regularly. The men and women are able to share their experiences, and they have an opportunity to participate in some worthwhile projects."

He shook his head and smiled. "I can't imagine my father ever doing something like that," Johann said.

"Stranger things have happened," Heike said lightly. "And now, my friend," she continued with a wink, "before I go, can I talk you into parting with some of your hard-earned cash for those less fortunate than we? I assure you the money is all spent wisely."

Johann surprised himself by giving Heike a twenty-mark banknote.

He was still thinking about his conversation with Heike when he entered his apartment. After discovering that Eva wasn't there, Johann noticed that he had two messages. Surprised, he exercised the self-test subroutines on his watch to see if there had been a malfunction in his personal communications system. There had not. Both messages had purposely not been forwarded.

Johann sat down in his living room opposite the huge video screen. The first message was from his mother's brother, Uncle Hermann, whom Johann had not seen for almost twenty years. From the coding on the video Johann could tell that the message had been transmitted from a Berlin hotel room the previous evening around dinnertime.

"Hello, Johann," a man dressed in a dark suit said on the screen. "In case you don't recognize me, I am your uncle Hermann, older and fatter than I was the last time you saw me." Hermann Kurz had a warm face. He smiled before continuing. "I am in Berlin for the weekend and would like to see you on a matter of some urgency. If you would be able to join me for drinks or dinner at the Schweizerhof Hotel on Saturday night, please phone and leave a message.

"I am not having this message forwarded because I do not want your parents to know of our meeting. At least not yet . . . Please, Johann, make an attempt to rearrange your schedule if you possibly can. I assure you that our conversation will be of the utmost importance to you and your family. . . . I am looking forward to seeing you again after all these years."

The astonished Johann only had a few seconds to think about his uncle Hermann before his message retrieval system automatically projected the second video onto the screen. Eva was sitting on a couch in a room that Johann did not recognize. Johann touched the pause button on the remote control and went into the kitchen for a drink of water.

Eva's face was still frozen on the screen when Johann returned. She was dressed casually, in a loose-fitting white blouse and blue jeans. Johann thought she looked unusually tired. Her eyes were red and swollen.

Eva's message had been transmitted a couple of hours earlier that morning, at five minutes before ten. "You're probably wondering where I am," Eva began, "and why I'm not in the apartment." The young woman hesitated. "I have not come home," she continued with difficulty, "because something happened last night, something unexpected, and I thought that I should tell you about it before we saw each other again."

Eva paused and fidgeted nervously on the couch. "The opening was a huge success, Johann," she said, forcing a smile. "You would have been proud of me. Everyone was extremely complimentary. Herr Freisinger even stopped by briefly, and virtually all the top city officials made an appearance. . . . Your cousin Ludwig was there with that new actress girlfriend of his. He was disappointed that you hadn't come."

Eva was distracted temporarily by someone who was out of the picture. Johann heard a woman's voice. "That's Gena," Eva said. "She's one of the other designers. You met her briefly once last month. I'm over at her apartment and will stay here until you phone."

"Anyway, I was really feeling elated when the official opening ended. Gena and I and Rolf Bachmann, the museum curator, went out dancing with several of the other members of the staff. We all drank too much and had a great time."

She stopped. Eva looked as if she were making an effort not to cry. "Johann," she said on the video, "I am very confused by what has happened. I guess I could blame it on the fact that I was drunk and got carried away, but that would be too easy. . . . At the end of the evening, Rolf invited me back to his apartment and I went.

"I don't know what to do now, Johann," Eva said slowly. "I thought that if I told you about last night this way, you could have some time to think before we talked. . . . I know that I have hurt you, and I am very sorry for that, but I also know that I love you. . . . Please call and help me understand where we go from here."

Johann glanced at his watch. It was three-thirty. In half an hour he would meet Eva and Rolf at his favorite café on the Unter den Linden, not far from the museum. Johann had purposely chosen a public meeting place to minimize the likelihood of an unpleasant scene. He was also delighted that Rolf was going to join them, for that would give Johann a chance to show the museum curator Helga Weber's journals.

He was surprised by how easy it had been for him to make the decision to end his affair with Eva. Her dalliance with Rolf, Johann had realized earlier in the afternoon, offered him a perfect opportunity to disengage himself from a relationship that had, in his opinion, become unsatisfying to both of them. Under normal circumstances, Johann mused, it might have taken them several months in a deteriorating situation to acknowledge that they should go their separate ways. Eva's spending the night with Rolf had, in reality, spared them both a lot of heartache.

Nevertheless, since Johann was by nature very cautious about changing any significant element in his life, he spent the final minutes in his apartment reviewing again the thoughts and feelings that were influencing his decision to terminate his affair with Eva.

Johann sat in the large armchair in the living room and stared briefly at a photograph of Eva and him, laughing and frolicking on the beach in Portugal. *In the beginning,* he recalled, *everything was so easy. We were so compatible, especially in bed.* Johann readily admitted that he would miss the sexual aspect of his relationship with Eva. They no longer had sex every day, as they had during the first months of their courtship. But they still made love three or four times a week, as regular as clockwork, primarily because Eva, whose insecurities were not hidden, believed that each sexual contact was a reaffirmation of their commitment to one another.

She has been an agreeable and intelligent companion, Johann told himself, continuing his inventory of Eva's assets. *We have enjoyed many evenings together at the theater, at restaurants, and with friends. We never really had any problems until . . .*

In fact, Johann recognized that the dynamics of his relationship with Eva had altered completely when Eva had started her work at the Third Reich Museum. Her personality had been transformed by the job. Previously, she had done more or less routine graphic-design tasks for mostly commercial applications and had not seemed particularly involved in her work. The high-profile position at the museum, however, had given Eva a taste of the limelight and rekindled her ambitions.

At first Eva had often brought her work home from the museum and shared what she was doing with Johann. For a while this mutual activity seemed to strengthen their relationship. But as Johann himself had become more knowledgeable about Eva's project, and had started expressing opinions of his own, their egos had begun to clash.

Johann still remembered clearly his astonishment and irritation with Eva the night he discovered, after a long discussion over dinner, that she was concerned only with the aesthetic concepts embodied in her exhibits, and was completely disengaged from the subject matter contained in the displays. She viewed the design of an exhibit depicting the death camps at Auschwitz, Treblinka, and Sobibor, for example, as an exercise in arrangement and lighting, without any overriding design principles based on the immorality of what was being displayed. The night had ended with Johann giving Eva a self-righteous lecture that had infuriated her. Subsequently, bitter arguments had erupted whenever Eva thought Johann was criticizing her work.

These disagreements had quickly spilled over into other parts of their life together, poisoning the rapport they once had shared. Eva became more openly critical of Johann, not just for what she called his "blind devotion and subservience" where his parents were concerned, but also for his insensitivity to many of the things that were important to her. Johann was often defensive and lashed out at the insecure Eva with emotionally damaging criticisms of his own.

In his final deliberation, Johann did not ask himself if he loved Eva. He knew that he did not. Maybe once or twice, in the early days of their affair, during a moment of sexual passion, Johann had felt something that he might have called love. But that had been a long time ago, and those feelings had long since been forgotten.

Johann continued to sit in the chair in his living room as he completed his review. *No,* he told himself at length, *there is no aspect of this situation that I have overlooked. I have made the correct decision.*

Realizing that he still had another ten minutes before his meeting with Eva and Rolf, Johann suddenly decided to examine more thoroughly the pocket in his waist pouch from which the peculiar white spheres had vanished that morning. This time he cut the entire pouch apart with some scissors and placed the exposed pocket directly under the light. To Johann's delight, in three or four places, down at the very bottom of the pocket, there were faint yet clearly identifiable tiny round imprints remaining on the material. Although the imprints did not explain in any way the mysterious disappearance of the spheres, they were a tangible proof that the unusual objects had indeed once been in the pocket.

Johann was so excited by the imprints that he started to leave the apartment without the Helga Weber journals that he intended to show Rolf Bachmann. *At least something good may come out of this meeting,* Johann told himself, tucking the journals inside his coat to protect them from the damp weather.

Uncle Hermann was already sitting at a table when Johann arrived at the restaurant in the Schweizerhof Hotel a little after six. The older man stood up when he saw his nephew and greeted him warmly with both a hearty handshake and a pat on the back. *"Mein Gott,"* Uncle Hermann said with a smile, "you are even bigger than I imagined. How tall are you?"

"I'm two meters eleven," Johann replied, slightly embarrassed.

"Sit down, sit down please," Uncle Hermann said. "Goodness, it's been a long time. . . . Seventeen years I think."

"At least," Johann said. "I was barely twelve when we visited you in Rothenburg, just before Christmas."

There was a short silence as the two men stared across the table at each other. "I'll explain everything, Johann," Uncle Hermann said, taking a sip of his wine. "But first, would you like some of this superb Poligny-Montrachet? I bought it to celebrate our reunion."

Johann nodded and his uncle poured the white wine into his glass. "Of course I want to know all about your job, and Eva, and everything else in your life, but first I have a couple of topics of my own to discuss. . . . Do you mind if we begin, right away, with the reasons I called you?"

"Not at all," Johann replied.

Uncle Hermann hesitated for a moment. "First, Johann," he then said, "I'm deeply troubled about your parents, as I'm certain you are as well. Their financial position is terribly precarious. Although your mother has never mentioned anything to me about their plight, I have done some investigating on my own and have discovered that they're in a woeful predicament. They may even lose the house if they don't pay the delinquent real-estate taxes in the next few weeks."

Uncle Hermann took another drink of his wine. From Johann's expression Uncle Hermann could tell that he had not told his nephew anything new or surprising. "I have also discovered," his uncle continued, "that you have been helping them substantially, for over a year now, and that without your assistance they could not possibly even have fed themselves." He shook his head. "I am appalled that my sister has never asked for *my* help, but I must admit that I am both impressed and deeply gratified that you have been so generous. It is very much to your credit."

"I have done what I could," Johann said quietly. "I only wish I could have done more."

"You are an admirable young man," Uncle Hermann said. "That's why it gives me great pleasure to inform you that you will never again need to provide any financial help to your parents."

Johann returned his wineglass to the table. "I don't understand," he said, his brow furrowed.

"Life has been very good to me," Uncle Hermann explained. "I

was lucky enough to anticipate this depression, and my assets have remained intact. It is of no consequence to me to assist your parents. Ac-
cordingly, I have, in the last three days, paid their delinquent taxes and
deposited enough money in my sister's bank account that they can live,
albeit frugally, for the next year or two."

Johann could not believe what he was hearing. As he began to comprehend fully what his uncle Hermann was telling him, Johann felt as if
an enormous weight was being lifted off his shoulders. "I don't know
how to thank you," he eventually stammered. "For them, for me, for all
of us."

"I assure you, Johann," Uncle Hermann said, leaning across the
table, "that the amount of money we are discussing is not that important
to me. It's the least I can do for my family."

Johann's shock did not quickly diminish. He sat quietly, sipping his
wine, although he wanted to stand up and shout with joy and relief.

"Did either of your parents," his uncle was saying, "ever tell you
why you never saw me again after our Christmas visit in Rothenburg seventeen years ago?"

"No," Johann said, shaking his head. "My father mentioned something about a quarrel, but he didn't give any specifics."

"So you don't know that I am a homosexual?"

Johann didn't know what to say. "No, Uncle Hermann," he said at
length. "Nobody ever told me."

"That's what the quarrel was about," Uncle Hermann said. "The
last night of your family's visit, after you were asleep, I 'came out,' as we
say. I even introduced them to my boyfriend at the time. Your father was
enraged and told me that I would never be welcome in your house
again."

After Uncle Hermann apologized for disappearing from his nephew's life
and Johann said, somewhat awkwardly, that his uncle's being a homosexual was not important as far as Johann was concerned, the focus of the
conversation shifted to the younger man. For some reason, the usually
taciturn Johann was eager to talk. As the meal progressed he told Uncle
Hermann about his work, about the conclusion of his affair with Eva,
even about Bakir and his confusing feelings of guilt. Uncle Hermann
seemed interested in every aspect of Johann's life.

"I went to that museum opening last night," Uncle Hermann said
in response to a comment Johann had made about Eva's work. "It was a
scary event. I agree with what *Le Monde* said this morning, that the representation of Hitler and the other Third Reich leaders, particularly in that

special exhibit entitled *Hitler und die Juden,* was devoid of moral comment, and therefore permitted the viewer to draw his or her own conclusions about what occurred. . . . Your cousin Ludwig, incidentally, reminds me of a Nazi SS officer from one of those early American films."

They talked and talked. During the main course Johann told Uncle Hermann about finding Helga Weber's journals in the family attic, and the excitement he had seen in Rolf Bachmann's face when the museum curator had quickly scanned the text. Johann also admitted that he felt strangely embarrassed that one of his ancestors had been such a Nazi fanatic.

"The museum will pay plenty for that kind of material," Uncle Hermann said. "But don't sell the journals to them too quickly. If the material is as powerful as you have suggested, I have some associates in the United States who would probably also want to buy them."

"But if the money is no longer needed," Johann asked, "why should I sell the journals at all?"

"They're too important to remain private," Uncle Hermann replied. "They can serve as a poignant historical reminder, if nothing else. . . . Besides, we can put the money into an account for your parents to use in the years ahead."

It was almost eight o'clock by the time the dessert was served. Johann and Uncle Hermann had finished the second bottle of wine. Johann was feeling pleasantly relaxed. He could not remember when he had enjoyed an evening so much.

Over dessert Johann told his uncle about his extraordinary encounter that morning with the double helix of sparkling particles. He first brought the subject into the conversation tentatively, to see whether or not his uncle was going to scoff or perhaps even belittle him. Encouraged by Uncle Hermann's initial response, however, Johann told the entire story, including all of the details.

Uncle Hermann was fascinated by the story. "And these imprints," he asked, "are they clearly visible? Could someone else see them?"

"Absolutely," Johann replied. "If you'd like, I could run back to my apartment now to get the pouch. I could be back in less than half an hour."

"That won't be necessary, Johann," Uncle Hermann said with a laugh. "I believe you." He took a bite of his strudel. "Johann," he then said, "have you ever heard of the Rama Society?"

"Yes, I think so," Johann said. "At least the name sounds vaguely familiar. . . . What do they do?"

"They are a group who catalog and study unexplained phenomena that might be related to nonhuman intelligence. They were formed ten years ago, right after the visit to our solar system by that cylindrical space-ship of unknown origin. Anyway, one of my closest friends is the director of the Rama Society. His name is Carlos Sauceda. I'm going to have him give you a call."

"So you think my double helix," Johann said excitedly, "may have come from somewhere in space?"

"I wouldn't go that far," Uncle Hermann said. "But Carlos has told me about some unexplained incidents that are remarkably similar. They have occurred all over the world. And not just in the last ten years either. I'm certain Carlos would be delighted to give you more of the details, and I suspect he will be anxious to study those imprints."

After the dessert, Uncle Hermann ordered two glasses of cognac. "Thank you very much for everything," Johann said earnestly as he sipped his cognac. "For helping my parents, for coming back into my life, and for this dinner. It has been a wonderful evening."

"It's not over yet," Uncle Hermann said with an unusually serious look on his face. "I have one more topic to discuss with you. . . . Do you by any chance remember the summer of 2122?"

Johann tried to clear his head and focus on his uncle's question. "Of course," he said at length. "That was the summer you took Mother and me to Paris."

"I will never forget your excitement in the Air and Space Museum," Uncle Hermann said. "You were certain that you were going to live on the moon or Mars someday."

Both men were silent as Johann returned to his childhood and re-membered his daydreams of space travel and the hours he had spent looking at the atlases of all the planets and their moons. His mother had kept that spacesuit Uncle Hermann had given him for his twelfth birth-day until after he had graduated from college. Somehow it all seemed so far away. . . .

"I realize that I may be intruding upon your life," his uncle said, breaking Johann's alcohol-induced reverie, "but something happened just two days ago that reminded me of the young boy I knew that sum-mer in Paris. One of my associates who works for the International Space Agency was complaining to me that he has been unable to find a properly qualified person to manage the largest water-distribution facility on Mars. The job seems a perfect match for your talents. I don't know if you still have any interest in that kind of thing, but . . ."

Johann's mind was swimming. He could barely concentrate on what his uncle was saying. He heard the words "Valhalla, excellent pay and benefits, two-year minimum term," but he had no concept of what they really meant. When Uncle Hermann handed him the business card with

the red ISA logo stamped across the top, Johann did not have the slightest idea that two days later he would have an interview that would irrevocably change his life.

Johann stumbled home to his empty apartment that night in a pleasant frame of mind. For the moment the good wine and the warm conversation with his uncle had restored his basic optimism. In fact, for the first
time in months, Johann was actually looking forward to the future with
eager anticipation.

VALHALLA

Giovanni Lamberti pulled the long lever back with his right arm. Through the goggles fixed tightly about his eyes, he watched as the huge scoop entered the shallow Martian ice trench. After a brief pause, he began exerting tension on the lever on his left. The scoop pulled toward him, its powerful teeth ripping through the ice and filling the body of the scoop with hundreds of kilograms of material.

"It's really not that difficult," Giovanni said to the young black man sitting beside him in the control room. "You just have to remember that Melvin is more than three hundred kilometers away, and allow for the delay in the reception of the signal."

Kwame Hassan was also wearing a pair of the strange goggles. He was sitting next to Giovanni, on a lower level, in what was called the copilot's seat. Kwame observed intently while his teacher Giovanni, handling both levers with consummate ease, lifted the full scoop out of the trench without dropping any of the ice, and deposited the contents in the open bed at the rear of the machine. He then returned the scoop to a position in front of the ice harvester and switched the controls to idle.

"Are you ready to try it on your own?" Giovanni said. He unstrapped his goggles and slid out of the large padded chair between the levers.

"I guess so," said Kwame, wishing that he had more time to learn his new job. "Johann told me that you'll be leaving early next week."

"That's right," Giovanni said with a broad grin. "After two and a half years, I'm finally out of here."

Kwame climbed the three steps and sat down in the chair. He adjusted his position several times until he felt comfortable with where his body was placed with respect to the levers. When he pulled the goggles over his eyes, Kwame found himself again in the middle of a scene far to the north of where he was physically located. Melvin the ice harvester was still sitting idly on that distant plateau on the Martian polar ice.

"Why don't we just use Melvin's automatic trenching subroutines?" Kwame asked. "The manuals I was sent to study said—"

"The manufacturers always exaggerate what these babies can do on their own," Giovanni interrupted. "Melvin's not nearly as smart and independent as his designers would have you believe. In the automatic mode, which we sometimes use at night if we're behind on our quotas, he rarely operates longer than two or three hours without going into safing. The machine simply cannot integrate and synthesize all the environmental parameters as well as a human operator."

"But the manual said that this particular version number had a mean time between failures of nineteen hours."

"That's marketing hype," Giovanni said, adjusting his goggles in the copilot's seat. "When Melvin first arrived, he would dig for ten or fifteen hours without stopping. But he was also likely to injure one of his subsystems by keeping them operating in stress conditions. The repairs damn near drove us crazy. Until Narong rewrote his software and adjusted all the fault tolerances, Melvin spent more time idle than he did working. Anyway, trooper, we can talk about all this later. Let's see what you can do."

The nervous Kwame went through the entire cycle very slowly, only spilling a fraction of the ice contents before reaching the open bed of the harvester. "Not too bad," said Giovanni. "At least you're going to be trainable. Not like that last character they sent me from Mutchville."

Kwame took a deep breath and started the operation anew. For just an instant, when he first touched the levers, he imagined that he was again sitting in his favorite crane, working on a construction site in the suburbs of Dar es Salaam. He shook the flashback off and concentrated on what he was doing. *I'm not in Tanzania anymore, he thought. Hell, I'm not even on the earth. . . . But at least I finally have a good job again.*

On the second pass, Kwame tried to speed up the process. Giovanni had finished his last full cycle in eighty-four seconds. Kwame knew that he would be expected, once he was fully trained, to complete thirty cycles per hour. Although he was pleased with the end result of his first attempt, it had taken more than six minutes.

Kwame's second trenching did not fill the scoop completely, and he spilled almost half of the ice before he reached the bed. The time for the cycle was just under four minutes. In the copilot's seat Giovanni was frowning.

"That was about a forty-percent run," Giovanni said. "You don't have to be a mathematical genius to figure out that it's better to take six minutes, and dump a full scoop, than to do a forty-percenter in four."

On his third cycle Kwame kept the scoop in the trench until it was completely full. Then, just as the scoop crossed the plane of the Martian surface, the system suddenly shut down.

"Shit," said Giovanni. "Not *another* problem."

"What do we do now?" Kwame asked.

"Melvin is running through self-test," Giovanni replied. "When he is done, if the difficulty was only a transient power surge, or any similar problem that did not persist, you'll see a green light on the panel on your right. If not, that blinking yellow light will change to red and Melvin's main computer will enter the elaborate diagnostic subroutines that Narong designed."

As Giovanni was speaking the yellow light on the control panel changed to red. Moments later a message on the panel monitor indicated that component HY442, located in the receiver processor, had failed, and that its redundant backup component was not properly responding to commands.

Giovanni pulled off his goggles. "That's it for the day, folks," he said to Kwame. "Melvin is dead in the water."

Johann was in the middle of preparing his requisition lists for his trip to Mutchville when Narong phoned. He thought for a moment about letting Narong handle the anomaly meeting by himself, but Johann reminded himself that he would soon be gone for two weeks and Narong would have enough decisions to make on his own during that period.

He stopped and knocked on Narong's office door before going to the meeting. Johann was the director of what was officially known as the VOF, or Valhalla Outpost Facility. Narong Udomphol, a Thai software engineer, was his deputy. Valhalla, as it was called by its sixty to seventy permanent residents and the occasional transient scientists who used the facility as a base camp for polar expeditions, was the northernmost inhabited outpost on Mars. Its primary purpose was to convert the Martian polar ice into water and pump it through pipelines to the other inhabited regions of the planet. Although there were two other similar facilities scattered in longitude around the planet, Valhalla was by far the largest, supplying roughly half the water used by the humans living on Mars.

Johann had been in Valhalla, except for business trips to Mutchville and one remarkable vacation week touring the volcanoes of the Tharsis region, for the entire eighteen months since his arrival on Mars. He had been promoted to director of the VOF only six months earlier, in June of 2142, as measured by the earth calendar.

"Melvin has crapped out again?" Johann asked, sticking his head into Narong's office. "Isn't that the third time this month?"

"No," Narong replied. He was a short man, early thirties, with a wonderfully open smile. "It was Martin the last two times," he said. "He's in the hangar now for a complete overhaul. We're just waiting on the parts."

All three of the Valhalla ice harvesters had been given names beginning with the letter M. Out of the total of six of the mammoth machines that had been manufactured to mine the Martian ice, three of them were working at Valhalla.

"So for the time being we have only Malcolm operating?" Johann said.

Narong nodded. "We'll be below our delivery quotas again this month," he said. "But there's nothing we can do about it. Considering the parts and personnel situations, we're lucky to be pumping any water south."

The two men walked down the hall to the conference room, where six other people, including Giovanni and Kwame, were waiting. The anomaly meeting, like most at Valhalla, was loosely structured. In the early discussion Giovanni pointed out that the backup HY442 in Melvin had supposedly just been repaired by the technicians, and that it was the second useless repair in the last ten days. Johann acknowledged that the lack of qualified technical personnel was causing them serious problems at Valhalla. He promised that he would not return from Mutchville until he had hired a competent test-and-repair engineer.

Narong then suggested that since Martin was in the hangar anyway, and there would be no other replacement HY442s available until the train arrived next week, perhaps their best course of action would be to pull the necessary components out of Martin and install them in Melvin out in the field.

Narong's plan was quickly accepted. But who would do the installation? Ordinarily that would have been Giovanni's job, since he was Melvin's cognizant engineer. But he was busy training Kwame, and also preparing to leave Valhalla for good. The only certified engineering re-pairman who could be gone from the outpost for the next two days with-out significantly compromising the site operation was Johann.

As the meeting was breaking up, Narong mentioned to Johann that the new Valhalla nurse, Satoko Hayakawa, had expressed a desire to see some of the "real Mars" at the first available opportunity. Since site pro-cedures prohibited any solo human activity outside the protective bubble, would Johann be willing to have Ms. Hayakawa join him? Johann agreed, and asked Narong to have the new nurse ready to depart at sunrise the next morning.

Satoko Hayakawa was a tiny woman, even by Japanese standards. Stand-ing beside Johann in the isolation chamber for a routine vacuum test of their spacesuits, she stood barely above his waist. "Can you hear me all right?" Johann said, checking the microphone in his helmet.

"Yes, I can," she said. Satoko flashed a wide smile. She was very excited.

The Valhalla operations team, using the most recent available data on the state of the ice sheet near the outpost, had plotted an optimal trek northward for the navigation computers of the rover and the icemobile. Johann had also input the planned route, as well as maps and emergency landmark information, into the portable computer he would be carrying in the waist pouch of his spacesuit.

Satoko and he said good-bye to Narong and the others half an hour before sunrise. They walked through the door separating the inner bub-ble, surrounding Valhalla proper, from the empty outer bubble which served as an environmental buffer for the facility. After waiting five min-utes for the required pressure changes, the pair stepped gingerly through another door, out onto the plains of Mars.

This was the first time that Satoko had ever stood on the outside surface of Mars. Remembering his own initial moments without the pro-tection of either a bubble or a vehicle, Johann paused and let Satoko savor the experience. She took a few steps away from the door and then turned around slowly, studying the nearby scattered rocks, the reddish Martian soil, and a small mountain range off to the southeast. *"Kirei des,"* she mumbled to herself.

Johann and Satoko next adjusted the filters in the translucent faceplates of their helmets. The glare of the Martian sun was too power-ful for their indoor settings.

They began to walk toward the rover. It had been parked about forty meters away from the bubble. Connected to the rear of the rover, the icemobile was mounted on a low, flat trailer. Once they reached a spot where the surface had changed to ice, Johann and Satoko planned to park the rover and travel in the icemobile for the rest of their journey.

The rover was an open, tracked vehicle, with three seats, suitable for a wide variation of terrain types. It moved comparatively slowly. The icemobile, on the other hand, had been designed especially for high-speed travel on the Martian polar ice. It rode on special skis and could reach a maximum velocity of eighty kilometers per hour on flat, unbroken ice.

After they had been riding in the rover for about ten minutes, Johann commanded the vehicle to turn around so they could look back at Valhalla. The geodesic dome covering their facility looked like a mirage, completely alien among the boulder-strewn, rusty fields of Mars. Johann waited while Satoko recorded some images of Valhalla with her tiny personal video camera. He then disembarked, carrying her camera, and took some pictures of her sitting alone in the rover in her spacesuit with the Valhalla bubble in the background.

During the first hour of their drive northward across the plains of Mars, Johann tried to engage Satoko in polite conversation. The young Japanese woman, however, was either too awestruck by the Martian landscape surrounding her, or too intimidated by Johann. She did not say much. Johann learned only that Satoko was twenty-four years old, that her father was a subway engineer in the northern Japanese city of Sapporo, and that she had lived her entire life on the island of Hokkaido with her parents and two younger siblings.

The Martian terrain around them gradually became more covered with ice. There was not a distinct break between the Martian polar cap and the plains, so the decision of where to transfer from the rover to the icemobile was a subjective one. Finally, more than two hours after leaving Valhalla, a long sloping incline lifted them onto what appeared to be a part of the main polar cap. Johann radioed back to Valhalla to confirm his position and then lowered the trailer bed so that the icemobile could be driven off.

Despite the fact that neither Johann nor Satoko could feel any wind inside their spacesuits, the sense of speed as they blasted northward in the icemobile was exhilarating. Within half an hour they had entered a totally white world. Ice mountains, ice canyons, ice plateaus—it was as if they had transferred to a totally new planet.

At one point the control panel on the icemobile flashed an overheating warning and Johann, laughing at himself, was forced to slow down. At midday, in the vicinity of a dangerous ice crevasse, Johann stopped the icemobile temporarily and invited Satoko for a short stroll to relieve the monotony of sitting. While they were staring down into the deep crevasse, Johann told Satoko the story of the early Martian explorer who had died in the vicinity.

They reached Melvin a couple of hours before sunset. Johann's first task was to deploy the tent in which Satoko and he would spend the night. Although the ice harvester repairs would only take a couple of hours at the most, it would be necessary for them to spend the night in the vicinity, for it was considered too dangerous to travel across the Martian ice in darkness unless special navigation aids were available.

After Johann set up the lights around Melvin to permit him to see what he was doing in the darkness, he passed the last hour of daylight reviewing the repair procedures that had been installed in his portable computer. His primary task was to replace the nonworking HY442 components. However, the engineering team at Valhalla had also decided that Johann should test another dozen or so of Melvin's critical components for any sign of stress or degradation, and replace them if they did not completely meet specifications.

Satoko volunteered to help Johann with the repairs. They trundled together across the ice, each carrying a small bag of tools and spare parts. Johann constructed a platform three meters off the ground so that he had easy access to the key electronic equipment buried inside Melvin's belly. Then he readjusted the lights to maximize his visibility in the area where he would be working. Soon after the sun had set, Johann was already busy repairing the ice harvester.

The mammoth gray machine dwarfed the two humans on the platform. Melvin was twelve meters tall and eighteen meters long. Its scoophead could contain more than ten cubic meters of ice at a time. When Melvin and his kindred machines had originally been designed, almost two decades earlier, they were considered to be precursor systems for the truly giant ice harvesters that would be necessary once the Martian population reached several hundred thousand.

In the early 2120s, long-range projections for Mars had predicted that the total planet population would pass a hundred thousand before the middle of the century, and reach a quarter million by 2190. The Great Chaos completely altered the development of Mars. The economic depression on Earth reduced the worldwide availability of discretionary revenue, from both governments and corporations, and brought an abrupt end to the miniboom that had been occurring on the red planet.

In fact, as the Great Chaos tightened its grip on Earth, budgets allocated to support endeavors on Mars plummeted below the sustenance level, leading to critical shortages and inadequate maintenance of the planetary infrastructure. In 2136 the population on Mars declined for the first time in the twenty-second century. In 2138 and 2139, many of the multinational corporations, including the one that had designed and built Melvin and the other ice-harvesting machines, completely abandoned their Martian facilities.

By 2141, when Johann Eberhardt first arrived on Mars, almost half the remaining Martian residents were on waiting lists to return to Earth. Nevertheless, attracted by guaranteed jobs at outstanding wages, as well as a sense of adventure, people still applied for positions on Mars, undaunted by what they believed were only temporary economic difficulties.

For both Kwame Hassan and Satoko Hayakawa, assignment to Mars had been a cause for celebration. Kwame had a wife and four young children to support. Since construction was at a standstill throughout Tanzania, there had been little work for him, despite his considerable skills, for almost four years. Before he had been offered the job on Mars, Kwame had been forced to move his family into smaller quarters nearer the center of the teeming capital city. The job on Mars paid enough that Kwame's wife and children were able to move back into the more comfortable suburbs of Dar es Salaam.

Satoko had graduated with honors from her nursing college in Sapporo. When she had begun her studies, she had hoped eventually to land a desirable position at one of Japan's leading research hospitals. Unemployment in Asia's leading economic nation, however, reached double digits in 2137, and was nearing fifteen percent in 2140 when the Japanese government passed a set of laws essentially creating, through an elaborate structure of tax credits, a strict pecking order in employment practices. Men were favored over women for all categories of jobs, and individuals with families were given preference over those who were unmarried and/ or had no children. After graduation the gifted Satoko had been unable to find anything but menial work. The opportunity to come to Mars and be the head nurse for the Valhalla Outpost Facility had been a godsend.

There were no surprises during the repair process. Johann replaced the pair of HY442s, as well as three other components that did not meet specifications, in slightly more than an hour. After Melvin, upon a signal from Valhalla, passed its entire system self-test, Johann dismantled the platform and returned it to its packing cases. Satoko and he, standing over by their tent a hundred meters away, then watched as Giovanni put Melvin through two trenching cycles to verify that the giant machine was again operational.

Inside the tent, Johann and Satoko played two quick games of gin rummy before settling down inside their padded sleeping bags. Johann had never mastered the art of sleeping in a spacesuit. After a few hours of sleep he awoke, feeling stiff, and decided to take a walk around. Outside, in the Martian night, it was pitch-black everywhere except over by Melvin, where Johann had left the powerful lights deployed, at Giovanni's request, in case Valhalla wanted to do anything additional with Melvin before daylight.

Johann strolled over toward the ice harvester without any particular purpose. After examining the trench that Melvin had been digging in the ice, he decided to walk around to the other, dark side of Melvin. He switched on his flashlight so that he could see where he was walking on the ice.

Just before Johann reached the rear of the ice harvester and emerged again into a lit area, his flashlight picked up an unusual reflection from Melvin's surface, about a meter above his head. Johann stopped and directed the beam back into the area where he had seen the reflection. What he saw sent a chill of terror through his body. A cloud of tiny sparkling particles, which had apparently been compressed and hidden underneath one of the slight overhangs in Melvin's uneven surface, began to drift slowly outward toward Johann. As it approached him the bright cloud formed into a figure-eight pattern in the air.

Johann's recognition was immediate. He knew absolutely that this was exactly the same phenomenon he had seen in the Tiergarten in Berlin twenty-one months before. He shone the flashlight beam directly into the pattern, which was about a meter long, and tried to quell the powerful fear that was telling him to flee. As before, the individual particles inside the formation were moving around freely inside the pattern, but the overall shape of the cloud remained fixed.

The response of Johann's body to the burst of adrenaline triggered the monitoring systems inside his spacesuit. As he continued to stare at the sparkling figure eight a meter above his head, Johann heard a computer voice in his ear saying, "Your pulse rate is abnormally high. You should consider resting."

Johann stood perfectly still and gazed at the cloud. He was determined to see what, if anything, the strange particles were going to do. After about fifteen seconds, the figure eight drifted down to his eye level. Johann followed its path with his flashlight. As the individual sparkling particles continued to dance around inside the pattern, the overall structure of the cloud turned on its side, so that each of the two bright circles in the figure eight were facing Johann's eyes.

While he watched, the particles began to clump together. They formed into eleven white spheres each about a hundred times as large as the original particles. These eleven spheres, which did not sparkle and were marked with a single narrow, circular red band, next arranged themselves into a slow procession that moved in a line around the entire figure-eight structure.

Johann was both fascinated and frightened. *Could this bizarre formation be alive?* he asked himself, astonished at what he was seeing. He
fought against another burst of fear and the urge to run away. Several
seconds later the spheres stopped for a brief moment, and then reversed
direction in their motion inside the figure eight. "Hello," Johann said
suddenly into his microphone, even surprising himself. "I am a human
being. . . . What are you?"

To his amazement, the moment he was finished speaking the
eleven little white spheres and the figure-eight outline coalesced into one
single large white sphere about the size of a baseball. This sphere
hovered in the air in front of Johann's eyes just long enough for him to
see the great circular red band around it, and then darted quickly forward.
Johann screamed involuntarily when it smashed into his faceplate. After
his terror subsided, he realized that there had been a vivid burst of light
just an instant before the sphere, the cloud, and the sparkling particles
had all disappeared. All that was left from the encounter was an unmistakable imprint on his faceplate.

2

Johann finished packing and carried the suitcase into the living room of his small apartment. He set it on the floor next to the other two bags, one of which contained the faceplate from his spacesuit, before glancing at the clock. There was still plenty of time to eat a leisurely breakfast before his final meeting with Narong. The train would not leave Valhalla for another two hours.

Narong arrived a few minutes late. "Sorry, Johann," he said with a worried look on his face. "I've been outside checking the supplies that came in with the train. Unfortunately, the manifest we received yesterday was accurate. We're short in nearly every category, especially processor parts. I've already phoned Mutchville, but they say there's nothing they can do."

"What about the new HY442s?" Johann asked.

"They're here," Narong replied. "But only three, instead of the six that we ordered . . . Unless you find someone who can repair complex components, we're never going to make our pumping quotas."

"I know," said Johann, forcing a smile. "Hiring a competent test-and-repair engineer is my second priority in Mutchville. My first, of course, is to find a software specialist who can replace you. You're a year over term already—"

"Lucinda now knows all our critical software," Narong interrupted. "She may be young, and not talk very much, but she's quite talented. A good test-and-repair engineer is more important for the site. Besides, unless you can somehow get me a reservation back to Earth before my currently scheduled date, you're stuck with me for another nine months at least."

"We shouldn't have waited so long to apply for your return."

"It's not your fault," Narong said. "I heard rumors about the wait lists over six months ago. I just didn't want to schedule my departure until I was certain Lucinda could take over. It never occurred to me that the demand for returns might be so great that I would be forced to wait a year."

"Maybe you won't," Johann said. "When I take the faceplate by the ISA office, I'll see if they can obtain a higher priority for you. It's the least I can do after all the outstanding work you have done here in Valhalla."

Narong glanced at Johann's bags on the floor of the apartment. "So you *are* going to take your faceplate to the ISA? I thought you decided last night not to make an official report."

"I'm not going to tell them all the details of the incident," Johann said. "At least not yet . . . I just want them to send the faceplate to the chemistry laboratory for an analysis."

"But they won't do that unless you fill out a report . . . you know how the ISA works."

"Maybe I can have it done unofficially," Johann said. "I was thinking of visiting the laboratory myself and talking to the chief chemist."

"Based on what happened to that woman at the Carr Outpost," Narong said, "that's a much better idea. Otherwise, even if you're not laughed at or put on psychological leave, you're bound to become bogged down in the ISA bureaucracy."

The two men looked at each other for several seconds. "You believe my story, don't you, Narong?"

"I think so," Narong said hesitantly, "but only because I've heard the story of what happened in that park in Berlin several times before." He smiled. "Johann, I would be lying to you if I didn't say that it's a huge stretch for me to believe your tale. Everything about it is incredible. As soon as my analytical mind kicks in with its questions, my doubt begins to grow. . . . I only accept your story because you've always told me the truth about everything else. However, I must warn you, someone who doesn't know you will think—"

"I'm a kook, or suffering from Martian syndrome, or worse."

"Exactly," said Narong.

Johann sighed and shook his head. "I feel the same way now that I did in Berlin two years ago. Half of me wants to ignore what happened and continue with my normal life, while the other half tells me I must pursue this thing somehow. . . . It could well be the most important event of my life."

"Have you ever followed up on your meeting with that Spanish guy in Berlin?" asked Narong.

"No," Johann said. "The interview was less than a week before I left Earth. And both he and his assistant seemed peculiar to me. I felt uncomfortable in their presence, especially after they started telling *me* stories."

Narong looked at his watch. "Well, it's your decision, one way or the other. Meanwhile I have a facility to run in your absence. Which reminds me, that inter-Asian science group that left last week did not check in again last night. Should I be concerned? Or should I just assume they're typical scientists who are too busy working to be concerned about our safety procedures?"

"They didn't act too impressed by our protocols before they left," Johann said. "So I wouldn't worry yet. . . . By the way, are we still following their navigation beacons?"

"Yes," answered Narong. "They have been in the same spot for four days now. They are about five hundred and twenty kilometers almost due north from Valhalla, not too far from where that Ukrainian team took the controversial ice core last year. I called their campsite this morning, but there was no answer. They were probably already working out on the ice."

"If they don't check in tonight," Johann said, hoisting the bags onto his shoulder and opening the apartment door, "wake them while they're sleeping. They'll be unhappy, but they need to be reminded of our safety procedures."

The train raced southward across Mars all afternoon before making its first stop at sunset. Johann slept most of the way. Giovanni woke him when they reached BioTech City.

"Goodness," said the startled Johann. "Are we there already?"

"Yes," said Giovanni. "Right on time for a change . . . They announced five minutes ago that all disembarking passengers should come to the forward car. Unless you've changed your mind, and would like to spend Christmas here with my sister and me, this is good-bye."

Johann stood up and shook Giovanni's hand. "We'll miss you at Valhalla, Giovanni," he said. "Both your skill and your sense of humor . . . Good luck wherever you go."

"Thanks, Johann," he replied. "I've enjoyed my term, and the friendships, but I must admit that I've really been homesick the last six months. It's a great feeling to know I'll be skiing at Cortina before the winter is over."

Giovanni picked up his bags and headed for the front of the car. Johann sat back down in his seat feeling strangely disoriented. He stared out the window of the train. The edge of the bubble surrounding Bio-Tech City was about fifty meters from where the train had stopped. A wide concrete sidewalk across the reddish Martian soil led from the train path to a door in the bubble. As Johann watched, the first of the passengers moved along the sidewalk toward the door.

Giovanni stopped in the middle of the walk and waved in Johann's direction. Johann had recognized his gait immediately, even though Giovanni was too far away for him to see any specific features behind the faceplate. As he waved back Johann conjured up a picture of Giovanni in ski clothes, preparing for a day of skiing in the Italian Alps. Johann was temporarily envious. *Maybe,* he thought, *I am becoming homesick too.*

Even after the passengers from BioTech City had come onboard, there were still only three other people in the car with Johann, and the nearest was several rows in front of him. The train quickly left the Bio-Tech City bubble far behind. Out the window the Martian landscape again looked harsh and inhospitable.

Will we ever really tame this place? Johann thought. He recalled how as a boy he had been thrilled by the grandiose plans for terra-forming Mars advanced by the scientists of the ISA. *But the engineers knew better,* Johann said to himself. *They tripled the time estimates and raised the predicted costs by an order of magnitude.*

It was a moot point now. Terra-forming planning and research had been one of the many casualties of the Great Chaos. There were even some people who thought human beings should withdraw altogether from Mars, ending a continuous presence that had already lasted over a hundred years.

Johann put the tiny headphones on his ears and activated the entertainment system in the arm of his seat. He scanned through the menus that appeared on the monitor. Johann briefly watched the local Martian news from the previous day, which was mostly about the continued high emigration of the Martian residents. He then switched over to the European news video. The feature story was about Christmas preparations in Germany. Despite the continuing depression, the commentator said, nothing could stop the Germans from planning for their favorite holiday.

Johann leaned back in his seat and listened to a group of freshly scrubbed German children singing *"Stille Nacht, Heilige Nacht."* As he remembered the wonderful Christmases of his childhood, Johann felt a profound loneliness. The happy memories of waiting in his room for his mother's call, and then bounding down the stairs to see what surprises were under the Christmas tree, were accompanied by a deep heartache that brought a rare tear to Johann's eye. For a moment he wished he had accepted Giovanni's invitation to spend the holidays in BioTech City. Giovanni had praised his younger sister's cooking, as well as her intelligence, and had even suggested that she might be a good match for Johann.

Johann switched off the video, removed his earphones, and retrieved the small bag from the rack above his head. He rummaged in the bag until he found a small videocube in a plastic wrapper. He inserted the cube into the proper spot in the arm of his seat. A moment later his mother's face appeared on the screen.

"Hello, Johann," Frau Eberhardt said. She was sharply dressed in a black silk blouse and looked as if she had just visited a beauty salon. "Your father and I send our greetings. And our love." His mother smiled. "Since these transmissions have become so expensive, this will be our last video before Christmas. . . . We will miss you during the holidays, of course. This will be only the second Christmas since your birth that we have not all been together."

Johann's mother gave him the news from Potsdam, mostly about people that he could only vaguely remember, and then his father appeared briefly on the screen. Herr Eberhardt spent most of his time extolling the virtues of Wagner's *Tristan und Isolde*, which he had seen at the Berlin Opera House the previous week.

In the last part of the video Johann's mother reported that the book made from Helga Weber's journals was still selling well, even though it was no longer on the national best-seller list. "Of course your father and I appreciate what you and Uncle Hermann have done for us," she said, "but we are disturbed at times by what some people, even our friends, say about the book. . . . There is a lot of talk these days about the Nazis and the Second World War. It seems that every week or two there is a commemoration of some terrible event that happened two hundred years ago.

"That American Jew activist, Rabbi Goldberg, has been in Germany again recently. In one of his speeches he insisted that all Germans should still feel guilty for what our ancestors did during the Third Reich, and he cited passages from Helga's book as an indication of how the ordinary Germans supported Hitler and the other Nazis. Neither your father nor I ever say anything when asked by the reporters, but I know Max is very angry with what the media have done with Helga's book. He told me last week that he wished the journals had never been published, even though without the money . . ."

Johann had watched the video quickly just minutes after it had been received at Valhalla two weeks earlier. At the time there had been a major crisis at the facility and he had been very busy. He had not had much time to think about his parents then. Now, however, sitting on a train during a long journey across Mars, he was listening carefully to everything that his parents were saying.

"Oh, I almost forgot," Frau Eberhardt said on the video after she finished discussing Helga Weber's journals, "you'll never guess who I saw in the supermarket only two weeks ago. Your old girlfriend Eva Haase . . . She was quite plump and was carrying a baby girl of ten weeks wrapped up in some kind of contraption. Would you believe it, she now lives in Potsdam. Anyway, Eva asked about you and was delighted to hear that things are going so well."

Johann did not hear his mother's good-bye. The image of Eva in a supermarket, carrying a new baby against her chest, had set off another sequence of memories. Again he was aware of a powerful loneliness. He switched off the monitor when he realized that the video had finished.

He tried unsuccessfully to fall asleep again. After half an hour Johann reactivated the video system and raced through the available selections. Smiling to himself, he selected a performance of Wagner's *Siegfried* to watch. It was the same production he had seen in his family home in Potsdam a month or so before he had left for Mars.

At New Dallas a long line of passengers boarded the train. Johann watched them file out of the city bubble and walk across the sidewalk in their spacesuits. When the train was moving again, the door to Johann's car opened and five people, all wearing the blue robes of the Order of St. Michael, entered. They were following a tall, pretty, copper-skinned woman who was obviously their leader.

"Good," the leader said, surveying the half-empty car. She turned to the others. "There is plenty of room here," she said. "Put your bags on the seats. I know you are all tired. We still have three hours until Mutchville. After we finish the collection, we'll come back here and try to stretch out and sleep. . . . Brother Adrian, why don't you and Sister Marcie take the front cars? Sister Nuba and Brother José, the two in the rear. I'll do this one myself."

The Michaelites placed their traveling bags on the empty seats and then dispersed. Their leader began canvassing the other passengers in Johann's car, holding a small, decorated tin can in her right hand.

"Hello," she said, when she finally reached Johann. "I'm Sister Vivien of the Order of St. Michael. As you know, this is a very difficult time on Mars. More people are facing a Christmas without proper food and clothing than ever before. Because of the long waiting lists to return to Earth, many destitute people have been forced to remain here, and do not have any money to pay for their housing. Members of our order work without pay to distribute resources to those . . .''

Johann stared back at Sister Vivien's beautiful brown eyes and did not interrupt her. The strong interplay between them caused Vivien to falter and blush slightly in the middle of her standard speech. Nevertheless, she recovered her composure and finished with a flourish.

"And how do I know," Johann asked playfully, "that you and your friends will not simply take the money I give you and spend it on a lavish Christmas dinner for yourselves?"

"With turkey, dressing, gravy, and even cranberry sauce?" Vivien said with a big grin.

Johann nodded. Vivien suddenly sat down in the empty seat next to him. "Look, whoever you are . . . what is your name, by the way?"

"Johann. Johann Eberhardt."

"Look, Johann Eberhardt," Vivien said. "I would absolutely love to have a turkey dinner with all the trimmings. And if you would like to come around to our church in Mutchville, and provide one for us, we would be more than happy to join you. But I have made a vow to the Big Man—that's probably God to you—that each and every cent I collect will be used for those in need. And I myself don't really qualify. Therefore—"

Vivien suddenly stopped talking and looked up and down at Johann one more time. "Good grief," she said, "you are one tall man. . . . How tall are you?"

"Two meters eleven."

"Hell," she said. "You're not a man, you're a giant." The door behind them opened and two Michaelites entered. "Hey," Vivien shouted at Sister Nuba and Brother José, "come over here. I'm having a conversation with a giant. . . . Now, you, Johann Eberhardt, why don't you stand up so my friends and I can see how tall you really are?"

Johann laughed and stood up, stooping slightly so that he didn't bump his head on the luggage rack. "Whooeee," said Vivien, putting a hand against the top of her forehead and gazing up at him, "I don't believe I have ever seen a man that tall except on a basketball court. And now that you're up," she said without a pause, "why don't you reach into your pocket, pull out some money, and make it a merrier Christmas for someone else?"

Johann shook his head and laughed again. "You are . . . incredible," he said, handing Vivien ten Martian dollars.

"Just serving God and my fellowman," Vivien said, laughing herself, "both of whom thank you, Giant Johann Eberhardt."

3

Johann's first two days in Mutchville were a disaster. First the manager of the travel office at the ISA
informed him that the only way Narong could obtain a place on an earlier
transport to Earth would be to buy a confirmed reservation from somebody else. "And that's illegal for an ISA employee or contractor," she said.
"If it became known that your friend had purchased his return ticket on
the black market, he could lose his service termination bonus."

Johann fared no better when he tried to file a protest with the ISA
quality engineer about the quantity of parts that had been allocated to
Valhalla. The bureaucrat in charge was decidedly unsympathetic, telling
Johann that he should consider himself lucky, since many of the outposts
were not receiving any of the parts they ordered.

In the afternoon of the first day Johann attempted to find someone
inside the ISA who could analyze the residue on his faceplate. He was
shuffled from office to office until one uncharacteristically honest young
man explained to him that the agency was currently in the process of
dismantling its entire chemical analysis capability on Mars.

Grumpy and discouraged, Johann visited the employment agency affiliated with Guntzel and Stern an hour after he left ISA headquarters. At the agency, after first reconfirming his intention to remain on Mars for another two years, Johann was told that there had been very few responses to his openings, despite the fact that unemployment was high and the positions had been aggressively advertised.

"You must realize," the agency manager said, "that we are in a state of quasi-panic here in Mutchville. Nobody is thinking about anything except returning to Earth. The idea of working for a minimum of six months in a distant outpost is simply out of the question, even for individuals who are unemployed and broke."

On the second day of his trip Johann interviewed the meager group of candidates who had responded to the employment office's call. One of the applicants was adequate for the semiskilled technician's job in the communications group. Nobody else met his minimum qualifications. Johann then spent the afternoon phoning people in Mutchville who appeared qualified for his engineering openings, based upon the comprehensive database lists, and were presently unemployed. He was not able to convince a single person to come in for an interview. Unwilling to accept that the situation was hopeless, Johann talked one more time with the agency manager before returning to his hotel.

"There is one other option," the man told Johann, "although it is decidedly risky. A new government policy allows outpost facilities to recruit employees from the penal colony at Alcatraz. Your counterpart from the Utopia Mine Facility had threatened to close down production altogether because of inadequate staffing. He found half a dozen recruits at Alcatraz who were willing to be indentured servants for six months in exchange for a gubernatorial pardon. . . . I don't know if you can match any of your skilled needs in the prison population, but you can probably fill all the other positions. . . ."

As Johann's train passed through the bubbles surrounding Mutchville, beginning the seventy-kilometer journey to Alcatraz, Johann was thinking about his videophone conversation the previous day with one of the deputy wardens at the prison. The deputy, a dark Swiss woman named Anna Kasper, had been extremely helpful. She had promised to make available the penal colony's complete computer files on all of the job applicants and also volunteered to assist Johann personally during his visit.

Ms. Kasper was waiting for him in the reception area just inside the Alcatraz bubble. She introduced herself before Johann had even finished removing his spacesuit. Ms. Kasper was in her midthirties, with striking brown eyes and a surprisingly attractive face that was much softer than it had appeared on the videophone. After a few minutes of conversation,

Johann could tell that Anna Kasper was one of those rare people who actually listens carefully.

Johann spent the rest of the morning screening applications on the computer monitor in Anna's office. Almost half the prison population had applied for one of his positions. It was easy to understand why. Although a free man might not want to live in the isolation of Valhalla for six months, a long-term prisoner was thrilled by the idea of a paying job for half a year plus a full pardon upon completion.

At Anna's suggestion, they narrowed the field by dividing the applicants into four groups, classifying each prisoner as either "qualified" or not, and "dangerous" or not. Anna classified a high percentage of the candidates as dangerous. Johann allowed her to remove from consideration all the dangerous applicants for the nonengineering positions; however, since there were only five qualified candidates for the two engineering openings in the entire prison population, all but one of whom were declared to be dangerous by Anna, Johann decided to interview them all.

"Well, how did it go?" Anna asked an exhausted Johann after the final interview of the first day was completed six hours later. She entered the small conference room and handed him a beer.

"All right, I think," he answered after thanking her for the beer. "Basically, I've already seen good candidates for all the nontechnical positions, except maybe the site supervisor, and that funny American Barry Watson is an excellent software engineer. . . . By the way, why is he here anyway? I haven't checked his prison files yet."

"He embezzled money, both here and on Earth, by breaking into bank computer systems. I should point out that Barry has shown no remorse. He may be difficult for you to manage."

"We'll talk about that tomorrow," Johann said, standing up and stretching. He took a long drink from his beer. "Or maybe later tonight, after I've had some food."

"Our normal dinner hour here was over long ago," Anna said, "but I've had a full meal prepared for you. It's sitting on the conference table in my office."

Anna sat opposite Johann while he ate. They talked about the applicants at first, but later the topic of conversation turned to the increasingly tense political and economic situation on Mars.

"I hate to be a pessimist," Anna said, "but I believe the conditions here are going to get much worse before they improve."

"So do I," Johann said between bites.

"They've cut our staff here again," Anna said, "effective two weeks from now. Neither the warden nor I think the number of guards that has been allocated will be enough to preserve order here. It's a frightening idea . . . the prisoners may take over Alcatraz."

"Did the warden explain this to the governor?"

"Yes," Anna said. "But it made no difference. From the government's point of view, Alcatraz is the least of their problems. After all, as one member of the governor's cabinet said, 'So what if the convicts revolt? What are they going to do out there in that isolated bubble all by themselves?'

"Look, I don't want to beat around the bush. . . . I'm worried about my safety and, quite frankly, I have had enough of this kind of work for a while. It seems to me that I am well suited for that site supervisor's position you have open at Valhalla. My experience here will be an added benefit if you decide to hire any of the prisoners. I hope you don't think I'm being too forward, but I have prepared a résumé for you to read tonight."

Johann stopped chewing and smiled. "So now the real reason for all your personal attention becomes clear. When you invited me to have dinner in your office I thought perhaps . . ."

"It did cross my mind," Anna said with a small laugh, "especially this morning. But my first interest is the job. And I assure you that I am a complete professional."

"I never doubted it for a minute," Johann said.

Johann stared across the table at the attractive, hard-looking woman with the bleached hair and sexy eyes. "Excuse me," he said, shaking his head slowly, "I don't think I understand."

"Yes, you do," Ludmila Krasovec replied. She began unbuttoning her blouse, exposing her ample cleavage. Johann felt an instantaneous surge of lust.

"I am not really a very good programmer, Herr Eberhardt," she said, leaning forward in her chair, "but I have superb talents in other areas . . . if you know what I mean."

She inhaled again on her cigarette. A slight smile played around her lips as she blew the smoke out slowly. Her eyes never left Johann's.

"I'm certain that your talents are considerable, Ms. Krasovec," Johann said, awkwardly forcing a smile. "But we are looking for someone with strong programming experience."

The Czech woman stubbed out her cigarette in the ashtray. "I bet the winters in Valhalla are dark and dreadfully boring," she said. "Imagine what it would be like to have a body like this next to you in bed every night."

"Thank you for your application, Ms. Krasovec," Johann said abruptly. He stood up on the other side of the table and motioned toward the door to the room.

"You'll think about me after I'm gone," Ludmila said cockily several seconds later. She turned around after she reached the door. "If you change your mind, my offer's still good. . . ."

Johann stared in disbelief as the door closed behind her. He rubbed his eyes. *Dammit,* he thought, *I am really losing my balance. For a few moments I actually found that woman enticing.*

He sat down again at the table and checked his interview schedule on the computer screen. He was already tired. Johann phoned Anna in the adjoining room and told her that he was going to take a fifteen-minute recess.

"Worn-out already?" Anna teased him with a laugh. "Did Ludmila use up all your energy?"

"Why didn't you warn me about her?" Johann asked.

"I suggested last night that you should read the prison files carefully *before* you begin each interview. Then you can avoid surprises. That's why we prepared all the information for you."

"There's not enough time, Anna," Johann replied. "I barely have time to catch my breath from one interview to the next."

"Well, make certain you study the files before you talk to this next applicant," Anna said. "Yasin al-Kharif is one of the most fascinating individuals I have ever met. . . . You would have seen him yesterday, except he was observing the Islamic sabbath and refused to meet with you until today."

During the recess Johann drank a Coke and read both the application and the prison files for Mr. al-Kharif. The application was sensational. The man had a master's degree in mechanical engineering from the University of Damascus. Yasin al-Kharif had also been a test engineer on several high-technology projects, including, just before his most recent conviction, a yearlong stint at Daewoo's Martian facility. Daewoo was the Korean firm that had manufactured the ice harvesters used at Valhalla.

Although Mr. al-Kharif had not worked directly on the ice harvesters, from his résumé Johann knew that he would definitely be familiar with Daewoo's certification procedures, their testing methods, and most importantly, their component lists. The man's experience was perfect! Johann chastised himself for not having read the man's application more carefully earlier.

When Johann read the first page of the prison files, however, he began having second thoughts:

YASIN AL-KHARIF

Sex: Male

Birth Date: May 11, 2110
Height: 1.55 meters
Intelligence: 4.04(!!)

Identification No: 283-482-11-1145
Birthplace: Alexandria, Egypt
Weight: 65 kilograms
Socialization: 0.29

CONVICTIONS:
(1) Sexual Assault, Mutchville, Mars, September 14, 2140
(2) Attempted Rape, Mutchville, Mars, August 22, 2138
(3) Sodomy of a Minor, Lahore, Pakistan, March 18, 2136
(4) Second-Degree Rape, Canterbury, England, July 4, 2134
(5) Sexual Assault, Damascus, Syria, February 11, 2133

Summary Psychological Profile: Genius intelligence; enormously arrogant, disdainful of "inferiors" and all females; resents and resists authority; self-sufficient and extraordinarily capable; loves challenges and arguments; broad basic knowledge, especially in engineering, science, and history; violent temper; practicing Muslim but not overly devout.

Johann was rereading the file when Mr. Yasin al-Kharif walked into the interview room. The applicant screwed up his nose and sniffed the air. "Cigarette smoke," he said with a sneer. "I hate it. . . . I hope you're not going to smoke."

"No," said Johann, extending his hand across the table. "I am not a smoker."

"Probably some bitch," Mr. al-Kharif said, sitting down in the chair and ignoring Johann's hand. "They love to smoke. Did you know that twice as many women are addicted to nicotine as men? It's another of their many weaknesses."

"I am Johann Eberhardt, director of the Valhalla Outpost Facility," Johann began. "Valhalla's function is to mine the polar ice and produce water—"

"I know all about Valhalla," Mr. al-Kharif interrupted, "or I wouldn't be here for this interview. . . . I'm not like all the other idiots you've been talking to. Let's cut through the crap, Eberhardt. The sheet that was circulating through the prison said you need a test-and-repair engineer. Exactly what kind of a job do you have available?"

Johann had the distinct impression, as the conversation progressed, that it was Yasin al-Kharif who was doing the interviewing. He certainly asked most of the questions. The little Arab was definitely intelligent, and he had firsthand knowledge of most of the components and subsystems contained in the complicated machines at Valhalla.

"You have to change the logic on those HY442s," he said at one point, "or you'll never obtain any reasonable lifetimes. There's one particular circuit that is notoriously weak. We added a K93 hyperchip to the HY442s on the bulldozer robots and doubled the mean time between failures. . . . Better still, don't those harvesters have QC14s in their navigation computers? You can take a pair of those, adjust five of the circuits, and perform all the HY442 functions."

Johann was staggered by the man's competence. And although he found Mr. al-Kharif's manner abrasive, he did not think it would be impossible to work with him. In his brief career he had already encountered more than one irascible genius.

"So," Johann said near the end of the interview, "do you have any other questions about the job?"

"Yeah," Mr. al-Kharif answered. "Tell me about the people I'll be working with, other than you. . . . I can tell you that I don't work well with cunts, especially outspoken ones."

Johann was shocked. He hesitated a few seconds before replying. "Mr. al-Kharif," he said slowly, "I must tell you that I find your repeated references to women as 'bitches' and 'cunts' offensive, to say the very least. A few members of the engineering staff at Valhalla are women and I won't—"

"I get your message, Ace," Yasin al-Kharif interrupted. "Good for you. You're an equal-gender employer. . . . I can work with women if I must, as long as they are competent and not too strident about feminism. What I can't stand are those dykes who argue that they've been discriminated against for thousands of years and should be favored over men in job assignments and promotions."

Johann stood up and walked around the desk. He shook Mr. al-Kharif's hand, which was limp. The small man barely reached Johann's rib cage. "I plan to make my decision in the next few days," Johann said. "You will be notified one way or the other."

"Don't think that just because you're so much taller than I am that I will be cowed or deferential," Mr. al-Kharif said in parting. "You may be the boss, but I know who's the smarter between us."

All that and a little man's complex as well, Johann thought as he watched the Arab leave the room.

On the train ride back to Mutchville Johann weighed the pros and cons of hiring Yasin al-Kharif. He did not make a decision, however, because he was constantly distracted by the antics of three young women who were passengers in his car. They were laughing noisily two rows in front of him, on the opposite side of the aisle. One of the young ladies, a vivacious blonde with adorable long ringlets, flashed a wide smile at Johann every time he looked in her direction. About fifteen minutes before the train entered the outer Mutchville bubble, the blonde walked back to Johann's seat.

"Excuse me," she said, "my friends and I were wondering. . . . Are you married?"

"No," Johann replied with an inviting smile.

"Hey, girls," the blonde yelled immediately to her friends, "he's single. . . . I was right."

For the remainder of the journey the blonde, a Danish girl named Margrethe, sat beside Johann, flirting unabashedly. Her two friends took the seats across the aisle and joined the light conversation. They talked about Christmas and parties and friends of theirs in Mutchville. The young women had spent the day at Alcatraz visiting a friend from the university who had made the mistake of having recreational drugs in her possession outside the Other Zone.

"What were you doing at Alcatraz?" Margrethe asked Johann. "Are you one of the guards?"

When Johann explained that he had visited Alcatraz to interview some of the prisoners for jobs at Valhalla, the young ladies started asking questions. It was quickly revealed that Johann did not spend much time in Mutchville, and that he would only be in town for a few more days. The young women politely continued the conversation until the train reached the station, but the flirtatiousness vanished from Margrethe's behavior as soon as she understood that Johann offered no long-term prospects. Johann bade the ladies good-bye with some sadness.

As he left the station and began walking toward his hotel, Johann realized that he was in desperate need of some sexual contact with a woman. The flirtations with Margrethe and Anna, Johann's initial response to the Krasovec woman, even the overtones in his conversation with Sister Vivien on the train to Mutchville—all the signs indicated that his horniness had reached an unmanageable level.

But what can I do about it? Johann asked himself. He remembered his last sexual encounter, a one-night stand with a pert Belgian scientist heading out of Valhalla to study the Martian polar region, and was astonished when he calculated that it had been nine months since that night. *No wonder I'm having so much trouble keeping my mind on my work.*

With thoughts of women and sex churning in his mind, Johann

turned onto the street leading to his hotel. There, on his right, he noticed a small neon sign flashing in the darkness. THE BALCONY—RESERVATIONS OFFICE, it said.

Johann stopped, standing in front of the sign. He remembered clearly a conversation he had had with Narong just before he had left Valhalla. Narong, who had none of the inhibitions about sex that Johann had inherited from his immediate family, had extolled the virtues of a particular brothel called the Balcony, saying it was better even than the famous Xanadu Resort near his boyhood home of Chiang Rai. "The Balcony is expensive," Narong had told him, "but worth every penny. By far the best in the Other Zone . . . You tell them what you want when you make your reservation, and boy, do they deliver."

At length Johann entered the door beside the sign and heard a soft chiming sound. The place reminded him of a doctor's office. There was a small waiting room, with a television screen, an electronic reader, and a rack of magazine and newspaper disks. On one side was a window with a counter. An attractive woman in a business suit appeared in the window several seconds later.

"May I help you?" she asked pleasantly.

Johann approached the window. "Perhaps," he said nervously. "I would like to ask you about your . . . services."

"You've never been here before?" the woman said.

"No," Johann replied. "But I have a friend who has come here a couple of times. He has recommended the Balcony very highly. I think I understand the process, but I don't know—"

"Let me suggest you watch our video first," she said, handing him a small cube. "The Balcony is a unique and very unusual establishment. Most of your questions will be answered by the video."

Johann sat down on the small couch after placing the cube in the television. The Balcony video began with a long procession of beautiful women dressed in every possible fashion, ranging from evening dresses, to sweatshirts and jeans, to bikinis. "The Balcony," the narrative voice intoned, "is not an ordinary brothel. The Balcony has been designed to satisfy the secret fantasies of the sexual hedonist in a safe and discreet way. . . ."

The video was only four minutes long. It explained that there were no set prices at the Balcony, that each "fantasy session" required individual design before a price could be established, and that all payments must be made at the time of the reservation.

"Do you have any questions?" the woman said when Johann approached the counter after watching the video.

"How do I explain what I would like?" Johann asked hesitantly.

"We have fantasy booths here in the office," the woman said. "You sit down in front of a recording camera and just talk about what you want your experience to be like. At times questions will flash on the monitor in the booth, prompting you to include more details, or seeking clarification of something you have said. When you are finished our designers will review what you have requested and will set a price on your fantasy, as well as define any limitations that must be imposed."

"How long does this evaluation process take?" Johann asked.

The woman checked a computer monitor behind her. "Right now it would take about twenty-five minutes. . . . I must remind you, however, that you are required to pay a nonrefundable fifty dollars for the evaluation itself. If you are not seriously considering making a reservation, please do not—"

"No," Johann interrupted. "I am definitely serious. I want to make a reservation for Christmas Eve." He handed her his identity card.

"May I make a suggestion?" she said politely after the business transaction was finished. "Since this is your first time at the Balcony, you may not know exactly what it is you're seeking. That is all right. Our designers and hostesses are both experienced and knowledgeable. It is very important, however, that you spell out any specifics that could detract from your appreciation of your fantasy encounter. For example, if you have preferences about the race, age, length or color of hair, dress, or other personal characteristics of your desired hostess, you should express them now. In the very few situations in which the Balcony has had a displeased customer, it has always been because the customer did not state explicitly what he was seeking."

Johann thanked the woman for her advice. She then pressed a button and the door next to the counter opened. Johann was surprised at his nervousness as he entered the indicated private booth and sat down. The monitor in front of him offered the first prompt.

"My name is Johann Eberhardt," he said. "I am thirty-one years old and my nation of origin is Germany. I am the director of the Valhalla Outpost Facility, which . . ."

Johann was in the booth for almost an hour. At first he talked about himself, his family, and his personal history. When it was obvious that he was becoming more comfortable, the prompts on the monitor invited him to describe his ideal sexual encounter, including the characteristics of his partner's personality. Johann had very clear opinions about what he liked and disliked in women. But when the prompts became more explicit, and sexual in nature, Johann had some trouble answering. He had never been comfortable talking about the details of sex. Eventually, however, when Johann allowed himself to think about what fantasies were the most stimulating during masturbation, he managed to communicate what he was seeking on Christmas Eve.

After he returned to the waiting room, Johann read an electronic magazine for fifteen minutes. Then he happened to notice a small placard on a table in the corner of the room. "The Balcony regrets to inform its clients that we will no longer be in business after March 30, 2143," it said.

Johann crossed the room and picked up the placard. *Another casualty of the depression,* he thought. *Even vice requires a healthy economy.*

"Your evaluation has been completed, Mr. Eberhardt," the woman behind the counter suddenly said. "We can confirm your reservation for eight o'clock on Christmas Eve. . . . You are a fortunate man. Our assistant manager herself will be your hostess."

"And what is the cost?" Johann asked.

"First I am pleased to tell you," the woman said, "that even though you made some unusual requests, requiring substantial setup time, the Balcony intends to fulfill all major elements of your fantasy except one. . . . We cannot provide a hostess who both meets all your other specifications and speaks fluent German."

"That's all right," Johann said. "I threw in the language request as an extra." He smiled. "I am quite comfortable making love in English."

There was a short silence. "The cost, please," Johann repeated.

"Including absolutely everything but the tip for your hostess, the cost of your fantasy experience will be seven hundred and fifty Martian dollars."

Johann whistled. "This had better be good," he said several seconds later when he handed the woman his identity card.

J ohann woke up early on the day designated as Christmas Eve on Mars. He worked out in the hotel swimming pool and recorded a short video to be sent to his parents. On his way back to his room to phone Narong at Valhalla, he passed through the hotel lobby, which was festooned with Christmas garlands. Johann stopped in front of the large, green tree in the center of the lobby and smiled to himself. The Christmas decorations made him think about the way the earth calendar had been superimposed on life on Mars.

Since the Martian day was actually about forty-two minutes longer than the days on Earth, adjustments were necessary to keep the two calendars compatible. Each Martian month except February had one less day than the equivalent month on the earth, and there were no leap years in the Martian calendar. The small differences that remained were straightened out at the end of each decade.

The Martian year was a more complicated issue. The working calendar essentially ignored the fact that a year on the red planet was actually six hundred and eighty-seven days. Since the human residents of the red planet spent virtually all their time in a controlled environment under the protective bubbles, they were not affected by the large temperature changes from one Martian season to another. Their lives were, however, impacted by the dust storms that usually occurred during the Martian summer. When these storms were intense and widespread, all travel and movement of cargo was halted. Neither the train system nor the shuttles could operate safely in the presence of the thick clouds of swirling dust driven by four- and five-hundred-kilometer-per-hour winds. For that reason, the Martian seasons were always noted on the earth-oriented calendars.

Johann had to wait more than half an hour before the operator managed to make a phone connection with Valhalla. At first Johann could not see Narong at all, and his Thai deputy sounded as if he were underwater. Five minutes into the call, the audio had cleared up, but Narong's image still faded from the screen occasionally.

"Mars Telephone has already informed us," Narong said while the two men were discussing the poor quality of the transmission, "that they do not intend to keep the video links operating north of BioTech. The ISA will no longer pay the maintenance costs."

"I'm afraid my news is not good either," Johann replied. "To begin with, I can't get an earlier reservation for you."

"I hadn't expected you would be able to do anything," Narong said. "But thank you for trying. What about the parts situation, though? Did you explain to those yo-yos that we cannot continue to meet our quotas if our equipment isn't maintained properly?"

Narong was not happy when Johann described his unsatisfactory visit to the ISA Quality Office. The two engineers groused about bureaucrats and institutional inefficiencies for several minutes, and then Johann summarized the status of his personnel search, focusing on the skilled positions.

"Watson and Kasper sound fine," Narong said. "I've dealt with warped hackers like Watson before. They're weird but relatively harmless. . . . Incidentally, I have no problem with the basic idea of hiring convicts—as long as they're not violent. In some ways, the regimen here at Valhalla is not unlike that in a prison. But this guy al-Kharif worries me. It would be great to have someone with his background, but what do we do if he assaults one of our female staff members?"

"It is understood that all the jobs, and the eventual pardons," Johann replied, "are contingent upon exemplary behavior. I will be acting essentially as al-Kharif's probation officer. I can return him to prison at any time, without cause, to serve the rest of his term."

"Damn," said Narong. "This one is a tough call. The only person even remotely qualified for our most important opening turns out to have a prehistoric attitude toward women."

"It's even worse than that," Johann said. "Al-Kharif is gifted, superbly qualified for the job. My guess is that he will overhaul the testing-and-repair processes and drastically improve our operating efficiency."

"If he doesn't rape somebody first . . . I would not want to be in your position. It sounds as if you're prepared to make a pact with the devil."

After a brief discussion of the demise of the ISA's chemical analysis laboratories and Johann's failure to find anyone to examine his faceplate, Narong told Johann that there had still been no communication between Valhalla and the scientists of the inter-Asian polar expedition.

"Tomorrow it will be a week since we had any kind of contact with them," Narong said. "We have radioed at least once each night, and we even tried during the day yesterday—in case they're on an unusual sleep cycle."

"Can you verify whether or not their communications equipment is working?" Johann asked.

"We have tried twice. Both times we have obtained ambiguous results. It's possible that their gear has malfunctioned."

"So we don't really know for certain that there is a problem," said Johann.

"And we don't know they're all right, either," replied Narong. "Yesterday I contacted ISA headquarters and asked for a charge authorization to send one of the drone rovers out to look for them. Do you know what they said? Can't pay for it unless a demonstrated emergency exists! The usual bureaucratic bullshit."

"Do we even have a working drone to spare?" Johann asked.

"That's the other difficulty," Narong answered. "Two are in the shop. The other four are fully engaged inspecting the conveyor lines."

"So what do you suggest?" Johann said.

"Let's try to contact them by radio for two more days. If we don't hear any response, we send a drone rover to the campsite. . . . Even if we must take the money out of our overhead."

"I agree," said Johann.

When his conversation with Narong was completed, Johann decided to take a stroll around Mutchville. After wandering around the town for almost an hour, Johann found himself in a residential area, surrounded by apartments, a few houses, and an occasional strip shopping center. He had already turned around, and was heading back toward the center of town by an alternate route, when he spotted, across a street on a small office next to a sports card shop, a sign that said THE RAMA SOCIETY. At first Johann thought his eyes were playing tricks on him. After verifying that he had indeed read the sign correctly, he crossed the street and entered the small office.

The front room was not much larger than a coat closet in an expensive home. Two folding chairs were against the window. Behind the small counter facing the door was a wall covered by a large white banner with the words THE RAMA SOCIETY printed in bold red. Both the side walls were bare. There was another door on the far right of the wall behind the counter.

Johann stood in the room and waited for at least two minutes. Nobody came. At length he walked up and pounded lightly on the counter. "Hello," he said. "Is anybody home?"

Johann heard footsteps only a few seconds before the door behind the counter was opened by a short, plump, bespectacled white man wearing a long red-and-white stocking cap on his head. He took one look at Johann and the color drained out of his ruddy face. "Oh my God," he said, quickly closing the door and disappearing.

"Clem," Johann heard the man shout. "You must come here. You won't believe who just walked into the office."

Half a minute later a woman, who looked like the man's twin sister, also wearing a long red-and-white stocking cap on her head, stuck her face into the room and looked at Johann. "Jesus," she yelled, immediately turning around and closing the door again. "You're right, Darwin," she shouted. "There's no doubt about it."

Johann waited patiently for the two strange people to return. He could hear them talking on the other side of the door, but he could not understand what they were saying. Finally he decided enough was enough. "Hello again," he said in a loud voice. "I'm still here."

The door opened slowly and both the man and the woman stumbled into the room. "We're sorry," the man said shyly, chewing on his bottom lip and not looking at Johann. "We didn't know you were coming and you kind of, well, you caught us by surprise."

"Hell, we didn't even know you were on Mars," the woman said. Emboldened by Johann's smile, she came around the corner and grabbed his arm. "He's real all right, Darwin. This sure ain't no damn costume."

The man now joined them and, as an afterthought, stuck out his hand. "I'm Darwin Bishop," he said. "And this is my wife, Clementine. You can call her Clem for short."

"I'm pleased to meet you, Darwin," Johann said. "My name is Johann Eberhardt. . . . You and your wife seem to have mistaken me—"

"So that's your name," Darwin interrupted. "Johann Eberhardt. We can finally fit a name to your famous face."

"Jesus, he is tall," Clem now said. "I had no idea from the video that he was such a big man. . . . What do you think, Darwin, maybe two-ten or so . . . ?"

"Two meters eleven," Johann offered.

"Hell, you're a damn giant," Clem said. "No wonder those funny particles singled you out for contact."

Johann was starting to understand. These two portly people, both of whom were now circling excitedly around him, had obviously seen the Carlos Sauceda video in which Johann had described in detail his strange encounter in the Tiergarten. At Carlos's suggestion, Johann had not identified himself in the video.

"This is just too good to be true," Darwin was saying. "What a wonderful Christmas present for all our society members here on Mars."

"We must send out a message immediately," Clem said. "Everyone will want to meet and question Mr. Eberhardt."

"If you don't mind"—Johann now spoke again, frightened by the prospect of meeting a covey of Darwins and Clems—"I would like to take this a little more slowly. Could we start with what you know about those funny particles you mentioned . . . ?"

Darwin and Clem took Johann into the back of the office, which was an amazing disaster of Christmas packages, boxes, computers, and other electronic equipment scattered in no apparent order around the large room. They found a table and Darwin set up three chairs around it. Clem brought Johann something to drink and they began to talk. The couple peppered him excitedly with questions, wanting to know what he had felt during the experience, what his theories were to explain what he had seen, and what he believed about the existence of intelligence either out in space or in some other, unperceived dimension. They were disappointed by Johann's unimaginative answers. Both Clem and Darwin had concocted creative, but different, explanations for the particles, neither of which appealed to Johann's logical mind.

The Bishops told Johann that his video had arrived four months previously and had immediately caused a sensation in their society, primarily because the chemical analysis of the imprints on his pouch had identified some complex molecules that were not manufactured on the earth. Johann asked some technical questions about the molecules, specifically about the likelihood that they could be waste products of fairly standard chemical reactions, but Darwin and Clem could provide no information.

A few minutes later the phone rang. Darwin located it behind a pile of boxes. "Guess who's sitting here in the office talking to Clem and me," Darwin said, after he and his friend Wyatt had exchanged greetings. "That German in the video, the one who captured the tiny spheres in Berlin . . . Really . . . I shit you not. . . . No, I can't show you because I don't remember where I put the video connection. . . . He just walked in the door, about an hour ago. Clem and I nearly passed out. . . . Can you believe it, Wyatt, we now have *three* people on Mars who have made contact with those funny particles. The odds against it must be astronomical. . . . I don't know, Wyatt, we haven't asked him. But we'll let you know. . . . Merry Christmas to you too. Good-bye now."

When Darwin hung up, Johann asked immediately about his reference to the "three" people on Mars who had made contact with the particles.

"It's two of those nuns from the Order of St. Michael," Clem said. "They were in England at the time of their encounters. They both saw the particles on the same day. Carlos managed to talk with one of them a week or so after he made your recording."

"One of our society members recognized the nun from the video," Darwin said. "He saw her supervising the food distribution at the homeless shelter in the Newport section last week. When he confronted her, the nun told him to go away, that she wanted nothing to do with the Rama Society."

"We don't really know who the other nun is," Clem added, "but Carlos wrote in the society newsletter that she is probably on Mars also. Carlos deduced that fact from some comments the first nun made after the interview."

"May I see their video?" Johann asked.

"Of course," Darwin said. "I should be able to find it here somewhere."

He rummaged through a couple of boxes for three or four minutes. "Here it is," he said brightly. "The label says 'Two Nuns on the Same Day,' received October seventeenth, 2142."

"Why did it take so long to arrive?" Johann wondered out loud.

"Carlos said that the Order of St. Michael gave him some trouble. They said they were concerned about the video's impact on their public image."

"Hell," added Clem, "according to Carlos, the order even tried to buy the video from him in exchange for a generous contribution to the society. . . . He didn't send out any copies until he was fairly certain that the Order of St. Michael had forgotten all about it."

Johann recognized Sister Vivien immediately, but he did not say anything to Darwin and Clem. Vivien told her story succinctly, emphasizing the angelic shape of the particle cloud and the fact that she had been in the process of making her ordination decision when the particles appeared. *That's probably why the order didn't want the video circulated*, Johann thought. *Even though I don't see why it would be damaging.*

Toward the end of the video, in a sequence lasting no more than a minute, Sister Vivien described another similar encounter by a fellow Michaelite priestess in Hyde Park in London on the same morning.

After watching Vivien's video twice, Johann stood up to leave. "Surely you're not going already," Clem said. "We've just started to talk . . . and we haven't even scheduled a time for you to meet with the society."

"I have a lunch appointment with a friend," Johann said, "and I still have some Christmas shopping to do."

"But when will you be back?" Darwin asked. "And how do we contact you?"

"I certainly thank you for all the information you have given me," Johann said, "and I appreciate your excitement about my incident. . . . But I would rather not have my address and phone number public knowledge among your members. My privacy is very important to me. I'm certain you can understand."

"Yes, we can," Clem said, clearly disappointed. "We're just delighted that you stopped by. Could we ask one favor before you go?"

"What is it?" Johann asked.

"Could we take some photos and a short video showing that you really were here? It would mean a lot to us."

"Certainly," said Johann.

While he posed alongside Darwin and Clem, Johann's mind was elsewhere. He was both fascinated and intrigued by the fact that Sister Vivien had also seen the strange particles. *I have a nun, or is it a priestess, to see*, Johann said to himself. *Before I leave for Valhalla.*

5

The Order of St. Michael was flourishing on Mars under Beatrice's
leadership. Three months after
her arrival, contributions and new recruits had both skyrocketed, despite
the difficult economic situation. Soon thereafter, Sister Beatrice supervised the design and construction of a new cathedral not far from downtown Mutchville. It took only seven months from groundbreaking to
completion of the building, primarily because of the extraordinary dedication of the Michaelite priests and priestesses who provided the labor.

The cathedral was the first major new building in Mutchville in
three years. Its towering spire reached within forty meters of the bubble
itself. At the front entrance stood a bronze sculpture of Christ, surrounded by birds and children. Underneath the bare feet of Jesus was
written, SUFFER THE CHILDREN TO COME UNTO ME. At the rear of the cathedral was a second bronze statue, this one of St. Michael standing on the
steps of the Victor Emmanuel Monument in the Piazza Veneto in Rome.
Around his head of thick curls was a great circle of flame representing the
nuclear blast that vaporized him instantly in late June of 2138.

The doors of the cathedral were open twenty-four hours a day. People could come for free food and clothing at any time. They were welcome to sleep on the cots and mats, use the toilets, see one of the Michaelite physicians, or if they were burdened by a problem, they could talk to one of the priests or priestesses who specialized in counseling.

Johann was astonished by the large number of people moving in and out of the cathedral on Christmas Eve. For ten minutes he stood across the plaza, leaning against a storefront. While he watched the activity at the church Johann planned what he was going to say to Sister Vivien.

He realized that even finding Sister Vivien might be difficult. *She might not even be in Mutchville at all,* he said to himself while he was crossing the plaza toward the cathedral.

While Johann was walking the door to the smoking kiosk beside the theater opened and a dark-skinned woman, wearing the blue robe and the blue-and-white headpiece of the Order of St. Michael, stepped out. Johann did not see her. Sister Vivien, however, recognized him immediately. She intercepted Johann in the center of the plaza.

"So, giant Johann, you didn't forget?" Vivien greeted him with a wide smile. "For how many people have you brought Christmas dinner? We may feed a thousand here at the church before tomorrow is over."

"Hello, Sister Vivien," a surprised Johann said. Then he laughed. "I'm afraid I forgot about the dinner."

"It's not too late," Sister Vivien said. "It's only Christmas Eve. The supermarket is still holding another thirty turkeys for us. Tell me, giant Johann, how many of them will you buy for your brethren?"

Johann stopped for a moment. "Do you really feed anyone who wanders into the church, no questions asked?"

"Yes, indeed," said Vivien with a serious look on her face. "And with the same enthusiasm that we ask the more fortunate people, like you, for money or time to be contributed to the benefit of others."

"Well," said Johann, "I came here specifically to see you. I know you're busy, but there's something I want to discuss with you. If I offer to buy, say, five turkeys for your Christmas feast, will you talk to me on the way to the supermarket and back?"

"Throw in twenty kilos of potatoes," Vivien said with a charming laugh, "and I'll even flirt with you in both directions."

Johann told Sister Vivien that he had come to talk to her because they had something unusual in common.

"What's that?" she asked lightly.

"We have both had encounters with clouds of dancing, sparkling particles," he said, immediately beginning to tell her about his experience in the Tiergarten.

Vivien stopped dead in her tracks. "That's exactly the same . . ." she said at one point, so overcome she could not finish her sentence.

When Johann described the imprints that the spheres had left in his pouch, Vivien began to tremble with excitement. "Imprints?" she shouted, grabbing Johann's shoulders. "The angels left imprints?"

Johann nodded and Vivien exploded with joy. "Oh, God," she said exultantly, "thank you, thank you for sending us yet another sign. . . . You have blessed us so much. Sister Beatrice will be ecstatic."

She started running toward the supermarket. "Come on, Brother Johann," she said. "We must hurry and get the food and return to the church."

"Wait," he yelled at Vivien. "There's more. . . . I saw them again, last week, here on Mars, near the north pole."

Vivien stopped and turned around. "What did you say?" she asked.

"I saw the bright particles again," Johann said as he approached her. "While I was on a repair mission on the polar ice, only a few days before I left to come to Mutchville."

Vivien's excitement turned to skepticism. "If this is your idea of a joke," she said, "I don't appreciate it. . . . Those Rama Society weirdos put you up to this, didn't they? They're the only ones here on Mars—"

"This is not a joke," Johann said. He stared directly at Vivien. "I am deadly serious. If you will just be patient, I'll tell you the whole story."

"Go ahead," said Vivien. She still looked as if she didn't believe him.

Near the end of Johann's tale, Vivien hailed a Michaelite priest who was passing on the street. "Brother Angelo," she said, "will you do me a favor?"

The priest came over beside them. Vivien asked Johann for the money for the food. "Take this to the market, please, Brother Angelo," she then said, "and buy five more of those Christmas turkeys Walter is keeping for us, plus as much dressing and potatoes as he will give us. Then take all the food back to Sister Darla. Tell her it's a gift from Brother Johann, and that I'll explain it all later."

After Johann had finished his description of his second encounter with the particles, Vivien asked him many questions. She wanted to know more about the details of the transformations that occurred in the nature and shape of the particles. She was also very curious about the baseball-sized sphere that smacked into Johann's space helmet.

"Now, why do you think it struck your faceplate?" Vivien said. "That seems odd, and out of character."

She started walking toward the church. "Out of character?" Johann said. "That's an unusual choice of words."

Vivien laughed. "I guess it is," she said. "Sister Beatrice and I . . . Well, I'll let her tell you herself, but we believe the bright particles are angels. Messengers from God, like in the Bible . . . And they appear only on very special occasions."

It was Johann's turn to be astounded. *"Angels?"* he said.

"Sister Beatrice will explain it to you," Vivien said. "She can be very convincing."

There were magnificent stained-glass windows on both sides of the cathedral sanctuary. The life of Jesus was depicted on the panels on one side; the life of St. Michael of Siena on the other. Because the scattered sunlight coming through the two bubbles protecting Mutchville did not show off the full beauty of the stained-glass windows, one of the Michaelite priests, who had been a motion-picture lighting director before his ordination, had designed a deployable lighting array, mounted on the roof, which permitted the full range of color and texture of the individual glass elements to be seen. Since it was Christmas Eve, the array was in place. Many of the hundred people who were in the cathedral when Johann and Sister Vivien entered had come just to look at the windows.

The back half of the sanctuary had been converted into a cafeteria. There were long tables, covered with simple white tablecloths, that were spread across the church. In front of the tables, toward the altar, four priests and priestesses were serving food to the short but steady flow of people having a meal at three o'clock in the afternoon. On both sides of the sanctuary, still in the back half, were clothes bins where sorted, washed, and marked-for-size outfits were available to anyone who wanted them.

Johann, who had been temporarily left by himself while Vivien attended to some order business, was surprised to find that he was emotionally touched by what he was seeing. The Michaelites seemed uniformly pleasant and dedicated. There was no doubt that they were performing a valuable service. *Maybe I shouldn't have been so cynical,* he told himself.

At that moment he first heard the computerized music system of the church. On the opposite end of the church, standing to the left of the altar, a solitary female figure, dressed in a blue robe with a wide white stripe, began to sing.

"O Holy Night . . . The stars are brightly shining. . . ."

Johann was thunderstruck. He had never heard such a clear and beautiful voice. The sound was mesmerizing, and heavenly.

"It is the night of the dear Savior's birth. . . . Long lay the world, in sin and error pining. . . ."

All other sounds in the cathedral had ceased. Everyone had stopped whatever he was doing, and was listening with rapt attention to the angel by the altar.

"Fall on your knees. . . . O hear, the angels' voices. . . ."

Without his even knowing it, tears filled Johann's eyes and began to run down his cheeks. When the amazing voice soared up the scale with the final "O Night, Divine . . . " Johann closed his eyes and focused his entire being on the magnificent sound. The pleasure was so intense he felt as if his spirit had been lifted out of his body.

She only sang one verse. When Johann opened his eyes, he noticed that Sister Vivien was watching him from a few meters away. Embarrassed, he pulled his handkerchief from his pocket and wiped his nose and eyes.

"She's really something, isn't she?" Vivien said softly after she was beside him.

Johann was speechless for a few moments. "That's an understatement," he eventually managed to say.

"Sister Beatrice wanted to try out the new sound system before the service tonight," Vivien said after a short silence.

"That was . . . Sister Beatrice?" Johann said, not even trying to hide his shock. "The other priestess who saw the particles?"

"Yes, indeed," Vivien said with a smile.

"God has blessed you, Brother Johann," Sister Beatrice said. "He must have some very important work for you."

Johann shifted uneasily in his chair. The three of them had been sitting in Beatrice's small office to the side of the altar for ten minutes. Johann had told shorter versions of his two encounters and Sister Beatrice had asked a few perceptive questions. He had answered awkwardly, for he was still in awe of this young woman with the radiant, smiling face, clear eyes that seemed to be peering into his very soul, and a singing voice that was incomparably beautiful. And she was the bishop of the Order of St. Michael, in charge of all church affairs on Mars! *How can she be real?* Johann asked himself as the long silence continued.

"So what do you think of Sister Beatrice's explanation?" Vivien asked, attempting to start the conversation again.

"That the particle clouds are angels?" Johann said. He wanted to be polite. "I guess it's possible," he continued, remembering his own thoughts in the hotel room. "Frankly, I never even considered that possibility until today."

He looked at Beatrice almost apologetically. "You see, I've never been very religious. At least not in the strict sense of the word. My family was Lutheran, like most northern Germans, but we didn't go to church regularly and didn't pray at home. I've always believed in God, of course, but not necessarily a personal God, who follows what you're doing on a day-to-day basis."

Johann paused. Neither of the priestesses said anything. "As for angels, I guess I've never thought much about them. . . . I think we discussed them in my medieval history course at the university." He smiled. "And I certainly remember Lucifer from Milton's *Paradise Lost.*"

There was another silence. Johann continued uncertainly, "As I said, it's possible that the particles are angels. . . ."

"But that's not what you think right now, is it, Brother Johann?" Beatrice said. "I have not convinced you."

"I must say, Sister Beatrice, that most of your references to biblical angels and others that appeared to the various saints went right over my head. Your argument sounded compelling, and I have no doubt that you have done all the proper research. . . ."

"So if the particles are not God's messengers, Brother Johann," Beatrice said, her eyes fixed on his, "what are they? Tell us *your* explanation."

Johann shrugged. "I don't have one, Sister Beatrice. . . . No explanation makes much sense to me."

Beatrice rose from her chair and walked over behind her desk. She turned on her computer, made a few entries, and printed out a list of books and journal articles, complete with page numbers. "What I have here, Brother Johann," she said, "is the primary set of source material I studied before I concluded that the particles were angels. I didn't just jump to that conclusion because the shape they took when they appeared to Vivien was so obvious. I can have copies of the articles made, if you would like, and I invite you to determine for yourself if my thinking has been 'logical,' to use a word that was bandied about in this room not too long ago."

"Sister Beatrice, I must be honest with you," Johann said after quickly scanning the list. "I'm an engineer with a scientific background. Even if I read all this material, I don't think there's any way I could ever actively embrace the idea that the bright particles I saw are angels sent by God. . . . It's just not consistent with who I am."

"Are you saying that you don't have an open mind?" Sister Beatrice said immediately.

"No . . . Well, maybe," Johann said. He laughed slightly. "I see your point. By the way, since you seem to have everything figured out, have you come up with any explanation of why the particles formed into a ball and bopped me on the faceplate?"

Beatrice crossed the room, knelt beside Johann's chair, and put her hand on his forearm. "Their behavior is very easy to understand," she said, her eyes burning with intensity. "Your angel was trying to wake you up, to snap you out of your complacency. You were granted a visit in the Tiergarten almost two years ago, and yet you have done nothing to show God that you understand you have been singled out for some special endeavor. The second apparition, Brother Johann, and the literal 'bop on the head,' as you call it, was to signal you that your special tasks are still waiting, and that it's time for you to discover them."

Johann stared at the earnest face only a meter away from his. He could not think of anything to say. He just kept thinking, *This is the most incredible woman I have ever met.*

Johann temporarily forgot about his rendezvous at the Balcony. In fact, at first he agreed to come back to the Michaelite church that evening and help Sister Vivien and the other members of the order serve Christmas dinner to the multitudes. His reasons for agreeing, however, were not altruistic. Vivien had told him that Sister Beatrice was going to sing during the services after dinner, and Johann desperately wanted to hear that beautiful voice again.

Of course he did not tell Vivien what his "other appointment" really was. Lying in the bathtub in his hotel room before dressing for the evening, Johann was a little ashamed that he was going to be indulging himself sexually while the brethren of the Order of St. Michael were going to be feeding the hungry. *But how can I not go now?* Johann asked himself. *I have already paid the seven hundred and fifty dollars. That's a lot of money for nothing.*

Several minutes later, waiting in front of his hotel for an electric taxi, Johann was full of anticipation, and just a trifle nervous. "The Other Zone, please," he said to the driver when he climbed into the cab.

"North gate or south gate," the taxi driver said in a monotone.

Johann consulted his map. "South gate," he said.

The ride took fewer than ten minutes. The taxi deposited Johann in the middle of a large parking lot, near the tollgate that was the entrance to the Other Zone. Johann watched some people walk into the narrow lanes defined by the restraining bars, insert their identity cards into the appropriate slots in a small pedestal, and then push through a turnstile.

Johann had never been in the Other Zone. When Martian tourism was flourishing in the late twenties and the early thirties, the Other Zone had been, along with the spectacular Valles Marineris and the volcanoes of the Tharsis region, one of the destinations on virtually every tourist itinerary. The three large, identical signs just outside the gate told why.

WARNING

YOU ARE ENTERING AN AREA WHERE CERTAIN ACTIVITIES
THAT ARE ILLEGAL ELSEWHERE IN MUTCHVILLE, NOTA-
BLY GAMBLING, DRUG USE, AND PROSTITUTION, ARE PER-
MITTED, CONTROLLED, AND TAXED. HOWEVER, NO
DISORDERLY CONDUCT, OBSCENE BEHAVIOR, OR EXCES-
SIVE PUBLIC DRUNKENNESS WILL BE TOLERATED. ANY-
ONE CONVICTED OF MISCONDUCT IN THIS AREA WILL BE
PROHIBITED FOREVER FROM RETURNING.

Next to the warning signs were smaller placards explaining that
each person entering the Other Zone paid both an entry fee and an additional small charge that was a function of how long he or she remained
inside.

Johann inserted his identity card and passed through the turnstile.
On the other side of the gate, he was immediately accosted by four young
men, each of whom offered to take him to a different brothel. They
brandished lewd photographs and spoke of carnal pleasures, but Johann
ignored them as he walked toward the main street leading into the business areas.

The Other Zone was a square, two kilometers on a side. Around the
perimeter were residential apartments, three or four stories high in most
places, that kept the sights and sounds of the zone from disturbing the
rest of the residents of Mutchville. There was no vehicular traffic inside
the zone. Everyone was on foot, or riding in a chair affixed to the back of
a bicycle that had been remodeled.

Johann was actually somewhat disappointed when he reached the
famous plaza in the center of the Other Zone. The large casinos surrounding the plaza were certainly brightly lit, but their illumination paled
beside the garish neon displays that Johann had seen in Las Vegas on his
one trip to the United States. He turned right at the New World Casino,
as his map indicated, and followed a street lined with alcohol and mari-
juana bars for about a hundred meters. At the end of the street Johann
entered what looked like a tastefully decorated lobby in a small, prestigious European hotel.

On one side of the main reception area in the Balcony was a handsome restaurant. Beyond the counter in the lobby, which was staffed by
two of the prettiest young women Johann had seen in Mutchville, there
was a small bar to the right of the elevators. He glanced at the clock
behind the counter and presented his identity card to one of the two

pretty receptionists. She checked her computer. "You're right on time, Mr. Eberhardt," she then said cheerfully. "Do you want to stop in the bar first, or are you ready to proceed with your appointment?"

"I guess I'm ready," Johann said, feeling a little foolish.

The young lady handed him a map. "Your appointment is not on-site," she said brightly. "This map indicates where you are going. Please read it before you leave the main building. If you have any questions, do not hesitate to ask."

Johann glanced at the map. The directions were easy to understand. He left the building, crossed a pair of side streets, and entered a lane in a residential section. Johann checked carefully to make certain he was in the right location before ringing the doorbell at the house indicated on the map.

A small camera, barely noticeable, was watching him from above the door. "Come in, darling," a soft, feminine voice said from a hidden speaker. "I'll be down in just a minute."

Johann heard the door click. He entered an open entryway dominated by a wooden stairway leading to the second floor. Through an open door to his right, Johann could see the living room. He went inside and sat down on the couch.

On the opposite side of the room, in the corner where it was away from the brick fireplace, a Christmas tree about two meters tall was standing. It had been carefully decorated with ornaments and popcorn strings. A star had been mounted on its very top. Underneath the tree were a dozen packages, each wrapped with a different kind of Christmas paper.

It's perfect, Johann said to himself, the scene evoking memories of his childhood. He picked up a framed photograph from the end table beside the couch. It was a head shot of a beautiful brunette woman in her late twenties. Across the left bottom corner was written, in a broad, open script, "For Johann, with my love . . . Amanda."

"I'm so glad you're finally home, Johann," the woman in the photograph said. She came into the room and gave him a light kiss on the lips. "But the kids will be sorry they missed you."

Johann smiled and examined the woman standing in front of him. She was wearing a simple black dress, not fancy, but not exactly what you would find on the racks at the Mutchville Emporium either. Most of her shoulders were bare, and the dress made a V drop in front, just enough to show a little cleavage. It was made of a knitted fabric and fit her exceptional body perfectly. The dress was not, however, so tight that it would have been called risqué.

Amanda's face was friendly and inviting. She was wearing very little makeup. Johann's first reaction was that Amanda looked like a sophisticated, adult version of Snow White. Her hair was black and hung down below her shoulders. Around her neck was a simple gold necklace with three diamonds in the front, the middle one slightly larger than the two on either side. Matching diamond studs were in her ears.

"So," Amanda said when it was clear from Johann's expression that his initial examination was over, "do you want to start work right away on Peter's train, or would you like a glass of wine first?"

"The wine, I think," Johann said. "It's been a long, hard day." On the way to the kitchen, Amanda stopped for a moment and flipped on the audio system. Johann heard a choir softly singing one of his favorite Christmas songs. "Do you hear what I hear? . . ."

As his eyes roamed around the room again Johann noticed another framed photograph, this one on top of the piano in the far corner. At first he couldn't believe what he was seeing. He stood up and crossed the room. The picture was a family photo, taken in casual clothes, of Johann, Amanda, and two children, a blond boy of seven or eight, and a gorgeous little brunette girl of four or five!

"Oh, there you are, darling," Amanda said. She was standing just inside the living room with two glasses of white wine.

"This is an amazing photograph," Johann said as she walked over beside him. "I can't imagine—"

"I have always loved that picture," she said, gently interrupting him. "It's the only one we have in which all four of us are smiling." She handed him his glass of wine. "Peter already looks a lot like you, but I don't think he'll be as tall as you are."

Before Johann could take a sip of his wine, Amanda touched her glass to his. "To our best Christmas ever," she said, reaching up and giving him a kiss.

"I will certainly drink to that," Johann replied.

They sipped wine and talked easily for half an hour. They were sitting comfortably near each other on the couch. Later Johann began to assemble the electric train and track that were his Christmas gift for his son, Peter. Amanda began to build a fire in the fireplace. Never once during the entire time did she slip out of character. She was Johann's wife, the mother of his two children, the keeper of the hearth.

Amanda brought him another glass of wine just before his work on the train was completed. She kissed him more boldly, teasing him playfully with her tongue. Johann loved it. "Come on, now," he said, "how do you expect me to finish this train if you're going to distract me?"

"That's your problem, Santa Claus," Amanda said. She kissed him again, first on the neck, and then around the ears. "I have other things on *my* mind."

Johann touched her face. He kissed her with passion for the first time and she responded perfectly, putting her hands behind his head and biting him very gently on the lower lip during the middle of their kiss.

"That was great," he said when their long kiss was over. He was somewhat surprised by the strength of his arousal. Johann glanced at the electric train on the table in front of him. "I guess I can finish this afterward," he said.

Amanda took Johann by the hand and led him back to the couch. She sat sideways on his lap, her arms wrapped around his neck, and they continued to kiss. Her kisses became more insistent, her tongue more provocative. She unbuttoned his shirt and began rubbing his left nipple, coordinating her titillations with her kisses.

"Should we go upstairs now?" he asked between kisses.

Amanda's eyes were seductive. "I thought it would be more exciting on the floor," she said. "In front of the fireplace."

She kept her arms around his neck and her mouth on his as he stood up from the couch. Johann pushed aside the remaining parts of the electric train and laid Amanda down in front of the fireplace. As he was taking off his clothes he accidentally kicked some of the other presents and caused the tree to shake noisily. They both laughed.

He looked at the firelight reflected in her beautiful brown eyes. "This is wonderful," he said.

"Merry Christmas, Johann," she said.

6

In the months that followed, Johann's life was full of stress. Mutchville and the rest of the Martian settlements were in a state of chaos and collapse. The infrastructure to maintain the entire human colony on Mars was rapidly deteriorating. Valhalla's survival was in jeopardy.

Throughout his life, sleep had been one of Johann's primary means of escaping from overwhelming problems. Unfortunately, during this period going to sleep did not offer him much relief. Indeed, his frequent dreams, still full of the people and images he had encountered during that extraordinary visit to Mutchville, became increasingly more vivid and bizarre. Eventually it became rare for Johann to sleep through the night without being awakened by a puzzling dream or a nightmare.

In one dream he was again sitting in the living room in the Balcony where he had first met Amanda. She arrived, looking magnificent, and Johann felt a powerful sexual desire as they kissed. Amanda then excused herself. Johann looked away for only a second or two, and where Amanda had been in the room there was now a formation of the dancing particles, shaped like a harp. He heard the beautiful music of the particle harp. Then another woman entered. It was Sister Vivien.

"Make love to me, Johann," Vivien said in the dream, taking off her Michaelite robe. "Sister Beatrice will not mind."

He touched Vivien's naked body and kissed her passionately. After a few kisses he opened his eyes and saw that Beatrice was standing less than a meter away, watching them carefully. She had a look of shock and disapproval on her face. Johann woke with a start.

Beatrice made many other appearances in Johann's dreams. Often he would see her standing in her bishop's robe on a distant hill. In those scenes she was always bathed in soft light. Occasionally, the Sister Beatrice in his dreams was a close friend and confidante. They would talk together for a long time and then she would sing to please him. Twice Beatrice even came to Johann during the night and sat beside him cozily on the couch in the Balcony. In those two dreams the photograph on the piano showed Johann and the two children with Beatrice, and it was her kisses that transported him into ecstasy. Johann surrendered gladly both times to the pleasure offered by his subconscious.

In real life Johann never contacted Beatrice and Vivien to find out what they had done with the faceplate he had sent to them by courier on the day he had departed from Mutchville. He had planned to surprise Beatrice and Vivien, and Darwin and Clem as well, with a visit to Mutchville in September or October of the following year. But his trip was postponed because of problems at Valhalla. Eventually it was canceled altogether.

As the economic crisis on Mars deepened Johann knew that without self-sufficiency, Valhalla had no chance of survival. He forced himself and the rest of the inhabitants of his polar outpost to work long hours preparing for the range of catastrophic events that might occur. Johann was determined that the group of humans for which he was responsible would survive the bleak months ahead.

"We will have more of everything from this crop, except for the tomatoes," Anna said. "Deirdre thinks we watered the tomatoes too much."

Johann and Anna were standing side by side in one of the long aisles out in the far greenhouse. To their right, corn was growing as high as the top of Johann's head. To their left was a beautiful plot of plump yellow squash and zucchini.

Johann glanced at the ceiling. "This place is an engineering marvel. Without the genius of Yasin and Narong, we never could have hoped—"

"From what Narong tells me," Anna interrupted, "there would

never have been any greenhouses without an original vision and some pretty astute systems engineering from a tall, blond German."

Johann smiled. "Thanks, Anna," he said. He didn't notice the loving look in her eyes. He had missed it consistently for over a year. "The truth is that the greenhouses have been a successful team effort from the beginning. You and Deirdre have improved every single one of the operating plans that we initially designed."

Johann bent down to touch one of the squashes. "How do you know when it's ready to pick?"

"It's all done automatically with that software Narong designed," she said. "Every day the overhead camera takes a picture of every square centimeter in the greenhouse. Algorithms compute growth rates, maturation coefficients, everything that is needed. Then that robot harvester Yasin assembled out of spare parts is turned on. It interrogates the database established by the algorithms and picks what is ready."

Johann stood up. "So with the increased yields from this crop, are you ready to declare the project a success?"

"Not yet," replied the always conservative Anna. "Our yields are still not high enough that we can easily survive a long duration dust storm like the one in 2133. . . . And despite my objections, you have not cut back the food allocations to allow me to stockpile vegetables for a simultaneous dust storm plus a major subsystem failure."

"We agreed several months ago to design only for single-point failures," Johann replied. "It does not make sense to keep everyone undernourished just so we can accommodate multiple-fault scenarios."

"Tell me that when everyone is starving," Anna said grimly. "When you assigned me this task, you challenged me to try to imagine how bad things could get. You said to assume we would be receiving no food or supplies of any kind from Mutchville. At the time I thought you were being unduly pessimistic. But now that the situation is even worse than you foresaw . . ."

"You've done a great job, Anna," Johann said, giving her a brotherly hug. "And we all appreciate it. . . . But now that we are nearing self-sufficiency, you should consider lightening up a bit. . . . Smile. . . . Enjoy your life a little."

They started walking back toward the greenhouse entrance. "There's another subject I've been meaning to talk to you about," Anna said hesitantly. "I promised Deirdre I would bring it up as soon as we began harvesting this crop."

"What is it?" Johann said easily.

"It's Yasin," Anna said. "He is becoming more and more abusive to all the women here, especially to Deirdre and Lucinda. It's not just his language, or his comments about women in general. Lately he has been making sexual threats."

Johann stopped. "Has he done this to you?"

"No," said Anna, "because he knows that I won't tolerate any of his shit. . . . But Johann, most of the women don't have either my self-confidence or my experience. They've never been around anyone who refers to them all the time as bitches or cunts. Or who believes graphic sexual jokes are acceptable in mixed company. They don't even know how to react to him."

"And what do you want me to do?" Johann said.

"Stop praising Yasin publicly, to begin with," Anna said sharply. "I know he is a genius and has helped Valhalla immensely, at least from an engineering point of view. But every time you talk about how critical Yasin's work has been, his ego becomes more inflated and he feels more indispensable. Then he figures he can treat the women any way he wants, without any consequences."

"But his work *has* been fantastic," Johann protested.

"That's the trouble with you men," Anna said, her voice rising. "I have never been able to figure out how you can so easily compartmentalize each other. If some guy's a brilliant engineer, or a fantastic home-run hitter, you overlook the fact that he's a jerk or a son of a bitch out of the office or away from the field. . . . Women do not look at men that way. We consider the *whole* individual, not just one or two parts. To us, it does not matter how smart Yasin is, or what he has done for the outpost. The way he treats women is disgusting, and he should be reprimanded and censured for his conduct."

Johann had never seen Anna so agitated. "All right," he said at length. "Give me more of the details and I will talk with Yasin."

"*When* will you talk with him?" Anna said. "I want to tell Deirdre and Lucinda."

"Soon," said Johann. He saw that Anna was not satisfied. "Tonight," he added. "No later than tonight."

Narong was in his office, working at his computer terminal. His door was open.

"May I come in?" Johann asked.

Narong smiled. "Of course," he said. "I always have time for the boss."

Johann slumped into one of the two large chairs in Narong's office and heaved a sigh. "I promised Anna I would talk to Yasin today," he said. "I need your help."

"More complaints?" Narong asked.

"Yes," Johann said. "Apparently he's getting worse. . . ." Johann squirmed in his chair. "I'm in an impossible situation," he continued. "I agree with the women that Yasin's behavior is intolerable, but I'm worried about what his response will be. Our system-failure rates are already astronomically high, and they're still increasing. Without Yasin we'll never keep up with the maintenance and repairs. . . . What do you think we should do?"

"It has been a Hobson's choice from the beginning," Narong said. "Yasin is both deeply talented and completely screwed up. During the first six months he was here, I thought he had reformed. But now I can see that it was just an act. After he was granted his freedom, he quickly reverted to his old behavior."

"Could we possibly maintain the outpost without Yasin?" Johann asked.

"You mean if he's confined to quarters, or decides to leave if and when another train ever arrives?"

Johann nodded. "I don't think so," Narong said slowly. "I wish it were otherwise, but the truth is that nobody else here at Valhalla knows electronics nearly as well as he does."

"That's what I expected you to say," Johann said. He stood up to leave. Narong handed him a five-page document.

"What's this?" Johann asked.

"Unfinished business," Narong said. "It's probably no longer a priority, since those few ISA staff members still in Mutchville certainly have bigger problems. However, this is the final report on those Asian scientists who disappeared over a year ago while you were down in Mutchville. The initial document was returned to us a few months ago, before the fax lines became inoperative. I had forgotten about it. It's now way overdue."

Narong shook his head. "You know, Johann," he said, "those guys at ISA headquarters didn't make a single substantive comment about any of the text. They recommended no changes to my description of the unsuccessful search conducted by our drone rovers, and they didn't question my surmise that the scientists had fallen into a crevasse or some other hazard on the ice. . . . All their comments were about the *form* of the document, including the numbering of the paragraphs."

Johann and Narong both laughed. "The stupid bureaucrats also informed me," Narong said, "that a report of this importance must be signed by a facility director or the equivalent. Without your signature the report is invalid."

Johann shrugged and signed the document without reading it. "What will you do with this now?" he asked.

"That's a good question," Narong answered. "I guess I'll put it on the train, assuming another one will arrive someday. Before this current communications blackout began six days ago, there was already a hint that a train might be coming in a couple of weeks. . . . As long as there were no dust storms."

There was a protracted silence in the room. "How much longer do you think it will be until there are no more trains at all, and no phone communications either?" Johann asked.

"I try not to think about that," Narong said, forcing a smile. "But I do know one thing. When the infrastructure on Mars collapses completely, I would much rather be in Valhalla than Mutchville, or anyplace else for that matter. At least we're somewhat prepared."

Courage is a strange word, Johann thought as he sat in his apartment, preparing for his meeting with Yasin. *It is applied most often to behavior during situations that are immediately life threatening. Sometimes it takes more courage to talk to another person about an unpleasant subject than it does to confront an armed lunatic, or to face down an animal in the wild.*

Johann brewed the last of his personal supply of coffee for his visitor, who was due to arrive any minute. They did not grow coffee in the Valhalla greenhouses—it was not considered essential—and there had been no deliveries of coffee from Mutchville for almost a year. Like many Muslims, Yasin did not drink alcohol. But he absolutely loved coffee. Johann was certain that Yasin would understand the significance of his gesture.

The Arab engineer was prompt, and in a good mood. He smelled the coffee the minute he walked through the door. "Why, that's damn nice of you, Ace," he said, accepting the cup that Johann offered him. "This must be a token of your appreciation."

"It is," Johann said, seating himself in a chair opposite Yasin. "I inspected the greenhouses today and we have a bumper crop. It goes without saying that it would not have been possible without your ingenuity."

"You're welcome," Yasin replied with a wide smile. "But I can't believe you requested a private meeting to thank me. There must be some other reason. There's no terrible news from Mutchville, is there? I thought the communications link was still not working."

"No, no," Johann said, "nothing like that." He hesitated, remembering what he had planned to say. "What I want to talk about is personal."

Yasin took a sip of coffee and his smile faded. "Let me guess," he said sharply. "One of your bitches has been complaining again."

Johann's eyes did not waver from Yasin's. "Several of the women have lodged a formal complaint, Yasin. Not just about your language, or your derisive remarks. They say you are making sexual threats."

"What a pile of shit," Yasin said, his eyes flashing. He set his coffee cup on the table and stood up. "Why should I have to put up with this?" he said angrily. "I bust my butt for you, and save this whole damn outpost, and what do I get for it? I have to listen to what a bunch of whining bitches say—

"Look, Ace, if there is some specific crime someone thinks I've committed, then charge me with it. But I'm not going to sit here and be upbraided because some lonely women have had their sensibilities offended."

For a moment Johann thought that Yasin was going to walk out the door. *What would I do then?* he thought fleetingly. "Yasin," he said hurriedly, "as the director of this facility, it is my duty to respond to the requests of my staff. . . . I am not charging you with anything at this time. I am simply conducting an unofficial investigation that is entirely consistent with my position. I have called you here so that I can hear your side of the issue."

Yasin's hand was on the doorknob, but he did not open the door. He hesitated for a moment. "All right, Ace," he said, coming back toward the chairs, "I'm going to take you at your word and presume that you do indeed have an open mind." He sat down in the chair and took another sip of coffee. "Now, why don't you tell me about these complaints so I can have a chance to defend myself."

Johann started slowly, first reminding Yasin that every time he referred to a woman, or women in general, as "cunts" or "bitches," he was demeaning all females in the same way that the term "nigger" or "kike" demeaned black people or Jews. Yasin did not say anything. Then Johann brought up Yasin's habit of telling sexual jokes in the presence of women. Johann had finished explaining that people had a right to choose not to hear such offensive stories, and had just begun to describe what Deirdre Robertson had called an explicit sexual threat, when Yasin interrupted him.

"That ugly bitch might say anything," Yasin said. "Don't believe a word she says. She's still pissed off because I wouldn't screw her. . . . Right after I came to Valhalla, she made a pass at me. I turned her down. She's been waiting ever since to get even with me. You know how women are."

Yasin told how Deirdre had tried to seduce him soon after his arrival at Valhalla. Even though Johann knew that Yasin was probably fabricating the story, there was little he could do. Yasin categorically denied ever saying to Ms. Robertson that if she didn't watch out, he'd pull up her dress and "slip her the big one."

Johann was no longer on the offensive. Yasin was smiling again, thinking the issue had been defused. He relaxed visibly. "All that bitch needs," he said with an easy laugh at the end of the conversation, "is a reaming from a real man. Then she wouldn't be so unhappy and frustrated all the time."

"It is exactly that kind of comment, Yasin," Johann answered harshly, "that alienates the women here at Valhalla. And many of the men, including me."

Yasin began backpedaling when he saw the anger in Johann's response. "You know, Ace," he said in a reflective tone a few seconds later, "the more I consider this problem, the more I think that what we're talking about is simply a cultural difference. The Islamic and Christian cultures have a completely different view of women and their role in society. I was raised to think of women as helpmates, supportive subordinates whose primary responsibility was to take care of the house and raise the man's children. . . . I use the possessive because under Islamic law, after a certain age all offspring belong to the father and the mother no longer has any legal rights to them.

"Please understand that being even the slightest bit concerned about what a woman might think is a foreign concept to an Islamic man. Can you imagine, for example, a woman in Saudi Arabia or Iraq making a complaint about a man's language? It would be unheard-of. . . . So you see, your European ideas, which proclaim the ostensible equality of the sexes—although I've met very few of your male colleagues who really believe it—are very difficult for me to grasp. I have tried to make some adjustments to my behavior, but I'm not always able to catch myself."

Very clever, Johann was thinking. *You have changed the whole tenor of this conversation. Now the problem is no longer personal. It's a cultural and religious issue. . . .*

"Kwame is very respectful of women," Johann said suddenly. "And he is also a Muslim."

"Kwame doesn't really count," Yasin retorted. "He's not that serious about his religion and black Africans practice a different kind of Islam anyway. . . . Besides, I think that Kwame's polite manner is an act. I bet he would screw any woman in this outpost, without her consent, if he thought there would be no consequences." Yasin leaned forward. "So would many of the men here at Valhalla, including your fair-haired Narong. . . . I don't know about you, Ace, I don't have you figured, but most men would force themselves on women if there were no laws to prevent it. That's biological, not cultural."

Johann was about to argue when there was a loud knock on the door. Both men stood up. "It's me, Narong," they heard. "I have some urgent news."

They opened the door. "Melvin dug up Dr. Won's body today," Narong said. "It's still encased in ice. One of the drones is bringing her to Valhalla. The body should be here in two hours or so."

7

Dr. Kyagi Won, a Korean geologist specializing in glaciers, was one of the four inter-Asian scientists who had mysteriously disappeared on the Martian polar ice over a year earlier. She and her male colleagues, Dr. Devi Sinha from India (the head of the expedition), Dr. Hiroshi Kawakita from Japan, and Dr. Ismail Jailani from Malaysia, had spent nearly a week in Valhalla before moving out on the ice to conduct their investigations. During their stay at the outpost, the Asian scientists had isolated themselves from the other residents. The quartet had eaten at their own table in the cafeteria and, unlike the free-spirited, bibulous Ukrainians from the previous year, had never attended any of the entertainments designed to enliven the evenings at the outpost.

Three of the Valhalla residents had trained the Asian scientists in the use of the icemobiles and other specialized equipment, and had gone with them to help establish the initial campsite on the ice. All three had returned with comments about the lack of warmth and personality in the Asian group. "They might as well be robots," one of the Valhallans who had assisted them had commented.

Dr. Won and her colleagues had come to the north pole of Mars for a specific purpose. They did not accept the results of the Ukrainian polar expedition that had won plaudits from many of the world's scientists. The Asians believed that both the core sample taken by the Ukrainians, and the ultimate analysis of the layers of that core, which resulted in a derived time history of the motion of the Martian spin axis, were seriously flawed. The Asian team intended to do the job properly. They expected to show that Dr. Kawakita's original theory for the evolution of the Martian spin axis, which had been thrown into disrepute by the findings of the Ukrainians, was indeed correct.

Johann and Narong had both briefed the scientists, on their last day at Valhalla, about the importance of checking in daily while they were out on the ice. Dr. Sinha had not been convinced that regular communications with the outpost were very important. "We have a lot of work to do," he had stated. "We will check in with Valhalla if it fits into our schedule."

Because of Dr. Sinha's attitude, Narong and Johann had been slow to react when communications from the Asian group out on the polar ice ceased. After over a week of silence, Valhalla had finally dispatched a pair of drone rovers to check on the scientists. The drones had located the campsite, where everything appeared to be in order, as well as an abandoned icemobile with a dead power system that was two kilometers away. However, the rovers found no sign of the people anywhere. A subsequent Valhalla investigative team headed by Narong also failed to find any clues related to the vanished group, even though the whole vicinity was searched. The team did determine, however, that there were peculiar malfunctions in all the communications equipment used by the inter-Asian scientists.

Under normal circumstances, the ISA would have sent a blue-ribbon commission to Valhalla to complete the investigation that Narong and his team had started. However, ISA headquarters in Mutchville had just received instructions to begin closing down all Martian operations when Narong's first investigative report reached them. The missing Asian scientists were not high on the ISA priority list at that time.

Dr. Won's body was still completely buried in ice when it arrived at Valhalla. Satoko Hayakawa supervised both the thawing and the autopsy, reporting that Dr. Won had no broken bones, no blood loss from wounds, and no cancerous tissues. Food was still present in her digestive system. When Satoko was pressed for a cause of death, she tentatively ascribed Dr. Won's death to a heart attack. "There are some peculiarities in the cardiac region," she told Johann, "but that's certainly not my area of expertise."

Dr. Won's portable computer was found in her waist pouch. Although it was no longer functioning, Narong and Yasin discovered after a careful component-by-component test that the memory was still operational. Working together, the two engineers jury-rigged an apparatus that permitted them to access the contents of the memory. The readout process was very slow, and fraught with difficulties. It took them two days to assemble a full translation of the contents, much of which was scientific gobbledygook that neither of them could understand. But Dr. Won's portable computer memory also contained her astonishing personal diary, beginning with the date that she and her colleagues left the Sri Lankan spaceport to rendezvous with the transportation platform in Earth orbit, and ending on the presumed day of her death. Narong and Yasin stored the entire diary on the memories of two separate processors at Valhalla. They then brought an edited, hardcopy printout of the last several days of Dr. Won's journal to Johann in his office.

"What you are about to read is incredible," Narong said.

"In my opinion, this Dr. Won lost her mind out there on the ice," Yasin offered, "and began imagining things. They must have been working her too hard. . . . Either that, or this whole damn story is part of some kind of complicated hoax that backfired. What's written in that diary is crazy and cannot be believed. Just what you would expect from a woman scientist who—"

"If you don't mind," Narong interrupted, "let's let Johann read it himself and draw his own conclusions."

"Have at it, Ace," Yasin said.

Johann began to read the sheets that had been handed to him.

20 DECEMBER 2142

I'm tired. We are all tired. We have been working twelve to fourteen hours a day, trying to find the right place to drill. Today we thought we had located a spot that met all our criteria. We inserted the drill and began the process. Only about forty meters down into the ice we saw indications that the layers were impinging. Dr. Sinha criticized me severely for my inept geological analysis. We moved to another site but found it unacceptable also.

21 DECEMBER 2142

The longest workday of the trip. I am completely exhausted. But the day was worthwhile. It looks as if we have finally found the perfect place to drill. It is only six kilometers from our new campsite, and more than sixty kilometers from where the Ukrainians took

their core. We are already over a hundred meters down and everything looks perfect. Dr. Kawakita has done a preliminary analysis of
the upper layers of the core and seems very pleased with the results.
Before going to bed, I reminded Dr. Sinha that we had not communicated with Valhalla for three days. He said we would send a message to the outpost tomorrow night.

22 DECEMBER 2142

Something bizarre happened when we returned to our campsite tonight. When we were still about a hundred meters away, I saw
a long, thin, white ribbon float out of our tent. It looked like the tail
of a high-flying kite. Inside the ribbon were tiny illuminated particles that appeared to be moving on their own, back and forth, from
side to side within the structure. The whole thing was twenty or
thirty meters long, and hovered in front of the tent for no more than
two or three seconds before zooming away at an unbelievable speed.

Drs. Sinha and Kawakita were talking, and not even facing the
campsite, when I first saw the ribbon. By the time they turned
around, the ribbon was disappearing in the distance. I believe Dr.
Jailani saw the object, too, but he wouldn't corroborate my story.
The men have all convinced themselves that what I saw was some
kind of transient polar atmospheric phenomenon. That doesn't
seem likely to me.

Our day, which had been so productive at the drill site (we are
now down over two hundred meters and everything still looks
great), ended on a dissonant note. Ismail was not certain that he
successfully transmitted our routine message to Valhalla. He reported to Dr. Sinha that even though the primary transmitter repeatedly passed self-test, there were peculiarities during the
transmission sequence. Dr. Sinha belittled Dr. Jailani. He said that
we would probably have a confirmation message from Valhalla while
we were sleeping. Dr. Sinha also reminded Dr. Jailani that it had
been his original intention to include a competent engineer among
our team instead of a fourth scientist.

23 DECEMBER 2142

I am alone in our campsite, still in a state of astonishment. It is
nearly midnight. I have been trying to use the backup transmitter to
send an important message to Valhalla, to tell them of our amazing
discovery today, for over an hour. Either I'm not following Ismail's
instructions properly, or this transmitter also is not working. I may
try again later, for I'm certain I will not sleep much tonight.

Today was the most extraordinary day of my life. Even now it's difficult for me to believe that what we saw and experienced could possibly have been real. Our team has discovered some kind of elaborate cavern structure, clearly built by intelligent beings, buried beneath the Martian polar ice. We are all certain that the cavern was not built by humans.

We are all well aware of the ramifications of what we have found. Before I left the other scientists three and a half hours ago to return to this campsite, we carefully composed a report to be transmitted to Valhalla. The report was purposely lacking in details, because we did not want to raise an alarm that might cause some of the outpost personnel to rush out here to join us. If we had said that we had found clear, incontrovertible evidence of the existence of extraterrestrials, we likely would have been besieged.

It's a moot point now. The report has not been transmitted. Valhalla does not know that the discovery of the century has been made on the Martian polar plains. Drs. Sinha and Kawakita do not need to worry about sharing their Nobel Prizes with anyone else.

Dr. Sinha woke us all exceptionally early this morning, more than an hour before sunrise. There was no confirmation from Valhalla that our message last night had been received, but Dr. Sinha was anxious for us to begin working out on the ice and did not want to waste any time troubleshooting the communications equipment. We ate our normal quick breakfast and were on our way to the drill site while it was still dark. Halfway along the trek, we all saw an extremely bright streak of light across the sky that seemed to terminate on the surface not far from where we were in the icemobiles. After a brief consultation, we moved off the pathway and headed toward where we believed the meteorite had fallen.

We searched for almost an hour. It was well after dawn when Dr. Kawakita, scanning the nearby terrain of small ice hills with his binoculars, saw something unusual. We parked the icemobiles and followed Dr. Kawakita on foot for about two hundred meters. What he had seen turned out to be a peculiar rectangular plate, twenty meters wide and almost a hundred meters long, elevated above the ice three or four meters by two dozen identical thick posts. The whole construction was the exact white color of the ice ("for camouflage," according to Ismail), except for thin bands of bright red along the borders and in rings around the posts.

The surface of the plate appeared to be metallic. It was exceptionally smooth to the touch. Dr. Sinha took many photographs while we conversed through the microphones in our helmets. Not

more than ten minutes after we decided to conduct a search of the
area around the plate, Dr. Jailani and I stumbled upon a large rectangular hole in the ice. We knew immediately that it was too perfect
to have been created by nature.

When Drs. Sinha and Kawakita joined us, we all took turns
shining our flashlights down into the hole. We could see some structure on either side of the hole below us, but nothing that we could
identify. Ismail suggested that we drop one of our emergency flares
into the hole and take photographs of what was illuminated. It was
an excellent suggestion.

The still pictures and videos were remarkable. They indicated
there was a multilevel construction underneath the surface, on both
sides of the hole. Both before and during lunch there was a long,
excited discussion of what we should do next. Although we did not
have with us the best equipment for beginning an exploration of the
subsurface tunnels, Dr. Sinha insisted that we should conduct at
least a preliminary investigation.

The men pulled out our two heavy-duty ropes, which we always carry with us in case there is an emergency on the ice, and
secured them around thick stanchions pounded into the ice at the
corners of the hole. By the middle of the afternoon all three of the
men had eased themselves down the pair of ropes to the first underground level and were busy taking pictures of the tunnels and corridors on either side of the central hole. It had been decided that I
would stay outside, not only out of concern for my personal safety,
but also in case something was needed quickly from the surface. For
the rest of the afternoon we communicated frequently on our
walkie-talkies. The men described what they saw, and I logged
their comments on my computer.

The men spent three hours exploring the maze of corridors on
both sides of the hole on the first level. They found occasional objects of unknown purpose, always white in color with some scattered
red surface markings, but nothing else. The extent of the subsurface tunneling was staggering. Someone or something has invested
an enormous amount of time and resources in carving these underground caverns in the Martian ice.

Around sunset the others climbed out of the hole and decided
that they were going to work for several more hours after taking a
short break. They were all still incredibly excited, and bursting with
energy. They asked me if I would return to the campsite, send the
report to Valhalla, and return with some other supplies and equipment by daybreak. Ismail volunteered to go to the campsite with

me, in case I was afraid to go alone, but I could see his expression through his faceplate and I knew that he really wanted to stay with the other men.

The last two hours before I departed the men removed one of the two ropes from its stanchion and tied it to the bottom of the other so that they would have access to the second subsurface level. When I reminded them that the two-rope configuration had been created originally for safety purposes, Dr. Sinha pointed out that after my return with the additional ropes, they would again have a safe, redundant means of descent. Just before I departed, the several small objects that had been removed from the tunnel were placed into one of our canvas bags. I was asked to return them to the campsite for safekeeping.

24 DECEMBER 2142

I will try to be coherent in this entry, but it will not be easy. I am frightened. I fear something dreadful has happened. I have not heard anything from my colleagues since I departed last evening to return to the campsite. At the present moment I am sitting on a tarpaulin on the ice, not more than ten meters from the entrance to the rectangular hole. It is about two hours before sunset. Around me are two bags of ropes, food, and other equipment that I carried over here from the icemobile this morning, as well as the packs and electronic apparatus that were here when I left last night.

I guess I should start at the beginning. I managed to sleep about three hours last night after another unsuccessful attempt to use the backup transmitter. When I awakened, it was of course still dark outside. I carefully assembled all the items on the requisition list and loaded them onto the back of the icemobile.

When the icemobile navigation system indicated that I was less than a kilometer away from the beacon we had placed next to the rectangular hole, I suddenly had an eerie feeling that I was being followed. I told myself that my fear was ridiculous, but nevertheless I turned around slowly in my seat and looked behind me. There, sparkling against the dark sky, no more than forty meters away, was a long white ribbon like the one I had seen coming out of our tent two nights earlier. I was paralyzed with terror. I could not drive. The icemobile bounced off the pathway and smashed into a small ice wall. The automatic brake activated and almost immediately the fault protection process switched off the icemobile.

I stared at the bright ribbon in the sky behind me for several seconds. It seemed to be hovering there, watching me. The tiny individual particles inside the ribbon moved in random patterns, up and down, and from side to side, bouncing back toward the center of the ribbon when they hit one of the sides of the formation. After what seemed to be forever, the ribbon curled upon itself and zoomed over my head, disappearing in the direction of the rectangular hole.

For a long time I could not move. My hands were trembling so violently I could not push the icemobile ignition button. I told myself to be calm, but it was impossible. Finally, after much effort, I managed to activate the icemobile, return to the pathway, and continue on my way.

I tried several times to reach the others using the walkie-talkie. I was afraid something was desperately wrong when I reached the other icemobile and saw that it had not been moved in my absence. Nevertheless, I still gathered up the two bags of equipment and supplies and carried them over the rough terrain to the vicinity of the rectangular hole.

Throughout the morning I made intermittent attempts to contact my colleagues. I also examined thoroughly the entire surface region around the hole. I was convinced that nothing had been touched since my departure the previous evening. The conclusion was inescapable. The men must have descended to the second subsurface level and never come out of the hole again.

So what should I do now? I have two possible courses of action. I can wait here beside the hole, hoping that I will eventually hear from my colleagues, or I can descend the rope myself and try to find them. If they are alive and so deep in the caverns that our walkie-talkies cannot communicate, then they will eventually emerge from the hole. They weren't carrying more than a day's worth of food and water in the packs and pouches of their spacesuits.

The option of descending myself into the hole is not very appealing. Despite the knots tied carefully in the rope at half-meter intervals, I do not trust either my strength or my balance enough to make a fifteen-meter climb in each direction. And what if something terrible happened to the others down at the second level? Is there any reason to believe the same thing would not happen to me?

No, a descent should only be considered as a last recourse. My best plan is to sit here and wait, hoping that one of them will respond to my communications before too much more time passes.

25 DECEMBER 2142

The sun rose about an hour ago. There is no change in the status here. As each hour passes it becomes more likely that my colleagues have all perished.

I am frightened and depressed. Last night, after waking from a nightmare, I found myself methodically reviewing everything that has happened in the last several days. I now realize how foolhardy and ridiculous it was for us to attempt to explore this cavern on our own. We should have noted its location, used our flares to take a few photographs and videos as evidence, and then returned to Valhalla immediately.

I have decided I will stay here and wait for the others no more than one day. I do not intend to descend into that hole. It is not a question of courage. It simply makes no sense for me to risk my life that way.

Before returning to the campsite and Valhalla, however, I plan to go back to our drill site and salvage what I can of our scientific investigations. That's the least I can do for the others. Dr. Kawakita's theories may be vindicated by the data already contained in the on-site computers.

I am no longer as terrified as I was yesterday. What I am feeling now is fatigue, sorrow, and disorientation. It would be an understatement to say that this entire experience has overwhelmed me. If I do not hear anything ever from the other scientists, I must summon all my resources and organizational skills for the journey back to Valhalla.

Narong and Yasin had left Johann while he was reading Dr. Won's journal. When he was finished, Johann took a deep breath and called Narong back into his office.

"Your face is pale," Narong said.

"I'm not surprised," Johann replied. "I have just read what may be the most amazing document ever written by a human being. If this journal is accurate, Dr. Won and her colleagues have made the most significant discovery in human history."

"Yasin still thinks it's all a hoax," Narong said.

"Perpetrated by whom, for what purpose?" Johann said. "And we know something that Yasin does not, namely that those bright particle formations have been seen before, by several different people. It is unlikely that Dr. Won—"

"But it is *possible* that she could have had access to the Rama Society information. And *conceivable* that this clique of scientists might have designed a clever plan, even involving Dr. Won's journal, to gain international recognition for themselves. Then the plan backfired and cost them their lives."

"No, Narong," Johann said. "Any conspiracy or hoax theory is too farfetched. I am convinced that this journal is telling the truth. . . . By the way, how do you imagine Dr. Won died?"

Narong shrugged. "It's impossible to know. She might have taken off on foot after the icemobile broke down, and lost her way. It's easy to become confused when there's nothing but ice in every direction."

Johann stood up. "So what do we do now, boss?" Narong asked.

"Ask Yasin to array all our radio transmitters in the direction of Mutchville. I'm going to report the discovery of Dr. Won's body, as required, and read selected excerpts from her diary." Johann paused for a moment. "I don't know if they can still hear us in Mutchville, even at full power, but we'll give it a try."

"Anything else?" Narong said, sensing that Johann was not finished.

"I'm going to go out on the ice myself," Johann said. "To verify as much as I can of the information in Dr. Won's journal. . . . I'll take Kwame with me. I want you to stay here and take care of things in Valhalla. The outpost needs capable leadership in case . . ." His voice trailed off.

"Will you descend into the caverns?" Narong asked.

"If they are indeed there," Johann replied.

8

K wame read the last part of Dr.
Won's journal in the conference
room that adjoined Johann's of-
fice. "What do you think?" Johann asked when Kwame handed the pa-
pers back to him.

"I don't know yet," the Tanzanian replied. "I haven't had any time
to digest what I just read. . . . It's such an incredible story. Could it
possibly be true?"

"That's the right question," Johann said. "For reasons I will explain
to you in a moment, I think there's some chance that Dr. Won's story *is*
true. More importantly, at least part of it is verifiable. The maps in her
journal are quite detailed. I intend to search for that rectangular hole
myself next week. I would like for you to join me in the search. It's your
choice either way, but before you answer, I want to share with you a
couple of my own unusual experiences."

Kwame listened intently as Johann described his pair of encounters
with the sparkling particles, as well as his discussions with Beatrice and
Vivien in Mutchville.

"Wow," said Kwame when Johann was finished. "So you believe

that the ribbon Dr. Won mentions is the same phenomenon you and the priestesses saw?" he asked. "And that all these incidents are somehow related?"

"Yes," Johann said. "Although I couldn't begin to tell you how or why."

Kwame smiled. "I like Sister Beatrice's concept. It would be comforting to believe that the particle formations might be messenger angels, sent by a benevolent God. Any other explanation would be frightening, especially in view of what happened to Dr. Won and her colleagues."

"Are you saying that you don't want to go with me?" Johann asked after a short silence.

"No, no," Kwame said. "Don't misunderstand me. I would be honored to accompany you. . . . But it's easy to imagine that those particles or whoever created the subsurface caverns Dr. Won described has capabilities that we could not even begin to understand. Or explain. That's why I like Sister Beatrice's idea of the angels. It makes a possible encounter with the particles somehow less daunting."

"Based on my own experience," Johann said, "I don't think we can conclude that the particles are hostile."

Kwame smiled again. "When the first Europeans appeared in Africa, they were welcomed by tribes who thought at the time that the white men were friendly gods. Little did the Africans know that their tribal way of life was about to be irrevocably destroyed by the newcomers."

"Narong and I were discussing something similar last night," Johann said. "If the particles and the caverns have extraterrestrial origins, and their technological prowess is as advanced as it appears, then contact between us and them could mean the end of human history as we know it."

"And it doesn't really matter if the aliens are friendly or hostile," Kwame said. "The end result will be the same. Look at what happened in the Amazon at the end of the twentieth century. The anthropologists who were the first to make contact with those reclusive Indian tribes meant well, but just by exposing the Indians to the *idea* that other ways of life existed, the anthropologists doomed their primitive lifestyle forever."

It was Johann's turn to smile. "I had no idea you were so interested in history," he said.

"I've been fascinated by history ever since I was a young man," Kwame said. "Even though I wasn't able to go to the university— mostly for financial reasons—I have managed to read and study. My interest in the historical significance of an extraterrestrial contact was piqued fourteen years ago, when that Rama spaceship zoomed into our solar system. I was in heavy-machinery school at the time. I followed the reports every day, thinking that some alien civilization had finally decided to announce itself to us. I was crushed when Rama disappeared without answering any of my burning questions."

"So you think there are alien civilizations out there among the stars?" Johann asked.

"Oh, yes," Kwame said. "It seems preposterous to me that only on Earth, on that one small planet, has life and intelligence evolved. The process that created us cannot have been unique."

Johann feigned a frown. "That doesn't sound like an answer I would expect from a good Muslim."

Kwame laughed. "There are all kinds of Muslims, just as there are all kinds of Christians. I have never believed that my religion constrained me to a particular kind of thinking. In my opinion, it is unlikely that either Allah or God expects us to be mindless followers."

Johann smiled at the tall, lithe African with the clear eyes. Kwame would be an excellent companion on the adventure of their lives.

Johann and Kwame spent three busy days preparing for their expedition. They each read Dr. Won's journal several more times, including her logs recording the comments the other three scientists made during the time they were below the surface in the caverns. As the two men planned together they began to appreciate one another's strengths. Johann was organized, efficient, deductive. Kwame was less obsessive, more creative, more intuitive.

The back of the icemobile that trailed behind their rover was over-flowing with equipment and supplies when they departed. Narong had helped Johann and Kwame wrap a heavy net around everything, and secure it tightly to the sides of the icemobile. Nevertheless, Johann was afraid that the jostling of the trailer would unsettle their cargo and they would lose something critical.

"If you'd like," Kwame said with a bemused smile the third time Johann stopped the rover to check that the cargo was still intact, "I could ride in the icemobile and make certain that nothing falls out."

Johann realized that he was being compulsive and tried to relax. He asked Kwame about his African childhood. Kwame had been raised in a small village in western Tanzania, not far from the Serengeti Reserve. Even Johann, with his limited imagination, could easily picture life in rural Tanzania, and see the fabled wild animals of the Serengeti, when Kwame told stories of his youth in his rich, descriptive language.

Their speed increased after they parked the rover and transferred to the icemobile. Johann stayed on routes across the ice that were well established until he reached the region of the ice hills and the small valleys where Dr. Won's map said the rectangular hole was located. Just before sunset they found the other icemobile and the long, white, flat rectangular plate. Soon thereafter they located the hole and set up their tent on a flat space in the vicinity.

Neither man was able to fall asleep at first. They talked through their helmets, lying side by side in sleeping bags, for over an hour. Kwame admitted that he was feeling apprehensive, and more than a little excited. He recalled for Johann a night he had spent out in the Serengeti, when he was a teenager earning extra money during the summer by being an assistant cook and dishwasher for a camera safari of Americans.

"This other boy and I decided we would sleep away from everyone else," Kwame said. "So we carried our sleeping bags several hundred meters to the south, near where the stream created a lovely pool beneath a small waterfall. It was a beautiful but hot moonlit night and we slept without a tent. I fell asleep counting the stars I could see. . . . A couple of hours later I awakened, feeling very sticky, and decided to take a midnight swim. When I was out in the middle of the pool I saw a huge crocodile watching me from about thirty meters away. It glided slowly toward me, its eyes reflecting the moonlight. I was terrified. . . . Fortunately, the crocodile was not hungry, otherwise I would not be here telling this story. But the mixture of excitement and fear I feel right now is similar to what I was feeling while I was treading water and watching that crocodile."

In the morning neither man had much to say. They followed the sequence of events they had designed together at Valhalla. They carefully unrolled the two long rope ladders and checked each rung for strength and stability. Kwame pounded four new stanchions into the ice near the corner of the hole (the two stanchions mentioned in Dr. Won's journal were still there, but there was no rope descending into the dark abyss) while Johann tested the small mobile camera units. The final step was to anchor one end of each heavy rope ladder around the stanchions and push the body of the ladder into the hole. There was no sound of contact at the bottom when either of the ladders finished unrolling. The depth of the hole was obviously greater than twenty meters.

Johann and Kwame attached mining lamps to their space helmets before they began their first descent. "Don't you find it peculiar," Johann said while adjusting his lamp, "that the icemobile has apparently not been touched in over a year, and the two stanchions put in place by Dr. Won's team have not been removed?"

Kwame shrugged. "No more peculiar than anything else," he said.

They climbed carefully all the way down the rope ladder, passing five pairs of broad, rectangular tunnels cut into the ice on either side of them. Using their flashlights while standing near the bottom of the ladder, Johann and Kwame could see that there were two more levels beneath them, and that the central hole was apparently no more than eight to ten meters deeper than the length of their ladders. They deployed the ten mobile cameras without incident, one in each tunnel at each level, and then returned to the bottom to begin retrieving their robot assistants. Eight of the ten cameras performed perfectly, showing up as expected at their assigned positions twelve minutes after starting their sequence. As planned, the two backups were sent into the tunnels from which two of the original cameras did not return. These backups were programmed with a shorter reconnaissance sequence.

Johann and Kwame spent the next two hours looking at the raw video information recorded by the mobile cameras. On one side of their tent they had set up an electronic system that included a television monitor. It turned out that very little of the video information recorded by the cameras was usable without the image-enhancement algorithms stored in the portable processors.

The work was tedious. Many of the frames were of blank walls of ice. It wasn't until late in the day, when Johann and Kwame were exhausted, that any sort of coherent picture of the subsurface world began to emerge.

"I believe," Kwame said during a short break, "that the first two levels are essentially without function. They are a combination of mazes and dead ends with no real purpose except to confuse and decoy anyone who happens upon this structure by chance."

"But what about the strange writing on the wall, if that's what it is, and that weird group of ice sculptures on the second level?" Johann asked.

"Unless there's something else beyond the range of the mobile cameras, deeper into the tunnels," Kwame said, "I still don't think the second level is important. My intuition tells me that what this place is all about does not begin until the third level beneath the surface. . . . And we can't tell what all that stuff the cameras photographed really is unless we go see it ourselves."

Johann and Kwame spent the rest of their waking hours studying the enhanced images from the third level and formulating their plan for the following day. They decided their first objective would be to examine a set of large objects with rounded corners, about a hundred meters away from the central hole, that was blocking the southwesterly tunnel on the third level.

Johann called Narong on the portable telephone just before Kwame and he climbed into their sleeping bags. He excitedly told Narong about everything they had discovered.

"What about the inter-Asian team?" Narong asked. "You haven't mentioned a word about them."

"Not a trace of evidence about what happened to the Asian scientists," Johann replied. "No bones, no bits of clothing, no pieces of their rope—nothing. And we examined the images with great care."

"They can't simply have vanished in thin air," Narong said. "Oh, well, be careful tomorrow, and phone as soon as you find anything unusual."

"It does not make any sense, now that I think about it," Kwame said after Johann hung up the phone, "that the bottom of the hole should have been so clean. We must have ourselves scattered some debris when we were deploying the ladders. And surely stuff blows in when the winds are high."

"I agree with you," Johann said. "Let's take a closer look at the bottom tomorrow."

Johann and Kwame climbed down the same rope ladder. They were on the side of the hole next to the southwesterly set of tunnels. Johann was below Kwame. Before he stepped off the ladder into one of the tunnels, he cast his flashlight beam below him, toward the bottom of the hole.

He couldn't see anything but darkness. "Weren't we able to see the bottom of this hole from the third level yesterday?"

"I can't remember," Kwame said from above him. "Maybe I should go down and look."

"No," said Johann. "We can do that later. . . . Let's go ahead and explore this tunnel first."

Kwame joined Johann in the tunnel entrance. They switched their mining helmets to full output. They could then see about fifty meters into the tunnel. After a short walk the strange rounded objects loomed up in the shadows ahead of them.

"Have you had any second thoughts about not bringing any weapons?" Kwame said into the microphone of his space helmet.

"My reptilian instinct tells me I should have a gun now," Johann replied. "But my cerebellum tells me it would be useless against whoever built this place."

Kwame chuckled. "Good point," he said.

The first of the strange objects, which was over against the left wall of the tunnel, resembled a giant bowling pin. It was taller than Johann, and much wider, with a smooth creamy-white surface broken only by a red band around its middle. Beyond the bowling pin were a pair of large spheres against the same wall. They were also smooth and white except for the red bands around their equators.

"It's a bowling alley," Kwame said.

Johann laughed as he walked past the spheres into the rest of the group of the smooth, rounded objects that stretched across the tunnel and blocked their progress. He paused, and then pulled himself up to the top of one of the smaller objects that looked like an overweight toadstool. From there Johann could see a large white door in the distance.

"Hey, Kwame," he yelled. "I've found something. . . . It looks like a door."

"That's just great, Johann," he heard Kwame say in a strange tone. "But what I have hanging over my head back here should probably be our first priority."

Johann whirled around and nearly slipped off the toadstool. A long white ribbon of sparkling particles was suspended over Kwame's head. Johann let himself down gently to the surface of the tunnel.

"Where did it come from?" Johann asked, his eyes never leaving the bright ribbon formation, which had now dropped to eye level.

"From behind us, I think," Kwame said. "I was rubbing this bowling pin here, and the ribbon thing suddenly materialized above my head. . . . Maybe it's the genie of the pin."

Kwame laughed nervously at his own joke. Meanwhile Johann was circling around, trying to come closer to Kwame. The ribbon kept moving also, staying between the two of them at eye level. The light from the ribbon was so bright that the two men could not see each other's faces.

Whenever Johann took a step toward Kwame, the ribbon became brighter and more active. Its formation danced about, as if it were agitated, and the individual, sparkling particles in its structure increased their speed. When Johann took a step away from Kwame, the exact opposite occurred.

"So, boss man," Kwame said after a moment, "do you have the feeling the ribbon thing is trying to keep us separated?"

"Seems to be," Johann replied apprehensively.

"Then why don't you just stop moving and lean against that toadstool. Let's see what happens next."

"All right," said Johann. "I guess we're not yet in any danger—at least not as far as I can tell."

As Johann and Kwame watched, the ribbon levitated another meter, danced briefly at its ends, and then transformed itself into a double helix exactly like the one Johann had seen in the snow in the Tiergarten years before in Berlin. Johann's heart went into overdrive. *It's not possible,* he was thinking. *It's just not possible.*

Only seconds later, before either man had yet uttered a word, the double helix changed into a figure eight. Johann's shock was so great that he almost stopped breathing. The figure eight turned on its side, the individual particles coalesced into eleven white spheres in rapid motion around the figure, and then the spheres reversed direction. Johann knew what was coming next. He ducked quickly as the white baseball with the red band darted over his head. The baseball turned around behind him, changed back into a ribbon, and flew back into the space between Kwame and him.

Johann tried to gather his wits. "Let's get the hell out of here, Kwame," he managed to say.

"I hear you, Johann," Kwame said. "But it looks like our problems are just beginning."

Beyond Kwame, coming from the direction of the central hole, was a large white thing, resembling a giant snowman riding on a skateboard. It was made of two huge snowballs, the larger one on the bottom resting on a flat white plate with six red wheels. This snowman had no eyes, no ears, and no arms. At least not until it reached Kwame. When the creature was less than a meter away from Kwame, the smaller, upper snowball suddenly convulsed and a white appendage appeared. The creature then wrapped its hand, or whatever it was at the end of the long skinny appendage, firmly around Kwame's arm and began pulling him toward the central hole.

Johann was paralyzed. When he recovered enough to try to help his friend, the ribbon transformed itself into a baseball again and began detonating against Johann's faceplate. Johann was blinded by the light and jolted by the frequent impacts. At length he gave up trying to help Kwame. The formation of dancing particles changed back into a ribbon and rose high enough in the tunnel that Johann could see what was happening.

Oh my God, Johann thought. *He's going to be thrown down into the hole.*

"Are you all right?" Johann screamed in panic.

"I'm scared shitless," Kwame replied. "This fiend has a vise grip on my arm and is dragging me toward the big hole. . . . When I struggle, the grip tightens. I'm afraid the son of a bitch is going to tear a hole in my spacesuit!"

"Jesus, Kwame," Johann said. "I'm sorry I got us into this. It was stupid, really stupid."

"It's too late for that, *Mein Herr*," Kwame said breathlessly. "We're almost to the— Wait, Johann, what is this? Johann, the hole's not there."

Johann was frantic. He could barely see Kwame and the snowman in the distance. "What, Kwame . . . What do you mean it's not there?"

"There's a platform connecting the two tunnels on either side. The snowman is dragging me— Shit, Johann, it's moving. It's a damn elevator. We're going up. Good-bye, Johann, good-bye."

9

The remaining two hours Johann
stayed in the subsurface world
were like a dream. Later, when
he would try to describe to someone what he saw during those two hours,
and what he felt, he would understand completely the meaning of the
word "ineffable."

The snowman, or another creature exactly like the one who kidnapped Kwame, disembarked from the elevator on Johann's level about
five minutes after Kwame had been kidnapped. The ribbon of particles
raced away down the tunnel as soon as the snowman was within ten
meters of Johann. An appendage shaped like a skinny tapered arm without a hand popped out of the snowman's torso after a brief convulsion in
the amazingly smooth surface, but Johann was not grabbed. The white
arm made a gesture that obviously meant "Follow me." The snowman
was Johann's guide for the next two hours.

They began in the area behind the ceiling-to-floor white door Johann had seen from the top of the toadstool. Beyond the open door the
tunnel, now illuminated by white lights mounted in the ice that formed
the ceiling, stretched in front of them as far as Johann could see. Objects

were stored in open compartments that lined both sides of the tunnel. Johann had no idea what he was seeing. All he could tell for certain was that all the objects were white, with smooth surfaces and rounded edges, that each of them had some type of red band or marking, and that each compartment contained only one kind of item. Every variation in size, shape, or marking had its own separate compartment.

Johann was dazzled by the profusion of white light that was everywhere. It reflected off the ice and all the white objects. He had to close his eyes repeatedly to keep from being blinded.

Johann followed his snowman guide for several hundred meters without stopping. He tried without success to make some sense out of his surroundings. The objects and their open compartments varied enormously in size. In one compartment cut into the ice, about the size of the box a large television set would occupy, there were thousands of identical tiny white rings, each smaller than a fingernail, each with a thin red band running completely around its midsection. Another compartment was mammoth, occupying the entire area beside the right side of the tunnel for twenty-five or thirty meters. It contained a dozen long white cylinders lying on their sides.

When the walls and the ceiling of the tunnel abruptly ended, the snowman stopped and extended its appendage upward. They had entered an enormous white warehouse whose towering ceiling could not have been far below the Martian surface. Johann felt giddy as he craned his neck to look around the vast underground room. The snowman then tapped him on the shoulder, and Johann followed his guide deeper into the warehouse.

From the middle of the warehouse floor, Johann could see all four of the ice walls. They were each at least fifteen meters tall and contained both more compartments and more objects. The floor itself was as large as an American football field and contained arrays of tall ice shelves that were laid out in perpendicular rows and columns. These shelves also were subdivided into compartments and filled with objects. As Johann gazed around the room a bizarre vehicle, a giant white bowl mounted on wheels and carrying a bunch of twisted pieces that looked like pretzels, passed by him on its way to some unknown destination. Down an aisle beside him, Johann saw a similar white bowl convulse, extend a very thin arm upward out of its center, and deftly pluck five screwlike objects out of their compartment.

The snowman allowed Johann to study the warehouse for a few minutes before it began sliding away down one of the aisles on its skateboard feet. Johann followed. They left the warehouse and entered a long, dark tunnel with blank walls of ice. The snowman was moving rapidly. It was difficult for Johann, in his spacesuit and backpack, to keep up with his guide. He was exhausted by the time they reached a platform elevator and went down several more levels in the underground realm.

Again the snowman marched Johann along a dark tunnel with blank walls. They made a right turn, then a left, entering new tunnels that looked just like all the others. At length they came to another tall white door. It opened when the snowman touched it, and Johann followed his guide into another large, illuminated room buried deep beneath the Martian ice.

On either side of the aisle were closed containers of different-colored liquids stored behind sheets of translucent plastic or glass. Sometimes two or three of these display cases were stacked on top of one another on one side of the aisle. The liquids were blue, green, or light brown.

Most of the display cases appeared to be empty. A few contained one or more of the white objects that Johann had seen in the compartments. In one case filled with a green liquid, a dark red thing resembling a starfish had affixed itself to the glass. It looked to Johann as if it were alive, but before he could study the creature and its motions, the snowman tapped him on the shoulder again. Later he caught a fleeting glance, as they moved quickly past another display case, of a long white object with some kind of intricate red webbing growing out of one end.

Johann had the sense that he was in some kind of museum or aquarium. Beyond that he did not have a clue about the nature of what he was being shown.

The snowman had some definite destination in mind. They made several turns—this room, too, was laid out with perpendicular aisles—before reaching a window behind which was a beautiful blue liquid that reminded Johann of a mountain lake. The snowman stopped and knocked on the outside of the container. At first Johann could see nothing at all in the liquid. Then he saw it, or rather *her*, swimming toward him. Johann nearly fainted.

What was swimming in the liquid was a white, blond, human girl, perhaps six years old, perfectly formed in every way except for flippers where her hands and feet should have been. She swam over to Johann, obviously saw him, and flashed a girlish smile. Johann was stupefied. The girl pirouetted in the water, blew bubbles out of her mouth, and tapped on the window with her flippers. Johann tapped back without thinking.

He stood there, transfixed, for several minutes. Never once did the girl leave the window. Johann's mind was asking a thousand questions. *Who is she? How did she get here? How is she breathing? What happened to her hands and feet?* Just before the snowman indicated that it was time for them to leave, Johann imagined that he saw the beginnings of fingers forming in the girl's hand flippers. At that point he knew that he had become completely insane.

The giant sea serpent with the dragonlike head was an anticlimax for Johann. Even though the creature pounded on the window with its enormous tail and made horrible, threatening faces, Johann hardly paid attention. He could not remove the image of the strange blond girl with the flippers from his mind.

In a daze he followed the snowman out of the aquarium and then through several more of the dark tunnels with the blank ice walls. Johann would vaguely remember later boarding the elevator platform and ascending to the surface. When he reached the tent, he collapsed in a heap on top of his sleeping bag. Kwame was unable to awaken him when he entered the hut a few minutes later.

It did not surprise them that neither of the telephones would work. Nor were Johann and Kwame surprised that their tent had been visited while they were inside the subsurface world, and that all their video information had been erased.

"So we have no proof of what we saw down there," Kwame said.

"Only our eyewitness accounts," Johann said. It was now dark outside. Johann had slept for nine hours. Although he had been awake for some time now, he was groggy, and still disoriented from his experience. Talking with Kwame was slowly bringing him back to reality.

"I wonder why they let Dr. Won escape with the maps and the journal," Kwame said.

"Maybe they didn't," Johann said. "Maybe the particles, or our snowman, or some other creature or thing from their world was instrumental in her death. Maybe they even sabotaged her computer, never dreaming that we would find her and extract the information about their existence. It was probably a million-to-one shot."

The two men continued to gather up their belongings and pack them in the large bags. "Why did they give you the complete tour?" Kwame said. "And keep me from seeing anything?"

Johann shrugged. "We can no more answer those questions than understand what they were trying to show me. . . . But I have learned something important, perhaps even profound, from this entire experience. I may be too close to it, and still temporarily out of my mind, but what I saw down there, beneath the ice, tells me that any aliens we ever encounter will be far stranger than we can imagine."

There was a short silence. "Do you think they'll let us leave now?" Kwame asked, hoisting a bag on his shoulder.

"I don't know," Johann said. "I guess that depends on whether they are threatened by what we know." He stopped his packing and looked at his friend. "Whatever they decide, it's obvious that we are completely in their power."

"That's not a very comforting thought," Kwame said.

"It wasn't supposed to be," Johann replied.

With the bags, which were much lighter now without the heavy rope ladders, upon their shoulders, Johann and Kwame trudged across the ice toward the icemobile. The ribbon of particles joined them while they were placing the bags in the back of the vehicle. To Johann's astonishment, the icemobile started without difficulty.

"Maybe they don't want to kill us too close to their home," Kwame said nervously.

The ribbon continued to hover above them as they drove south across the Martian ice. Johann began to worry about a new problem. "What if the ribbon of particles follows us all the way to Valhalla?" he said. "Are we going to expose everyone else at the outpost to some terrible new danger?"

"There's no way we can know," Kwame replied. "But I bet that the particles and their friends already know all about Valhalla, and that the damn ribbon is following us for some other purpose."

The icemobile suddenly stopped functioning when the men were near the edge of the main polar cap, no more than a kilometer from where they had parked the rover. "Uh-oh," said Kwame. "I don't like this at all. . . . This would not be a good place to die."

The ribbon moved closer to them. "Leave everything," Johann said suddenly. "Take off all your packs and pouches and put them in the back of the icemobile. We'll show them that we're willing to leave behind every shred of evidence."

Kwame looked at Johann quizzically. "All right," he said after several seconds. "If you think it's important."

They continued on foot in the direction of the rover. The bright ribbon of particles dropped down to eye level and stayed between them, no more than fifty centimeters away from Johann. His fear grew every time he looked over at the glowing ribbon. Finally his nerves overwhelmed him. "Look, whatever you are," he screamed. "If you're going to kill us, just get it over with."

The white ribbon curled itself into a halo and slowly levitated. It danced back and forth above their heads for a few seconds. Then, suddenly, there was a burst of light that temporarily blinded both men. They didn't see the ribbon explode into thousands of tiny, tiny particles that flew down and adhered to both of their spacesuits. To Johann and Kwame, it seemed as if the ribbon had simply disappeared.

Valhalla was in the middle of its own crisis when Johann and Kwame returned. "I know you have many things to tell me," Narong said to Johann, "but I need your immediate help. Deirdre Robertson has accused Yasin of attacking her last night in her room. She says he was about to rape her when Anna came to her rescue. I've scheduled a hearing two hours from now. . . . Since you're back, you'll have to preside."

"Shit," said Johann. "I have just had the single most amazing experience of my life, maybe of *any* life, and now must I really deal with Yasin?"

Narong shrugged. "Noblesse oblige and all that," he said. "Everyone will know that you've returned. I certainly can't hold the hearing without you, and if we announce a delay we'll infuriate every woman at the outpost. But suit yourself."

"No, no," Johann said. "Let's get it over with. If anything will give me a dose of reality, it will be listening to Yasin arguing with two women." He turned to Kwame. "We'll need you as an official adviser at the hearing. You are at least a nominal Muslim, so Yasin will not be able to claim the hearing is culturally biased. . . . Although I must warn you, Yasin has a history of vengeful acts."

Kwame smiled. "After what just happened to us, Johann, Mr. Yasin al-Kharif does not scare me one iota. I would a hundred times rather face *his* rage than ever again feel that snowman's grip on my arm."

"Snowman?" Narong said with a look of surprise. "Maybe we should delay the hearing."

Both Johann and Kwame laughed. "Let's have some lunch," Johann said. "We'll tell you the short version of our story."

10

The hearing took place in the only room at Valhalla large enough to accommodate comfortably all the people who wanted to attend, the gymnasium that was part of the recreation complex. Johann would have preferred a private hearing, but Narong convinced him that the widespread interest in the case dictated an open meeting. As the audience continued to file into the gymnasium, Johann leaned over to Kwame. "From the sublime to the ridiculous in a few short hours," he said.

"The real world always imposes itself," the Tanzanian replied.

Johann and his advisory board, which consisted of Narong, Kwame, and Lucinda Davis, sat behind a long table on the gymnasium floor. Yasin was seated in a folding chair on their right. Deirdre Robertson and Anna Kasper, who had jointly filed the complaint, were to the left of the table. Most of the remaining residents of Valhalla sat on bleachers that pulled out from the wall.

"As the director of the Valhalla Outpost," Johann began when everything was quiet, "one of my duties is to investigate any conduct by a resident that may have violated the statutes governing the entire Martian colony. If I find that there is sufficient reason to believe a law has been broken, I am required to remand the individual who has been accused to the authorities in Mutchville for a proper trial in a court of law. . . . I recognize that under the unusual conditions currently existing on Mars, it may be difficult, if not impossible, to accomplish the transfer of the accused to Mutchville. Nevertheless, I intend to conduct this hearing as the proper first step in due process."

Johann paused. He felt very peculiar. Somehow this whole hearing didn't seem very important after what had just happened to him. He summoned all his willpower and focused on Yasin.

"Mr. Yasin al-Kharif, you have been accused of the attempted rape of Ms. Deirdre Robertson. How do you plead?"

"Not guilty."

"Let the record of the hearing indicate that Mr. Yasin al-Kharif pleads not guilty," Johann now said. "Each of the three of you"—he motioned to Deirdre, Anna, and Yasin—"will be given ten minutes to tell what you know about the alleged attempted rape that occurred in Ms. Robertson's room last night. . . . I would like to remind each of you that you are under oath. Watch the light above the computer in front of you when you are giving your testimony. If a red light flashes, the subroutine converting your speech into a written transcript has missed a word or words and some repetition may be necessary. When the three of you have finished, my advisory board and I will almost certainly ask some questions."

The testimonies contained no substantive disagreements about the basic events that had occurred prior to the alleged assault. Yasin had told Deirdre that he had some new ideas about how to improve the efficiency of the greenhouses. They had agreed upon a meeting, but because of both of their near-term work schedules, the most convenient time for them to get together had been the previous evening after dinner. Deirdre had been wary of seeing Yasin in the office complex at a time when there might not be any other workers around. After consulting with Anna Kasper, she had decided to hold the meeting in her room in the living quarters.

Everything had been fine for about an hour. Deirdre admitted that Yasin had had some "intriguing" ideas for improving the performance of the greenhouses. She also acknowledged that Yasin's behavior had been proper and professional during the first part of their meeting. Toward the end of their discussion, Deirdre felt safe enough to close the door to the noisy hallway, despite Anna Kasper's earlier suggestion that she keep it open the entire time.

What happened next varied sharply in Deirdre and Yasin's accounts.

According to Yasin, who was by far the more eloquent of the two, Deirdre began flirting with him after closing the door, suggested that the two of them sit side by side on the couch to review some diagrams he had brought with him, and repeatedly caressed him before he kissed her. Deirdre said she was friendly, not flirtatious, that it was only natural that the two people talking about the same complicated diagram should be sitting on the same side of the table, and that although her hand may have accidentally rested on Yasin's shoulder "once or twice," she definitely did not caress him.

Yasin had kissed her suddenly and vigorously on the mouth. He had then grabbed Deirdre's breast near the end of the kiss. She had slapped him and called him a "prick." He had become enraged, pulled down his pants, and showed her what a prick really was. When Yasin had threatened to use it on her, Deirdre had begun screaming and Anna had rushed into the room, catching Yasin with his pants still down.

Johann could barely focus on the testimonies. Images from the previous day continued to flood his mind and capture his attention. He almost didn't hear Deirdre's weeping summary, in which she decried the fact that women are always on the defensive.

"Why must we always prove," she complained, "beyond *any* doubt, that we have done absolutely nothing to encourage a man's sexual attack, before anyone will even consider a charge of rape." Just before her summary, Johann had been buried deep in his memory, standing again in front of a window in an underground ice cavern, playing tap-tap with an unusual six-year-old girl immersed in a blue liquid.

The three members of his advisory board did an excellent job interrogating the witnesses. Johann never asked a single question. His mind continued to drift away from the proceedings. *Pay attention, this is important,* he chastised himself at one point. *This hearing is critical in these people's lives.*

But what happened to me yesterday, Johann responded to that first inner voice, justifying his mental wanderings, *may well be critical in the life of every human who will ever be alive.*

All the advisory board members, plus Yasin, Deirdre, and Anna, were all staring at Johann. "We have no further questions," Narong repeated.

"All right," said Johann, quickly gathering his wits. "In that case the board and I will adjourn to deliberate."

At that moment the gymnasium door burst open and a young man, one of the programmers who spent all his free time playing computer games, raced into the room. "A train," he shouted breathlessly. "A train has arrived. . . . With passengers. There are priests and nuns waiting in our air lock."

The advisory board meeting was postponed so that the outpost could accommodate the unexpected train. Sisters Beatrice and Vivien, along with three other Michaelites, had already removed their spacesuits and were inside the arrival hall by the time Johann arrived. For several seconds Johann just stood and stared at the visitors. His brain simply refused to process the visual input.

"Why, Brother Johann"—Beatrice's lilting voice snapped him out of his stupor—"how delightful that you have come to meet us yourself. We apologize for not alerting you that we were coming, but we made the decision on such short notice, and communications aren't what they once were. . . ."

Her eyes still had the same burning intensity. Several seconds later Johann heard another voice he recognized. He turned and smiled at Sister Vivien. "When your report reached Mutchville," she said, "one of our priests was on duty in the communications office. Sister Beatrice says that his presence there was the work of God. We commandeered a train immediately to make certain we left before the dust storm reached Mutchville."

Narong had just walked up beside Johann. "A dust storm?" he said. "Where? How big?"

"Sister Vivien, Sister Beatrice," Johann said, "this is the deputy director of Valhalla, Mr. Narong Udomphol."

"Delighted," Narong said hurriedly. "But please tell me about this dust storm. If it's coming this way, it could have serious consequences for the outpost."

"All we know," Sister Vivien said pleasantly, "is that the storm is huge, and it was approaching Mutchville from the south a couple of days ago. Before we left we heard one of the forecasters say that this storm is better organized than the one in 2133 and may become global in scope."

Narong abruptly excused himself to talk to the chief engineer of the train. Meanwhile Johann felt as if his life were spinning out of control. *No more,* he thought. *Nothing else . . . I can't deal with everything that's already happening. Not the bright particles and Sister Beatrice and a dust storm too.*

". . . We're pretty tired from the journey," Sister Beatrice was saying. "Is there somewhere we could take a shower, and maybe then a nap? We realize that Valhalla is pretty small, but don't you have some quarters for transient scientists? One of our priestesses visited here several years ago—"

"The train is going to leave tonight," Narong interrupted the moment he was again beside Johann. "They want to guarantee they'll reach

BioTech City before the storm. We have eleven staff members on the departure request list. I don't need to remind you that at least four of them are in critical positions."

"Here, Sisters," Johann said, ignoring Narong for the moment, "take my keys. You can use my apartment. It's number eleven, at the end of the hall in the white stucco building directly across the plaza. There are two extra towels in the linen closet in the hallway."

"Why, thank you, Brother Johann," Sister Beatrice said brightly. "That's very generous indeed. We'll try to keep everything neat and tidy."

She turned to talk to the other Michaelites. Sister Vivien flashed Johann a smile and made a thank-you with her lips. When the robed visitors had all left the arrival hall, Johann put his hands on Narong's shoulders.

"My friend," he said, "I am going to let you deal with all those staff members who want to leave Valhalla. You know our needs as well as I do. I hope you can convince most of them to stay, but if you can't, I won't hold it against you."

"You aren't going to talk to any of them yourself?" Narong asked.

"Nope . . . And I'm not going to convene the advisory board in Yasin's case until tomorrow morning, nor will I talk to the good sisters again until after dinner." He smiled. "And I'm not available to discuss our dust-storm contingency plans until tomorrow afternoon."

Narong was puzzled. "Then what are you going to do for the rest of today?"

"I will be in my office," Johann said, "by myself, with the door locked and the telephone disconnected. I may be thinking, I may be sleeping, I may even be crying. But whatever I am doing, I will be doing it all alone."

Johann turned around and walked out of the arrival hall.

Johann was only allowed one hour's peace in his office. Yasin started banging on the door and would not go away. "Come on, Ace," Yasin said, "I know you're in there. . . . I've looked everywhere else."

At length Johann reluctantly opened the door. Yasin's eyes searched every corner of the room. "Where is she?" he said with a leering grin. "Have I finally discovered a dark secret about our buttoned-up outpost director?"

"There's nobody here but me, Yasin," Johann said wearily. "I have just been sitting at my desk thinking. . . . Incidentally, I must remind you that both the audio and video recorders are on, for my protection as well as yours. According to the hearing procedures, we are not supposed to have any contact, except in an emergency, until a decision is rendered."

"In my opinion this *is* an emergency," Yasin said. "I, too, am faced with a decision. According to the terms of my release and pardon, I am free to leave here whenever I want. The train is departing from Valhalla five hours from now. Whether or not I will be onboard depends on the outcome of the hearing. I would like to know—"

"I'm not going to convene the advisory board now just to fit in with your schedule," Johann interrupted. "There are a few other important things occurring at the present time."

"All right, Ace," Yasin said with a shrug. "But I thought I was pretty damn important to this operation. If you can't answer any of my questions, I guess I'll be forced to assume that you intend to punish me for teaching that bitch a lesson. In that case, I have no choice but to leave Valhalla."

"Such threats have no impact on your case, Yasin," Johann said harshly. "You will be judged based on your actions, not on your value to the outpost. In my opinion, what you did last night was unacceptable, and constitutes sexual assault. Unless the advisory board convinces me I'm wrong, I will recommend confining you to your quarters here until the authorities in Mutchville can decide what should be done with you."

"You're a real shithead, Ace," Yasin said angrily. "All this time I thought we had an understanding. . . . I busted my butt for this place! And you know goddamn well that I wasn't going to rape her. Would I be that stupid? Huh? To attack a woman in her own room, when the door wasn't even locked?"

"Yasin," Johann replied, "whether or not I think you would have raped Deirdre is irrelevant. The fact remains that you purposely exposed yourself to her, and made sexual threats. You admitted as much. . . . Whether you accept it or not, that is unlawful behavior."

"Have it your way," Yasin said bitterly. "You just lost yourself the best fucking engineer this outpost has ever had. I'll be on that train when it leaves. And I know my rights, you can't keep me here against my will."

"No, Yasin, I can't," Johann replied. "But I can see to it that the transcripts of this afternoon's hearing, and this meeting as well, are carried on the same train and handed over to the authorities in Mutchville. Based on your past record, I would not expect the courts to be lenient."

"I'll take my chances, Ace," Yasin said. "From what I've heard about Mutchville, the law is barely functioning there." He stormed out in a fury.

Despite what he had said earlier to Narong, Johann spent the rest of the afternoon talking to the four important staff members who had departure requests on file. Johann was very persuasive. He convinced all four of them that it was in their own best interests to remain at Valhalla. Those who were planning to leave the outpost had completed their terms of service. They were going to Mutchville only as the first step in the process of returning to the earth. To decide to stay in Valhalla meant acknowledging that there was little or no chance, in the near future, of securing passage from chaotic Mutchville to Phobos and eventually on to Earth. Johann underscored in his discussions with them that Valhalla was isolated from the anarchy that existed elsewhere on Mars, and comparatively self-sufficient. He counseled the individuals to consider staying in Valhalla as a safe haven until economic conditions improved.

Although Sisters Beatrice and Vivien accepted Johann's offer to sleep in his living room, it was not until well after dinner that Johann had any time to visit privately with them. Earlier the two priestesses were busy making certain that their brethren were comfortable in their new quarters. The other three Michaelites, Brother Ravi, a striking young Tamil of Dravidian ancestry, Sister Nuba, and Brother José (Johann had met both Nuba and José at the time of his original encounter on the train with Vivien), had all been moved into the apartments only recently vacated by the three Valhallans, including Yasin, who had left on the train. Beatrice and Vivien did not return to Johann's apartment until quite late, more than an hour after he had watched the train pull out of the station.

Although they were very tired, both Beatrice and Vivien wanted to talk to Johann. He prepared a soothing warm drink, mostly water but lightly flavored by the inedible parts of the greenhouse fruits and vegetables, and served it to the two women at the small table in his nook.

"We were, of course, fascinated," Beatrice began, "by that Dr. Won's description of her encounters with the angels. Both Sister Vivien and I were certain that it was another sign that God still has some purpose for us here on Mars."

Johann smiled. He had forgotten how refreshing Beatrice's certitude was. "Another sign?" he said.

"Yes, Brother Johann," Sister Beatrice continued with her characteristic earnestness. "Only two weeks ago we finally received the message from Siena—it had been delayed several months because of all the communications problems between Mars and Earth—that both Vivien and I had been reassigned."

"Sister Beatrice has been appointed as the Bishop of Montevideo," Vivien said. "It is a very important position. We have thousands of priests and priestesses in Uruguay."

"Congratulations," Johann said immediately. "You must be pleased."

"I am thankful that the order has found my service satisfactory," Sister Beatrice said, "but I must admit that I wasn't expecting a reassignment. I had never considered leaving Mars. The situation in Mutchville, especially since those criminals from Alcatraz arrived, has been so dire, and we have been providing so much that is essential to the populace—"

"I'm sorry," Johann gently interrupted, "I don't understand. . . . What happened at Alcatraz?"

"The prisoners took over the penal colony," Vivien said. "They killed what was left of the staff and distributed all the weapons. They came riding into Mutchville on a train they hijacked and established their own fiefdom in the western part of the city."

"I had no idea it was that bad," said Johann.

"God has offered me many challenges in my life," Sister Beatice continued after the brief digression. "I assumed that this reassignment was part of His attempt to show me that we should not become too personally involved in any one of His endeavors. But I still have so much to do here on Mars. I asked God to show me how I could best use the time remaining."

Sister Beatrice sipped her drink and smiled. "This is not bad, Brother Johann. You have learned well how to use what is available. You would make an excellent priest in our order."

"Thank you, Sister Beatrice," he said.

"Last week I received an answer to my prayers," Beatrice said. "During my early-morning meditation, I was outside in the dark, kneeling beside the large statue of St. Michael that is behind the cathedral, when a bright light filtered through my closed eyes. I opened them slowly and saw, hovering around St. Michael's head, a formation of the sparkling particles. I was overwhelmed with joy and thanked God immediately for having sent an angel to guide me.

"I rose and walked around the statue, studying the white outline and watching the tiny particles dance back and forth. When I was directly in front of St. Michael, I recognized the shape the angel had taken. It was a faceplate, Brother Johann, identical to the one you left us after your visit!"

Johann showed his surprise but said nothing.

"I ran inside the church and awakened Vivien," Beatrice said, her face still glowing, "but the angel had gone before we returned. . . . Even that day Vivien and I discussed whether what I had seen indicated that we should make a trip up here to see you. When, two days later, our priest at the communications office read us those excerpts from Dr. Won's diary, we knew that God was calling us to visit Valhalla. . . . Oh, Brother Johann," Beatrice said excitedly, "we must go out there, on the ice, and see what wonders God has created."

"I've already done that, Sister Beatrice," Johann said. "In fact, I just returned from the ice this morning."

The two priestesses looked at him in consternation. "You've already found the rectangular hole?" Sister Beatrice asked.

Johann nodded. "And was there something down below, some kind of structure in the ice?" Vivien said.

"Was there ever!" Johann said. "A world unlike any I had ever even imagined."

"Why didn't you tell us this before, Brother Johann?" Beatrice asked. Her brow was knitted and she appeared momentarily confused.

Johann laughed. "There hasn't been any time—this is the first chance I've had."

Beatrice and Vivien savored every word of Johann's story. They asked questions, requested more complete descriptions, and even drew a map and pictures on sheets of paper on the table. Sister Beatrice became more and more excited as the story progressed. When Johann described the blinding flash and the disappearance of the ribbon, Beatrice positively exulted.

"Like Elijah, Brother Johann," she said. "You are like Elijah. . . . Or maybe even Moses . . . God has favored you and this friend, this Kwame, over all others. He must have something very, very important for you to do."

Tears had begun to stream out of Beatrice's eyes and down her cheeks. She reached out her two hands, one to Vivien and one to Johann. Johann had never touched Beatrice before. He was amazed at how comfortably their hands fit together.

"Pray with us, Brother Johann," Beatrice said, leading both Vivien and Johann to a place in the living room where they could kneel together. "Open your heart to God, as He has opened Himself to you."

They knelt side by side, with Beatrice in the middle. The two women clasped their hands in front of them and closed their eyes. Johann followed their lead, although he felt incredibly self-conscious.

"Thank you, O God," Beatrice said fervently. "Thank you for having shown us again and again the wonders of Thy creation. Help us all, dear God, including Brother Johann kneeling here beside us, to comprehend these miracles Thou hast chosen us to witness, and to use our knowledge of these miracles in such a way that human spirits everywhere shall be uplifted and Thy name universally praised. We pray in the name of Thy son Jesus, and all the saints who have served Thee, including our beloved St. Michael."

11

J ohann did not fall asleep immediately. For a while he listened to
the murmur of the two women in
the next room. He could not understand their words, but he loved the
sound of their voices. It was an unusual experience for him to be sharing
his apartment with others, especially women.

As he lay in bed with his eyes closed, his mind jumped from event
to event in the hectic last two days of his life. Johann smiled as he recalled Sister Beatrice's response to his admitted astonishment that the
ribbon had changed into all the different manifestations of the particles
that he had personally seen before.

"It's not surprising, Brother Johann," she had said, "that the angels
know about all your previous encounters with their kind, even if they
occurred on another planet. God's angels all communicate with each
other, wherever they are, and an interaction with a human is a major
event in their realm. . . . What astonishes *me* is that you have been
blessed by all these extraordinary events, and you *still* can't or won't
acknowledge the guiding hand of God in your life."

Johann finally fell asleep thinking about Beatrice. She dominated his dreams, most of which were short, disconnected vignettes dealing with the mundane details of daily life. In one of them Beatrice accompanied Johann through a routine inspection of the outpost. He remembered thinking in his dream how natural it seemed for the two of them to be together.

Someone was shaking him lightly. "Brother Johann," the woman's voice said, "wake up please. . . . Something has happened."

He was slow to realize where he was. Johann sat up in his bed and automatically looked at the clock on the end table. It was not yet four o'clock.

"I'm sorry to bother you, Brother Johann," Beatrice said, "but something unusual is happening very near to Valhalla. . . . I had just begun my meditation up on the observation deck when I saw a pair of bright lights flashing across the dark sky. I was thinking they landed fairly close to the outpost when I saw three more, following approximately the same path."

The sleepy Johann stared at the beautiful, eager eyes no more than a meter away from his. His first impulse was to tell Sister Beatrice to return to her meditation, or whatever in the hell she had been doing, and come back in three hours to tell him again about the bright lights in the sky. *But no,* Johann thought to himself, *I'll go with her up to the observation deck, and give her my standard lecture on meteor showers. . . . That might actually be fun.*

He slipped out of bed in the dark and found a shirt and a pair of slacks. They tiptoed through the living room, being careful not to wake the sleeping Vivien, and began climbing the winding stairs that led to Valhalla's only observation deck.

"I couldn't sleep at all," Beatrice whispered from above Johann on the narrow staircase. "I kept thinking about your story last night."

Johann had to slow himself down as they climbed to keep from becoming tangled in the bottom of Beatrice's robe. Once, he was seized by a boyish impulse to lift her robe and see what was underneath, but he managed to restrain himself.

"All of the lights originated there, in that sector of the sky," Beatrice said once they reached the deck. She pointed to a group of stars not far from the tiny moon Deimos. The view was sensational. Valhalla was one of the sites on Mars which, for astronomical purposes, had special viewing windows built into the bubbles. A pair of those windows was directly over the observation deck.

"They seemed at first to be flying directly toward us," Beatrice said. "But at the last moment they veered away and landed nearby, out on that plateau in the west, I believe."

Johann had turned to face Beatrice and was about to start his meteor-shower lecture when her face began to glow from reflected light. "Look, Brother Johann," she said. "There's another one!"

Holy shit, thought Johann as he turned to face the viewing windows. His first impulse was to duck. It looked as if the spectacular light heading in their direction was indeed going to hit Valhalla. It was all over in a few seconds. Whatever had been the source of the bright light had apparently impacted Mars a few kilometers to the west, near where Beatrice had indicated that the earlier objects might have landed.

"We must be passing through a swarm of meteors," Johann said after he recovered from the shock. "That was quite a sight."

"Can we go out there and see where they landed?" Sister Beatrice asked.

Johann looked at her with incredulity. "Now?" he said. "At four o'clock in the morning?"

Beatrice smiled. "I'm ready if you are," she said.

While they were in the air lock and Johann was checking out the rover and its ancillary systems, he was seized by a fit of uncontrollable laughter. Beatrice heard him laughing on the earphones inside her spacesuit. She walked over directly in front of him. "What is it?" she said.

Johann gazed at her through both their faceplates. "This is so certifiably insane," he said, struggling not to laugh again, "that it's comical. I wish I could be there to see Narong's face when his alarm wakes him and he listens to my recorded message. 'Dear Narong, Sister Beatrice and I saw some unusual bright lights about four o'clock this morning. We have taken Rover 14A out on the western plateau to investigate.' "

A minute later Johann was still chuckling intermittently. They were now sitting side by side in the rover, waiting for the ambient environment in the air lock to become that of Mars.

"Are you making fun of me, Brother Johann?" Beatrice asked. "It's all right if you are," she added. "I'm not offended. I appreciate your doing this to satisfy my curiosity."

Johann turned to face his companion. "No . . . Well, yes, maybe a little," he said. "I've just never met anyone quite like you."

"I could say the same thing, Brother Johann," she replied.

They drove in silence toward the west, away from the late-summer sun that was rising in a low arc behind them. It was a spectacular early morning. The millions of stars above them receded as the polar sun inched higher in the Martian sky.

"I will miss this planet," Beatrice said as Johann steered the rover up a long slope that led to the plateau. "It is a harsh place, not really meant for human habitation, but it has a raw and unique beauty."

"Someday," Johann said, bouncing in his seat from the rough terrain, "if we ever straighten out our problems on Earth, we will transform Mars into a paradise."

"Only if God is willing, Brother Johann," Beatrice replied.

The plateau was several hundred meters higher in altitude than the position where Valhalla was located. Behind them, in the direction of the rising sun, the geodesic bubbles looked out of place on the barren plains. There were many more boulders here on the plateau than there had been in the immediate vicinity of the outpost. Some of the boulders were quite large and blocked their view. Often it was not easy for Johann to find a path through the profusion of rocks.

"These rocks are all ejecta," Johann said, "deposited here by a major impact millions of years ago. There's a huge crater nearby."

Johann made a sharp left turn to avoid a chaotic boulder field. They had continued south only a few hundred meters when the sky above them, now a light rusty color, flashed with another bright light. They stared together as the light hurtled toward them. Sister Beatrice reached out and grabbed Johann's arm just before the bright flash narrowly missed them, landing only half a kilometer or so away.

Johann drove the rover as fast as he dared. They came over a small hill on the plateau and saw a sight, down the slope in front of them, that they would both remember for the rest of their lives. The object that had just landed, a large white sphere, had extended a pair of strange, scissor-like contraptions from its midsection, and was cutting itself out of a multilayered bag that had obviously cushioned its impact on the surface.

The large white sphere was on the right side of a small, flat plain. Around the rest of the plain were other empty bags with gaping holes, as well as a wide variety of white objects with smooth surfaces, rounded corners, and occasional red bands or other red markings. Most of these strange objects were standing still, but a few were in motion, using their retractable appendages to sweep rocks and other debris away from the two big construction projects in the middle of the plain.

The newly arrived sphere, once free of its bag, retracted its scissors and began rolling toward the larger of the two construction projects. Hovering over each of the projects were long ribbons of sparkling particles. Although these ribbons were much larger than any of the formations Johann had seen before, from a distance they appeared to be identical in kind to the one that had followed Johann and Kwame for so long on the polar ice.

Johann parked the rover and aimed both of the rover cameras at the incredible scene below them. Beatrice began to pray. Johann was silent until she finished.

The new sphere had by this time convulsed several times, each time radically changing its shape. It currently resembled a freight car, with tracks instead of wheels, and was hauling six or eight of the other white objects from where they had been standing to the vicinity of the larger construction project.

"If I had not seen this with my own eyes," he said, "I could not possibly have believed it. . . . I must thank you for suggesting we come out here this morning."

"God called us both, Brother Johann," Beatrice said simply.

They climbed out of the rover and stood side by side, watching the activity below them. White, hulking things with hands like scoops were digging in the Martian soil and carrying their collected material over to what looked like bloated furnaces. From time to time a tall, skinny, white object would stick its long hand into the furnace and retrieve something that would subsequently be stacked in one of the many piles forming around the two construction projects.

Only the smaller of the two projects had begun to take any shape. It already looked like a hatbox erected on short stilts. Johann checked his watch and then opened up the back of the rover. He found enough tools and parts that he could construct two makeshift tripods, upon which he mounted the two rover cameras after carefully removing them from the vehicle. Johann also deployed a portable transmitter and hooked it to the cameras so that they would be able, once back in Valhalla, to view in real time what was occurring on the plateau. He verified with the newly awakened Narong that the pictures were being received in the outpost communications center.

Beatrice could not take her eyes off the scene on the plateau. When Johann told her that it was time for them to return to Valhalla, she was disappointed. "Don't you think we should go down there, Brother Johann," she asked, "and actually be *among* the angels?"

"No, I don't," Johann replied. "I believe if we were meant to intercede in any way, we would have been given a sign."

Beatrice responded with an appreciative smile. "Well spoken, Brother Johann," she said.

Nobody did any work in Valhalla that day. Everyone stayed glued to one of the television monitors scattered throughout the outpost, all of which displayed the amazing scene unfolding on the plateau a few kilometers to the west. In the middle of the morning drone rovers were sent to the site to set up more cameras, guaranteeing that both wide-angle frames of the entire scene and narrow-angle close-ups of the two construction projects would be available even if camera-system failures occurred.

At first Johann himself supervised the small operations center, reviewing the incoming signals and choosing, as a function of what was occurring out on the plateau, which of the signals would be routed to the outpost monitors. Sister Beatrice was not content simply to watch the monitors along with everyone else at Valhalla. Whenever Johann glanced up, or talked to the technician seated beside him, he saw Beatrice standing on the other side of the glass window.

The moment Johann left the operations center, Sister Beatrice accosted him and launched into a long explanation of how important it was that she personally witness everything the angels were doing. She would not be denied. At length Johann acquiesced and let her occupy one of the chairs behind the control panels, but only after she promised not to touch any of the switches or interfere in any way with the monitoring process.

By the late afternoon the smaller construction project on the plateau had been completed. All the mobile white objects were now concentrating their attention on the larger project. The small white hatbox stood alone, glistening in the afternoon sun, raised a meter above the Martian surface by its peculiar stilts. Next to it, a skinny white rectangular plate, accented by a striking red line around its perimeter, had been erected facing Valhalla. The plate had been built quickly, after the hatbox was essentially finished, by two mobile white giraffes.

The purpose of the plate was not clear until after the sun had set. Then the lights scattered around the plate began to flash. Narong was the first to figure out the pattern in the lights and to predict accurately the future behavior of the flashes. He explained to Johann in the operations center that the pattern would reach its "logical conclusion" in a little more than an hour.

"But what does it mean?" a puzzled Johann asked.

"Beats the shit out of me," said Narong. "Maybe it's some kind of communications or scheduling device for all the objects."

"It's a clock all right," Sister Beatrice said quietly. "But it's meant for us, not them. . . . The angels all communicate with each other using other means." She smiled. "Something important is going to happen when the pattern is completed."

Both men looked at her in astonishment. "*What* is going to happen?" Narong said.

"I don't know," Beatrice said. "We'll just have to wait and see."

Activity on the other construction project on the plateau ceased altogether as the flashing lights continued through their predicted sequence. Johann and Narong decided to take advantage of the temporary lull by visiting the cafeteria for a quick meal. Sister Beatrice declined to join them, choosing instead to remain at her post in the operations center. She told Johann and Narong that she would phone them if there were any new developments.

"That is one amazing woman," Narong said as the two men began walking toward the cafeteria. "Her intensity must be seen to be believed."

"Didn't I tell you?" Johann said. "And wait until you hear her sing. Her voice is even more unbelievable . . . if that's possible."

Before they even reached the cafeteria, Johann's phone began to ring. He smiled knowingly at Narong and took the small receiver from his waist pouch. "Yes, Sister Beatrice," he said. "What is it?"

"It's Anna, Johann," an excited voice on the other end said. "I'm over in the arrival hall. The train has returned."

"The train that left last night?" Johann said.

"Yes," Anna answered. "Yasin, Jaime, and Torok are all here, with me, along with the engineering personnel from the train. . . . They reached the outskirts of BioTech City and then turned around. Yasin says he needs to speak to you immediately."

"All right," Johann said. "Bring him over to the cafeteria."

Johann and Narong were halfway through their sandwiches when they were joined by Yasin and Anna. "It's the worst dust storm of the century, Ace," Yasin said before even sitting down. "It's probably hitting BioTech as we speak. Everything to the south is shut down and in total chaos. . . . They would not even let us enter BioTech because they're worried about running out of food."

"Any idea how fast the storm is moving?" Narong said.

"The stationmaster at BioTech told us that it will definitely go global by early next week," Yasin replied. "Top winds were measured at eight hundred kilometers per hour before the gauges at Mutchville broke. The dust is already higher than the Tharsis peaks in the midlatitudes."

"How long can we survive without sunlight?" Johann said to Narong.

"Six weeks to two months," Narong said. "Maybe ten weeks if we're lucky and have no major failures."

"I was thinking about it on the train," Yasin said. "If we take all the emergency steps now, before the storm arrives, we can probably buy an extra month. But it would be necessary to halt all water production completely, and use the big machines to help supply power to the outpost."

"During the storm of 2109, just after Valhalla became operational," Narong said with a worried look, "there was no incident sunlight here for ninety-two days. That kind of storm would wipe us out."

A tiny alarm went off on Narong's watch. "I had almost forgotten," he said, turning around and pointing at the monitor above them. "Our sequence of flashes will reach its end point in one more minute."

In a quick thirty seconds Johann and Narong tried to explain to

Yasin what had happened at Valhalla in the twenty-five hours since the train had departed. At length they gave up, fell silent, and stared at the monitor.

The images on the television screen showed the rectangular plate, with its flashing lights, and the hatbox sitting nearby. Since it was night outside on the plains of Mars, and the robot cameras with their lighting were far away, the hatbox was hard to see. When the countdown finished, there was a brilliant burst of light underneath the hatbox and it lifted off the surface. Everyone gasped. The technician in the operations center had the presence of mind to switch to the wide-angle camera an instant later. All of the residents of Valhalla watched in awe during the four or five seconds it took the hatbox to accelerate upward and out of the field of view.

12

Once Johann announced that a major dust storm was coming and proclaimed a state of emergency at Valhalla, the entire outpost switched into high gear. The astonishing events out on the plateau were temporarily forgotten in the rush of activity to prepare for the storm.

Johann and Narong, after a detailed executive planning session, met with the personnel from each department and developed a full set of emergency procedures. The meetings lasted until after midnight. Johann was already tired when he received a message from Anna urging him to spend a few minutes with Deirdre and her most vocal friends, all of whom were incensed that Johann had suspended action on the complaint against Yasin.

Deirdre was livid. "The son of a bitch shook his penis at me," she trumpeted during a small meeting with Johann in his office. "He admitted it in front of everybody. . . . By not taking action immediately, you are condoning his action."

"It is my opinion," Johann replied slowly, "that to guarantee this outpost will survive the coming dust storm, we need Yasin's talent and cooperation. I am not willing to risk everyone in Valhalla to redress your grievance. Yasin has given me his word that there will be no more incidents. I *promise* you that I will convene the advisory board and address your complaint again as soon as this emergency is over."

"His word doesn't mean a damn thing," Deirdre said bitterly. "And you know as well as I do, there will be no judgment against him after that much time has passed. Yasin will suffer no consequences, *again*, for his abusive behavior."

"I'm sorry, Deirdre," Johann said. "It was not an easy decision. I admit that—"

"If you were a woman," she interrupted, "you would understand how I feel." She shook her head. "You men just don't get it," she said, stalking out of the room.

The others followed. Johann glanced at his watch and rubbed his eyes. It was almost one o'clock. When he reached his apartment he was surprised to find that Sister Beatrice was not in the living room.

"She's still over in the operations center," Sister Vivien said, sitting up from the bed she had made herself on the floor. "She may sleep some there—but Sister Beatrice told me on the phone two hours ago that she has become very friendly with the night-shift technician Fernando Gomez. He has agreed to awaken her immediately if he sees any new or unusual behavior among the angels."

Johann smiled to himself and said good night to Vivien. He went into his bedroom and fell asleep, fully clothed, on the top of his bed. A little more than an hour later he was awakened from a deep and dreamless sleep by the gentle touch of Sister Beatrice.

"Jesus, Sister," Johann said crossly when he realized who was touching him. "Can't you leave me alone for just one night?"

He rolled over on his side with his back to Sister Beatrice. "I'm sorry to disturb you, Brother Johann," she said pleasantly. "I know that you were up late planning for the dust storm, but I believe we have an emergency situation."

Johann sighed heavily and sat up. He switched on the lamp on his end table. "What is it, Sister Beatrice?" he said, making no attempt to disguise his irritation.

"Late last night the activity among the mobile angels accelerated rapidly. Fernando noticed it also. I believe that the timetable for the larger construction project has been revised."

So what? Johann thought to himself. He gazed at Sister Beatrice, waiting for her to continue. Her blue eyes were extraordinarily clear. She looked so eager, so fresh. . . . *How is that possible?* Johann asked himself. *She has had no more sleep than I have.*

Sister Beatrice had sat down on the side of the bed. "Brother Johann," she said, leaning toward him and trembling with excitement, "the angels are building another hatbox. Only *this* one is much larger, and has an open door with a small ladder to the surface. Fernando programmed one of the cameras to use its zoom lens and look inside the door. We saw seats, Brother Johann. Seats that appear to be a perfect size for human beings."

Johann took a slow, deep breath and tried to comprehend what he was hearing. "I would not have bothered you," Beatrice now said, "except half an hour ago a second rectangular plate was erected beside this new hatbox, and lights began to flash. . . . Unless Fernando and I have made an error in reading the pattern, the sequence will conclude in three hours, just after dawn."

Johann was now completely awake. "And you believe that this hatbox, too, is about to launch itself from Mars?"

"Of course," she said with a smile. "That's obvious. Otherwise there would have been no point to everything last night. The smaller hatbox was just a demonstration, to make certain we understood what they were doing."

Her eyes became even more intense. "They have come to rescue us, Brother Johann," she said. "From the dust storm, and from the collapse of our community on Mars. God has sent His angels to carry us away."

Johann was speechless. His mind was exploding with questions. "You think the hatbox was built for *us*?" he said.

"Yes." Sister Beatrice nodded. "At least *some* of us . . . Nothing else makes any sense. I have prayed earnestly to God, imploring Him to tell me if my conclusions are wrong. I have shared what I am thinking with all my brethren, and with Fernando and his girlfriend Satoko. Everyone agrees that I have properly interpreted the signs. They are all preparing to leave at this very moment, but of course we need your help. . . . There is not much time."

Johann jumped up from the bed immediately. He now understood why she had awakened him. "Let me get this straight. You want me to take all of you out there," he said, "*now*, in the middle of the night, so that you can board an alien spacecraft that you believe was sent by God to rescue you?"

Beatrice smiled and nodded again.

"Then you, my dear bishop, or whatever it is that you are," Johann said, now pacing around the bedroom, "are absolutely crazy. . . . You have no idea *at all* where that hatbox might go, or who is controlling it, or why it came here in the first place. This whole thing may be some kind of an alien trick. . . . The damn thing may blow up as soon as you are onboard."

"I didn't expect you to understand, Brother Johann," she said in an even tone, "for you have so little faith. And people *with* faith always seem crazy to those *without*. . . . But all this is beside the point. The eight of us who want to be inside that hatbox when the light sequence finishes cannot accomplish our goal without your approval. Mr. Udomphol says it must be your decision for us to use the rovers."

"You've already awakened Narong?" Johann said.

"Yes," said Beatrice. "He is over at the operations center now, verifying the pattern in the flashing lights."

His doorbell rang. Sister Vivien, dressed in a fresh robe and headpiece, answered the door before Johann did. Brothers Ravi and José, Sister Nuba, Fernando Gomez, Satoko Hayakawa, and Anna Kasper all filed into the room.

"We're all ready," Brother Ravi said.

"Anna," Johann shouted. "What are you doing with these people?"

"I want to go too," she said with a smile, "if there's enough room. . . . I can't say that Sister Beatrice has convinced me that the white objects and the particles are angels, but from what you've said about your encounters with them, I think my chances in that hatbox are at least as good as if I stay in Valhalla for the dust storm."

"Well, I'll be damned," was all Johann could say.

The rovers at Valhalla could accommodate three passengers each. Johann drove 14A again, with Sister Beatrice and Anna Kasper beside him. Narong, Kwame, and Yasin drove the other three vehicles.

"I would have thought you would be the *last* person to take part in such a harebrained scheme," Johann said to Anna as he steered the rover onto the slope leading up to the plateau.

"So would I," Anna said, laughing into the microphone. "In fact, when I stopped by the operations center late last night, I was thinking about nothing but the dust storm."

"What made you decide to go?" Johann said.

"Sister Beatrice," Anna replied. "Somehow what she was saying, even without the angel part, made sense to me."

"She allowed God to speak to her, Brother Johann," Beatrice said. "I was just His temporary agent."

"She is a very persuasive agent," Anna said.

"I can certainly believe that," Johann commented, turning his head to smile at Beatrice through his faceplate.

When they reached the site, they parked the rovers next to the robot cameras that were still sending real-time transmissions to Valhalla, and walked down the steep incline toward the hatbox and the rectangular plate. Narong interpreted the flashing lights, informing everyone that there were forty minutes left in the sequence. He walked over beside Johann.

"Don't you think it's dangerous to stand so close?" Narong asked. "We don't really know what's going to happen. If an explosion, or excess radiation, were to wipe all of us out, Valhalla would have a hard time surviving the dust storm."

Johann agreed. He asked everyone to step up the pace so that the four drivers would be able to watch the liftoff, if it occurred, from beside the rovers.

The long white ribbon of particles hovering over both the hatbox and the plate seemed to brighten as the twelve humans made their way down the incline. Johann stared at the ribbon and watched the sparkling motes dance back and forth inside the structure. He remembered vividly each of his previous experiences with the particles and found himself wondering if this would be his last encounter with them.

Sister Beatrice marched directly over to the hatbox and ascended the ladder without hesitation. The other four Michaelites were right behind her. "There are eleven seats altogether," she announced several seconds later, "placed against the walls. There is plenty of room inside."

Anna was the last of the eight to climb the ladder. When she reached the top rung, she turned around and waved to the four men standing on the Martian surface. "This ought to be interesting," she said, her voice betraying her nervousness.

There were eighteen more minutes remaining in the sequence. The sun had just begun to rise in the east. The four drivers turned their backs on the hatbox and headed for the rovers.

"Hey, Ace," Yasin said. "After this launch or whatever is over, can we spend some time examining those things over there?" He motioned toward the collection of white objects two hundred meters to the west.

"I don't think that would be such a good idea," Johann said, turning around to look at Yasin. It was then that Johann noticed the two smaller ribbons flying toward them. The men froze as each of the two ribbons formed into a torus and came up beside them. One ribbon ended up hovering over Johann, the other over Kwame. Johann felt a strange tingling sensation all over his arms and legs.

"There are still three seats left," they heard Sister Beatrice say. She was watching from the doorway to the hatbox.

Kwame craned his neck backward and stared at the halo of particles over his head. "Well," he said after several seconds, "that's enough for me. . . . I know when I'm being called."

He reached over and shook hands with the other men. "Wish me luck," Kwame said. Johann could see him grinning through his faceplate.

"And what about you, boss?" Narong said as they watched Kwame walking toward the hatbox. "There is definitely something hovering over your head as well."

"I'm not going," Johann said, starting to walk toward the rovers again. "It's too crazy. . . . Besides, I'm needed at Valhalla."

"We could manage without you," Narong said. "And remember what you told me about your first experience. . . ."

There was no time for Johann to respond. The particles had formed into a baseball and were poised in midair above his head, a few meters up the incline. When he took another step up the slope, the baseball smashed against his faceplate.

"Brother Johann," he heard a beautiful voice say inside his helmet, "come with us. You have been selected over and over."

The baseball resumed its position. It was poised to strike Johann again if he walked up the hill. The tingling in his arms and legs intensified. Impelled by something beyond rational thought, he turned around and headed down the incline.

"Hooray for you, Brother Johann," Sister Beatrice said into her microphone. "Some faith at last."

Johann reached the ladder while there were still six minutes to go in the sequence. As he climbed the rungs he was aware of both his palpitating heart and an inner voice telling him that he was a complete and utter fool.

Sister Beatrice greeted him at the door with a small hug and ushered him inside. The room, which was shaped like a hexagon, was the size of a small bedroom. With one eye on his watch, Johann made small talk with the others and tried to calm his nerves before taking the seat farthest from the door.

"Someone else is coming," Fernando Gomez said as the countdown entered its last minute. He was seated closest to the door. Both Johann and Sister Beatrice rose instinctively to see what was happening.

A solitary figure in a spacesuit was racing across the Martian plain. He bounded up the ladder and entered the door to the hatbox. "I'll take the last seat," Yasin said with a grin. Fifteen seconds later the door closed.

THE
DIVINE COMEDY

I t was dark inside the capsule for a
brief moment after the door shut.
Then lighting was provided by a
dozen small light sources in the floor, two in each part of the hexagon.
Around the capsule, two people were sitting against each of the five solid
walls. Fernando's seat shared the sixth wall with the closed door.

Everything happened very quickly. A few seconds after the lights
came on, Johann felt bands wrap around his forehead, his chest, and his
thighs, pinning him to his chair. There were a couple of cries of fear, but
they were drowned out by the roar beneath the floor. The force of the
acceleration was enormous. Johann felt as if the pressure was going to
push his eyes out of his head. Across the capsule, Sister Beatrice strained
against the bands, finally succeeding in clasping her hands in prayer.

In less than a minute the acceleration diminished to a normal level.
When the bands holding him against the chair loosened and retracted,
the wall behind and above Johann slid to one side and revealed a tall thin
window. The hatbox was already thirty kilometers above the surface of
Mars and climbing rapidly. Valhalla could no longer be identified as a

separate entity, but the angry growing dust storm, now covering two thirds of the planet, was a spectacular sight below them.

"Well, Ace . . ." Yasin was the first to speak. He had risen from his chair and was standing next to Johann, looking out the window. "Where do you think we're going?"

"I have no idea," Johann answered. He stared at the huge, swirling clouds of dust covering the region directly below them. He thought about Narong, and Valhalla, and the struggle the outpost would have to survive the dust storm.

"They'll make it all right, Ace," Yasin said, as if he were reading Johann's mind. "They have eleven less mouths to feed. . . . And your boy Narong is extremely competent."

"Brother Johann," Sister Beatrice said. She was standing on his left side, also staring out the window. "We are going to offer a prayer of thanks to God. Would you care to join us?"

"To which God are you going to pray, Sister?" Yasin asked. "The Christian God, Allah, or some other?"

Sister Beatrice faced Yasin directly. "Mr. al-Kharif," she said into her microphone, "we have not had a formal introduction. I am Sister Beatrice of the Order of St. Michael."

"I know who you are, Sister," Yasin said. "You are famous, or infamous, all over Mars. Hell, we even had two of your clowns working at Alcatraz."

"Mr. al-Kharif," Beatrice said, ignoring the taunting tone of his voice, "members of our order believe that there is one God, not just for all humanity, but for the entire universe. Whether that God be called Allah, or Jehovah, or something else is not important. What is important is our worship of Him, and our love and respect for one another. . . . In a moment we are going to share a prayer of thanks, a collective expression of our humility in the presence of the miracle we have experienced. We would be delighted if you would share this prayer with us."

Outside the window, Mars continued to recede from the spacecraft. Now, for the first time, the full globe was visible. All that could be seen of the surface, however, was the region near the north pole and the very top of Mount Olympus. The rest was obscured by the awesome dust storm that had covered the planet with a light brown shroud.

Yasin and Johann looked at the planet below them. "Dear God," they both heard Sister Beatrice say. They turned around. The other nine members of their group were kneeling on the floor of the hexagon, their hands clasped in prayer.

"What are you doing, Hassan?" Yasin said sharply. "You're a Muslim, not a Christian."

Kwame was kneeling between Sister Vivien and Sister Nuba. "At this moment, Yasin, that distinction seems especially insignificant," he said. "Now, if you will permit us, we would like to continue with our prayer."

Johann left the window and knelt beside Sister Beatrice. She turned to smile at him. "Dear God," she began again.

"All right, Sister," Yasin interrupted, determined to have the last word. "I am willing to participate, but only on one condition. Can you include a sura from the Koran in your prayer?"

"Of course, Mr. al-Kharif," Beatrice said without hesitation. "In fact, we shall begin with one." She motioned to the empty spot in the cirle. "Will you join us please?"

Yasin knelt down awkwardly. "Dear God," Beatrice said, "we would like to start our prayer of thanks for Your majesty and compassion with a sura from the one hundred and twelfth chapter of the Koran, 'Say He is the One God. . . .' "

Their orbit carried them completely around Mars every seventy minutes. Since the size of the planet below them did not appreciably change, Johann concluded that they were flying in a near-circular orbit. On the first revolution each of the occupants spent at least a few minutes at the window. Johann and Yasin were the only two members of the group with any detailed background in physics. They took turns answering questions about the motion of their vehicle, the appearance of the terminator below them, and the location and size of the two Martian moons.

The hatbox attitude-control profile was simple. The window always pointed at the closest point on Mars. Thus no stars were visible through the window, except during that brief period of time when the disk below them was completely dark. Then a few stars could be seen at the edge of the window.

Toward the end of the first revolution, Johann organized a thorough examination of their small capsule. Sister Vivien discovered a storage area below the center panel in the floor. It contained several vessels of water and almost a hundred soft cylinders. Yasin danced up the side of the room, enjoying the weightlessness, and opened what turned out to be a door in the ceiling.

"There's a closet up here," he announced, "with shelves and peculiar white objects with red markings. . . . There's even a hole that might make a perfect toilet, if we weren't in these damn spacesuits."

By the beginning of the third orbit, it was obvious from the drop-off in conversation that everyone was becoming anxious. The excitement that had followed the launch had waned, and the thrill of experimenting in the weightless environment had passed. Every square centimeter of the small capsule had already been investigated.

Johann was sitting in his chair. Anna came over beside him. "Not that I'm worried or anything," she whispered into her microphone, "but for how long will these suits keep us alive?"

"These are all Barclay's, Version D," Johann replied, "designed for up to eighteen hours without air-supply replenishment. . . . Although you might be hungry and uncomfortable by then."

"Did we bring any instruments that would tell us anything about the environment in this capsule?" Anna asked.

"No, dammit," Johann said. "It was an oversight on my part. In our haste this morning, there wasn't much time for planning." He yawned and slumped down in his chair. "I don't know about anyone else," he said, "but I'm going to take a nap."

"How in the world," Anna said, "can you possibly sleep now? We're in a strange spacecraft built by someone or something unknown, orbiting the planet Mars, and we have absolutely no idea what is going to happen next. I couldn't sleep now even if you gave me a bottle of sleeping pills."

"I can," Johann said. He yawned again and smiled behind his faceplate. "Ask that woman over there why," he said, pointing at Beatrice. "She's the reason I have had no more than five hours' total sleep the last two days."

Toward the end of his nap Johann began to dream. Scenes and places from his childhood were frequented by people he had known as an adult. In one dream he was back in his family home with his parents, in the kitchen where his mother was preparing dinner. Beatrice and Vivien were talking easily with Frau Eberhardt and helping her with the *Kartoffelsalat*. They were both dressed in the robe and headpiece of their order.

"Such nice girls, Johann," his mother said, taking him aside, "but which one is yours?"

He tried to explain to his mother that Beatrice and Vivien were both priestesses, and had taken vows of chastity. In the dream his mother didn't understand. "But they are women, aren't they?" she said. "And it's obvious they find you attractive."

Johann became frustrated with his mother because she couldn't understand that Beatrice and Vivien were different from other women. He was about to shout at her in his dream when he was awakened by a touch on his shoulder.

He opened his eyes slowly and looked through the faceplate. Sister

Beatrice was standing beside him in her spacesuit. She was wearing a broad smile.

"I'm sorry to disturb you, Brother Johann."

"I've heard that before, Sister Beatrice," Johann said. He shook his head and rolled his eyes. "What is it with you, anyway? Have you taken over management of my sleep along with all your other duties?"

She could tell that he was teasing her. Beatrice laughed. "I guess so," she said. "Although I did not do it knowingly."

"So what is it *now*, Sister B?" Johann said with a flourish. "Bright lights in the sky? Hatboxes out on the western plateau? Some new crisis?"

She became serious. "You've been asleep, Brother Johann, for four revolutions. During that time my brethren and I have been talking, meditating, and praying for guidance. Some of the other passengers on this capsule are becoming quite agitated and, in my opinion, are starting to act irrationally."

"*Starting* to act irrationally, Sister?" Johann said with a chuckle. "What we all did seven hours ago was the height of irrationality. Even now, when I look out this window at Mars, and realize that I don't have the foggiest idea what is going on here, I still can't believe that I actually walked up that ladder. . . ."

He didn't finish his thought. "You came with us, I believe," Sister Beatrice said after a short silence, "because you had faith. At least for a moment. Faith, Brother Johann, is a powerful force." She put her hand on his arm. "It is because of faith that I am going to take off my spacesuit now."

"Whaaat?" he said, standing up from his seat. "Did I hear you correctly? You are going to take off your spacesuit when you have absolutely no knowledge about the environment in this capsule? Are you completely crazy? This vehicle was *open* to Mars, Sister Beatrice, only seven hours ago. At that time the pressure must have been close to the same as it was on Mars. Do you know what will happen the moment you expose yourself to six millibars of pressure? Every gas molecule in your entire body will push against your skin, forcing itself in the direction of lower pressure. You will die in excruciating pain in a matter of seconds."

Johann was almost shouting. When he was finished everyone was looking at Beatrice and him.

Beatrice began by addressing Johann, but as she spoke she wandered slowly around the capsule, her eyes meeting the eyes of all the others in the group. "During my prayers," she said, "I realized that it did not make sense that God's angels would build this capsule for us unless it had been designed to accommodate our needs. There is water beneath the floor for us, and both Sister Vivien and I believe those long cylinders are some kind of food. But we cannot drink this water, or eat the manna God has provided for us, as long as we are inside these spacesuits.

"God and His angels could have come for us immediately, as I am confident they will do in the near future, but He decided first to test our faith. He has given us a spaceship to deliver us from the perils of Mars, chairs in which to sit, and fancy seat belts to spare us injury during launch. Do we really believe that He would not also provide a safe and comfortable environment inside this capsule?"

Beatrice was now standing by herself in the middle of the room. Her voice modulated and became softer. "In my prayers I beseeched God to show me where my thinking was wrong. He sent me no signs, nothing to indicate that I was incorrect. Therefore, I am going to show Him that I have faith. I am going to remove my spacesuit."

"Wait a minute, Sister," Yasin said immediately, rushing over beside her. "It may be your right to kill yourself, but not to take any of us with you. If the ambient pressure in here is a vacuum, or roughly the same as it was on Mars, then parts of your helmet may become projectiles when you depressurize. . . . It could be dangerous for everyone else. Give us just a moment."

Yasin and Johann conferred over the front of Johann's seat. Yasin wanted to restrain Beatrice forcibly, to render her somehow incapable of taking off her spacesuit. Johann pointed out that what Yasin was recommending was not practical. The suit had been designed to make it easy for the occupant to take it off. There were even emergency controls inside the faceplate, for example, that could be activated by a bite.

Yasin made a quick estimate of the likely velocity that any pieces of Beatrice's helmet might attain, but both Johann and he soon agreed that the uncertainties were so great the computation was meaningless.

At length Johann and Yasin asked Beatrice to stand against one wall of the hexagon, and suggested that everyone else lie down on the floor, as far away from her as possible, with their arms protecting the back of their faceplates. At this point Sister Vivien inserted herself into the discussion.

"This is ridiculous," she said, her voice rising. "Look at us. . . . Sister Beatrice is willing to risk her life on an issue of faith, and all we can think about is whether we will be hurt by flying pieces of her helmet. I am appalled."

Vivien walked over beside her friend and mentor. "I also will remove my spacesuit. Not without some trepidation, I will admit. But my devotion to Sister Beatrice is stronger than my fear."

Beatrice and Vivien stared into each other's eyes through their faceplates for a moment, and then moved over against one of the walls. "Now, those of you who are afraid may cower if you choose," Vivien continued. "We will say a short prayer and then count to three. On the sound of 'three' we will take off our helmets."

Only Yasin tried to protect himself. Johann stood transfixed in the middle of the room. The two women prayed together and then counted to three. Nothing happened when they broke the seals on their helmets. A few seconds later their heads were uncovered.

Beatrice and Vivien immediately knelt on the floor. "Thank you, dear God," Sister Beatrice said, "for showing us again the importance of faith. We pray that we will continue to grow in our understanding of Thee, and our ability to do Thy work. In St. Michael's name. Amen."

Two days passed with no change in the physical conditions of their existence. The capsule continued to orbit Mars, the window always pointed at the planet, with monotonous regularity. Inside their tiny worldlet, the eleven passengers moved freely about. Their spacesuits were stored on shelves in the closet. They drank the water and ate the curious cylinders, which tasted like unprocessed wheat flavored slightly with lemon. Yasin even figured out how to use the toilet, and enjoyed being in the spotlight when he explained its use to everyone else.

Sister Beatrice's enormous energy and resolute good humor were an example for the group. Yasin, jealous of the respect accorded her by the others, tried to bait her regularly, but she never showed any signs of anger or irritation. Despite Yasin's antagonism and thinly veiled insults, never once did Beatrice respond in kind.

Not everyone was tolerant of Yasin's acrid remarks. Kwame Hassan and the Mexican technician Fernando Gomez, neither of whom had the studied nonviolence of the Michaelites, each nearly struck Yasin on separate occasions. It was necessary for Johann to restrain Kwame when Yasin, during a discussion with Sister Vivien about the Order of St. Michael and its vow of chastity, made a derisive, crude reference to Vivien's private parts.

Johann enjoyed observing the dynamics among his fellow passengers. He watched the admiration for Sister Beatrice, even among the non-Michaelites, grow with each passing hour. He knew that Yasin's arrogance and truculence would eventually lead to his ostracism from the group. Johann was correct. After two days, only Johann and Sister Beatrice responded to Yasin with any civility.

Without the task of managing the Valhalla Outpost, Johann became contemplative. He found himself thinking about his life as an entity, and asking questions about purpose, love, religion, and friendship that he had never before considered. Occasionally he tried to imagine where this hatbox they were occupying would take them, but he knew it was a useless exercise. *Wherever we go,* Johann told himself, *it will be far more amazing than anything I can create in my imagination.*

Everyone but Satoko Hayakawa was sleeping when the capsule changed its attitude. The roll-and-yaw maneuvers took place without imparting any significant disturbance to the inside of the spacecraft. Satoko only noticed the change when she came over to the window for a look at Mars. What she saw instead was a glittering array of stars shining in the blackness of space. In the center of the window was a bright light, not yet distinguishable from all the rest of the lights in the firmament.

By the time Satoko had shown the bright light to her boyfriend Fernando, and the pair of them had awakened Johann, the light was already dominating the scene out the window. Johann watched for a few minutes, estimated the approach velocity of the light, and made the decision to awaken the others.

Within an hour all eleven of the passengers on the capsule were clustered around the window, staring apprehensively at the white sphere that was continuing to rush toward them. It looked oddly alive, this polished white ball with two red circles symmetrically placed in its upper hemisphere, a red polar hood on its top, and two distinct red bands, separated only by the thinnest of white lines, running completely around its equator.

As the sphere drew closer Johann and the others began to grasp how enormous it was. Its sheer size engendered fear. The two equatorial bands remained in the center of the window as first the hood, and then the two red eyes, disappeared off the top of the window. For another ten minutes the only nonwhite color that could be seen out the window was the red of the constantly growing equatorial bands.

There was not much conversation in the capsule. Someone would occasionally ask a question, or make an isolated comment, but most of the remarks went unanswered. Each of the eleven humans was both excited and terrified, aware that he or she was witnessing something never before seen by any member of the species.

The window remained pointed at the exact center of the thin white line between the two lips. At one point the red equatorial bands filled the view, except for the white between them, and then they, too, began to disappear off the top and bottom of the window.

"How big is that damn thing?" Fernando asked nobody in particular.

"Huge," Johann replied. He had been doing some mental calculations. "At least twenty-five kilometers in diameter."

"More," Yasin said. "I bet it's closer to fifty."

"As big as a large asteroid," Johann said.

The red vanished in the next few minutes and the scene outside the window was again a sea of white. In the middle of the picture, on the true equator of the sphere, they could discern the slightest marking running from one side to the other.

"Is it going to hit us?" Anna asked, unable to hide the terror in her voice.

"Looks like it," Yasin said.

At that moment the top hemisphere of the oncoming object started to separate from the bottom along the thin marking. Inside the separation, nothing at all could be seen. As the gap became wider, the white on the top and bottom of the screen rapidly disappeared. Soon there was nothing but blackness outside the window.

"It has eaten us," Sister Vivien remarked.

"We are inside it, that's for certain," Johann said.

Even Yasin knelt in the circle when Sister Beatrice suggested that it might be a good time to say a collective prayer.

2

They were not surprised when the door opened. They had discussed that likelihood many times during the half hour they had been waiting. When the window behind Johann had closed automatically a few minutes after Beatrice's prayer, everyone had started talking at once.

"Hold it, hold it," Johann shouted. "One at a time . . . Let's hear what everyone has to say."

The others had directed questions at Johann and Sister Beatrice. Neither of them had any answers. Beatrice remained upbeat, and confident that no terrible fate awaited them in the enormous sphere. Johann had been more sanguine, and advised prudence in all situations.

Anna asked if they should put on their spacesuits again, or perhaps carry them along if and when the door should open and they left the capsule. Sister Beatrice had said no, that it was obvious that God and His angels understood thoroughly their environmental requirements. Johann laughingly remarked that he was going to take his spacesuit with him, not because he did not have faith in God's ability as an engineer, but because

He might have left some of the more mundane specifications to a lesser being.

Then the door had opened. At first nobody moved. In front of them was a long illuminated corridor with white walls and a white floor. They could not see the end of the hallway. Yasin walked over to the door. Holding on to the capsule, he looked up, into the sphere.

"I can't see a ceiling," he reported.

The Michaelites formed a line, with Sister Beatrice at the front. "Are we ready?" she said, moving toward the door. Johann, Yasin, and Anna retrieved their spacesuits from the closet and took positions at the back of the queue.

They walked into the white corridor. No more than five seconds after Anna, the last person in the line, exited from the capsule, the door closed behind them. She took a deep breath. "Now there is no going back," she said.

"There never is," Johann said.

Anna reached for Johann's hand. "Am I the only one who's terrified?" she asked.

"*Au contraire,*" he said with a nervous laugh. "The only ones in this line who are *not* terrified are those in the front. . . . And at times I have my doubts about their sanity."

The corridor was very long and turned slightly to the left. Sister Beatrice led the procession, followed by Sister Vivien, Brothers Ravi and José, Sister Nuba, Fernando and Satoko, Kwame, Yasin, Johann, and Anna. After they had been shuffling forward in the weightlessness for five minutes or so, with no change of any kind in their surroundings, Beatrice called for a brief rest. She and Vivien passed the water vessels around.

"Tell me, Sister," Yasin said after he had satisfied his thirst, "does this look like heaven to you? Are we going to meet your St. Peter at any minute?"

Beatrice came over to where Yasin was standing. "Mr. al-Kharif," she said, "I have no pictures of heaven in my mind. I am confident that God can create a heaven more magnificent and wonderful than anything I would ever imagine."

Yasin smiled. "But what might be considered heaven for you might not even be pleasant for me. And vice versa. If there is only one God, as you have told us, I presume there's only one heaven. How does God create a single place that pleases both of *us*, let alone anyone else? Does He make some kind of least-squares fit to everybody's specifications?"

Yasin laughed at his own cleverness and glanced around at the others, soliciting appreciation of his wit.

Beatrice drew closer to him. "Your simplistic views about our reli-

gion remind me of an Alexander Pope couplet," she said in a friendly
tone. " 'A little learning is a dangerous thing; drink deep or taste not the
Pierian spring.' You have not yet drunk deep enough, Mr. al-Kharif. . . .
Heaven to the thinking Christian is not a place, it is a concept. It is the
promise of the soul living forever in harmony with the universe, surrounded by the fellowship of similar souls. There is no requirement that
your heaven be my heaven. God can create as many heavens as He
chooses."

"Your knowledge of Islam is equally shallow, Sister," Yasin said
sharply. "Just because you can quote a few suras—"

"I would welcome the opportunity to learn more about your religious views, Mr. al-Kharif," Sister Beatrice interrupted, "and to share
mine with you. But now is not the appropriate time."

She turned away with a smile. At the back of the line Johann saw
anger flash briefly in Yasin's eyes. *He does not like you, Sister Beatrice,* Johann thought. *And not just because you are a woman, although that's part of
it . . .*

After they had shuffled for another five minutes, the corridor expanded
into a tall, cylindrical room with the same white floor and walls. In the
center of the large chamber was a pair of intertwining helical slides, also
white, each of which had a broad red band running down the center of
the slide. The two helices ascended into darkness at the top of the room.
All the illumination in the chamber came from lights in the lower two
meters of the wall.

Around the periphery of the circular floor, many doors and cabinets
had been cut into the white walls. In short order the group found a pair of
toilets, a large shower with stalls and showerheads to accommodate three
people, some peculiar white towels with red trim, eleven sleeping mats,
two cabinets full of what the group decided must be underwear, and
eleven pairs of red-and-white shoes.

Sister Nuba was the first to try on the shoes. "Hey, look at these,"
she shouted, before becoming embarrassed by her outburst. Nuba took a
few steps. "They're very light," she said in a less expressive tone. "And
they're magnetized or something. It's easier to walk."

Everyone wanted to take a shower. The women went first, although
Yasin entered a mild protest. Kwame joined Johann at the foot of one of
the slides while the first group of women was in the shower.

"So are we supposed to climb this thing?" Kwame asked.

Johann turned and smiled. "Your guess is as good as mine," he said.

Kwame leaned his head back and stared at the darkness above his
head. "There can only be one reason why it's not lit up there," Kwame

said. "Whoever it is that has brought us here does not want us to see what's there. Therefore, my logical mind says that we are not supposed to climb the slide."

"Makes sense to me," Johann said.

Across the room, Yasin was already climbing the other slide. As he ascended into the darkness he waved down at the others.

"Do you think that's wise?" Sister Beatrice shouted at him. She had just come out of the shower.

Yasin shrugged. "Why else would it be here?" he said. He glanced above him and then switched on his pocket flashlight. "Here I go," he said.

Yasin disappeared into the dark. From time to time the others on the floor could see the beam from his flashlight. After about two minutes they heard a sharp cry, almost a yelp, far above them. Several seconds later Yasin flew out of the dark, tumbling in midair as he headed for the floor.

He landed on his back. Yasin was not seriously injured, but his usual cockiness was gone for a few minutes. "Something grabbed me and threw me off the slide," he told those who had come over to help him. "I don't know where it came from, or what it was, but it was very strong."

"What was it like up there?" Johann asked.

"The slides go on and on without any change," Yasin answered. "I was probably fifty or sixty meters high, and everything was still the same above me. Even the walls—"

"Listen," Brother Ravi said suddenly. "Do you hear that rumbling?"

Everyone became quiet. Above them in the darkness they could hear a noise that was steadily growing louder. It did not take them long to figure out that something was coming down the slide or slides. As the sound came nearer it became more distinct. Johann and Yasin both identified it as metal sliding on metal.

The two identical vehicles carrying their food and water showed up at exactly the same time, one at the bottom of each slide. The vehicles were rectangular, flatbedded with low restraining sides, white with red markings, and mounted on sliding wheels that traveled on the side rails of the helical slides. One carried eight large vessels of water, the other forty-four food cylinders stacked in piles of eleven. As soon as all the cargo was unloaded, the bizarre vehicles departed.

"Shit," said Yasin to Johann as they watched the second carrier scurry away. "I wanted to take a closer look at one of those things." He saw Beatrice approaching and winked at Johann. "To see what kind of engineers God's angels are."

"Pretty damn good, I would say," Johann said. "At least based on the evidence so far."

Johann had not yet fallen asleep on his mat when Kwame Hassan came over beside him.

"Are you too tired for a little talk?" Kwame asked.

Johann sat up. "What's on your mind?" he said.

The lithe Tanzanian squatted next to Johann. "What do you think is really going on here, Johann?" he said, still in a subdued tone. "Have we been kidnapped by the white ribbons?"

"My best guess, Kwame, and that's all it is, is that we have hitched a ride aboard a spacecraft built by an incredibly advanced extraterrestrial species, and we have been brought to this giant sphere for some specific purpose. . . . Although I agree with Sister Beatrice that the hatbox was designed for our use, I have no idea why, or what is going to happen to us now."

"But *who* are these aliens?" Kwame asked. "Where did they come from? What do they want from us? What were they doing on Mars? Are they in any way related to that Rama spaceship that visited the solar system fourteen years ago?"

Johann smiled. "As usual, Kwame, you're asking all the right questions," he said. "But I'm afraid I don't have any of the answers."

"But what are they going to do with us?" Kwame asked. "Isn't it likely that they are going to kill us eventually? Why would they take care of us forever?"

Johann lay back down on his mat. "My guess," he said, "is that whatever the aliens do with us, any kind of normal life we might ever have had is indeed over. . . . Even if they were to return us to Earth tomorrow, and leave me in Berlin and you in Dar es Salaam, neither of us would ever again be able to function in the normal world. We have gone through the looking glass, Kwame. . . . We have had what the psychologists call a life-shattering experience."

Yasin suddenly appeared beside them. "Jesus, Ace," he said, "I had no idea that you were such a philosopher. . . . But I came to discuss another problem. It's that crazy nun. She seems to have appointed herself the leader of this damn group. We three should pool our resources and put her in her place."

"You may have difficulty believing this, Yasin," Johann said, "but I am quite comfortable with Sister Beatrice and her role. I may not agree with her assumptions, or her motivations, but on balance I find her to be intelligent and capable. And she's absolutely tireless."

"Still," Yasin said, "no matter how competent she is, it galls me that all of us are playing second fiddle to a female religious fanatic."

"Good night, Yasin," Johann said. "And good night, Kwame."

The white ribbon entered the chamber sometime while they were sleeping. For an entire day it stayed in virtually the same spot, hovering near the helical slides about one meter above the humans' heads. Its presence cast a pall on the conversations. Voices were lower and more subdued. People were careful with what they did, and said, for they had the feeling that the ribbon was monitoring their actions.

Anna Kasper spent most of the day in the toilet or shower, trying to hide from the ribbon. She did not want it to see her, and she definitely did not want to think about it. The bright ribbon terrified her, sitting there in the air, its dancing particles drifting aimlessly about. When she did come out into the chamber, she kept her eyes focused on the floor.

The intruder completely discombobulated the gentle Japanese nurse Satoko Hayakawa. She was mesmerized by the ribbon. Satoko stood as close to it as she dared for several hours, staring at the individual particles and following trajectories from side to side. Eventually she began talking to the ribbon in a low voice, and at one point she suddenly started weeping hysterically. Not even Fernando could console her. "It's going to kill us," Satoko kept repeating. "I know it's going to kill us."

The prevailing mood was somber when the wall lights finally dimmed. Several members of the group stretched out immediately on their mats. Sisters Beatrice and Vivien approached Johann. "Maybe everyone else would feel better," Beatrice said, "if we each told our encounter stories again."

Johann reflected for a moment. "I don't think so," he replied. "Remember, those encounters all took place in familiar surroundings. The particles were bizarre, to be sure, but everything else in the scene was completely normal. . . . What is frightening people here is both the ribbon *and* the sense that we are all strangers in a strange land."

Beatrice smiled. "I grok," she said brightly. "But I wish there was something I could do to give everyone more peace of mind. . . . Not even prayer seems to help them."

"Maybe you should sing," Johann said. "I can't speak for the others, but that would certainly cheer me up."

"That's a great idea, Sister Beatrice," Vivien said enthusiastically. "It would take everyone's minds off our worries."

"But what should I sing?" Beatrice asked, her brow knitted beneath her headpiece.

"Anything upbeat, preferably not religious," Johann said. "Didn't you mention you sang in a lot of popular musicals before you joined the order? Pick some of your favorites, even Disney, if you prefer, as long as it's light."

"I don't know," Sister Beatrice said, momentarily taken aback.

Johann was already on his feet. He clapped his hands three times. "Attention, everyone," he then said. "We are all in for a treat. Sister Beatrice has agreed to sing some songs for us before we go to sleep."

There was some scattered applause. Everyone looked at Beatrice. "Just you wait, Brother Johann," she said with a smile. She then switched to a cockney accent. "Just you wait, Brother Johann," Beatrice repeated.

Beatrice sang for half an hour. She started with pieces from the halcyon days of musical comedy in the twentieth century. Then she switched to some of the better tunes from the mid-twenty-first century, when the musical theater had staged a robust rebirth.

The mood in the chamber changed. Even Satoko came out of her depression. Sister Vivien was becoming louder and more animated with each song. "Do the *Phantom*, B," Vivien shouted after Beatrice had finished with the title song from the political musical *Gorbachev*.

The Phantom of the Opera was Johann's favorite musical. It was the world's favorite, too, and was still being revived at regular intervals a hundred and fifty years after it had been originally created. Johann had seen the live play only once, in Berlin as a university student, and he had been disappointed because the young woman playing Christine could not hit the exceptionally high notes. Beatrice sang "Think of Me," and then "Angel of Music," her lute-clear, flawless voice giving a new meaning to each of the songs. Johann recalled the first time he had heard Beatrice sing while he was listening to the two songs from *Phantom*. He led the others in hearty applause when she was finished.

Beatrice extended a hand to Johann and another to Sister Vivien. "Could we all join hands, please?" she asked.

When everyone was standing in a circle, Beatrice turned around and glanced at the ribbon. "Let's show our visitor," she said, "that we are united, and not afraid of anything that might happen.

"Blessed be the tie that binds," she sang. "Our hearts in Christian love . . . The fellowship, of kindred minds . . ."

Johann felt her warm hand in his and squeezed it lightly. Beatrice squeezed back, a gesture of friendship, and her response sent a pulse of lightning through his entire body.

The second day the ribbon no longer frightened them. When it started moving around, seemingly eavesdropping on private conversations, nobody became unduly alarmed.

"I threw water on it," Kwame told the others after the ribbon had followed him into the shower. He was laughing. "It wriggled a bit, shaking itself like a wet dog."

Fernando and Brother José purposely walked over to where the ribbon was hovering and conducted a long and animated conversation in Spanish. "Now *that* ought to confuse it," Fernando said with a broad smile when he rejoined Satoko.

None of them saw the snowman until it appeared at the edge of the room, near the entrance to the corridor. Sister Vivien uttered a short, shrill cry and pointed in the snowman's direction. The room became silent immediately. Johann, who had been talking with Brother Ravi about the terrible living conditions in south India as a result of the depression, felt a sharp pang of fear when he saw the snowman.

This creature was identical to the one Johann and Kwame had encountered in the tunnels beneath the Martian polar ice. It consisted of two large, stacked white balls without any markings, the bottom one slightly larger and resting on a white plate with red wheels. The snowman stood in place for nearly a minute and then rolled slowly toward them. The ribbon, as if on cue, moved over to the bottom of one of the helical slides.

When it was about ten meters away from the closest human, the middle of the snowman's upper body convulsed and a long, skinny white arm with two fingers and an unusually fat thumb extended outward. Everyone backed away as the snowman approached the group. It made a beeline for Sister Beatrice. She did not try to run away.

The strange being wrapped its hand around Beatrice's forearm and began slowly pulling her toward the helical slide where the ribbon was hovering. Sister Beatrice did not resist. Johann thought he saw her mumbling a prayer.

After the snowman had released her underneath the ribbon, at the entrance to the slide, it rolled back toward the other humans. This time it selected Johann. He winced when he felt the firm grip on his forearm, but he also did not try to fight. Johann let the snowman pull him slowly over to where Beatrice was standing.

The ribbon started moving up the helix, staying a fixed altitude above the slide. The snowman lifted its arm and pointed upward, toward the ribbon. "I think we're supposed to ascend," Sister Beatrice said gamely.

"I guess so," Johann replied, struggling against the alternating waves of fear and panic that were coursing through his body.

She took the first step up the slide. Johann followed. When they were a couple of meters above the others, Yasin ran across the room. Dodging the snowman, he tried to enter the bottom of the slide. The alien creature seized him in its powerful grip.

"Stop," Yasin yelled, "you're hurting me."

When the snowman released him, Yasin scrambled up to where Sister Beatrice and Johann had momentarily stopped. The snowman's torso convulsed again, and its arm immediately doubled its length. This time it lifted Yasin off the surface and threw him in the direction of the other humans. The startled Yasin slid across the floor into Kwame's feet.

The ribbon moved higher. The snowman pointed upward again as Johann and Sister Beatrice edged into the darkness.

3

The helical slide wound around its identical partner many many times. Beatrice and Johann quickly reached an altitude so far above the chamber that they could no longer see any light at all below them. The only illumination was provided by the ribbon. *At least we're not fighting gravity too*, Johann thought after they had been walking for twenty minutes.

"Well, Brother Johann," Sister Beatrice said between breaths from in front of him, "I wonder what miracles God has in store for us now."

He could tell from her gait and her posture that she was tiring. They had been moving at a brisk pace the entire time.

"It must be all right for us to stop," Johann said. "Why don't we take a short rest."

"That's a great idea," Beatrice said. She turned around to face him. At first, because the ribbon was directly behind Beatrice, Johann could not see either her expression or her eyes. He stepped slightly to the side and she did the same.

"Isn't this fantastic?" she said brightly. "Did you ever even dream, when you were a child, that you might experience something like this?"

He searched her face carefully. There was not a trace of fear any-where. "Are you *never* afraid, Sister Beatrice?" Johann asked. "I mean, here we are, inside a giant spherical worldlet created by beings of un-imaginable capability, walking in the dark up a never-ending helical slide toward an unknown destination. And you act as if we're on some kind of a tour, or in an amusement park."

Beatrice smiled down at him. "Hey," she said, "this is neat. . . . Now I know what it would be like to be as tall as you are."

Johann shook his head and threw his arms up in mock despair.

Sister Beatrice laughed. "Relax, Brother Johann," she said. "Every-thing will be all right. That's what faith is all about. Once you put your-self in God's hands, and accept whatever He may have in store for you, then all your fears and worries are over. *Qué será, será*. And you can take the time to smell the roses. Or to enjoy an exhilarating walk up a helical slide built by God's angels . . . Or by aliens if you prefer."

"Aha," Johann said. "So you do acknowledge the possibility that all this may have an extraterrestrial origin?"

"Of course, Brother Johann," she said, "but it really makes no dif-ference. Aliens or angels. Both are God's creatures. And I would not pre-sume to understand His methods."

Johann thought for a moment. "You have an answer for everything," he said.

"No," said Beatrice teasingly. "But God does. . . . Now, should we continue? Our guide appears to be agitated."

In front of them the ribbon was cavorting, twisting at the ends and dancing around in the air. They resumed the climb.

They must have walked three or four kilometers before they finally reached the top of the slide. Johann and Beatrice were both tired. From what they could see, they assumed they were in a very large, open room. The floor was still white. They could not see any walls.

After following the ribbon for another five or six minutes, they came to a canal that was about thirty meters wide. The ribbon stopped and hovered above the swiftly flowing water. Beside the canal, a few meters to their right, were two sleeping mats identical to those they had been using in the chamber, two vessels filled with water, and a half-dozen food cylinders.

Sister Beatrice, weary from the long walk, plopped down on one of the mats and immediately had a drink of water. Johann explored a little first, going along the canal in both directions to the edge of the territory illuminated by the ribbon.

"There are no bridges," he said when he returned.

Beatrice was already eating one of the cylinders. "Mmm," she said. "This dark green one is new, Brother Johann. It almost tastes like chocolate." She offered it to him.

He was still standing, staring across the canal. "Will you sit down, please," Beatrice continued. "You're even starting to make *me* nervous. . . . The other side looks exactly like this. Nothing new, no surprises. Meanwhile you must be hungry and thirsty."

Johann sat beside her on the mat. She handed him the water jug. "The ribbon has stopped, the sleeping mats are here, there is food and water," she said. "Ergo, this is where we are spending the night."

He took a long drink. "And that's *all?*" Johann said, wiping his mouth with his arm. "You don't ask where are we now, or what's the purpose of the canal, or why were we separated from the others?"

"No," she said, taking a bite from another cylinder. "Because I have already accepted that we cannot answer those questions. No matter how much time we spend discussing them. And I am comfortable with that fact."

"But where's your curiosity, Sister Beatrice?" Johann asked. "If your faith is so strong it allows you to accept *anything*, then there is no motivation to learn—"

"Not so fast, Brother Johann," Beatrice interrupted. "You're almost as bad as Mr. al-Kharif in your simplistic notions about modern religion." She finished chewing the bite that was in her mouth. "Faith and curiosity are in fact good partners, not competitive attributes. As St. Michael said in one of his most famous lectures, 'That which can be learned, should be learned. Man glorifies God by pushing one of His most spectacular creations, the human mind, to its absolute limit. But we should not therefore conclude that the total universe of knowledge will ever be accessible to us. Only God is omniscient. What He knows, and we have not yet learned, or can never know, belongs in the realm of faith.' "

Johann had picked up a food cylinder and taken a bite while Beatrice was talking. When she was finished he continued to chew methodically for a few seconds. "How many of these pithy sayings by St. Michael have you memorized?" he then said. "I've been hearing them now for several days and I don't believe you've repeated a single one."

Sister Beatrice smiled. "I don't consciously memorize them," she said. "But I've studied St. Michael's sermons as much or more than the Bible, and since I actually *heard* some of them, and remember the impact they made on me, I retain them very easily in my memory."

"What was he like, your St. Michael?" Johann said. "Along with everyone else, I have seen the video of the moment of his death many times, and I once watched one of his televised lectures entitled 'The New Evolution.' His German was exceptionally good, I remember, and his ideas were quite provocative, but other than that one lecture, I didn't follow his life."

Sister Beatrice gazed at Johann for several seconds. "St. Michael was the most unusual human being I ever met," she said slowly. "He taught me how to live, how to give, how to be happy with myself."

She paused and reached over to touch Johann on the arm. "I cannot talk about my experiences with Michael without becoming very emotional. My days with him are the treasures of my life. . . . Please don't misunderstand me, Brother Johann, but I am not yet ready to share those treasures with you. Only when I am certain that my experiences will be very special to you as well can I open up my heart and talk about St. Michael."

When Johann awakened he could see Sister Beatrice sitting beside the canal in the lotus position. She was about five meters beyond the end of their mats. Her eyes were closed. She looked remarkably peaceful. *And where does this meditation stuff come from?* he asked himself. *That's not part of any Christianity I know.*

He was careful not to disturb her. He propped his head up on an elbow and continued to watch her. Her face reflected the light from the ribbon, which remained where it had been all night, hovering over the canal. *She's really a beautiful woman,* Johann told himself. *I wonder what she would look like without that awful robe and headpiece.*

Johann recalled all his memories of Sister Beatrice. He did not have a single image of her without her bishop's habit. He had seen Sister Vivien, a couple of times in his apartment, without the prescribed clothing of the Order of St. Michael. But not Beatrice.

He waited until she had finished her meditation before starting breakfast. Beatrice joined him. She was unusually quiet while they were eating. Johann asked her about her practice of meditation. Sister Beatrice was not forthcoming. All she said was that St. Michael had learned to meditate when he was in India and had included it in his recommended daily regimen because of its ability to "center" an individual.

Johann was about to ask Beatrice if anything was bothering her when the small boat suddenly appeared in the canal. It emerged from behind them, coming downstream, and then stopped on their side of the canal no more than ten meters away. Sister Beatrice brightened immediately.

"Look, Brother Johann," she said. "God's angels have sent us a boat. And it even has a picnic basket, and a pair of oars."

The boat was white, with a red stripe on its side. Inside were two white benches. A pair of wide, cushioned seats with low backrests were on each of the benches.

Beatrice boarded the boat and began examining the picnic basket. "There's plenty of food and water," she said. "And even a big blanket on the bottom . . . Are you ready for another adventure?"

Sister Beatrice laughed when Johann asked if he should bring the sleeping mats. "You should go through our training, Brother Johann," she said. "Then you wouldn't be so concerned about *things*. . . . We don't need the mats. There will either be some wherever we are when it's time to sleep again, or we'll do without. Come on, let's see where this boat is going to take us."

Johann had expected he would have some difficulty balancing on the boat. He had forgotten that they were still in a weightless environment. He sat down on the right seat facing the back of the boat. Beatrice was on the right side of her seat also, so there was ample room for their legs. The picnic basket was behind her. The two oars were below the bench behind him.

The boat started moving as soon as they were both seated. The ribbon remained where it was. As the light faded away Johann grew uncomfortable. "Is your faith strong today?" Beatrice said teasingly. "Or do you need some support from me?"

"I can always use your support," Johann replied.

They rode in total blackness. Neither of them could see anything at all. The small boat seemed to be moving faster. At times Johann could hear the gurgle of the rushing water.

"This is really fun," Beatrice said. "It reminds me of a water ride in the dark at Paul Bunyan Land."

"What's Paul Bunyan Land?" Johann asked.

"One of those huge family destination centers," Beatrice answered. "It's right outside Minneapolis. My father used to take us there when I deserved a special reward. You know, good grades in school, or an unusual commendation for one of my performances."

"When did you start singing?" Johann said.

"At birth," Beatrice replied. He could tell that she was laughing. Johann wished that he could see her.

"There's a light up ahead," Beatrice announced.

Johann turned around. They moved quickly into the light. Their canal had now become a river, surrounded on both sides by tall monoliths of brown rock. Above them, beyond the rocks, they could see what looked like blue sky. The vast scope of their spherical world was becoming clear.

The river wound through several turns before the rocks beside them began to show any variation. After one turn the river widened and on Beatrice's right side the rock walls slowly changed to terraced rock fields sprinkled with occasional large boulders. Farther on, there was a brown sand beach lining part of the riverbank. Behind the sand, up the sloping rocky terrain, a landscape of varied rock formations was reminiscent of the American southwest.

It was a spectacular sight. A strong, solitary source, above them and in the direction of the back of the boat, was providing all the light. Johann shaded his eyes and tried to find the fake sun up in the pure blue sky, but he could not look at it directly.

The huge brown cliffs remained on Beatrice's left. After another bend in the river, their channel split into two parts and a solitary snow-capped mountain appeared in the far distance on her right. Behind it, a few kilometers later, an entire jagged range of breathtakingly tall mountains, their tops all painted by the same white brush, was a feast for their eyes. In the foreground the varied rock formations looked as if they had been shaped by artists.

"I feel as if we should be listening to Dvorak's *New World Symphony*," Sister Beatrice said, breaking a long silence.

"I can hear it in my head," said Johann. He was watching the scenes on his left with a growing ache in his heart. The incomparable beauty of the sight reminded him of Earth, and he was aware of an acute yearning to see it once again.

"They've done a great job, don't you think?" Beatrice said.

"Yes," Johann said. "Whoever *they* are."

The river split into three more channels. Their boat followed the smallest, middle rivulet and entered a dark tunnel as soon as the other two channels were no longer in sight. "Are you thirsty?" Beatrice asked when they had been riding in the dark for five minutes.

"A little," Johann said.

They fumbled clumsily, laughing at themselves, but she eventually managed to hand him one of the water vessels from the picnic basket. He sucked hard at the drinking tube and felt the refreshing water in his mouth. Several seconds later they emerged from the tunnel into an altogether different world.

On Beatrice's right was nothing but placid water for the few kilometers they could see, and darkness beyond that. To their left was a grass-covered bank, sloping gently down to the water's edge. They could also see flowers and trees, and grassy knolls.

"Listen," said Beatrice. "Can you hear the birds?"

The boat was moving more slowly now, hugging the left bank. Johann could indeed hear what sounded like birds. He could make out at least three or four distinct and different chirps and cries.

"How in the world . . . ?"

"Look, Johann, over there, at the bottom of those trees. Do you see the squirrels?"

The boat pulled into a slight indentation in the left bank and came to a halt. Sister Beatrice reached behind her and gathered up the basket.

"Well," she said, pointing over at a small hill beside the trees, near where the squirrels were playing, "could you imagine a more heavenly place for a picnic?"

"You took the words right out of my mouth," Johann said.

4

Lying on the blanket, staring at the blue sky over his head and listening to the medley of songs from the unseen birds, Johann finally stopped torturing himself with questions he could not answer. They had both enjoyed the lunch. The conversation had been light. Sister Beatrice had asked him to talk about his childhood, his family, and his university days. She had been very interested in his competitive swimming career and had compared his feelings when he represented Germany in international meets to her emotions when she had appeared in her first musical on Broadway.

She was sitting beside him on the blanket, trying to coax the squirrels to eat from her hand. Beatrice shredded part of one of the food cylinders, but the animals were not interested.

"When I first joined the order," she said, giving up on the squirrels and moving over closer to Johann, "I went through a peculiar antianimal phase. . . . I was stuck on the idea that people were showering love on their pets that should have been saved for other humans." She laughed. "I actually asked St. Michael about this issue one night, if you can believe it. . . . He was so kind. He smiled at me and then said, 'Sister

Beatrice, is it your belief that people have only an allocated amount of love and affection to share? And if they give it to one special person, or even a pet, they won't have any more left?' Just two days before I had listened to Michael's 'Infinite Love' sermon, so I was pretty embarrassed. . . ."

Johann loved to hear her talk. Her speech was rich with inflections and emphases, and there was almost a musical modality to the way she constructed her sentences. For some reason, as Beatrice continued to reminisce, Johann suddenly remembered a conversation he had had with his high-school chum Heike back when they were both sixteen. It had been a gray, damp, cold day in Potsdam, the third or fourth in a row, and Heike had been irritated at the weather.

"I can't wait to get to heaven," she had said, "because the sun will shine every day. And there will be no mud, and no wet grass."

No mud and no wet grass, Johann thought. *And thou beside me in the sunlight.*

". . . I went to Lake Bemidji every summer from the time I was ten until I was seventeen," Beatrice was saying. "There were a group of foreign-language camps scattered around the lake. My father wanted me to be fluent in at least two other languages. Because he was still hoping I would use my voice training to be an opera star, he thought I would choose to study Italian and German. . . . But I fooled him. I learned French and Japanese instead."

"Japanese? Why did you decide . . . ?" said Johann. He had turned over on his side to look at Beatrice. He was not able to complete his question. She was running her fingers through the long blond hair that fell down to the small of her back. It looked like silk.

"When," he stammered eventually, "when did you take off your headpiece?"

"A couple of minutes ago," she said, "after I finished trying to feed the squirrels." Beatrice laughed. "That's right, you've never seen my hair down before." She turned her head from side to side. "What do you think?"

"It's beautiful," was all he could think of to say.

Beatrice talked again about Lake Bemidji and Johann listened silently from beside her on the blanket. He carefully studied her long hair, her blue eyes, and her radiant face. *You are beautiful*, he thought.

They had only been back in the moving boat for a few minutes when the first scattered houses appeared on the left bank. The large, handsome, and freshly painted homes were just beyond the thick forest that Johann and Beatrice had been able to see from their picnic site. Some of the houses were brick or stucco, but most looked as if they were made of wood. Each of them had trees and well-trimmed grass in the front yard, with either an orderly garden plot or more grass in the rear.

The houses began to cluster. What was obviously a church stood on the top of a small hill. The boat passed a school, a small factory, and then some office buildings. Everything was neat and clean.

They entered another tunnel. Johann and Beatrice recognized many of the sounds they were hearing long before they came out into the light. A modern Western city was now on their left. Cars were driving on the boulevard along the bank of the river. Beyond the boulevard, trolleys climbed shop-lined streets up the gently sloping hills. Johann and Sister Beatrice were astonished that people were suddenly everywhere. Some were fishing in the river. Some were eating in restaurants along the shore. A hundred or so had gathered in an outdoor amphitheater to hear a man speak or sing. Nobody paid even the slightest attention to the two strangers in the white boat moving slowly down the river.

Children were playing soccer on a large green field. Two boys and their dogs were flying kites nearby. A woman pushed a baby carriage on the walkway beside the river. Johann and Sister Beatrice stared at the diverse scene without comment. They were both dumbfounded.

On the outskirts of the city a collection of palatial homes, each with its own private boathouse, lined the water. Through the open windows Johann and Beatrice could see luxurious furniture, fine art, and people dining at long tables. Fancy cars were in the garages. At a private dock near them, four teenagers, two boys and two girls, clambered into a small motorboat.

The motorboat came right at them. Only when their boat swerved to avoid a collision did Johann and Beatrice look at the other side of the river. They had not glanced in that direction a single time since they had come out of the last tunnel.

On the opposite bank of the river, about four hundred meters in front of them, was another city scene. Only this one was vastly different. Tumbledown clapboard shacks were strewn along the bank. Clothing was hanging everywhere, on porches, on trees, on lines stretched between the houses. Naked children of all colors were swimming in the garbage-infested water. Every conceivable kind of boat, most looking as if they might sink at any moment, was going to and fro in the portion of the river nearest the bank.

Johann and Beatrice's boat was headed for a wooden dock where twenty-five or thirty bedraggled people were standing, waving and hollering in their direction. Elsewhere along the shore, small groups were piling into the canoes and other small boats and coming toward them.

"I don't like the looks of this," Johann said, starting to feel tense. He instinctively reached behind him and picked up one of the long oars.

A huge barge passed in front of their boat when they were in the middle of the river. When the barge was gone, three boats from the poor city were nearly upon them. Johann and Sister Beatrice could clearly see the occupants of the first vessel. An old, wizened Asiatic woman, her hair matted and unkempt, was holding out her right hand and yelling something they couldn't understand. Three bright-eyed silent children, two girls and a boy, were sitting on the floor of the boat behind her. Their hands were outstretched as well.

Johann was now standing in the boat, holding an oar across the front of his body. He put the oar in the water and paddled fiercely to soften their impact with the ramshackle vessel carrying the old woman and the children. The two boats bumped, but not hard enough that anyone was injured. The children laughed.

Sister Beatrice reached into the picnic basket and pulled out two food cylinders. One she placed in the hands of the old woman and the other she broke into pieces and distributed to the children. The woman smiled appreciatively. The three children greedily ate the food.

A chorus of shouts came from the crowd on the dock when Beatrice passed out the food. More people rushed to the boats. Johann's inchoate fear escalated into terror as he counted all the small boats headed in their direction.

He quickly surveyed the entire scene around them, located another tunnel, downstream on his left, and began to ply the water with long, powerful strokes of his oar. A second boat pulled alongside, this one occupied by a dark brown man and two sullen teenage boys. None of them smiled. They held out their hands. Beatrice gave them one food cylinder each. There was no acknowledgment of the gift.

Johann rowed even faster. Half a dozen boats were closing in on them. Johann tried to remember how many cylinders had originally been in the basket, and how many they had eaten during the picnic. A black family, a man, a woman, and three children, were in the next boat that reached Johann and Beatrice. She gave the family the two remaining food cylinders and showed them that the basket was now empty. The man grunted, said something in a strange language, and made a drinking motion with his hands. Beatrice handed the man the fuller of their two water jugs.

It was obvious to Johann that they were not going to reach the tunnel entrance without being intercepted by at least two more of the boats. "And what will you give them *now*?" he said to Sister Beatrice in between the furious strokes of his oar.

She was still calm. There was no fear or panic in her eyes. "I'll simply tell them that we have no food or water left," she said.

There was no time for him to argue with her. The two boats, operating in tandem, drew up on either side of them. Three adult males were on each boat. A burly brown man with a mustache and a leering smile, who was standing in the boat on Johann's right, was obviously in charge. He said something in a demanding tone to Sister Beatrice. She smiled and shrugged, showing him the empty basket. He motioned at the remaining water jug. Beatrice handed it to him. Still they did not go away.

After a short discussion with two of his compatriots, the burly man started to climb into their boat. "NO," Johann said emphatically, brandishing the oar. The man looked at Johann and reconsidered. With a quick swipe of his arm, he grabbed the picnic basket out of Beatrice's hands. She fell down on the seat.

"Now *go!*" thundered Johann, using the oar and his enormous strength to push away first one boat and then the other. They were still a hundred meters from the tunnel. More boats were coming at them from both sides. *"Stay away,"* Johann shouted, flailing at the closest boat with the oar.

None of the other boats came any closer as Johann paddled hard toward the tunnel entrance. He kept moving his head from side to side, glaring at the occupants of the nearby vessels. They reached the darkness of the tunnel without any more encounters.

"Are you all right?" Johann asked Beatrice after they were safely in the dark tunnel.

"Physically I am," she said, "but . . ." She did not finish her thought.

Johann took several deep breaths and tried to slow down his raging pulse. "But what?" he said after a long silence.

"Now is not the time to talk about it," she said. "The incident is still too fresh. . . . And I don't want to hurt your feelings."

"Hurt my feelings?" Johann said. "What on earth are you talking about?"

He felt her hand reaching for his in the darkness. "That's just my point, Brother Johann," she said. "I'm not talking about anything on Earth. We are not on Earth. . . . We are either in an alien spaceship, or in some kind of purgatory, depending on which of our interpretations is correct. . . . In either case, I believe we were just given a test. And we probably failed."

"I've completely lost you," Johann said.

"That's why we're not going to talk about it now, Brother Johann," she said.

When Johann and Sister Beatrice came out of the tunnel, they could not see well, for the artificial sun had vanished. On their left, however, was a town with lights shining through the windows of the buildings beside the river. A few of the buildings looked familiar to Johann.

"Well, how about this, Brother Johann," Sister Beatrice said. "We're in downtown Mutchville again."

The boat pulled over to the left and stopped against a small dock. Beatrice stood up and started to disembark.

"Before we get out, Sister Beatrice," Johann said, "will you at least answer one question?"

"If I can, Brother Johann," she replied.

"Were those real people like you and me back there, on and around the river?"

"I don't know what you mean by the expression 'real people,'" Beatrice said. "After thinking some about it, I believe that the entire scene was created expressly for us—by God, or the aliens, take your pick —to see how we would react."

"So you don't think all those people were captured or abducted from the earth and are now living in this huge sphere?" Johann said.

Beatrice smiled. "No," she said, "and you don't either, Brother Johann, even if it makes it easier to justify your actions."

"But they might have harmed you," Johann insisted.

"Only if it was God's will," Sister Beatrice said. She stepped out of the boat. "We can discuss this more later," she said. "It looks as if our hosts have something else prepared for us now. This reproduction of downtown Mutchville is definitely not an accident."

Four square blocks of the center of Mutchville had been faithfully replicated beside the shore of the river. At least the outside of the buildings was right. The correct signs, although unlit, were on the exteriors of the buildings, and lights were shining through many of the windows. But all of the doors were locked. Johann quickly became frustrated.

"What are we supposed to do here?" he said testily after neither door to the Mutchville Emporium would open.

"Be patient, Brother Johann," Sister Beatrice said. "I'm certain it will become clear eventually."

They turned into another street. In front of them, on the right side halfway down the block, a neon sign was blinking. THE BALCONY—RESERVATIONS OFFICE, it said.

Johann's heart nearly leaped out of his body when he saw the sign. He stopped and struggled to control his emotions.

Even in the dim light Sister Beatrice could see the pained expression on his face. She, too, had noticed the sign. "What is it, Brother Johann?" she said.

Johann did not respond. His first thought was to run, or at least to suggest that they should return to the boat. But he knew that was impossible. His internal turmoil continued to grow as he reluctantly followed Sister Beatrice down the street.

"The Balcony was a famous brothel, wasn't it, Brother Johann?" Beatrice said pleasantly as they approached the sign.

"Yes, it was," he mumbled.

She could tell that he was uncomfortable. Out of kindness, she did not say anything else until they reached the door.

"I'll let you open it," Sister Beatrice said.

"You're certain that it's going to open?" he said nervously.

"Yes, I am, Brother Johann," she replied. "This must be where we are supposed to go. This is the only outside sign that has been working since we left the boat."

The door yielded. Johann pushed it open, expecting to see the small office in which he had arranged his Christmas Eve rendezvous. Instead, Sister Beatrice and he walked into a perfect reproduction of the living room where he had met and had sex with his hostess Amanda.

Johann was stupefied. As he looked around the room he thought he was going to lose consciousness. A million thoughts and feelings crashed upon him so swiftly that he could not sort them out. He sat down on the couch before his knees buckled.

Sister Beatrice wandered around the room. "What a beautiful Christmas tree!" she exclaimed. She played a few notes on the piano before she noticed the photograph above and behind the keyboard.

"Why, it's you, Brother Johann," she said. "With a lovely wife and two handsome children." She turned and looked across the room at him. "But you told me you had never been married? I don't understand."

Sister Beatrice stood there in her robe and headpiece, smiling patiently at Johann. He could not remember ever having been so embarrassed before. "It's a long story," he said, after fidgeting uncomfortably for several seconds. "But I haven't lied to you. . . . I've never been married."

"Then who are these people?" Sister Beatrice asked.

"Oh, there you are, darling," another voice said. "I expected you hours ago."

Johann glanced up from his hands with a look of sheer terror on his face. Amanda, or her ghost, or a simulation, was striding across the room toward him. She was wearing the same black dress that she had worn on Christmas Eve.

Johann was powerless to respond in any way. His entire being was one large short circuit. Amanda kissed him enticingly on the lips and then snuggled into his lap with her arms around the back of his neck.

"You can do better than that, darling," she said. "After all, it's Christmas Eve and I've been waiting for you all day."

Before Johann could say anything, Amanda began kissing him again. Even her kisses were a perfect match! Johann finally gained control of himself and struggled away from her embrace.

"Amanda," he said, "there's someone else with me. Sister Beatrice. She's the bishop of the Order of St. Michael."

"Oh," Amanda said. She stood up and straightened her dress. "You didn't say you were going to bring another woman," she said. "I don't know if—"

"There has been a mix-up, a terrible mix-up," Johann said.

Sister Beatrice walked over and the two women exchanged greetings. From time to time Beatrice looked over at Johann with a curious expression on her face.

"Is there anything I can get for you, Sister?" Amanda asked.

"No, thank you," Beatrice replied. "But I am very tired, and I don't know where I am going to sleep tonight."

"We have an extra room with two twin beds," Amanda said. "It's at the top of the staircase, on the left. There's a small bathroom as well."

"That's great," Beatrice replied. "Now, if you don't mind, I think I'll turn in." She started for the door. "Good night, Johann," she said. "I'll see you in the morning. . . . I think." She still had that peculiar expression on her face as she left the living room.

Johann leaped up from the couch. "Wait a minute, Sister Beatrice," he said. "I'm coming with you."

He turned to Amanda. "There's been a change of plans," he said. "I'm going to sleep in the other bed, in the same room as Sister Beatrice."

"But—" Amanda started to protest.

"No, really, don't take it personally. It's better this way."

"Suit yourself," Amanda said as Johann rushed out the door.

5

J ohann lay on his back in the small bed. His eyes were still open. The room was dark. Beside him, on top of the white bedspread on an identical bed, he could barely see the outline of Sister Beatrice. She was sleeping on her side, facing the wall, still wearing her robe and headpiece. From the sound of her regular breathing, Johann surmised that she was sleeping peacefully.

He had not slept at all during the three hours since they had come up the stairs to the bedroom. They had hardly spoken before Beatrice had gone to bed. Johann had tried once, awkwardly, to start a conversation, not knowing himself either what to say or how to say it. She had been washing her face in the bathroom at the time. A little later she had passed close to him in the bedroom.

"You don't owe me any explanation, Johann," she had said. "I am very tired," she then added. "If it's all right, I would like to go to sleep."

Johann had turned off the lights after Beatrice assumed her sleeping position on the bed. He stood quietly in the room for several minutes, staring at her silhouette, talking to her in his mind but not saying anything out loud. Finally he had lain down in the adjoining bed, hoping to escape into the soothing world of sleep.

But Johann had not been able to turn off either his mind or his emotions. His mind had bombarded him with question after question about what he had experienced during the day. *How and why had all those scenes been created? Who had created them, and how did they have such intimate knowledge of his personal history? What were the people Sister Beatrice and he had encountered, including Amanda, if one accepted the proposition that they were probably not real?*

On and on his mind had raced. But it was not only the questions his mind was asking that had caused Johann discomfort and prolonged his sleeplessness. What was still making him squirm, three hours later, were his feelings of guilt and embarrassment about the reconstructed scene from the Balcony. He was positively mortified that Sister Beatrice had seen him in such an environment. Johann could not decide whether to tell her the truth about what had happened in the Other Zone on Christmas Eve, or to ignore the subject altogether. Either way, he was certain, based on the expressions he had seen on her face earlier in the evening, that her opinion of him had been irrevocably compromised.

Lying in that strange room in the dark, Johann had not yet admitted to himself that he was falling in love with Beatrice, and that this new feeling was responsible for his monumental angst and indecision. All he knew was that he was feeling hopeless and depressed. He wished with all his being that he had canceled his appointment at the Balcony and had gone instead to hear Beatrice sing at the church.

Johann must have eventually fallen asleep for an hour or two, for the light from the ribbon awakened him from a dream. It sat there in the dark room, hovering just below the ceiling. As he stirred into consciousness, opening his eyes intermittently to look at the ribbon, Sister Beatrice sat up in the bed next to him.

"Goodness, Brother Johann," she said, covering her mouth while she yawned, "it feels so early. . . . Have we had a full night's sleep already?"

"I don't think so, Sister Beatrice," he said.

The ribbon flew over to the door and made some twists and turns. Sister Beatrice headed for the bathroom. "There's no rest for the weary," she said idly.

Nor for the wicked, Johann thought, his unresolved feelings from the previous night erupting in a new wave of guilt. *And what should I do now?* he asked himself.

He used the bathroom after she was finished. When he came out, Sister Beatrice was standing in the doorway with one hand on the wall. "The ribbon is already halfway down the stairs," she said. "I guess we're in a hurry today."

Out on the streets of pseudo-Mutchville, it was completely dark. None of the interior lights that had been shining through the windows the night before was illuminated. The Balcony sign was also off.

Johann and Beatrice followed the ribbon down to the river. Their boat was waiting for them, with a new supply of food cylinders and water vessels. They sat down in the same seats they had occupied the previous day. The boat began to move immediately, in the same direction as the ribbon, which was already thirty meters in front of them.

It was dark everywhere. Johann and Beatrice could not see anything except the ribbon and its reflection on the water of the river. He started to speak. "If it's all right," she interrupted him, "I would like to meditate first." She handed him the food and water. "It's the way I begin every day."

For thirty minutes they rode silently in the boat. Beatrice had her eyes closed. Johann took occasional bites from a cylinder, sipped the water, and gazed at the reflections of ribbon light on Beatrice's face. His internal turmoil had not subsided. He had still not decided whether or not he was going to say anything more about the scene from the Balcony. As they rode along the river Johann again envied Beatrice. *It must be wonderful*, he thought, *to be so totally accepting. . . . But how is that possible for someone like me?*

The ribbon flew off to the right, following a separate branch of the river, only moments before Johann and Beatrice entered a long tunnel. When they emerged the sky was just beginning to show some light on Johann's left, and the river was quite narrow. They could see forests on both banks. Scattered here and there, among the trees, were typical Japanese country dwellings with blue tile roofs. Their boat passed under a bridge. Beatrice opened her eyes as they came into a city. An old train, moving along the river's edge, caught up with them. The cars were marked with Japanese characters, and were half-full of people.

The sky became lighter as dawn approached. A middle-aged Japanese woman, wearing a simple blue-and-white *yukata*, was out in her vegetable garden. She looked over at Johann and Beatrice with a baffled expression as their boat slowly passed. Beatrice waved.

Suddenly there was a blinding light at Johann's back. An instant later he felt a terrible, searing hot wind that knocked him off his seat, onto the floor of the boat. When he looked up, already feeling the burning pain in his back, Sister Beatrice was lying facedown across her pair of seats. Johann reached over to help her. At that moment he heard an enormous sound behind him.

His ears ringing, Johann looked in the direction of the noise. He saw a giant fireball, awesome and terrifying, with a mushroom-shaped cloud rising rapidly above it.

Beatrice was now sitting up, staring at the boiling cloud in the sky. "Hiroshima," she said.

Johann shuddered the moment he saw her. The right side of her face was a brilliant pink, and some of the skin had already started to peel.

"Oh, my God," he said. "Your face—it's burned."

"I know," Sister Beatrice said. She screwed up her face and winced from the pain. "I can feel it."

"Is there anything I can do to help?" Johann asked.

Beatrice reached over into the river and grabbed some water in her cupped hand. She splashed it against the raw skin on her face. Johann watched her with a feeling of utter horror and helplessness. Beatrice winced a second time. Then she took a deep breath and shrugged.

"I can't think of anything, Brother Johann," she said. "But thank you for asking."

Johann looked behind him again, in the direction the boat was moving. The monstrous cloud continued to expand and race upward. On both sides of the bank people were now scurrying about and pointing in the direction of the cloud.

He felt Beatrice's light touch on his shoulder. "Your back is badly burned, Johann," she said.

He had been so deeply in shock and so concerned about Beatrice that he had been oblivious to his own pain. Now that she called attention to it, however, Johann realized that his back felt as if it were on fire. Suddenly he also noticed for the first time the desperate cries that were all around them, coming from the people on the shore.

Near them on the left bank two young Japanese children, both wailing at a high pitch and holding their faces, plunged into the river and started swimming toward them. Johann watched their frantic strokes with a bizarre fascination. He cringed as they drew near the boat. Their disfigurement was awful.

"We must help them," Sister Beatrice said.

Johann was near panic. Although he had heard what Beatrice had said, he did not understand what she meant.

"We must help them," she repeated. "Hand them an oar."

Johann mechanically picked up an oar and put it gently into the water near where the two children were swimming. They grabbed the oar and moved along it toward the boat.

"Now pick the children up and bring them into the boat," Sister Beatrice said. She spoke slowly and softly, aware from Johann's eyes and body language that he was having considerable difficulty coping with the confusion around him.

Johann sat on his knees and extended his long arms into the water. First he reached the little girl. He lifted her with his forearms and handed her to Beatrice. The girl dripped water all over Beatrice's robe and began to wail as soon as she caught her breath. Sister Beatrice cradled the girl in her arms and brought the water jug to her lips. "There, there," she said in Japanese, "everything is going to be all right."

Johann had momentarily forgotten about the boy. The oar brushed against his legs, nearly slipping out of the boat, and Johann grabbed it just in time. The boy was now flailing around in the water. Johann leaned over the edge of the boat, almost losing his balance, and retrieved the boy.

Beatrice handed Johann the water vessel. He studied the way she was holding the girl and copied her. The cries from the boy began to diminish when Johann gave him some water to drink. The boy, about seven or eight years old, stared at Johann with wide-open eyes as he sucked at the drinking tube.

Both children were badly burned over the upper half of their bodies. The smell of the seared flesh was sickening. Johann fought against nausea as he tried to comfort the boy.

They had passed under another bridge. There were now many people swimming in the water around them, all burned and most crying out for assistance. Beatrice motioned for Johann to hand the boy over to her. "Try to help the others, Brother Johann," she said. "We still have plenty of room in the boat."

The black rain began before Johann could reach an old woman struggling to follow the oar. The droplets of thick, dark muck fell out of strange clouds, unlike any Johann or Beatrice had ever seen, that apparently had been created by the atomic bomb. The black raindrops splattered the old woman's face as Johann pulled her into the boat.

When he handed her the water jug, the old woman at first turned away. She spat twice into her hand. With a look of astonishment and bewilderment the old woman showed Johann the three teeth that had come out with her spittle. While she was drinking, she touched her head and a thick tuft of hair fell out.

The black rain continued. People swam up to both sides of the boat. Johann began pulling them in, one by one, and passing the water vessel to the newcomers. The boat filled rapidly. The drinking water was almost gone. Sister Beatrice pointed over to the shore.

"I think we should go over there," she said.

On a gentle, grassy slope along the riverbank, a makeshift outdoor hospital had been established. Lying in rows on the grass were over a hundred people, most of them suffering from terrible burns. Two doctors and a nurse were racing from patient to patient, injecting painkillers and spreading a cream on the burned skin. Occasionally one of the doctors lingered over a patient long enough to perform a quick examination. Sometimes he would then drape a cloth over the face of the victim he had just examined.

The black rain ceased while Johann was guiding the boat to shore with the oar. Many of their passengers did not have enough strength to disembark on their own. Johann carried each of them up the slope and laid them gently in one of the rows. Sister Beatrice, meanwhile, was talking to the Japanese doctors and the nurse about what she could do to help. The entire time she was carrying in her arms that first little girl who had swum to their boat. When she at length laid the girl gently down upon the grass and placed a small cloth over her innocent face, Johann saw Sister Beatrice cry for the first time.

He walked over to comfort her. "It's all right, Brother Johann," she said, forcing a smile and wiping away her tears. "God has given her release from her pain."

Beatrice told Johann that the lead doctor had requested that the dead be removed, and placed in the back of a nearby truck. That would create more room on the grassy slope for those who were still alive. For nearly an hour Johann lifted weightless dead bodies and carried them fifty to a hundred meters to the truck. During this time Sister Beatrice helped the nurses, moving among the wailing patients with her bright smile, trying to assuage their physical and emotional pain.

Some of the dead were children. Some were very old. Johann found himself wondering, each time he stooped to lift another victim, what kind of life that person had had, or might have had if he or she had lived to be an adult. When he had already carried twenty victims to the truck, he picked up a beautiful young pregnant woman. For some reason, thinking about this particular woman and her unborn child, and imagining the anticipatory joy in their family that had been interrupted by this man-made disaster, caused Johann's emotional reservoir to overflow. Tears came into his eyes and ran down his cheeks. They continued to flow steadily until he had removed all the dead from the slope.

Johann looked for Sister Beatrice after he was finished with his task. He found her singing Japanese songs with a group of burned children. Her eyes were also red and swollen and her face was covered in white.

"Turn around, please," Sister Beatrice said to Johann as soon as she saw him. He jumped when her hands first touched his back. "Some Japanese soldiers have arrived to help," she said as she rubbed the cream gently against Johann's fried skin. "We are no longer absolutely necessary here."

They shared a short silence. "Never, Sister Beatrice," Johann then said, "have I experienced anything even remotely like this. . . . I had no idea it was so horrible."

"The reality of Hiroshima was much, much worse," she said. "I once read an eyewitness account. . . . God's angels have given us only a small taste. So that we never forget."

While she was applying the soothing cream Johann thought again about all the dead bodies he had carried in the last hour. Tears were again swimming freely in his eyes when he turned around to face Sister Beatrice.

"Thank you," he said. He saw that she was studying his face. "I'm not crying from the pain, Sister—" he began.

"I know, Brother Johann," she interrupted. "These tears are coming straight from your heart."

6

Johann and Beatrice returned to
their boat after more soldiers and
additional medical personnel ar-
rived. As soon as they were onboard, the boat edged out into deeper
water. The river soon made a sharp turn and entered another dark tunnel.

"Did you have a chance to talk to the Japanese nurse?" Sister Beatrice asked while they were in the tunnel.

"No," Johann replied. "I was too busy with the bodies."

"She looked exactly like our Satoko," Beatrice said. "She even
talked like her. . . . It was eerie. Once I mistakenly called her Satoko
and she gave me a curious look."

"And what do you think is happening to us now?" Johann asked
after a short silence.

"I don't know, Brother Johann," Sister Beatrice said. "But I'm certain it wasn't chance that the nurse looked like Satoko. Whatever we are
experiencing has definitely been personalized for us."

When they came out of the tunnel they encountered artificial daylight again. For a while the boat moved slowly along the left side of the
river. On the bank beside them was a two-lane highway, with a thick

forest on the other side of the road. On Beatrice's right, on the far side of the river, a towering white stucco wall rose high above the water. Johann and Beatrice were discussing the random red stripes on the stucco wall when the boat pulled over to the shore on the left and suddenly stopped.

They looked at each other for a few seconds and then climbed out of the boat. They walked up the small bank and stood beside the highway. "What should we do now?" Johann asked after they had been standing for a minute or two.

Sister Beatrice laughed. "Are you still so impatient, Brother Johann?" she said. "Have you learned nothing yet?"

Johann grinned. "Maybe a little," he said.

" 'He also serves who only stands and waits,' " Beatrice quoted.

"That's not my style," Johann said. "And not yours either, if you don't mind my saying so."

"Voilà," Beatrice said as a car appeared on the horizon heading in their direction.

The car, a near-new 1937 Volkswagen, slowed gradually as it approached them. The driver studied the unlikely pair standing beside the country road for several seconds before deciding to stop. The dark-haired man then leaned across the car, with the motor still running, and rolled down the window.

"Kann ich Sie helfen?" he asked.

"Vielleicht," Johann answered. He was not surprised, after having seen the car, that the man spoke to him in German. Following a quick introductory exchange, Johann explained to the man that both Sister Beatrice and he had been burned in an accident a couple of hours before and thought it might be a good idea to have a doctor look at their injuries.

"Jawohl," the man said. *"Ich bin Arzt. Ich heisse* Helmut Goldschlag. . . . If you would like, I can take you to my office in town and give you an examination."

Sister Beatrice climbed into the front seat beside Dr. Goldschlag. Johann tried to make himself comfortable in the tiny backseat.

Soon after the car began to move, Johann informed Dr. Goldschlag that his friend was an American nun who spoke only a little German. The doctor glanced over at Sister Beatrice from time to time during the drive. "I know it hurts," he said after several minutes, "but your face looks much worse than it is. You'll be surprised by how fast it will heal."

Initially Johann did not talk very much, limiting himself to translating Dr. Goldschlag's occasional comments for Beatrice. Later, however, after the road began winding through the woods and passing occasional signs identifying that they were in the Black Forest region of Germany, Johann leaned forward and carried on a steady conversation with the amiable doctor.

Johann told Dr. Goldschlag that he was a civil engineer from Berlin, and that Sister Beatrice's family and his had been friends for many years. According to Johann's story, Beatrice and he had rented a boat for the day so that they could have their own private tour of the Schwarzwald. Although Johann did not explain any details, he suggested to Dr. Goldschlag that their burns had resulted from an accident with the extra fuel on the boat.

During the conversation their driver often referred to his wife, Stella, and his daughter, Elke. "We are going to spend this coming weekend up at Hinterzarten," he said with a broad smile. "I have just driven up there today, in fact, to make certain that all the arrangements are in order."

They approached a country restaurant on the left. *"Möchten Sie etwas zu essen?"* Dr. Goldschlag asked. "Or would you rather continue on to my office and have your burns treated right away?"

After Johann and Beatrice both said that they were hungry, the doctor pulled the car into the small parking area. Four other cars were parked in the same dirt lot. One was marked with a large, official-looking insignia that Johann did not recognize. Dr. Goldschlag noticed the car and its insignia while they were walking toward the restaurant. He hesitated a moment, a frown upon his face, and then returned briefly to the car. When he rejoined Johann and Sister Beatrice, he was wearing an armband signifying that he was Jewish. "It's the law," he said grimly.

The large, converted farmhouse contained both a shop and a restaurant. The shop was full of cuckoo clocks of all shapes and sizes. Sister Beatrice and Johann spent a few minutes browsing through the clock collection while Dr. Goldschlag was in the rest room. As soon as the doctor returned, several of the cuckoo clocks signaled that it was exactly noon. All three of them enjoyed the elaborate displays, laughing at the antics of the carved wooden figures marking the time.

Dr. Goldschlag's laugh abruptly vanished, however, as they approached the main room of the restaurant. Beside the entrance was a simple sign. JUDEN VERBOTEN, it said.

"I will wait for you in the car," Helmut Goldschlag said.

"Absolutely not," Johann said immediately. "We will not eat without you."

Sister Beatrice, who had seen the sign and understood the gist of the conversation, followed the two men out the door and into the parking area. As Dr. Goldschlag turned his car onto the highway, all three of them noticed a tall blond man in a greenish uniform, staring at them from the doorway of the restaurant.

The talk in the car was about politics. Dr. Goldschlag told Johann and Sister Beatrice that his office had been destroyed a year earlier and he had been told he could no longer practice medicine in Germany. He had salvaged some of his equipment and supplies, however, and was still seeing many of his patients, most of whom were not Jewish, in the two back rooms of his house.

"My brother, who is also a doctor, went to the United States in 1935," he said, "just after the Nuremberg laws were promulgated. He was one of the lucky ones. Stella, Elke, and I have been trying to obtain emigration permits for almost two years. My wife and daughter have even become fluent in English. But it's hopeless. The Americans are no longer accepting ordinary Jewish refugees."

When they reached the outskirts of a small town, Dr. Goldschlag turned down a dirt road on the left. Soon thereafter he stopped in front of a large, typical German house.

"This is my home," he said proudly. "My wife and I have lived here since our marriage eight years ago."

He took them in the back entrance of his house and then disappeared briefly. When the door to the small room where Johann and Sister Beatrice were waiting was opened again, the doctor was accompanied by a woman and a six-year-old girl. Johann's recognition was instant. Stella Goldschlag was an exact reproduction of Sylvie Demirel, the wife of Johann's Turkish engineering friend Bakir from Berlin.

"These are my jewels," Helmut Goldschlag said as Johann struggled to control his emotions. "Stella, Elke, I would like for you to meet Johann Eberhardt and Sister Beatrice."

The bright-eyed little girl was not shy. "What happened to your face?" she said to Sister Beatrice in perfect English.

Beatrice bent down to the girl's level. "I burned it," she said softly. "That's why I have come to see your father. He is going to make it better."

"I'm preparing some lunch," Stella Goldschlag announced. "After Helmut has examined you, would you please join us?"

"We would be honored," Johann replied. He continued to stare at Frau Goldschlag until she left the room.

Dr. Goldschlag cleaned their wounds thoroughly and applied a soothing salve. The whole process was very painful for Johann and Sister Beatrice. They both endured the examination without comment, however, expecting, based on their experiences of the last two days, that at any moment some new and untoward event would occur.

They talked hurriedly during the minute or so that the doctor left them alone in the examining room. Johann and Sister Beatrice asked themselves if they should try to warn Dr. Goldschlag, by explaining to him that they were from the future and knew for certain what was going to happen to all the Jews who remained in Germany.

"I don't think that's what we're here for," Sister Beatrice said. "Besides, how could he believe such a fantastic story?"

Stella Goldschlag served them a typical German lunch, with three different kinds of wurst. Helmut opened one of his few remaining bottles of good wine. The girl, her mother, and Sister Beatrice conversed in English, talking about America mostly. At one point Elke asked Beatrice why she had become a nun, and if it was true that she could never marry.

Helmut and Johann discussed Hitler, the Nazis, and world politics. Dr. Goldschlag suggested that since the Poles had now been defeated, perhaps the leaders of Europe would declare a truce and some semblance of normality might return to everyone's life.

The doctor had just offered Johann a postprandial cigar when there was a loud pounding on the front door, followed swiftly by a brick crashing through the window of the living room.

"Jew Goldschlag," a nasty voice called. "Open the door. . . . We have come to take you away."

Helmut Goldschlag acted immediately. "Will you help us?" he asked Johann.

"Of course," Johann replied.

The doctor handed Johann the car keys. "You know how to drive, *nicht war*? Take Stella and Elke to your boat. The river runs into the Rhine after twenty-five more kilometers. If you wait until nightfall before moving out into the Rhine, you can make it to Switzerland before daylight tomorrow."

He handed a slip of paper to Johann. "Please take them to this address in Basel. I will cooperate with these hooligans and make my own escape later."

Stella and Elke had vanished from the dining room the instant the pounding on the door had begun. They returned now, each with her own suitcase, dressed for travel. The family had obviously been prepared for flight.

The beating on the door became louder. Another brick was hurled through the window. "Jew Goldschlag," the voice said. "Open this door now or we will break it down."

The doctor hurriedly embraced his wife and daughter. "Now go," he said, fighting back the tears.

Johann picked up the little girl and her bag and raced out the back door. The four of them jumped into the car. Johann followed Stella's directions, leaving the house in a direction that could not be seen from the front door.

They were back on the two-lane highway in less than five minutes.

It was not until they passed the country restaurant with the cuckoo clocks that Johann noticed that they were being followed. He increased his speed. The other car remained the same distance behind them.

Sister Beatrice recognized the spot where they had been standing beside the highway. Johann stopped abruptly, pulling the Volkswagen off the road on the river side. The Goldschlags and their bags were barely out of the car when the men who had been pursuing them came to a screeching halt on the other side of the road. Three security policemen, all wearing greenish uniforms with Nazi armbands, leaped out and ran across the highway.

"What are you doing here?" the oldest policeman said menacingly to Johann. He was the only one with a gun.

"We decided to stop and take a look at the river," Johann replied.

The lead policeman screwed up his face. "Here?" he said. "What is so special about this place?" He glanced at Stella and Elke Goldschlag. "And why do the woman and the little girl have suitcases?"

Johann did not say anything. "This is very suspicious," the policeman asserted, his eyes narrowing.

One of the other men had climbed down the bank toward the river. "There is a boat here," he shouted as he came back up the slope to rejoin his colleagues.

The lead policeman drew his gun and waved it at Johann. *"Was heissen Sie? Was tun Sie hier?"* he yelled.

"I am Johann Eberhardt, a civil engineer from Berlin. These are my friends, Sister Beatrice, and Stella and Elke Goldschlag. We decided to stop—"

"Goldschlag?" interrupted one of the two other policemen. "I know them. They are Jews. . . . The Jew doctor is her husband."

Johann struck the lead policeman a thunderous blow across the forearm. The gun flew out of his hand and into the bushes. "Run," Johann shouted. "Go to the boat now."

Another of the policemen grabbed Elke, but he released her when Johann smashed him in the face with his fist. "Nazi pigs," Johann roared, picking up the smallest of the men and hurling him against the ground.

He had no time to see if Sister Beatrice and the Goldschlags reached the boat. He was too busy fighting. He was winning, too, in spite of the fact that he had three opponents, until one of the officers hit him in the back of the head with a club. Dazed, Johann was not able to continue his ferocious fight. Sensing that he was weakening, the policemen moved in for the kill. Over and over Johann was struck on the head with the club. Finally he fell to the ground and lost consciousness.

His head ached when he awakened an hour later. Sister Beatrice and Johann were again on the boat, moving slowly down a narrow river between two towering white walls of stone. Johann was lying across his pair of seats.

"What happened?" he said to Sister Beatrice.

"They knocked you out," she said. "We had already reached the boat, but one of the policemen waded into the water and grabbed us before we could escape."

"Where are the Goldschlags?" Johann asked.

"They were taken into custody by the Nazis. . . . The policemen were going to arrest us, too, until your cousin Ludwig arrived."

"My cousin Ludwig?" Johann said, sitting up and looking at Beatrice with astonishment. "What are you talking about?"

"While you were still lying unconscious beside the road," Sister Beatrice said, "a bigger car with the same insignia arrived. It was driven by a young man in a fancy green uniform. He asked a few questions about the situation, and then told the others to take Stella and Elke to town. When they were gone, the new officer informed me that he was your cousin Ludwig, and that he would not be able to intercede on our behalf again."

Johann shook his head. "This whole thing is just too bizarre," he said.

"Is there a real Cousin Ludwig back in Germany?" Beatrice asked.

"Yes, there is," Johann said. "And he is indeed an officer with the National Security Police."

Johann talked to Sister Beatrice for several minutes about Cousin Ludwig, the NSP, his friend Bakir, and the general problem of the foreign workers in Germany. He also explained in more detail why he had been so startled when Stella Goldschlag had looked exactly like Sylvie Demirel.

Sister Beatrice was quiet for several seconds at the end of Johann's long monologue. "Are you familiar, Brother Johann," she said, "with the English word 'expiation'?"

"I have heard it," he said. "But I don't know exactly what it means."

"It's a great word," she said, "generally used in a religious context. . . . Anyway, to 'expiate' is to 'atone for.' I believe what we just experienced was God's way of giving you a chance to expiate your earlier mistakes. And maybe those of Germany as well . . . You did very well, Brother Johann. I'm proud of you."

7

J ohann and Sister Beatrice talked easily as their boat drifted slowly downstream between the two white walls. Beatrice suggested that God and His angels were still testing the two of them in some way, attempting to obtain more information about the character and values of the human species. Although Johann readily admitted that her explanation was plausible, he still favored the idea that the astonishing scenes replicating Hiroshima and Nazi Germany had been designed by aliens.

Their long conversation then turned to their childhoods, hers in the Minneapolis suburb of Edina and his in Potsdam. Johann and Beatrice shared a few poignant memories from those earlier, innocent days of their lives.

" 'There was a time when meadow, grove, and stream,' " Sister Beatrice quoted, " 'the earth, and every common sight, to me did seem apparelled in celestial light . . .' I lost that light for several years, Brother Johann," she said. "And I did not find it again until I met Michael."

"When I was a child," Johann said, after Beatrice explained how St. Michael had introduced her to a new and different kind of God, "I thought that God was a superfather of some kind. . . . Like my own in some ways, only much better and more powerful. I guess I let Him go at the same time it was becoming apparent to me that my father was just another man, with all the warts and foibles of every other member of our species."

They were approaching another dark tunnel. Sister Beatrice leaned forward. "I think our respite is about to end," she said. "God or the aliens or whoever is choreographing our lives must think we are ready for something else."

The tunnel was not very long. When they emerged, the towering wall was still on Beatrice's right, but on the left side of the boat, right next to the shoreline, a train track now ran parallel to the river.

The boat moved over closer to the shore. They heard a loud whistle. "Here we go again," Sister Beatrice said as a train came into view behind them.

Riding in the engine at the front of the train were three men wearing the green Nazi police uniforms. The engine had a swastika painted on its side. One of the officers leaned out of the engine window and waved at Johann and Beatrice.

"That is your cousin Ludwig, isn't it?" she asked.

"Yes, indeed," a bewildered Johann answered, shaking his head again. He waved at his cousin without enthusiasm.

The engine passed them. The first car was packed with passengers. Dozens of people were leaning out the windows, occupying every square centimeter of space. The passengers did not look happy. From their faces and their clothes, Johann deduced that they were Jewish. An empty feeling settled in his stomach.

"Look, Brother Johann," Sister Beatrice exclaimed. "There, in the middle of the car . . . It's Dr. Goldschlag, and Stella, and Elke."

The boat was no more than twenty meters from the train. Johann could clearly see the Goldschlags, hanging out the window and waving in their direction. Beatrice and he waved back. The little girl, Elke, who was apparently being held off the ground by her father, broke into a wide smile. "Hello, Sister Beatrice," they heard her say.

The car was very long. Its sides were marked with a Nazi flag at the front and rear. In the middle the word *"Deutschland"* was written on its side.

The first car finally passed. The second car was identical, except it was a different set of forlorn Jewish faces staring out the crowded, open windows. As the middle of the second car approached, however, what Johann saw sent a chill through his body. Helmut Goldschlag, his wife, Stella, and their daughter, Elke, were in this car also! Again they exchanged waves and the little girl said, "Hello, Sister Beatrice."

The Goldschlags were surrounded by another group of Jews being transported by the Nazis in the third car. They were also in the middle of the fourth car, still standing at the window and waving at Johann and Sister Beatrice in their little boat.

The train increased its speed. The cars continued to pass. The sign on the side of the car changed from DEUTSCHLAND to FRANKREICH and then to POLAND. The train was interminable. From every car the Goldschlags waved.

Johann could not watch any more. The empty feeling in his stomach had changed to nausea. As another packed carload of Polish Jews sped by, Johann leaned over the side of the boat and vomited into the river. His forehead broke into a sweat. He glanced up, watched two more cars pass, and retched again.

"It's not my fault!" he shouted at the train in between attacks of nausea. "It's not my fault!"

He felt Sister Beatrice's comforting hands on his shoulders. "No, it's not your fault, Brother Johann," she said softly. "Not specifically . . . Yet in some measure all of us are to blame. Not just you, or even those Nazis who plotted to systematically exterminate the Jews. I am guilty too. Every human being is accountable in some way for every inhumane act committed by another person. . . . That's what the Order of St. Michael is all about. Michael often said that only—"

"Don't talk to me about God or St. Michael now," Johann shouted angrily. "If there is a God, how could He have let all this occur?" He motioned at the train. "Look," he said, "it goes on and on."

As they gazed together at the train Johann and Beatrice noticed that there had been some changes. Nazi flags were no longer painted on the sides of each car. And the faces staring out were no longer Jewish. The car passing them at that moment, in fact, had American flags at the beginning and end. The people looking out the windows, except for the Goldschlag family, who still occupied the middle of each car, were American Indians.

The train was now moving so fast that an entire car passed the boat in less than five seconds. Johann and Beatrice watched silently as more carloads of Native Americans raced by them. Then came three cars marked with the Australian flag. The aboriginal inhabitants of these cars stared blankly out the train windows as if they did not see anything at all. The Goldschlags were in these cars as well, still waving at Johann and Sister Beatrice.

Behind the boat the train stretched to the limit of the horizon. The next cars that passed Johann and Beatrice were emblazoned with the bold-colored flag of the Council of Governments. The passengers, except for the Goldschlags, were all emaciated black people, their starving eyes bulging out of their pitiful faces. The African cars hurtled by one after the other. Johann's discomfort became unbearable.

"No more, please," he yelled, tears streaming from his eyes. "Stop this goddamned train."

"Dear God," Sister Beatrice said from beside him. She was kneeling on her seat. "We see only too clearly what horrors human beings are capable of in the absence of Thy guidance. Forgive us all, we beseech Thee, not only for the terrible mistakes we have made, but also for our callous indifference to the suffering of our brethren. Share with us Thy wisdom and understanding so that we may create a world of harmony for our entire species. In St. Michael's name. Amen."

Only a few seconds after she concluded her prayer, the lights were extinguished. Johann and Sister Beatrice were plunged into total darkness. They could hear nothing as well. The sound of the train had vanished.

"Are you all right, Brother Johann?" she asked after a protracted silence.

"I'm alive, Sister Beatrice," he replied. "And I guess I have control of myself again. But I certainly wouldn't say that I'm 'all right.' What we just saw must either be a taste of hell, or some sadistic alien's way of reminding us how imperfect we humans are. In either case, I'm considering filing a complaint with the management."

He could hear her laugh in the dark. "It's good to see that you have retained your sense of humor," she said.

"It's my final self-protection mechanism," Johann said. "My head is hurting in at least a dozen places, my back is completely roasted, and both my self-image and my view of the human species as a whole are at all-time lows. . . . I have neither the courage nor the means to commit suicide. So I might as well laugh."

"You could try praying, Brother Johann," she said. "It works for me."

"I'm glad it works for you, Sister Beatrice," he said. "I really am. . . . But I would feel like a hypocrite. I have not genuinely prayed for many years, since I was a child and believed in the trinity of God, Santa Claus, and the tooth fairy. . . . And despite what we have experienced, I can't conceive even at this moment of a God who listens to our prayers. I would be inclined, based on the evidence, to believe in a God who didn't really give a shit about us at all."

"That would be a start," Beatrice said several seconds later. "Acknowledging even a God who doesn't give a shit could start the process."

The sudden forward acceleration of the boat pinned Beatrice against the back of her seat. Johann was thrown on the floor between them. He had just managed in the darkness to scramble back onto his seat when the boat made an abrupt ninety-degree turn, downward. Johann and Beatrice were thrown forward, away from the boat, by their horizontal momentum. They were now floating in space, surrounded in their weightlessness by some of the water from the river that had also been thrown free by the sharp turn.

"Brother Johann," Beatrice cried in the dark, "are you still there?"

Johann turned to respond to the cry and began to tumble out of control. "Where are you?" he said as his disorientation became complete.

"Over here," he heard her say somewhere behind him.

He seemed to be twisting and turning in all directions at once. Never had Johann's senses been so utterly useless. He no longer had any idea which way was up or down, or where Beatrice might be with respect to him. Each time she called his name she seemed to be farther away.

It was an amazing flight. For almost two minutes Johann was in total dark and without any kinesthetic references. Since there was no gravity until the last hundred meters of his free fall, his speed did not increase significantly. His fear, however, moved to progressively higher levels. Toward the end, Johann had convinced himself that he had been condemned to tumble forever in the unrelenting darkness.

He saw the distant light to his left only moments before he heard both the splash and Beatrice's cry. Seconds later he, too, plunged into the tepid water. Johann started to swim, but with no light and little gravity, it was difficult to find the surface. He finally worked out a search pattern and reached the surface with plenty of breath to spare.

His first act when he broke the water was to yell her name. There was no response. Johann frantically searched the area around him in the water. The distant light provided enough illumination that Johann could see what looked like churning water about twenty meters to his right. There were no other signs of Beatrice. Adrenaline pouring into his system, he raced over to where the water was disturbed.

Still he found nothing. Johann shouted Beatrice's name. He waited a few seconds, and then in desperation began swimming again.

He was underwater when he brushed against her leg the first time. Beatrice was floating unconscious just beneath the surface. Johann lifted her head out of the water and began to swim toward the distant light. Only twice during the next fifteen minutes did he allow himself to look briefly at her face. There was no sign of any life.

Johann was exhausted when he finally reached a sandy beach dimly lit by the distant overhead light. He pulled Beatrice up on the sand, surprised to discover that there was some small gravity working against him as he lifted her. He immediately began mouth-to-mouth resuscitation. For five minutes he tried to force air into her lungs and pump the water out.

When she wouldn't wake up, Johann became frantic again. He started talking wildly to himself, and then addressed his raving to his unseen and unknown hosts.

"I really don't give a shit," he shouted at one point, pausing for a moment in his efforts to revive her, "if you are aliens or angels. . . . But I damn sure do care about this woman, and she doesn't deserve to die. She is the best human being I have ever met. . . . If one of us must die, then take me instead, and let her live."

He returned to the resuscitation with renewed vigor, increasing both his tempo and the amount of pressure he was applying to Beatrice's chest. "You will not die. . . . You will not die," he kept saying over and over.

After one forceful push, a heavy stream of water burst out of her mouth and her body shook slightly, as if it were trying to cough. Encouraged, Johann pushed hard again and more water streamed out of Beatrice's mouth. This time she did indeed cough. She was alive! The exultant Johann continued to press rhythmically on her chest until her violent coughing finished the task of emptying the water from her lungs.

He sat beside her on the sand and held her up while her coughing slowly abated. When Beatrice was finally able to draw a clear breath, she smiled wearily at Johann and then lost consciousness again.

Johann stayed awake until he convinced himself that Beatrice was all right. He carefully monitored both her breathing and her pulse. At length he permitted himself to lie down beside her on the sand. Johann fell asleep instantly.

In his last dream he was swimming alone in the middle of a vast ocean. Johann called Beatrice's name repeatedly, but she never appeared. He saw something in the distance that he thought might be her body, but when he reached it in the dream, it was only a piece of driftwood.

Johann awakened with a start and sat up. The darkness had been replaced by artificial daylight. Beside him Beatrice was still sleeping. He checked her pulse, stood up, and stretched. Then he took a few cautious steps on the sand before jumping into the air. Based on the time it took him to return to the sand, Johann estimated that the gravity level was roughly a tenth of that on Earth.

But how are they creating gravity at all? he wondered briefly as he began to look around. *And why?*

To Johann's left the placid lake stretched into the distance as far as he could see. To his right, beyond the white sand beach that was about forty meters wide, lush tropical plants grew up the side of a gentle slope. The unruly, thick vegetation bordered the beach everywhere except in an area about a hundred meters to the right of him, where there was a tidy grove of unusual trees. With his sharp eyes, Johann could see bunches of large, brown spheres hanging from the lower branches of these trees. He decided to investigate the grove.

He walked barefoot across the sand, stopping every ten meters or so to look back at the sleeping Beatrice. When he reached the trees in the grove, which had thick, white trunks, Johann pulled down the bunch of brown objects nearest his head and plucked one of them out of the tree.

The object was the size of a basketball, with a hard brown covering. Looking around on the floor of the grove, he found a wide, flat rock. He sat down, still in view of Beatrice, and hit the top of the brown object against the rock progressively harder until major cracks developed in its surface.

With his powerful hands Johann pulled away parts of the outer shell. A thick, red gelatin oozed out. He pinched off a piece with his fingers and held it under his nose. There was no smell. He was about to taste the red material when he felt the brown sphere move in his hand.

Startled, Johann sat very still for a few seconds until the movement recurred. Then he set the object carefully down on the flat rock so that he could watch it. It jiggled back and forth ever so slightly several times during the next minute. Before anything else happened, however, he heard Sister Beatrice calling his name. In a flash, Johann bounded out of the grove and across the sandy beach.

She was sitting up on the sand with her robe wrapped across her torso. Beatrice smiled as he approached. "I figured that tall man over in the grove of trees must be you," she said. "Either that or I was dreaming again."

He dropped down beside her. "How are you?" Johann asked.

"As well as can be expected," she said. "For a moment, when I first opened my eyes and saw the sand, the water, and all the vegetation, I thought I had died and gone to heaven." She laughed. "I assume you must have rescued me. . . . My last memory is of being hopelessly entangled in my robe and trying to swim, without knowing which way was the surface."

"It was fortunate that I found you," Johann said. "And even more fortunate that you had not already drowned."

"God must not have been ready for me to die yet, Brother Johann," she said teasingly. "Or maybe He wanted to make it absolutely clear to you how dependent we all are on one another, in case you had missed the earlier, more subtle messages."

She laughed again. A moment later she was more serious. "I thank you for my life, Brother Johann," she said with her characteristic intensity. "I have no idea how I will ever repay you."

Johann did not know what to say. He suddenly felt awkward and embarrassed. Inside his head, however, he heard the words that he might have spoken if he had not been so confused by his own emotions. *You have repaid me already. Your smile and your laughter are all the payment I could ever want.*

Before they started to explore their new domain together, Sister Beatrice convinced Johann that it was all right to drink from the lake. It was not an easy task. Despite his thirst, Johann was reluctant to accept that it could possibly be safe to drink from a large pool of standing water. Sister Beatrice stated matter-of-factly that the lake water must be all right, otherwise their hosts would have provided drinking vessels for them, as they always had in the past. In the face of her certitude, Johann eventually waded out into the lake about twenty meters and took a long drink.

Beatrice wrapped her wet robe around her shoulders, wearing it like a shawl over her long underwear. They walked along the beach, and Sister Beatrice started to feel better. Johann wanted to show her the unusual grove and the brown spheres that he had found.

Instead they first inspected the vines, leafy plants, and shrubs that were in their immediate vicinity. The flora was unlike anything they had ever seen. One of the vines, for example, enmeshed in a bush covered with black berries, had peculiar cylindrical rods growing perpendicular to its stem and extending almost half a meter out from the main body of the vine. Another shrub had many prominent offshoots that reentered the ground, forming a protective circle around what appeared to be, based on its size, the central growth of the plant.

During the time they were examining the vegetation, Johann and Sister Beatrice only saw one species of animal, a brightly colored flying creature, about the size of a butterfly, with two pairs of long, narrow wings and eight tiny legs. They saw three of these creatures, each of them sitting on a horseshoe-shaped red fruit growing in the center of a large leaf.

Together they found many shrubs with berries, and what looked like fruit on half a dozen different kinds of plants. Johann and Beatrice decided not to eat any just yet, mostly because of Johann's earlier experience with the brown spheres.

Despite her growing fatigue, Sister Beatrice eventually accompanied Johann to his special grove. His brown object was still resting on the flat rock. Where Johann had pulled away the covering, a hole had been burrowed through the red material. He picked up the object and handed it to Beatrice. She stood still for over a minute.

"I don't feel any movement, Brother Johann," she said.

He held it for a while and then shrugged. "I know I felt it move," he said. "I even *saw* it wiggle while it was sitting on the rock."

Beatrice smiled. "I'm sure you did, Brother Johann. . . . But it's not moving now. And among the set of events that we have experienced in the last few days, the movement of this nut or seed or whatever it is does not rank as one of the greater mysteries."

He stared at her for a few seconds. "You're patronizing me," he said.

"A little," she replied apologetically, putting her arm through his and heading back toward the lake. "These last few days I have grown to understand your need to analyze and explain every phenomenon you encounter," she said while they were walking. "But as I have mentioned to you before, that kind of compulsive need inevitably leads to frustration. Only if there is faith and acceptance in the presence of that which is beyond our understanding can we ever achieve any inner peace."

"Sister Beatrice," Johann said a little later, "I'm not comfortable with your notion of blind acceptance. It seems to be antithetical to the whole thinking process. Without thought, and the understanding that comes from an analytical approach to what we see and experience, we are no different from all the billions of other molecules trapped in insentient rocks, plants, and lesser animals. Thinking is what has allowed the human species to be aware of who and what we are in the overall scheme of things."

They had reached the lake. Beatrice turned to face Johann. "St. Michael taught that the ability to think and reason is our single greatest attribute. He encouraged research and learning of all kinds. But he also reminded us repeatedly that thought was only one of God's gifts to mankind. . . . Love and faith are two others. Neither can exist, Michael said in one of his sermons, in a person who believes that the only path to truth is a rigorous combination of logic and analysis."

Johann stared at Beatrice's intense blue eyes and was flooded by a myriad of simultaneous emotions. *How can I argue with her*, he said to himself, *when just hearing her voice, or seeing her smile, brings me such pure happiness? Is this not the very point she is making, that we are not simply thinking creatures, and that we must learn to accept concepts and feelings that we cannot logically explain?*

He had a sudden and powerful desire to kiss her. Beatrice must have sensed what he was feeling, for she took a step backward and looked away.

"And now, Brother Johann," she said lightly, "if you have had enough philosophy for the time being, I would like to take a nap. When I wake up, if we still have light, let's look for something to eat. Without food in our stomachs, we are not likely to resolve many of the fundamental issues of the universe."

Johann smiled. *I love you,* he thought.

8

Sister Beatrice was surprisingly full
of energy after her nap. When Johann and she walked half a kilo-
meter down the beach and noticed a small mountain rising behind and
beyond the thick vegetation, Beatrice insisted that they should climb the
peak.

Johann tried to dissuade her, reminding her that she had nearly
drowned less than twenty hours earlier. She dismissed his concerns and
plunged into the vegetation, heading in the direction of the small mountain. Sister Beatrice quickly discovered that her robe was a cumbersome
nuisance in the thick growth. "Would it be too immodest," she asked
Johann, "for me to leave my robe on the beach?"

Johann agreed that given their circumstances, it did not make much
sense for Beatrice to continue to wear her Michaelite robe. She returned
to the beach, neatly folded the robe, and placed it on the sand in front of
a group of shrubs with bright blue berries. As she skipped barefoot across
the sand in his direction, wearing only her standard long underwear, Johann realized, for the first time, that Beatrice's body was as beautiful as

her face. With that realization came a surge of lust that he instantly suppressed.

They found a stream several hundred meters inland and decided to follow its course up toward the peak. The vegetation was not as thick on the banks of the stream as it was elsewhere, and climbing was not difficult in the low gravity, so their progress was quite rapid. The air temperature was mild, but they both began to sweat eventually from the constant activity.

Beatrice sat down beside the stream when they were slightly more than halfway to the top. She splashed some water against her face and then bent over to take a drink.

"How do you know that this water also is safe?" Johann asked.

Beatrice glanced up at Johann, shook her head, and then broke into a smile. "Look around you, Brother Johann," she said. "Isn't this place absolutely marvelous? Is it even conceivable that a paradise like this wouldn't have perfectly pure water? Besides, you didn't die or become sick after drinking from the lake; why would you suspect that the water in this stream would be different?"

Johann didn't answer immediately. He turned slowly around, surveying the plants on both banks of the stream. "What are we doing here, Sister Beatrice?" he said eventually. "Why was this place created, and by whom? Why were we taken to Hiroshima and Nazi Germany? What was the purpose of that endless, painful train?" He threw up his arms in despair. "None of this makes any sense to me."

"Brother Johann," Beatrice said with a bemused look on her face, "sometimes I think that you are indeed hopeless. . . . Here we are, surrounded by beauty on all sides, and you can't enjoy it because you can't explain everything that has happened to us. Haven't you heard a word I have been saying to you? We do not need to understand the universe to be happy. There will always be things that we can't comprehend. That's why faith is so important. . . . Brother Johann, I'm afraid you're going to continue to have a hard time unless you can somehow learn to experience life without analyzing it to death."

Johann looked away from Sister Beatrice. From the set of his body, she guessed correctly that she had hurt his feelings. "I'm sorry, Brother Johann," she said sincerely. "What I said was unduly harsh, and presumptuous as well. Please forgive me."

He walked over, bent down beside the stream, and took a long drink. When he was finished, Johann wiped his mouth with the back of his hand and stared at Sister Beatrice.

"Not knowing what's going on doesn't bother you even one little bit?" he asked.

She came over beside him and touched his shoulder. "I *wonder* about it, Brother Johann, and I might even try, now that you have raised the issue so often, to see if I can come up with a reasonable explanation for this island. But not understanding doesn't *bother* me, and I would never, ever let it interfere with my appreciation of all this beauty."

They discovered that they were on an island when they reached the top of the small mountain. The island was long and comparatively narrow, roughly ten kilometers by two kilometers. The mountain peak, rising four hundred meters above the level of the lake, was almost exactly in the island's center. The sandy beach on which Johann had resuscitated Beatrice stretched down one long side of the island. On the opposite side there was no beach at all. There, the calm blue waters of the lake that surrounded the island lapped against the bottom of steep cliffs.

Where the beach and cliffs came together, at either end of the island, there were fascinating rock formations that were dotted with caves. Johann and Beatrice decided to explore these rock formations next. After taking one final look at the spectacular view, Beatrice headed down a path that led through the vegetation toward the caves closest to their initial landing spot on the beach.

They reached the rocks when the artificial daylight was almost gone. The first two caves they explored were right opposite the lake. Both were large, empty single rooms with surprisingly flat floors. Their structure suggested that the caves had been at least partially created by intelligent beings.

As they rounded one corner during their exploration among the rocks, Johann and Beatrice saw a flickering light reflecting off a very large boulder about twenty meters in front of them. They stopped and watched for several seconds. Ahead of them, a pathway through the rocks turned sharply to the left. The light was coming from somewhere beyond that turn.

Johann edged forward slowly, touching the rock wall with his left hand and listening for any sounds he might be able to identify. He heard nothing. His pulse rate increased as images of white ribbons and snowmen came into his mind. He eventually reached the corner. Beatrice was only a couple of meters behind him.

"Here I go," he whispered, thrusting his head around the edge of the rocks and looking to his left.

In front of him, above a hole in the center of a circular plaza virtually surrounded by rock walls five to six meters in height, a large fire was burning. Johann motioned to Beatrice to join him. They walked slowly into the plaza together. They stood there, mesmerized, staring at the dancing yellow flames that seemed to be rising out of the ground.

"He has given us also the gift of fire, Brother Johann," she said reverently. "To provide us with heat and light."

Johann walked over as close as he dared to the fire and looked down into the hole. He could not see anything but yellow flame. "So you think this fire was meant specifically for us?" he asked.

"Yes, Brother Johann," Beatrice said. She had a faraway look in her eyes. "I now believe that this entire island, including everything on it, was carefully crafted by an omniscient and omnipotent designer, the one I call God and you barely acknowledge, for our exclusive use. . . . We are meant to live here, in these caves, to drink the water from the lake and streams, to eat the fruits and berries that are so plentiful. . . . God has given us a paradise to share."

Her face was radiant in the reflected firelight. Despite her burns, which had already started to heal, Johann had never seen her look so beautiful. He knew that he was falling hopelessly in love with her.

"I don't mean any disrespect, Sister Beatrice," he said after a long silence. "But would you mind telling me how you *know* all these things already? Have you seen something that I haven't?"

They were standing together beside the fire. The artificial daylight was completely gone. Beatrice turned to Johann and took his hands in hers. "Not with my eyes, Brother Johann," she said. "But I have sensed His presence here with my heart and soul."

The next day, after sleeping side by side near the fire, Johann and Sister Beatrice found the storehouse cave. It was huge, and contained an astonishing array of virtually everything they could possibly have wanted or needed. Just inside the entrance, on white shelves with the occasional characteristic red stripes, were four empty water vessels and several hundred food cylinders. They had been juxtaposed to an assortment of the berries, grains, and fruits that Johann and Beatrice had already encountered on the island. The meaning of the arrangement was unmistakable. Johann no longer had any doubt about whether or not they were supposed to eat the produce of the island.

In cabinets and shelves behind the food and drinking vessels were sleeping mats and pillows, towels and washcloths, familiar tools of all sorts and sizes, building materials, ropes and strings, wheels, vast stacks of fabric pieces along with sewing instruments, pots and pans, dinnerware, and hundreds of other objects, some of which neither Johann nor Beatrice could readily identify. Every item was white in color, with a red mark or band somewhere on its surface.

They were overwhelmed by the contents of the storehouse cave. They spent over an hour wandering from shelf to shelf, and cabinet to cabinet, taking an inventory of what had been provided for them. When Johann and Sister Beatrice finally returned together to the entrance to the cave, she was beaming.

"Well, Brother Johann," she said. "Would you say that we have been adequately supplied?"

"That would be an understatement, Sister Beatrice," he replied. "It certainly looks as if God or the aliens intends for us to stay here for quite a while . . . as you suggested last night."

"Who knows," she said coyly, "we may be here forever."

"Sister Beatrice," he said in a light vein, "if my fate in life is to be marooned forever on this island with you, I will try my hardest to be *accepting*. Otherwise, I will never find that inner peace you talk so much about. . . ."

She raised her arm to strike him, but Johann laughed and jumped away.

They quickly settled into a regular routine. They slept in the cave closest to the fire, each on a separate mat, within an arm's length of one another. Each morning at the first sign of light, Beatrice would wake Johann. While she was meditating down on the beach he would use the toilet cave, a small open room with a very deep hole in its center. Then he would take his long exercise swim in the lake. After sharing a leisurely breakfast, usually the coarse brown grain mixed with fruit juices and berries, Johann and Sister Beatrice would decide what they were going to do for the day.

Most of the time they explored the island together. On several of their exploratory hikes they went all the way to the other side of the island. Most of the individual caves on the opposite side were larger, with many rooms, as if they had been designed for groups. The general layout of the other cave system, however, was similar to theirs. It also had a perpetual fire burning in a circular plaza, and a vast storehouse that contained several hundred useful items.

"So we don't *have* to live together," Sister Beatrice said lightly one day after they had visited the other caves. "If we ever decide that we can't stand each other, we can live on opposite sides of the island. . . . Or maybe, just for variety, we can use the other caves from time to time. Like a vacation home . . ."

Sometimes Beatrice would tell Johann that she wanted to spend the morning, or the entire day, by herself. On those days she would commune privately with God, or use the needles, thread, and fabric from the storehouse to make them some simple clothing. Johann would explore on his own, or build something with the treasure trove of materials and tools that had been supplied to them by their hosts.

At night, they always ate dinner around the fire. Afterward, Johann would ask Sister Beatrice to sing. She always sang at least one song, usually two or three. She had an enormous repertoire, including religious music, opera, the musical theater, and even some popular songs. Johann was delighted to discover that Beatrice could sing several of the pieces from Wagner's Ring Cycle, including Brunhild's famous aria when Siegfried's kiss awakens her from sleep. Johann often closed his eyes when Sister Beatrice was singing. The intensity of his pleasure never ceased to amaze him.

Before going to bed they generally made a soothing drink of mixed berries and water and heated it over the fire. It was a peaceful, easy existence for both of them. They rarely argued. Johann grew accustomed to Beatrice's religious devotion. She never stopped trying to convince him that he would be happier if God played a more important role in his life, but she did not push too much.

They lost count of the days after twenty or so. The passage of time no longer mattered to them. Sister Beatrice was happy with her relationships with both God and Brother Johann. He was delighted to be spending every waking hour with the woman he loved.

9

Eva and he were quarreling in his apartment. It was a weekend, and Johann felt that they should spend at least one of the two evenings with his parents in Potsdam. Eva told Johann that his parents were boring, and that *he* was boring.

The buzzer sounded. "Who is it?" Johann asked crossly.

"It's me, Sister Beatrice," a lovely voice said on the intercom. "May I come up?"

He released the door locks. "Who is Sister Beatrice?" Eva asked, her expression partly quizzical, partly displeasure.

"She's a bishop of the Order of St. Michael," Johann said proudly. "She's beautiful, and has an amazing singing voice, and has dedicated her life to helping others."

"She sounds too good to be true," Eva said scornfully, walking toward the bedroom.

There was a knock on the door. "Good morning, Brother Johann," Beatrice said lightly. "I was in your neighborhood and thought I would drop by and say hello."

"I'm delighted that you did, Sister Beatrice," he said. He invited her into the apartment. "In just a moment," he said confidentially, "I'm going to introduce you to my friend Eva. We're still engaged, but we won't be much longer."

"I'm glad to hear that, Brother Johann," Sister Beatrice said. "She certainly doesn't seem like the right woman for you. . . . By the way, it's very hot outside, and I've had a long walk. Do you mind if I use your shower?"

"No, of course not," Johann replied. "It's right down the hall."

"Where did your friend the nun go?" Eva asked when she returned a few seconds later.

"Sister Beatrice is taking a shower in the guest bathroom," Johann said.

"That is certainly peculiar behavior," Eva said, "stopping off at a friend's house for a shower."

Johann looked down the hall. The door to the guest bathroom was still open. Sister Beatrice was standing in her long underwear with her back to Johann. Her folded robe was on the floor beside her. She tested the shower water with her hand and then started to take off her underwear.

He walked toward the bathroom. "Where are you going?" Eva asked Johann.

"I'm going to see if she needs anything," Johann said.

Beatrice was now naked. She stepped gingerly into the shower, without closing the curtain, and turned sideways, letting the jets of water splash against her full, round breasts. Johann was standing at the bathroom door.

"Hello again, Brother Johann," Sister Beatrice said sweetly. "I can't tell you how divine this water feels." She placed both of her hands on her breasts and began to massage her nipples with slow, circular motions.

"I came to see if there was anything you needed," Johann said with difficulty.

Beatrice gave him a look unlike any Johann had ever seen before. She was still massaging herself. "Why yes, Brother Johann," she said. "As a matter of fact, there is something that I need."

She motioned for him to come over closer to the shower. When he was beside her, she leaned out, dripping water on both Johann and the floor, and kissed him passionately on the lips.

"Now take off your clothes," she said softly, "and join me in here."

Johann removed his clothes and left them in a heap on the bathroom floor. Beatrice moved back so that there was plenty of room for him in the shower. When they were standing facing each other in the stream of water, she took both his large hands and placed them on her breasts. Then she kissed him again.

Johann was overwhelmed by desire. When the kiss was completed Sister Beatrice reached down approvingly and touched his swollen penis. It was then that Johann realized that Eva was watching them from the bathroom door.

He woke up abruptly from the vivid dream, opened his eyes, and looked around. For a few seconds Johann was completely disoriented. The sound of running water reminded him of the shower in his dream. It took him a little while to realize that he was hearing the island sprinkler system, which was turned on for half an hour, three times a week, always in the middle of the night.

Sister Beatrice was sleeping peacefully an arm's length away from him. Johann was still feeling the powerful sexual arousal from his dream. He closed his eyes again, hoping to recapture the image of an amorous Beatrice standing beside him in the shower.

A picture of Beatrice, naked and desirable, did come into his mind, but it was not the image from his dream. This picture was a real memory, from two days earlier, when he had watched her bathing in the cove on the far side of their caves. Johann had not meant to spy on her. He had been out exploring on his own, and was bringing back for observation and study another pair of the brown nuts from the grove next to the beach. He had heard Beatrice splashing and had headed in her direction, without thinking about the fact that she might be taking a bath.

Johann had first seen her standing naked on the sand, no more than twenty meters away. Instead of calling to her, or respecting her privacy by going in the opposite direction, he had watched her in silence, even hiding himself when she began to dry off. Johann had been unable to take his eyes off her body. Sister Beatrice had never seen him.

He lay on his back on the mat, tormented by her naked image and his own arousal. After glancing over to make certain that she was still asleep, Johann slipped his right hand into the underwear that Beatrice had made for him.

They had found a new kind of fruit on the far side of the island. It had a yellow meat that was soft, juicy, and delicious. Both Johann and Sister Beatrice were in good spirits after they finished their late dinner.

"I have a surprise for you tonight, Brother Johann," she said. "I have decided to share some of my very special memories about St. Michael. . . . I have never before told these things to anyone who is not a member of our order, and I know that you are somewhat cynical about many aspects of religion, so—"

"My affection for you, Sister Beatrice," Johann interrupted, "is greater than my cynicism. I assure you that I will treasure anything that is important to you."

"I suspected that, Brother Johann," she said, "but thanks for the reassurance." Sister Beatrice smiled. "Okay, fire away, ask me anything you want to know about Michael."

"I have only a vague idea about how you became involved with the order in the first place," Johann said. "Why don't you start at the beginning, when you met Michael for the first time?"

Beatrice turned and stared at the fire. "It seems like so long ago now," she said. "Almost as if it were another lifetime . . ."

She paused for several seconds. "It was late in the winter of 2138, the twenty-fifth of February to be exact, when my touring company reached Florence. We had been playing the Continent for six weeks and had already been to London, Paris, and Berlin. The company was doing four different musicals in a one-week stay at each venue. I had the lead in *Follow Your Heart*, and minor roles in the other shows.

"I was twenty-one at the time and a junior, majoring in music with a minor in English literature, at the University of Minnesota. I had taken off a semester from school both because I was tired of studying and because I wanted to make some money.

"The American Theater Group, or ATG as we affectionately called it, was the most prestigious touring company in the nation. To be selected for it as a university student was considered quite an honor. My parents were very proud."

She took a drink of water from one of their cups. Johann studied her face in the firelight. It had healed magnificently. No one would have known that she had been badly burned not more than two months earlier.

"We had a day off between each of the shows," Sister Beatrice continued. "One of the members of our company had heard Michael preach the day after we had arrived in Florence and had come back raving about his insight and charisma. Several of us went with her, mostly out of curiosity.

"The morning was beautiful. Quite crisp, I remember, but with a hint of spring in the air. Michael was preaching outdoors, in an amphitheater in the suburbs of Florence used for popular-music concerts during the summer. The title of his sermon that morning was 'The Circulation System of the Human Species.'

"The service began with a pair of hymns. There was a choir of twenty-five or so Michaelites in their blue robes standing on one side of the stage. Michael came out without any ceremony and joined in the singing, first standing beside the choir and then moving among the front rows of the audience. He greeted the members of his flock with a smile and a nod of his head. He also stopped from time to time to shake hands with the people he had never seen before.

"Michael was in a good mood. His smile was warm and inviting, his small dimples on both cheeks were pronounced, and his robin's-egg-blue eyes were magnificent in the early-morning sun. We had arrived early and were in the fifth or sixth row. When he passed in front of us, it was at the end of a hymn. He stopped and listened to me sing. I remember my pulse rate shot up under the intensity of his gaze. When the song was over, he took my hand and said simply, 'You have a beautiful voice. I hope you find what you are looking for today.' "

Sister Beatrice stopped, took a deep breath, and swallowed. Tears had welled up in her eyes. "It's impossible for me to describe, Brother Johann," she said, "the amazing feelings that I had that morning, beginning at the moment that Michael touched my hand. I felt as if a towering wave, soft, gentle, and comforting, had swept over me. When I looked into his eyes, I felt an inner peace unlike any I had ever experienced before. Later, while I was listening to him speak . . ."

She turned and looked at the fire. Her cheeks were glistening with her tears. "My whole life was transformed in one hour. It was not only what Michael said, but how he said it, full of warmth and humor and boundless love. . . . He seemed to be speaking directly to my soul. I remember having the feeling that nobody else was present, only Michael and I, and that he had come to be my guide, to show me God's plan for my life."

Sister Beatrice turned back to Johann, smiled quickly, and then stood up. "The sermon was in Italian," she said, starting to walk slowly around the fire, "but Michael had prerecorded it in six other languages. He was a brilliant linguist, among other talents. . . . Anyway, the timing wasn't exactly the same on the English version I was hearing, but it was close, and Michael's verbal idiosyncrasies and inflections were certainly captured on the tape.

"His message was simple. In order for there to be lasting peace on the planet Earth, another major step in evolution was necessary. This step would be as complicated and important as the great breakthrough that produced multicellular creatures in the Precambrian oceans after two billion years of uninspired unicellular evolution. That next great step forward, according to Michael, will result eventually in one grand, harmonious human organism, working for the advantage of all, comprising each and every human being on this planet.

"His goal in life, Michael said, and his charge to those who accepted him as their spiritual leader, was to design an organization that could become the circulatory system of that great new human organism, distributing the resources of food, clothing, shelter, love, education, and health care wherever they were needed. By establishing a worldwide organization of dedicated men and women whose only purpose in life was to serve their fellow humans, Michael hoped to demonstrate that it was indeed possible to create large-scale social systems that would support the final evolution."

She sat down again directly opposite him. "I bought it all in that hour, Brother Johann. . . . Michael, his vision, the idea of being the blood vessels of mankind. I stayed after the sermon and asked what I needed to do to become a Michaelite. That evening I withdrew from the touring company and spent the night in the barracks with his followers. The next morning at dawn I met personally for an hour with Michael, made my commitment, and put on my blue robe for the first time."

Johann reached over and took her right hand in his. They sat together in silence, alternately staring at each other and the fire, until Sister Beatrice removed her hand, walked over to her sleeping mat in the nearby cave, and lay down to go to sleep.

They were eating dinner together after a game of soccer on the beach and an invigorating swim. Johann was trying to explain to Sister Beatrice what he had learned about the brown nuts from the special grove. She was making his explanation difficult, laughing and teasing him at the end of almost every sentence.

"It is clear that it's the worms that are making the nuts move," he said. "I have established that fact beyond a shadow of a doubt. . . . But the nut doesn't wiggle unless part of its outer shell has been removed. Somehow the worms inside *know* when the integrity of the shell has been compromised."

Beatrice was eating a bunch of the little black berries from beside the stream. "But, Brother Johann," she said, her eyes dancing playfully, "you still haven't answered my first question. How do the worms penetrate that hard covering? You said yourself that even those nuts with no holes in the shell contain worms. Where do they come from?"

"My working hypothesis," Johann said, not noticing her mirth, "is that the worms, or perhaps some less advanced egg or larvae form, are deposited in the nut bud at the beginning of its growth, when its exterior has not yet hardened. . . . I collected some of those buds today. If you would like, I could bring them over now and we could test my hypothesis together. Although without a microscope—"

"Dear Brother Johann," Beatrice suddenly interrupted, "I would dearly love to know more about your fascinating plants, but I would much prefer a stroll beside the lake tonight. Would you care to join me?"

"Of course," he said, standing up. "Look, Sister Beatrice," he then said defensively, "if you really have no interest in what I am learning . . ."

"Don't be silly, Brother Johann," she said, laughing and taking his hand. "I enjoy sharing your research. I just like teasing you even more."

She led him down to the beach. It was not totally dark. The light in the sky or ceiling that had originally led Johann to the island always shone when the artificial daylight was gone, providing illumination roughly equivalent to light from a half-moon.

"So what should I sing for you tonight, Brother Johann?" Sister Beatrice said merrily as they walked along the sand hand in hand. "You've been such a good sport about everything, I feel I owe you at least one request."

"Do you know all the songs from *The Phantom of the Opera?*" he said, remembering her medley soon after they and their ex-Valhalla colleagues had all been gobbled up by the great extraterrestrial sphere.

"Certainly everything that Christine sings," Beatrice replied. "I played that part for three weeks at the Minneapolis Summer Festival in thirty-six."

"Then I'd like to hear 'All I Ask of You,' " Johann said.

"It's a duet in the show, I'm sure you remember. Do you want me to sing for both Raoul and Christine?" she said. "Otherwise, it wouldn't make much sense."

Johann nodded. Sister Beatrice let go of his hand and bounded out in front of Johann on the sand. She was wearing a one piece, white jumpsuit with red stripes on the shoulders. She turned, smiling, and began to sing.

"No more talk of darkness, forget these wide-eyed fears; I'm here, nothing can harm you, my words will warm and calm you."

Her voice had never sounded more beautiful to Johann. What he was watching was even better than the fantasies that his mind and heart had been creating during his moments alone ever since he had realized how much he was in love with her. The woman he adored was singing a love song for him.

". . . Say you love me every moment."

I do, Beatrice, I do, Johann thought, *more than I would ever have believed possible.*

As the song continued Johann was swept away by the beauty of the moment. His heartache became so fierce that he could barely breathe, and a flood of tears burst forth from his eyes.

". . . Love me, that's all I ask of you."

He could not say anything when she was finished. Johann stood unmoving in the sand, transfixed, tears running down his cheeks. Sister Beatrice approached him warily.

"Are you all right?" she said after she noticed the tears.

He still could not speak.

"Dear Brother Johann," she said, kissing him lightly on the cheek.

He was awake most of the night arguing with himself. In the early morning, while Sister Beatrice was meditating, he swam several extra kilometers, trying to use up enough nervous energy that he could think through his dilemma with calm, measured thoughts. The extra swim did not help much. As soon as Johann started thinking again about the idea that had taken control of his mind, he became nervous and agitated.

He knew that Beatrice was planning to take a bath after breakfast. He knew also that he wanted to see her naked again. What Johann could not decide was whether he should be sneaky, and watch her bathe from a convenient hiding place, or just boldly walk down to the beach and start a conversation, as if it were a completely normal thing to do.

And what will happen then? he asked himself for the hundredth time. *If she asks me to leave, how can I then violate her trust by watching from behind the rocks?*

But is that any worse, another voice in Johann's head said, *than being a Peeping Tom without her knowing it? Isn't that an even bigger violation of trust?*

Johann had gone through many many scenarios, each with a different outcome. He was so preoccupied with his decision, which he had not yet completely made, that he hardly spoke to Sister Beatrice during breakfast.

She noticed his unusual behavior. "What's wrong, Brother Johann?" she asked. "Are you not feeling well this morning?"

He mumbled something about a stomachache. "It could be those brown cereal grains," Sister Beatrice said. "I'm not sure our digestive systems can handle them after they dry and harden."

Johann continued to eat his breakfast without saying anything. "So what are you going to do while I take a bath?" Beatrice asked innocently.

I'm going to spy on you, he thought instantly, *so that I have more images to drive me crazy in the middle of the night.*

"I don't know," he said. "I might go back to sleep. . . . I swam a long way this morning."

"You really don't look well," she said after studying his face. "I wonder if there are viruses and bacteria in our paradise after all." She leaned over and felt his forehead. "You certainly don't feel as if you have any fever."

My fever is of a different kind, he thought. *One that I don't think you would understand.*

When Sister Beatrice departed, taking with her the soap they had made by heating and cooling a mixture of herbs and thick fluids from some of the plants, Johann plopped down on his mat. *I am not going to move until she returns,* he told himself. *I am stronger than my desire.*

He tried to concentrate on what his next round of experiments with the brown nuts should be, but images of Beatrice kept coming into his mind. After several minutes Johann stood up and left the cave, heading toward the beach where she was bathing.

He crept up noiselessly to a vantage point he had selected the previous afternoon. She was not in her usual spot. In fact, although he could hear Sister Beatrice singing softly to herself, he could not see her at all. Johann left his safe hiding place and moved in the direction of her voice.

She was on the sand on the other side of an unusually tall group of shrubs and bushes that were surrounding a single tree. Using one of the branches of the tree to support himself, Johann tried to lean around the bushes. When he still couldn't see Beatrice, he leaned farther. The branch snapped and broke. Johann fell to the ground.

"You startled me, Brother Johann," he heard Sister Beatrice say a few moments later. She had hastily wrapped a towel around her midsection.

"I was coming to see you," he said, getting to his feet. "I slipped and fell."

Sister Beatrice's eyes surveyed the entire scene, including Johann's imprint on the ground, the shrubs and bushes, and the broken tree branch. Johann felt certain she knew what he had really been doing.

"Brother Johann," she said at length, looking directly into his eyes, "please don't come upon me suddenly like that. Especially when I'm not wearing any clothes. It's an issue of common courtesy."

Johann finished brushing himself off. "I'm sorry, Sister Beatrice," he said. "I'll try to give you more warning in the future."

She turned and walked back onto the beach. "That soap is all over my body and it's starting to itch. I'm going into the water. . . . I guess as long as you're here, you might as well bathe too. The lake is certainly big enough for both of us, and I brought an extra towel."

Sister Beatrice dropped her towel on the sand beside the soap and dashed into the lake. Johann watched her naked body disappear under the water. He took off his clothes and rubbed the sticky soap all over. Johann noticed that Beatrice was looking away from the shore and not paying any attention to him. His heart already pounding furiously, he carefully fixed her location in his mind, took a deep breath, and dove into the water.

Johann swam with powerful strokes, well beneath the surface of the clear water. He could see Beatrice's lovely naked bottom when he was still ten meters away. Johann swam up to her, grabbed her legs, and turned her upside down.

"You sneak," Sister Beatrice said with a laugh, splashing him wildly when she was again standing upright. "I didn't hear you coming."

He splashed her back. Beatrice dove under the water and grabbed his legs, trying to topple him. She was not strong enough. She surfaced right in front of him, her breasts barely underneath the water. Her wooden Michaelite amulet was resting just above the top of her cleavage.

"You're just too damned big, Brother Johann," she said. "It's not a fair fight."

He reached down and kissed her on the lips. To his surprise and delight, she returned his kiss. He opened his mouth a little. Her soft lips parted and their tongues touched, first ever so lightly, and then, as the kiss endured, her tongue began to move about, tickling his, driving him into an uncontrollable desire.

"I love you, Beatrice," he said when their lips separated. "Oh, how I love you." He kissed her wet neck, then her forehead.

"And I love you, Brother Johann," he heard her say just before their lips touched again.

The second kiss was even more passionate than the first. Johann lifted Beatrice out of the water. With one hand on her buttocks, and the other behind her back, he carried her, while they were still kissing, all the way to the beach. She had both her arms around his neck. He laid her gently on the sand and knelt beside her.

Johann removed his lips from hers. His mouth moved quickly down her body to her right nipple, which he caressed softly with his tongue before widening his mouth and engulfing as much of her breast as he could. He had never known such desire. Johann reached down with his powerful arms and forced her legs apart, sliding his body on top of her.

"I can't, Brother Johann," he heard her say. "Please don't."

Johann opened his eyes and saw the face he adored only a few centimeters away. She was frightened. "Please don't," Sister Beatrice repeated entreatingly.

In an instant both of his options flashed through Johann's mind. His exploding desire told him that Beatrice couldn't possibly stop him now, and that she certainly would forgive him eventually. After all, she had enticed him with her kisses. . . .

With enormous willpower, Johann threw himself away from Sister Beatrice and onto the sand beside her. Trembling from the effort, he lay on his back for several seconds. Then he stood up, uttered a long, horrible wail, and dashed at full speed into the water.

10

"It will be better if we talk about
what happened," Sister Beatrice
said that evening near the end of
dinner. "We can't just ignore it."

Johann put his plate of sliced fruit on the ground. "I've already told
you once that I don't want to discuss it," he said sharply. He stood up
and turned his back on Sister Beatrice.

"I don't understand why you're so angry, Brother Johann," she said.
"I have not accused you of forcing yourself upon me, and given the circumstances, I would expect that my right to be upset about the situation—"

"I do not want to have this conversation, Sister Beatrice," Johann
interrupted her. He spun around, pain and frustration showing on his
face. "Certainly not now . . . Maybe not ever."

"But that's childish," she persisted. "How can we not talk about
something so important? Up until now, our friendship has been based on
honesty and trust. If we don't share our feelings about last night . . ."

Johann started walking away from Sister Beatrice and the fire.
"Where are you going, Brother Johann?" she said.

"I don't know," he answered. "Somewhere else, at least until I understand what I am feeling. Someplace where I can't see you, or hear your voice."

She heard his footsteps on the path. "Good night, Brother Johann," she said.

He slept on the beach not far from where the incident had occurred. When he awoke in the morning, Johann went for a very long swim. It was almost the middle of the day by the time he returned to their cave area.

Beatrice was sitting in the cave nearest the fire. For the first time since they had arrived at the island, she was wearing a robe and a headpiece. Johann assumed that she must have made them either the previous night or earlier that morning.

"I'm glad you came back, Brother Johann," she said. "I missed your company. . . . And I was worried about you."

"Thank you, Sister Beatrice," Johann said without emotion.

"Have you had any breakfast?" she asked solicitously. "I completely peeled one of those large green melons, the ones you like so much."

She pushed a plate with the melon slices in his direction. He picked it up without comment and sat down with his back against the rocks.

"I've been doing a lot of thinking, and praying, Brother Johann, because of what happened yesterday," Sister Beatrice said tentatively. "Please don't be offended. I'm not asking you for a discussion—it was wrong of me last night to try to force you to talk about it—but there are some things I would like to say to you, to clear the air, so to speak. . . ."

Johann continued to chew his melon in silence.

Beatrice took a deep breath. "In my heart," she said, "I guess I have known for some time that you were in love with me, and that you desired me physically. I deceived and deluded myself, Brother Johann, by insisting in my open thoughts that you and I were just good friends, like a sister and a brother, and that there was nothing wrong with the flirtatious play that we both enjoyed so much. . . . Yes, Brother Johann, I enjoyed it too. More than I was willing to admit. It was a fantastic ego trip for me to be the object of your adoration."

She stopped, struggling, and looked away from Johann. "The worst part, Brother Johann, is that I tried to deceive God also. In my prayers and communion with Him, I never acknowledged what I thought you were feeling about me, or what I was truly feeling about you. It's obvious why I didn't. Had I suggested, even one time in a prayer, that I thought you found me sexually desirable, or that I could not stop myself from wondering what it would be like to kiss you, then I would have been forced to change my behavior. . . . By not telling God what was really happening between us, I violated His trust, and undermined a relationship with Him that it has taken me years to develop."

Sister Beatrice paused again. When Johann still didn't offer any comment, she continued. "I swore to God last night that henceforth I would tell nothing but the truth, to Him and to you. I promised that I would be alert to my self-deceptions and would set aside time every day to commune with Him about my feelings. As an outward manifestation of my renewed commitment to the vows of the Order of St. Michael, which are responsible for the greatest happiness I have ever known, I also promised Him that I would again wear the robe and headpiece of the order at all times, to remind me, in case I might ever again forget, who and what I am.

"It is now time, Brother Johann," she said with increasing tension in her voice, "for me to tell *you* the truth. I *do* love you, as I told you yesterday, more than I have ever loved another human being except Michael, but I will not abrogate my vows to God because of my love for you. I can now admit to you, to myself, and to God, that I wanted you to kiss me with passion and desire. Yesterday was thrilling, Brother Johann, and very very special to me. But it was wrong. Wrong for both of us. Wrong for me because I have sworn an oath to God to have no sexual encounters of any kind. Wrong for you because my behavior was misleading, and it most certainly confused and frustrated you.

"What happened yesterday will not be repeated. Last night and this morning I apologized to God for my deception, and I asked for His forgiveness and love. I am telling you now, my dear, dear Brother Johann, how sorry I am for any pain that I may have caused you by my earlier actions, and I promise you they will not recur. Please forgive me if you can."

Sister Beatrice smiled and held her hands out to Johann. He stared at her, a blank expression on his face, and then walked away toward the beach.

Their lives changed in many ways. Sister Beatrice was true to her word. Johann never saw her when she was not wearing her habit. She suppressed her playful side, fearful that he might misinterpret any play as flirtation.

Each of them spent more time alone. They continued to have their meals together, beside the fire, but they no longer slept in the same cave. Their conversations had unspoken boundaries, and focused on safe topics such as her sewing, or her experiences as a priestess of the Order of St. Michael, or his botanical investigations.

They no longer swam together in the lake. His morning swims became more therapeutic in nature. Johann would continue to swim until he was so fatigued that he could not feel the dull heartache that was his constant companion. The heartache always increased in intensity each time he was about to see her again.

Sister Beatrice did not sing after dinner. Sometimes, when he would return to the cave area after a trek across the island, Johann would hear her singing to herself. Usually the songs were religious. Nevertheless, it was many days before he could hear Beatrice singing anything without feeling a painful contraction in his chest.

In time a numbness replaced Johann's heartache. Beatrice no longer appeared in all his dreams. He still had no enthusiasm, however, for anything else in his life. Not even when he discovered that the worms were somehow a part of the brown nuts, and formed naturally inside the shells, without any external intervention, did he feel real excitement. His swims, his hikes, and even his scientific experiments were only planned diversions. At least as long as he was engaged in one of those activities, Johann did not torture himself too much with thoughts about his unfulfilled love.

"I'm becoming very worried about you, Brother Johann," Sister Beatrice said cautiously one evening after they had finished dinner. "You have not been yourself for a long time. . . . At least not the Johann I thought I knew."

Johann stared at her for several seconds before replying. "How perceptive of you, Sister Beatrice," he then said sarcastically. "Perhaps you're also able to identify the cause of my affliction?"

The anger in his response was not hidden. "Goodness, Brother Johann," she said, clearly distressed, "do you still dislike me so much? Even after all this time? Will you never be able to forgive me?"

He looked away, struggling with his emotions. "I do not dislike you," he managed eventually to say. "But I have not been able to forget the Sister Beatrice who was with me when we first came to this island. . . . Those were very happy days for me."

Johann was surprised to hear his own words. He had never acknowledged his sense of loss before, not even to himself.

"That was not the real Sister Beatrice," she said, choosing her words carefully. "The woman who flirted with you was someone else, a hybrid of a Minnesota teenager and a priestess paying lip service to her sacred vows. I'm sorry, Brother Johann, but that person will not return, no matter how much you want—"

"Why not, Sister Beatrice?" Johann said, standing up suddenly. "Why won't she return?" He was nearly shouting. "It was *that* Beatrice I loved, not this pious, self-satisfied old woman who is afraid even to laugh. . . . Oh, God," he said, raising his arms toward the sky, "this is so stupid, so fucking stupid."

He stopped for a moment and then moved abruptly toward her. "Has it ever occurred to you that those vows of yours are now absolutely meaningless? Beatrice, you and I are stranded on an island in the middle of an alien spaceship. No sane person would continue to cling to ridiculous religious vows made years ago on Earth. . . . If you really love me, as you have indicated, then we should be living here as lovers, as husband and wife, enjoying each other in every way, instead of—"

"You are very wrong, Brother Johann," Sister Beatrice interrupted him with an emotional outburst of her own. "I *do* love you, as a woman loves a man. That's why I wanted to kiss you. That's why I deceived both God and myself. . . . It has not been easy for me. I put my soul in jeopardy because of my love for you."

She stopped a moment and lowered her voice. "I love you at this very moment, Brother Johann, and it distresses me terribly to see how much pain I have caused you. However, I made a sacred pledge years ago, a pledge that included a vow of chastity. . . . I made that pledge to God, Brother Johann, not to another human being, and not to a church. I swore to refrain from sex for the rest of my life, and I did not qualify my oath in any way. I did not ask to be excused from my vow if I was no longer on the planet Earth, or if I found someone, like you, who was the epitome of the men in my adolescent fantasies.

"Whether you believe it or not, where we are now is still part of God's creation. We may not know what is happening to us, but He does. My vow is every bit as meaningful here as it was on Earth, maybe more so, because it is now more difficult for me to honor my oath."

Johann had started to laugh. Sister Beatrice looked at him quizzically. "This is crazy," he said to her. "I can't fight you and God both. I'm giving up, as of this moment. . . . That's *my* vow, Sister Beatrice, and I intend to live by it."

It was not that easy, of course. But Johann told himself, whenever he felt that he had chosen an impossible course, that the benefits of his new life far outweighed the disadvantages. Sister Beatrice was friendlier. They spent more time together. There were occasional moments when it was difficult for him to contain his physical desire, but for the most part he accepted his new role as a fond brother.

He was not at all unhappy with his life. Beatrice was not so solemn and so guarded. Their conversations were lively, and sprinkled with humor. She sometimes sang religious songs after dinner. At least the pleasure of hearing her magnificent voice was not proscribed. Johann's two favorites, which he requested over and over, were "Ave Maria" and "Amazing Grace." He almost convinced himself that he could now enjoy her singing even more, because he was not distracted by sexual thoughts.

Sister Beatrice invited Johann to sleep beside her again, in the cave closest to the fire. He declined her invitation, without giving any explanation. It was during his solitary night hours that Johann loosened up the rigid reins he held on his desires. He allowed himself to masturbate, although he often felt guilty afterward. Always Beatrice was his partner in his sexual fantasies.

Late one afternoon, when the artificial daylight was almost gone, Johann and Beatrice were standing on the beach, arguing gently about how long it had been since they had first arrived on the island. She said that it was just under a hundred days, explaining that as a woman, she had nearly perfect ways of measuring the passage of time without keeping a calendar. Johann insisted that the actual duration was closer to a hundred and twenty days. He suggested to Sister Beatrice that the combination of low gravity and an unusual diet might have caused a significant change in her biological clock.

Johann was carefully justifying his calculation when he saw Sister Beatrice's eyes suddenly widen. "Well, I'll be . . . Brother Johann," she said. "We have a visitor."

He spun around and looked in the direction she was pointing. Down the beach, three meters or so above the ground, a white ribbon of sparkling particles was flying in their direction. Johann felt a surge of fear and apprehension. He had forgotten what a spellbinding sight the ribbons were. Sister Beatrice stared fixedly at the ribbon as it flew into their vicinity and then hovered, ten meters away, dancing and twisting at its ends.

As always, Johann found himself staring at the thousands of individual particles inside the illuminated structure of the ribbon. They drifted from side to side, apparently randomly, always reversing direction when they encountered the edge of the formation.

The ribbon moved away from the beach, toward the cave area. Johann and Sister Beatrice followed. The ribbon entered the darkest cave of all, the one most shielded from the fire and the night light in the sky, and began to dance against the rock wall. Once Johann and Sister Beatrice were both inside the cave as well, their visitor suddenly split itself into two parts, continuing to dance as each half slowly transformed its shape. One of the bright ribbons became what was unmistakably a naked Johann. The other changed into an eerily accurate, glowing white representation of Sister Beatrice without her robe and headpiece.

At first the new particle formations, which were roughly half scale, perfect in comparative size, and anatomically correct, simply hovered in the cave against the wall, allowing their human observers to recover from the shock of witnessing the unusual transformations. Later, the two glowing figures turned and faced each other. The particle Johann bent down and passionately kissed the Sister Beatrice. She returned the kiss with her arms around his neck. He lifted her, his arousal showing, and pulled her against his body. She wrapped her legs around his buttocks and began moving slowly up and down. Locked in this erotic embrace, the two white particle figures twisted slowly around, showing Johann and Sister Beatrice a full three-hundred-and-sixty-degree view.

"Incredible," she said softly. "And absolutely beautiful."

Johann, too, was struck by the aesthetic beauty of what they were seeing, but his primary feeling was a raw and powerful sexual desire. It took a monumental amount of self-control for him not to kiss Beatrice at that very moment.

The two figures in front of the cave wall merged and became a ribbon again a few seconds after the full turn was completed. Moments later it flew over Johann and Sister Beatrice's heads, out into the darkness.

To Johann, the meaning of the visit from the ribbon was obvious. The aliens, or whoever it was that was responsible for the island and their presence on it, were expecting them to mate. No other explanation made any sense.

Sister Beatrice did not agree with his interpretation. She readily admitted that she was not certain why the ribbon had come, but couldn't part of the purpose have been to show them they were being carefully watched? Or maybe to remind her that she had violated the spirit of her oath of chastity? Or some other reason that they couldn't begin to fathom?

Johann became increasingly frustrated as they talked through dinner and into the night. Sister Beatrice stubbornly refused to accept Johann's explanation of the apparition. "What is it with you, Sister Beatrice?" Johann said at length. "Do you have so much invested in your precious chastity that you can no longer think straight? What can I say that will possibly convince you that our hosts think we should become lovers?"

"Brother Johann," she replied, "I have listened carefully to everything you have said, but I have not changed my mind. I still have doubts about the purpose of the ribbon's visit. And I cannot, in good conscience, abrogate my oath of chastity as long as I have a shred of doubt. Furthermore, I must admit that I am somewhat dismayed by your aggressiveness on this subject. I am starting to believe that you are not nearly as accepting of our situation as you have led me to think."

"Crap, Sister Beatrice," Johann said. "This whole discussion has been useless from the beginning. It's absolutely clear why the ribbon came, whether you can see it or not. The aliens think our love-without-sex relationship is absurd."

"Brother Johann," she said angrily, "your attitude has become both patronizing and demeaning. I find it totally unacceptable. . . . And by the way, if love without sex is absurd, how would you classify sex without love? Or is that a different situation altogether?"

He glared at her. "What are you talking about *now*, Sister?"

"I have never brought it up before, Brother Johann, out of respect for your feelings," she said. "But you have never mentioned it either, not once in all this time we've been together. . . . Your reaction during our visit to that brothel in Mutchville was a tacit admission, in my opinion, that we were replaying a scene from your earlier life. If you can ridicule me about love without sex, then it seems only fair that I can confront you about sex without love."

Beatrice had never seen him so angry. Johann's face turned red, and he started to snarl. With great effort, he backed away. "I'm going to leave you now, Sister Beatrice," Johann said, his voice charged with emotion. "Before I say or do something I will regret."

He turned and ran away from Beatrice and the fire. When he was gone, she stared out into the dark for almost a minute.

Johann returned the next afternoon. He could not conceive of living by himself on the other side of the island. The idea of swimming across the lake, to discover what he might find, did cross his mind, but he dismissed it as foolish.

He had spent most of the morning trying to analyze his feelings for Sister Beatrice. Johann had finally admitted to himself that it was unlikely he would ever be able to suppress completely his physical desire for her. But he had also acknowledged that sharing a life with her, in a brother-sister relationship, was not exactly a terrible hardship.

Sister Beatrice apologized profusely when Johann appeared. In his presence she castigated herself for needing to be right, for arguing unfairly, and for losing her temper. She also reasserted her love for him and promised never again to behave the way she had the day before.

After ten days the contretemps was forgotten. Johann and Beatrice settled back into their established routine. Slowly but surely even Johann became more or less content with the situation. *After all*, he told himself, *there are far worse fates than mine. There is only one element missing from my life.*

They were both startled when a second ribbon appeared one morning just after breakfast. The ribbon was agitated, dancing and twisting about, until Johann and Sister Beatrice started following it along the path toward the mountain peak in the center of the island. It zoomed quickly in front of them, urging them to hurry. When they reached the top of the mountain, the ribbon flew off toward the opposite side of the island.

"Now, what do you suppose that was all about?" Johann asked as they were catching their breath.

"I have no idea," Sister Beatrice said. "Look, the ribbon is already to the edge of the island. It's heading out over the lake."

They both saw the floating object at the same time. The ribbon was several hundred meters offshore, hovering over whatever it was that was floating on the water.

"Can you see what it is?" Johann asked.

"No," said Beatrice, "but my guess is we're supposed to find out."

They hurried down the path, reaching the beach not far from the other set of caves. They could still see the ribbon hovering over the water. Johann plunged into the lake and started swimming in that direction. When he was about twenty meters away, he saw that the object was a man, either dead or unconscious, partially sprawled across a broad, flat piece of driftwood.

The ribbon flew away as Johann approached the target. He swam around to where he could see the man's battered face. It was Yasin al-Kharif.

I t was not until the third day after
they found Yasin that Sister Beatrice slept for more than an hour
at a time. Only then was she able to convince herself that their visitor was
going to survive without her constant care and attention. Yasin still looked
wretched. His eyes were no longer swollen shut, and he had stopped
coughing up blood, but his face was still badly bruised and discolored.

By the third day Sister Beatrice and Johann had set, bandaged, and
rendered immobile Yasin's broken leg. They had wrapped his chest to
ease the pain of his suspected broken ribs. She had patiently cleaned and
doctored all his open wounds and had spent many hours spooning minuscule amounts of water, warm soup, and juice into his mouth.

It still hurt Yasin to part his lips. He had not yet said anything, but
his expressive eyes indicated his pain every time any part of his body
moved. The same eyes also showed what Sister Beatrice interpreted as
gratitude whenever she would feed him or minister to his wounds.

They set up headquarters in the largest of the caves on the opposite
side of the island. Johann brought sleeping mats, pillows, and what they
needed for medical supplies from the nearby storehouse. While Sister

Beatrice was keeping her vigil at Yasin's side, Johann searched the island for the foods and medicinal plants she requested. Sometimes he even crossed the island to their caves on the other side to obtain a particular special item.

Beatrice was totally obsessed with Yasin's recovery. She talked about nothing but his health. She told Johann of every sound, movement, and grimace that their patient made. Her prayers were full of requests for God to help and guide them in their task of caring for their injured comrade.

She refused to speculate about what might have happened to Yasin. On the second day after they found Yasin, when Johann commented that Yasin looked as if he had received "a thousand blows," Beatrice responded harshly.

"Our task here, Brother Johann," she said, "is to do our utmost to ensure that Yasin will heal completely. *How* he came to be injured is irrelevant to what we are doing."

Johann watched Sister Beatrice's single-minded devotion to Yasin with a mixture of awe and inchoate jealousy. For himself, he could not imagine ever being so dedicated to the health and well-being of another person. At one point he lightly criticized her for not sleeping enough. He suggested that Yasin might benefit more from her care if she was rested, and able to think more clearly. Sister Beatrice told Johann to mind his own business.

After a week Johann was aware that he was feeling lonely, and sorely missing the rambling fireside conversations with Sister Beatrice that he enjoyed so much. He chose not to say anything to her about his feelings, however, not just because he felt guilty about his selfishness, but also because at some level he understood that caring for Yasin was an integral part of Sister Beatrice's nature.

Johann already knew for certain that he was not happy about Yasin's arrival. To say that he was anxious about their collective future would have been an understatement. He did not relish the prospect of sharing his Beatrice with any man, and certainly not with someone like Yasin.

At Yasin's request they had moved him over to where he could lean against the wall of the cave. He was propped up on both sides by pillows. The reflected firelight kept the cave from being in total darkness.

"I know," he said, after thanking them for their care while moving him, "that both of you must be wondering why I was in such terrible shape when you found me. During these many days that I have been recuperating, I've been thinking about what happened. . . . I'm not sure I can explain it in a way that makes any sense, even to me."

Yasin paused. Sister Beatrice urged him to conserve his strength, saying that there would be plenty of time later for conversation.

"No, no," Yasin said, lifting to his lips a cup of hot, herbal tea mixed with berry juice, "now is as good a time as ever. I want to tell the story and be done with it. Besides," he said, forcing a smile and then wincing from the pain, "I know Ace Eberhardt very well. He needs to have everything explained. That's his nature."

Sister Beatrice gave Johann a quick, curious look. "It's easiest if I start at the beginning, when the two of you left the rest of us in that first room in the sphere," Yasin said. "We spent another two days there. Then a pair of the snowmen showed up and herded us up the long helical slide behind one of those glowing ribbons. When we reached the top, we walked for what seemed like forever until we came to the edge of a lake.

"We slept on mats that had been laid out beside the lake. In the morning, we followed the ribbon along the shore for a kilometer or two. . . . We came upon a large boat that was obviously waiting for us. We boarded it and set out across the lake, following the ribbon. After three or four hours of sailing in the near-darkness, we reached the other side. The ribbon then guided us up a long path surrounded on both sides by what appeared to be tall trees.

"Several of the women in our group—especially the Japanese nurse, who I believe completely lost her wits sometime after we left Mars—became increasingly frantic during this last march. At one point Satoko sat down on the path and refused to move. We all stood around nervously for over an hour until a snowman appeared out of the woods and picked her up with two of its peculiar arms. It then carried her, screaming hysterically, along the path behind the ribbon.

"Eventually we reached our destination, a clearing in the forest, where five white conical structures, like American Indian tepees, were arranged in a circle around a large, continuous fire that seemed to be rising out of the ground. The snowman and the ribbon then departed."

Yasin stopped and took a drink of his tea. Johann and Sister Beatrice were both listening attentively.

"Two of the five tepees were obviously meant to be toilets. They had nothing inside except deep holes in the middle. The other three tepees each contained three mats, with very little room between any of them. There were also three—I guess 'boxes' would be the best descriptive word—in the tepees. They were little rectangular solids, with tops, in which we could store our personal effects."

Yasin laughed. "You would not have believed all the fuss that ensued. How were we going to divide ourselves up into three groups to share the tepees? We argued the issue for about an hour, standing in the dark around the fire. There was no split that pleased everybody. Finally your friend Sister Vivien, who was exasperated by the whole discussion, went into one of the conical structures and dragged out a sleeping mat. 'I'll sleep out here,' she said. 'That ought to make it easier to come to some kind of an arrangement.'

"I followed her lead, pulling a mat out of one of the other tepees. Fernando and Satoko then occupied one of the two mat houses, Anna and Sister Nuba the other. That left the two male Michaelite priests and Kwame Hassan to share the third tepee."

Yasin now shook his head. "During that first week we must have looked absurd to the aliens who were watching us. We were hopelessly disorganized. It was apparent to me immediately that we had been placed in a more or less permanent living situation. When our first daylight came, and we began to explore, we found a stream of running water, another group of conical houses stuffed with supplies, and plenty of things to eat in the immediate vicinity. Our 'village,' as we called it, was near the center of a twenty-five-square-kilometer area that was bounded on three sides by the lake, and on the fourth by a deep chasm, or canyon, the bottom of which was in total darkness."

"Was there any gravity where you were?" Johann asked. "Or were you still weightless?"

"Good question, Ace," Yasin replied. "Yes, a little, about one tenth of a g, I would guess . . . Hassan and I both noticed it first after we crossed the lake."

"So our sphere must be spinning," Johann said.

Yasin shrugged and grinned. "Not necessarily. Who knows what kind of technological magic these guys may have developed. They may even have local gravity machines. Anyway, we don't want to bore Sister Beatrice with our engineering talk."

"It might surprise you to know, Mr. al-Kharif," she said, "that I took a full year of physics at the university."

"Good for you, Sister," Yasin said, in a condescending tone. "Ace and I will call on you if we need any help distinguishing leptons from muons. . . . Going back to the story, it was not long before the group decided that we needed some better method of organizing ourselves. We elected Kwame Hassan as our chief, with Sister Vivien as his deputy. That was the first of our many mistakes.

"Hassan took his election very seriously. He thought it gave him authority to tell everybody what to do. On the second day after he was elected, he allocated the community responsibilities among the group. I didn't mind that so much, even though most of my tasks involved working with Ravi and José. . . . No offense, Sister, but neither of those two have had an original idea since puberty. However, Hassan's attitude really pissed me off. He began monitoring everyone's tasks *and* behavior, and giving us performance evaluations. Really. Can you believe it? He became really angry when I told him I didn't give a shit what he thought."

Yasin stopped abruptly, his brow furrowed. "This is too much detail," he said, after thinking for several seconds. "I'm going to quickly summarize the next hundred days. . . . Hassan and Sister Vivien became lovers and anointed themselves as our king and queen. Ravi and José moved out of their tepee so that the royal pair could use it as their castle. All kinds of unnecessary rules were established, with stupid punishments for breaking them. I was placed in solitary confinement in one of the toilet tepees, for example, and guarded by that Mexican thug Gomez for an entire day for refusing an order from Sister Vivien and calling her a bitch.

"Hassan did none of the ordinary work, nor did he or his queen help when Ravi, José, and I built a large and comfortable house that could accommodate everyone. Meanwhile Satoko's mental condition continued to deteriorate, as much from the possessiveness of Gomez as anything. . . . I tried to be her friend, and to help her, but Fernando warned me to stay away from her."

A look of strong, unidentifiable emotion passed over Yasin's face. "Satoko had been excused from all regular duties," he said. "That often left her alone during the day in the village. For some time she had been signaling to me that she needed to see me in private. One morning, while everyone was out doing his allocated task, I doubled back to the village to talk to her.

"Satoko was delighted to see me. She greeted me with a long passionate kiss and asked me if I would come inside her tepee and have sex with her. When I declined, saying that I had only come back to see if I could help her in any way, Satoko thanked me effusively and began telling me about the red demons that flew out of the canyon to rape her whenever she was in the village alone. When I expressed some doubt about her tale, she insisted that I accompany her, that very minute, to the meadow beside the wall of the canyon.

"As we walked down the path toward the canyon, Satoko started tearing her clothes off, saying that she wanted to be ready for the demons. She then bolted into the meadow, naked and screaming at the top of her lungs. I was afraid she was going to jump into the canyon. I tackled her and held her on the ground. She continued to scream.

"Hassan and Gomez burst into the meadow from another direction, took one look at the scene, and set upon me without asking any questions. I tried to defend myself, but they were much too large for me. They struck me over and over with their fists, until I was nearly unconscious. Then Gomez picked me up and hurled me into the canyon.

"It seemed as if I were falling forever. Somewhere during the fall I lost consciousness. The next thing I remember was hearing your soothing voice, Sister Beatrice."

She had tears on her cheeks. "I'm so sorry, Yasin," she said. She touched his hands. "I had no idea it was so terrible."

Johann was in a gigantic turmoil. As soon as he was certain that Yasin was asleep, he crawled quietly across the cave to where Sister Beatrice was sleeping.

"Wake up," he whispered in her ear several times. When she finally stirred and opened her eyes, he said softly, "I must talk to you," and put his finger to his lips.

She followed him out of the cave and down the path to the beach. "What is it, Brother Johann?" she said. "What's the matter?"

Johann could not contain himself. "That story Yasin told before dinner," he said, "is almost certainly the biggest pile of bullshit you have ever heard in your entire life. And you fell for it, hook, line, and sinker."

Sister Beatrice eyed him curiously. "Calm down, Brother Johann," she said. "You are very upset. . . . And I don't understand why."

"Yasin al-Kharif is a pathological liar," Johann shouted. "And a sexual sociopath as well. You should see his record. He was convicted of sexual assault *five* times on Earth and Mars. He even attacked a member of my staff at Valhalla. It's virtually certain, knowing Kwame Hassan and Fernando Gomez as I do, that Yasin was trying to rape Satoko when they caught him."

For several seconds Beatrice said nothing. "Brother Johann," she finally said, "Yasin has gone through a traumatic experience, whatever the reason. Do you doubt that he was beaten and thrown over the cliff, in more or less the way that he described?"

"That part was probably true," Johann said. "It may have been the only truth in his story. But he probably deserved his fate. I don't believe for a minute—"

"You believe there are justifiable reasons, Brother Johann," she interrupted, "for one human being to kill another? Did I hear you correctly?"

"No, no . . . not except under very unusual circumstances," Johann said. "But I also don't think that a rapist deserves much sympathy."

Again Sister Beatrice was quiet. "Is that why you're so upset, Brother Johann?" she said at length. "Because I showed some sympathy for Yasin?"

"Yes . . . yes, I guess so," Johann said slowly.

"Brother Johann," Sister Beatrice then said, "it is my duty as a priestess of the Order of St. Michael to have compassion for all my fellow human beings, no matter what terrible deeds they may have committed. I don't know if it makes you feel any better, but my sympathy for Yasin has nothing to do with whether or not I believe his story. Can you understand that?"

Johann stared at her in silence. "Is there anything else, Brother Johann?" she asked.

Yes, there is, he thought without saying anything. *But I'm not certain I can tell you yet.*

"Then can I go back to bed now?" Sister Beatrice said at length. "I am very tired."

She turned to walk back to the cave. "There is something else," Johann said, feeling suddenly uncertain.

"What is it?" Beatrice asked. She had turned around.

"I'm convinced that Yasin was purposely sent here by the aliens or angels," Johann said. "Because we did nothing in response to the sexual apparition in the cave."

Sister Beatrice stared at him for a long time. "I thought we had finished with that topic," she said wearily. "I seem to recall an agreement not to—"

"But that was before Yasin showed up," he interrupted. "Can't you see?" he said earnestly. "It can't be just coincidence that he arrived so soon after the apparition. . . . If we were meant to mate, and couldn't or wouldn't follow their explicit instructions, then the appearance of another man might catalyze our behavior, or perhaps he even—" Johann stopped.

Sister Beatrice frowned and her eyes showed anger. "I don't like what you're suggesting at all, Brother Johann. God's angels would certainly not be that interested in our sexual behavior. . . . I am going to terminate this conversation now and return to my mat, before I become any angrier."

That won't change my opinion, Johann said to himself as he watched her walk away. *Or the fact that it was not a coincidence.*

12

Yasin's leg was slow to heal. Even a month later it was too early to remove the makeshift splint. But his facial bruises and his ribs had mended by that time, and he was generally in good spirits.

The three of them were still living on the opposite side of the island. They ate dinner around the fire in the plaza not far from their cave. Often after their meal they would talk until it was time for bed. Yasin would dominate these conversations with his assertive personality and his lightning-quick intelligence.

Yasin had not developed his own personal explanation for either the gigantic sphere in which they were living or the hatbox spacecraft that had rescued them from Mars. When he suggested that the two vehicles might have unrelated origins, and that different alien species, with no knowledge of one another, might be responsible for them, Johann and Sister Beatrice looked at each other in astonishment.

"Why do you think there must necessarily be some coordinated plan or purpose behind all this, Ace?" Yasin said with his characteristic grin. "Just because all the bizarre creatures we have seen share this red-

and-white motif? Your attitude is decidedly unenlightened. Look at what we have now learned about nature. Chaos is the governing principle, not the orderly design of some careful master planner. Even the simplest phenomena, like the weather, defy our attempts to dominate them with our mathematical models. Why would you think that our puny minds could possibly comprehend these creatures . . . ?"

Yasin was not concerned about whether their hosts were aliens or angels, or if they were friendly or hostile. In fact, after their second conversation on the subject, he told Johann and Sister Beatrice that he considered discussions about their spacecraft and its creators as nothing more than "intellectual masturbation." He preferred to talk about other things.

Yasin was a natural storyteller. Johann doubted if all the tales he told of his youth were true, but he agreed with Sister Beatrice that Yasin's images of life in the teeming Egyptian city of Alexandria and the sterile, fundamentalist Islamic stronghold of Medina were both provocative and fascinating.

Yasin was surprisingly candid about his childhood and adolescence. He had lived in Alexandria until he was thirteen. During that period Yasin's father, a native of Saudi Arabia, was a professor of Islamic history at the University of Alexandria. His mother's older brother had been one of Professor al-Kharif's first graduate students.

Yasin's mother, as intelligent as she was beautiful, had married the handsome professor when she was only seventeen. She had immediately become pregnant with Yasin, and three other children had quickly followed. Yasin's early years were as full of the daily prayers, the quotations from the Koran, and the other manifestations of Islamic religious devotion as if he had been raised in one of the cities of Saudi Arabia. Outside his Islamic enclave, however, cosmopolitan Alexandria offered many distractions to the young and curious boy. Whenever he could, he escaped into the excitement of the city, obtaining a diverse street education to complement his outstanding academic record at the Islamic school.

When he was almost twelve, Yasin heard for the first time his mother's protests about the restrictions placed upon her by both her husband and his fundamentalist interpretation of their religion. The resulting divorce was inevitable. One evening soon after his thirteenth birthday, Yasin's father told him to gather up his belongings and to help his siblings pack all their things. With Yasin's mother softly weeping in the living room of their Alexandrian home, Professor al-Kharif took his property, including the four children, and departed for Medina, in his native land of Saudi Arabia. Neither Yasin nor any of his brothers or sisters ever saw their mother again.

Yasin definitely took his father's point of view in this story. He didn't mourn for his lost mother. In fact, he spoke as if she had transgressed against the marriage, and his father's actions had been justified by her inappropriate behavior.

"It is impossible for us," Sister Beatrice said to Johann one morning when they met on the beach after his swim and her meditation, "to comprehend the cultural gulf that separates us from Yasin. Our lives have been so fundamentally different. He has no regard for women because he has been taught since birth that women exist only to serve men. His father and his strict religious training have brainwashed him."

" 'No regard' is not strong enough to describe Yasin's attitude toward women," Johann said. " 'Disdain' would be a better word. . . . You don't know him as I do. Remember, I worked with Yasin for eighteen months. He considers women useful only as sexual partners, or as mothers for the children of men."

"But how could he feel otherwise, Brother Johann?" Sister Beatrice said. "His mother disappeared from his life at a crucial time in his development, and in Yasin's opinion it was *her* fault that he lost both the security of his family and the rich, exciting Alexandrian life that he loved. It's only natural—"

"I'm sorry, Sister Beatrice," Johann interrupted gently, "but I can't accept that either Yasin's attitude, or his antisocial behavior, can somehow be justified by the emotional deprivation of his childhood and adolescence. I have heard similar arguments explaining criminal behavior many times and I've never been able to swallow them.

"Perhaps when he was still a young man, Yasin's background should have been a consideration in judging his actions. But not now. Has his adult experience meant nothing? He has lived in England, and even briefly in the United States. Was this obviously brilliant man not able to see that the rest of the world, including most of his Arab and Muslim colleagues, has a much more humane attitude toward women?

"No, Sister Beatrice, I have no sympathy for Yasin. Millions of others have been raised in identical backgrounds and have never been guilty of a single incident of sexual assault. My problem with Yasin is not that he is an Arab. What makes him a pariah to me is that he is an unrepentant rapist. From my point of view he is a confirmed sociopath, and we would be wise to be wary of him."

Sister Beatrice stared at Johann for a long time. "It saddens me, Brother Johann," she said finally, "to realize that you harbor such uncharitable opinions about another human being. Don't you believe that individuals are capable of change, even later in their lives? And if they are not, then doesn't that mean that the human species is itself doomed?"

Johann gazed out at the lake before replying. "Most of the time I am an optimist, Sister Beatrice," he said. "Nothing thrills me more than the human potential for goodness and growth. I have even met some people—and I would put you in that category—that actually live up to that potential. Most, however, do not. Why doesn't each individual human being realize his or her potential? That's the puzzling question.

"I suspect that each of us is indelibly imprinted by our experiences during our development from an embryo to an adult. Much of this imprinting is permanently stored in what might be called 'firmware,' and can only be overwritten in a few rare cases. As we age, this firmware limits us, and prevents the personality changes necessary for us to realize our full potential.

"From my point of view, the utopia you and your Michaelite brethren seek can only be achieved if this imprinting process can be significantly influenced. The set of human beings alive today, for example, couldn't achieve what you call the 'final evolution.' Their firmware would never allow them to accept the selflessness that's required. Only if you can design and monitor the development process of subsequent generations do you have a chance of reaching your stated goal."

The look in Sister Beatrice's eyes was respectful. "Very interesting, Brother Johann," she said. "I certainly do not agree with you that Yasin al-Kharif and others like him are a lost cause and cannot be guided into more constructive living, but my experience has definitely taught me that to change the world we must start with the children. On that point you and the Order of St. Michael are in accord. That's why we focus so much on the very young."

She turned inland and put her arm through Johann's, something that she had not done in a long time. "You have an unusual way of looking at things, Brother Johann," she said. "I still have much to learn from you."

For a few brief moments, as he walked arm in arm with Sister Beatrice up the path toward the caves, the feeling of impending doom that had been Johann's constant companion since Yasin's arrival temporarily disappeared. The foreboding returned, however, when Johann saw Yasin watching them, a leer upon his face, from the top of the flat rock just outside their cave.

"So much of the history they teach in your Western schools is hopelessly inaccurate," Yasin was saying as they finished their dinner. "When I looked at the secondary-school textbooks in both England and the United States, I was absolutely flabbergasted. The cultural bias is astounding."

"What are you talking about?" Sister Beatrice asked.

"To begin with," Yasin said, "there is the implicit suggestion that Western civilization, loosely defined as some sort of historical continuum from Greece through Rome to Victorian England and the twentieth-century United States, is vastly superior to all other civilizations that have ever existed. My father was outraged when I returned to Medina and showed him the world-history book being used in the high schools in Texas. There was virtually no discussion of Islam at all, except where our culture interacted with the history of the Europeans.

"My father and I read that our civilization was characterized by nomadic hordes of ruthless warriors who swept on horseback across North Africa, most of Asia, and Southern Europe during the Dark Ages. There was no mention of the fact that we invented the modern number system, performed the first real astronomical observations, and supplied the words 'algebra,' 'almanac,' and 'chemistry,' among others, to the precious English language. . . . What was written in that textbook was insulting."

There was passion in Yasin's voice. "My father taught a course in comparative history at the University of Medina. It was the best course I ever took, and not just because my father was teaching it. The thesis of the course was very simple. My father taught that all history, from Sumeria up until the emergence of the Asian powers in the middle of the twenty-first century, has essentially been a struggle for supremacy between two racial groups, one European and typified by the Aryan/Teutonic people that settled Scandinavia, England, and Germany, and the other Middle Eastern, the purest strains of which can be found in Arabia and the Levant.

"In his course my father compared the total contributions of the two races to today's modern civilization, and reached the unmistakable conclusion that *our* accomplishments, especially when the Jews are properly counted among the Levantine peoples, far outweigh those of the blond, blue-eyed Nordic types usually given credit for the successes of Western Europe and the United States. . . ."

Yasin would declaim on any subject with very little prompting. History and science were two of his favorite topics. He used a facile mixture of fact and opinion to buttress his conclusions. Sometimes Johann or Sister Beatrice would catch him in a misrepresentation, or factual error, that seemed to undermine what he was saying. But he would remain unwavering in his convictions, as if the major truth he was propounding were not dependent in any way on the supporting facts.

There weren't many outright disputes in the discussions around the fire. Johann was not naturally argumentative in conversation. He preferred to think carefully about what he was hearing before saying very much. Despite her wealth of knowledge, Sister Beatrice was gracious to a fault. As a result, many of Yasin's proclamations, some of which both Johann and Sister Beatrice thought to be bizarre, or even ludicrous, went unchallenged.

One evening, however, just two days after Yasin's splint was re-

moved and he began to move about freely, the evening discussion centered on religion. At issue was the Islamic tenet that the use of force, and
even the killing of nonbelievers, if necessary, was an acceptable way to
spread the word of the prophet. Yasin became angry and defensive when
Sister Beatrice continued to ask probing questions and to cite historical
facts that did not support his point of view.

"Yes, yes, Sister, what you are saying is true," Yasin said at one
point, "Muhammad did sanction, on a few occasions, the killing of cap-
tives after a battle between his followers and his opponents. But you have
taken the historical events out of context again. Muhammad believed he
had no choice. He was in desperate straits. The word of God had to be
defended. His opponents were engaged in a concerted attempt to destroy
him utterly, and any show of mercy would have been considered a sign of
weakness."

"Unless my knowledge of history is incorrect, Yasin," Sister Beatrice
said, "Muhammad did not just 'sanction' massacres 'on a few occasions.'
Often after a battle the conquered were slaughtered mercilessly. And
wasn't it Muhammad himself who made armed conflict one of the cornerstones of Islam? Did he not say that the quickest means of entering
paradise was martyrdom in a battle with infidels? Are there not passages
in the Koran exhorting the faithful—"

"Hold it a minute, Sister," Yasin interrupted imperiously, showing a
flash of anger. "There's just no way that either of you can appreciate how
the individual elements of Islam are woven into the overall fabric of the
religion. You are attacking one small component of our belief, without any
understanding of the structure into which it all fits."

Yasin took a deep breath before continuing. The tone in his voice
was that of an adult talking to young children. "One definite problem in
this discussion is that the only religion the two of you know anything
about, Christianity, is essentially a feminine religion, extolling compassion, forgiveness, and monogamous marriage, as well as the sanctity of
human life. These are virtues generally embraced by women.

"Islam, by contrast, is a masculine religion, with its own, different
set of virtues. Spreading the faith through armed conflict, polygamy for
the general benefit of the society, and a defining role for women as helpmates for men may be distasteful to you, but that does not make them
wrong. What is important here is not what you or I or any specific human
being thinks religion should be, but what Allah intended for those who
are to worship Him. We accept that both Christ and Muhammad were
His prophets, but only Muhammad, the true Messenger of God, heard
Allah completely and correctly."

"Are you suggesting, Yasin," Sister Beatrice said, an edge in her
voice, "that of the three of us, only *you* are able to be objective about

both Islam and Christianity? I remind you that I have made religion my life study, and may well know as much about the doctrine, history, and practices of Islam as you do."

"But you are both a woman *and* a Christian," Yasin said, glancing over at Johann with a superior smirk on his face. "It's unlikely that any amount of study would allow you to look at Islam without the prejudices that accompany your sex and religion."

Sister Beatrice rose abruptly. She was visibly shaken. "Good night, Yasin," she said. "I am going to bed before I become any angrier. . . . Not since I was a teenager has anyone purposely tried to make me feel so insignificant."

She walked away from the fire. Yasin looked at Johann again and shrugged. Johann jumped up and followed Sister Beatrice into the cave.

Johann did not sleep much that night. The argument between Sister Beatrice and Yasin had heightened his sense of foreboding. Now that Yasin was healed, and no longer needed Beatrice to care for him, Johann feared that his disregard for her would become increasingly more obvious. There did not seem to be any way to avoid more clashes in the future.

In his last brief conversation with Sister Beatrice before she had lain down on her mat, Johann had sensed, for the first time, that even she was beginning to have doubts that the three of them could live in harmony in their island paradise. *There may come a day*, Johann thought, *when she will wish that she had not nursed Yasin back to health so diligently.*

13

Once Yasin was healthy, his attitude toward Sister Beatrice did indeed change. He began by belittling her devotion, including not only her prayers and meditation, but also her wearing of the robe and headpiece of the Order of St. Michael. At first his comments were fairly innocuous, usually in the guise of humor, but as time passed they became more frequent and insulting.

Sister Beatrice did not fight back. She would not even allow herself to mention that Yasin was far from rigorous in his observation of the rules of Islam. She also entreated Johann not to intercede. Although she admitted to Johann that she was hurt by Yasin's disdain, her bigger concern was finding some way for the three of them to live together in harmony.

Yasin moved into his own cave, ostensibly so that he could have more privacy, leaving Johann and Sister Beatrice to share the large cave near the fire. Yasin spent his days in and around the storehouse, tinkering with the supplies and building whatever he thought might be needed. Johann and Beatrice had to admit that both the wheelbarrow and the large wagon Yasin constructed were extremely useful.

Yasin always showed up promptly for meals, correctly assuming that

Johann and Sister Beatrice would include enough food for him in their dinner preparations. One night he announced, with great fanfare, that he had decided to design and build a house on the beach for the three of them. When neither Johann nor Beatrice showed much interest, Yasin sulked for the rest of the evening.

The nighttime discussions around the fire ceased altogether after another argument in which Yasin made it clear that he thought Sister Beatrice's opinions were completely meaningless. Johann upbraided him for his arrogance, and some angry words were exchanged, but Beatrice managed to effect a reconciliation between the two men by suppressing her own feelings.

She started meditating after dinner as well as in the early morning. Clearly troubled by her inability to reach a compromise with Yasin that allowed her even a modicum of self-respect, Sister Beatrice turned to prayer and introspection for comfort. She tried gamely to put on a happy face when she was around either or both of the men, but Johann could tell that it was only an act. Not even singing consoled her. One evening after dinner, when the three of them had had an unusually cordial conversation, Johann asked her if she would sing a few songs for them. In the middle of her second song, she suddenly stopped and retreated to the cave. She told Johann later that Yasin had been looking at her in an "unseemly" way while she was singing.

Johann had suggested to Yasin that he should pitch in and help with the gathering of their food, but Yasin had dismissed the activity as "woman's work." Johann was therefore pleasantly surprised one morning when Yasin volunteered to accompany him on his twice-weekly trip to obtain food. Sister Beatrice was encouraged, telling Johann that this was the "first real sign" of Yasin's willingness to be accommodating. The two men, each carrying one of the large baskets Beatrice had made from the thin wood strips in the storehouse, walked away from the caves together in a relaxed and easy mood.

All morning Yasin seemed genuinely interested in Johann's lessons about harvesting the ripe fruits and berries. He even expressed real admiration when Johann gave him a tour of the farm, a cleared area of several thousand square meters not far from Johann and Beatrice's original caves. On the farm they had planted a dozen or so rows of the principal grains that they had discovered on the island.

"So do you gather the seeds and plant them at regular intervals?" Yasin asked.

"They don't have seeds, at least not in the way that we define them," Johann answered. He bent down next to one particular plant. "Each kind of grain has only one specific part, which, if rooted in the ground, will grow and become a full plant. It took us a long time, and a lot of patient observation, to figure out the critical part for each plant."

Their baskets were nearly full by midday. Yasin acknowledged that he was both tired and hungry. The two men sat on rocks beside one of the larger streams and had a leisurely lunch. They were about three fourths of the way up the mountain. From their vantage point they could see the cave formations where they lived. Beatrice was swimming in the lake not far from the caves.

"She is the strangest woman I have ever met," Yasin said.

Johann smiled. "Sister Beatrice is amazing," he said. "I have never met anyone even remotely like her."

Yasin popped a couple of berries in his mouth and turned toward Johann. "I'm sorry I cramped your style by showing up, Ace," he said with an unusual smile. "You must have really been horny before I moved into my new cave."

Johann gave Yasin a puzzled look. "Excuse me," he said.

"Come on, Ace," Yasin said, a lecherous grin spreading across his face, "I'm not *that* dumb. I've noticed how you and the sister look at each other." He leaned toward Johann. "I'm dying to know if she's a good fuck. Does she moan and thrash about, or is she as uptight during sex as she is the rest of the time?"

Johann was too stunned to reply. At first it was impossible for him to believe that he had properly heard what Yasin had said. Then Johann felt a surge of anger and his face started turning red.

Johann stood up and looked away. Yasin misinterpreted his response. "I bet she's great," he said. "The quiet ones usually are. Once she takes off that abominable robe, I bet she goes completely wild."

"Shut up, Yasin," Johann said, spinning around. His body was trembling with rage.

Yasin saw the anger in Johann's eyes and put his hands up in front of his chest to defend himself. "Simmer down, Ace," he said. "No need to come unglued . . . I was just wondering. You know, here we are, two guys on an island with one bizarre bitch. It's only natural that I—"

"For your information," Johann suddenly blurted without thinking, "Sister Beatrice and I are not lovers. . . . Her religious order requires a vow of chastity and she has remained committed—"

Johann stopped himself. Already he wished that he had not said so much. He picked up his basket. "Let's go," he said, avoiding Yasin's eyes.

Dammit and double dammit, Johann was thinking as he led Yasin rapidly down the path toward the caves. *I do not trust that son of a bitch. I should have let him believe that Beatrice and I are lovers.*

———————

Johann was exasperated. Sister Beatrice would not take his warnings seriously. They were lying on their mats in the cave and whispering back and forth.

"Surely you don't believe, Brother Johann," she said, "that Yasin would try to *force* himself upon me. He has never given the slightest indication. . . ."

Johann's whisper was charged with emotion. "He has been convicted of assaulting *five* women," he said. "God knows how many others he may have attacked. . . . I'm telling you, Sister Beatrice, I saw it in his eyes when he asked me if you were 'a good fuck.' He wants to have sex with you, and would rape you if he thought he could get away with it."

"Brother Johann," she said after a long silence, "isn't it possible that you're overreacting? Or perhaps you're jealous, or feeling guilty, because of what we almost did. You could be transposing what you're feeling to Yasin. . . . I admit that his questions about us were awful, but Yasin is a crude person, and what he said to you is not out of keeping with his nature."

"Spare me the amateur psychology," Johann said sharply. "I know what I saw, and what I heard. If you're such a trusting fool that you choose to ignore what I'm telling you—"

"I don't like it when you call me names, Brother Johann," Beatrice said. "I think it's time to end this conversation. . . . Good night and sweet dreams."

Neither Johann nor Yasin mentioned their discussion again. In the days that followed, Yasin stopped insulting Beatrice so much. He also accompanied Johann on two more food-gathering treks and even made a couple of new, larger baskets to replace the original ones.

Sister Beatrice cited Yasin's improved behavior as evidence of his new, more congenial outlook. Johann admitted that their companion's attitude had apparently changed, but his basic distrust of Yasin remained.

Johann's schedule during this time was completely predictable. Every morning he swam for at least half an hour. Every fifth day he extended his swim and stayed in the water for over an hour. Several weeks later, on a day when he was planning to make an extra-long swim, he had a peculiar, uneasy feeling when he plunged into the lake at dawn.

Usually, when he was breathing while swimming, Johann was not conscious of looking at anything. He would be aware that the island scenery was there when he breathed on one side, and that the lake stretched endlessly into the distance on the other, but he never really looked at anything specific. On this particular morning, however, he found himself searching the island shore while he was breathing on the right side. Over a period of thirty seconds or so, covering half a dozen breaths on each side, Johann was certain he saw Yasin staring at him from the outcropping of rocks above the cave formations.

Johann puzzled about what he had seen as he continued to swim. Yasin was a notorious late sleeper. They hardly ever saw him until just before breakfast, after Johann was finished swimming and Sister Beatrice had completed her morning meditation. Johann looked again at the outcropping. Yasin had gone. Had he imagined that he had seen him? No, he had definitely seen Yasin five or six times. But why was he awake so early? And why was he standing there watching Johann swim?

Johann's debate with himself was over in a couple of strokes. If his fears were meaningless—as they probably were, he told himself—he could always take a longer swim tomorrow. It was compulsive to remain too rigorously tied to his schedule. He turned around and started swimming back toward the caves.

He heard Sister Beatrice yelling when he was still thirty or forty meters out in the lake. Fueled by a burst of adrenaline, Johann surged out of the water, across the beach, and up to the large cave in a matter of seconds.

"Stop, Yasin, stop," Johann heard Sister Beatrice say just before he rounded the corner and entered the front of the cave.

"Relax, Sister," Yasin replied in a strangely calm tone. "This will all be over in a minute."

Yasin was astride Sister Beatrice on her sleeping mat. His left hand was pressing against her chest while his right hand was tugging on her long underwear. Beatrice's robe had been ripped off and was lying beside them. She was flailing with both her free hands, striking Yasin with useless blows.

Johann raced across the cave and grabbed the startled Yasin from behind. Lifting him over his head with superhuman strength, he carried Yasin to the nearest cave wall and hurled the smaller man against it with all his might. Yasin, dazed by the force of the impact, fell on the floor and was momentarily motionless. Johann was upon him in an instant. His rage uncontrollable, he picked Yasin up under the shoulders and began banging him against the wall with terrible force.

Blood began to gush from Yasin's many wounds and from his mouth. His eyes showed that he was about to lose consciousness.

"No, Johann, no," Sister Beatrice was screaming from behind him.

Johann did not know how long her arms had been around his chest, trying to restrain him. He finally let go of Yasin, who collapsed in a heap on
the cave floor. Johann bent down and shouted in Yasin's bloody face.

"If you ever, *ever* touch her again, you are a dead man, Yasin al-
Kharif. Do you understand? A *dead* man!"

Yasin started to say something, but the blood in his mouth made
him cough. Sister Beatrice tried to move around Johann to help him.

"NO," Johann shouted, grabbing her arm fiercely. "You will not
help him. Not after what he tried to do to you."

Sister Beatrice saw the wild look in Johann's eyes and decided not
to argue. Still holding on to Beatrice, Johann turned back to Yasin.

"We are going to return to the caves on the other side of the island," he said. "You are not to come near us under any circumstances. Is
that clear?"

Both Sister Beatrice and Johann thought they saw Yasin nod before
his eyes closed and he became unconscious. When they faced each other,
Beatrice buried her head against Johann's chest and allowed herself to
sob for a long time.

14

Twice during the next few days Sister Beatrice implored Johann to accompany her across the island to make certain that Yasin was all right. The first time Johann refused angrily. The second time, six days after the incident, he reluctantly agreed to check on Yasin himself so that Beatrice would stop worrying about the possibility that he might have died from the injuries he received during the fight.

Johann decided to go in the middle of the night to minimize the likelihood that Yasin would see him. His reconnaissance trip was successful. He found Yasin fast asleep on a mat in one of the smaller caves. A new basket of food was not far from his mat, near a collection of the same medicinal plants with which Sister Beatrice had treated Yasin's wounds when he first arrived on the island. An odd array of tools and other objects from the storehouse was stacked just outside the entrance to the cave.

Sister Beatrice was reassured that Yasin had not died. As the days passed, however, she started to feel anxious again about their tenuous situation.

"Sooner or later," she said to Johann one evening around the fire, "we are going to run into Yasin again. This island is just too small for us to avoid each other forever. . . . Wouldn't it be better if we went to him, and tried to reach some kind of understanding? Otherwise, I fear . . ."

Johann was adamant. He did not want any kind of accommodation with Yasin. He was still angry with himself for not having protected Sister Beatrice better. In spite of her repeated entreaties, Johann refused even to consider forgiving Yasin for having attacked her. Beatrice's occasional pleas for what she called a peace conference always fell on deaf ears.

Johann cut down one of the larger trees and made two clubs from the sturdy wood. The smaller one he gave to Sister Beatrice, insisting that she keep it within range whenever the two of them were separated. The larger club he carried with him at all times.

He stopped swimming in the mornings altogether. Johann was not going to give Yasin an opportunity to sneak up and attack Beatrice while he was gone. In place of his swim, he rose early each day and climbed up the mountain, stopping at one of several locations from which he could spy on Yasin.

He became completely familiar with Yasin's morning routine. Soon after waking, Johann's adversary would douse the pair of torches that had stood outside his cave as sentinels throughout the night. Next he would say his morning prayers facing the beach, prepare and eat a large breakfast, and then begin work on one of his many construction projects.

Over a several-day period Johann watched Yasin build a small boat, much like a canoe, and test it in the lake not far from his cave. Early one morning Yasin set out across the lake. Johann stayed at his observation post until he could no longer see the boat on the horizon. That night Sister Beatrice and he rejoiced, thinking that the cause of the tension in their lives had disappeared.

The next morning, however, Johann saw the canoe pulled up on the beach near Yasin's cave. Yasin himself did not appear until well after the middle of the day. Johann and Sister Beatrice spent their evening beside the fire speculating about what might have happened to cause him to return to the island.

"Maybe there was no place for him to go," Sister Beatrice said. "Perhaps there are physical barriers around the distant edges of the lake."

Johann was deep in thought. "All three of us 'fell' into this lake," he said, "if that is the right word. So there must be a passageway between this region and the rest of the spacecraft."

"Unless it's been sealed by our hosts," she said.

"That's what is bothering me," Johann said in a serious tone. "I watched Yasin's preparations. He was carrying a lot of stuff with him in that canoe. He definitely intended to leave our island forever. . . . That he had no choice except to come back adds more strength to my conviction that the aliens purposely brought him here to this island in the first place—"

"*That* again, Brother Johann?" she interrupted sharply. "Can't you just leave it alone? Especially now, when we have enough to worry about?"

"All right," Johann said. "But I do want you to remember one thing. I have no intention of forgiving Yasin for what he did to you. He is the lowest kind of scum. . . ."

Sister Beatrice listened to Johann's diatribe. It was clear that his feelings about Yasin, instead of softening in time as she had hoped, had turned into an implacable hatred.

Yasin was building a house on the widest part of the beach, around a curve in the island that was almost a kilometer away from his cave. Every morning after breakfast he would load supplies and tools in his new, larger wagon and carry them over to the house construction site. There he would work all day, sometimes continuing into the night by torchlight.

Johann had found several excellent vantage points from which he could watch Yasin working on the house. He coaxed Sister Beatrice into joining him on the mountain for a peek at Yasin's creation the morning after the framing on the house was finally completed.

"Yasin is certainly industrious, isn't he, Brother Johann?" she said.

"Nobody ever said that the man was not talented," Johann grudgingly replied. "At Valhalla he often accomplished in a single day what would have taken an ordinary engineer at least two weeks. . . . But, on a larger scale, his abilities cannot begin to compensate for the fundamental flaws in his nature. Yasin may be a genius, but he is still a dangerous sociopath."

Sister Beatrice was quiet for several minutes. Johann launched into another tirade about Yasin. This morning he was talking about how peculiar it was that neither of them had ever seen any sign of Yasin's presence on their side of the island. "The man is either extremely clever," Johann said, "or he is completely ignoring us. He has probably convinced himself that we will come forward with an olive branch eventually. That's where he is dead wrong."

"Brother Johann," Beatrice said during a break in Johann's monologue, "please don't be offended by my question, but since you knew about Yasin's convictions for sexual offenses ahead of time, why in the world did you hire him to work at Valhalla in the first place?"

Johann shrugged. "Mea culpa," he said. "At the time I thought Yasin's engineering talent, and the outpost's need for it, was more important than his criminal record. . . . Now I realize that I made a terrible mistake." He smiled. "I'm not too old to learn new things, am I?"

No, you're not, Sister Beatrice said to herself. *And I'm hoping that soon you will learn the most difficult tenet of Christianity. Everyone, no matter what heinous deed he or she may have committed, is entitled to forgiveness.*

The smell awakened Johann about an hour before dawn. It was unmistakable. There was a fire on their island.

He walked outside the cave and stood on a tall boulder. Johann could see a glow in the distance. He inhaled deeply, verifying the smell of smoke, and then returned to the cave to awaken Sister Beatrice.

"There's a fire somewhere," he said. "I'm going to climb the mountain and see if I can locate it."

Beatrice took a whiff of the air. "I smell it too," she said. "If you'll wait just a minute for me to wash up, I'll come with you."

Johann led Sister Beatrice slowly up the path toward the top of the mountain. As they climbed in altitude the raging fire became visible. It was already quite large, covering at least five percent of the island. The fire was mostly at the lower elevations, although it was creeping slowly up the slopes of the mountain. It appeared to be centered near where Yasin had been building his house.

Johann and Sister Beatrice both saw the long ribbon at the same time. It first appeared as a distant glow, far out over the lake. The bright ribbon flew toward the island at an enormous velocity, swooping down low over the fire, circling it a couple of times, and then zooming back out across the water.

They watched the ribbon until it disappeared into the darkness beyond the lake. Sister Beatrice crossed herself and said a silent prayer. "I forget sometimes," she then said, "that you, Yasin, and I are not alone in this world of ours. Our angels are obviously still present, even if they appear only occasionally."

Johann was studying the fire. Because the wind on the island was steady and very light, the fire was not moving very fast. However, the vegetation was so thick everywhere except near the two cave formations that there was nothing to stop the fire from burning the entire island.

The artificial daylight came abruptly, as it always did, forcing Johann and Sister Beatrice to close their eyes to adjust to the sudden surge of light. The fire did not look so ominous in the daylight. Johann and Sister Beatrice could now tell that the fire had started in the vegetation immediately behind Yasin's unfinished house, and then spread in three directions, both up the slope and up and down the beach. Yasin's house on the beach was untouched by the fire; however, there was now only a blackened wasteland at the edge of the beach behind the house.

Johann and Sister Beatrice spent a few minutes standing on the side of the mountain, searching carefully for Yasin. They looked around the edge of the fire, along the beaches, and near the cave where he lived. They did not see him.

"I hope he escaped safely," Beatrice said.

"I'm sure he did," Johann said. "He probably tripped or stumbled, carrying one of his torches, and started the fire inadvertently. Unless he was seriously injured, he could easily have outrun the fire. . . . At this moment, however, I'm not worried about Yasin. I'm concerned about what we're going to eat if—"

Johann did not finish his sentence. Feeling the ground moving underneath his feet, he reached out and grabbed Sister Beatrice's arm. "It's an earthquake," he said in astonishment.

The shaking in the ground intensified. It became impossible to stand up. Johann and Sister Beatrice sat down, holding hands. Without warning, a powerful force thrust them to the side, throwing each of them against the ground. Johann's face was scratched by the branches of a nearby shrub. He tried to regain his sitting position, but it was impossible. He could not overcome the unknown force.

Both Johann and Sister Beatrice began to slide down the slope. They were not able to hold on to each other any longer. "Are you all right?" Johann yelled as he rolled into a bush that temporarily stopped his descent.

"I'm okay for now," Beatrice shouted back. "But I won't be if we slide down the whole mountain."

The force jerked Johann free from the bush. He tumbled into Sister Beatrice just before the force pushing them down the hill suddenly stopped. They scrambled toward each other and stood up, laughing.

Before Johann could say anything, Sister Beatrice pointed behind him, a look of disbelief in her eyes. "Look, Brother Johann, look what's happened to the lake!" she exclaimed.

He turned around. "Oh, my God!" was all Johann could say. Before the earthquake and the strange force, Yasin's house had been thirty meters from the water. Now the lake had retreated at least three hundred meters from the house, exposing an enormous expanse of sand beach. Johann scanned around the perimeter of the lake. The amount of new beach dropped off steadily on either side of Yasin's house. On the other side of the island, near Johann and Sister Beatrice's caves, the lakeshore had hardly changed at all.

"This is very peculiar," Johann said. "The lake has receded in a symmetrical pattern around the area where the fire started, as if someone deliberately designed the change."

The fire had not been affected by the earthquake. While Johann was studying its extent, Sister Beatrice noticed a strange ripple on the lake far in the distance. It seemed to be headed toward them. She pointed out the ripple to Johann.

As they watched, the ripple grew and grew into a wave of staggering size. It hurtled toward the island, still building, taller and taller, until Johann guessed that it was at least a hundred meters high.

Raw fear gripped them both as they stared at the immense wall of water about to smash into their island. Johann tried to calculate the size of the wave. Forcing himself to be calm, he told Sister Beatrice that he was certain they were safe near the top of the mountain. "Of course," he then said, as much to himself as to her, "what a perfect way to put out the fire."

The gigantic wave bearing down upon them was an awesome, breathtaking sight. When it hit the island, it broke with a thundering roar. Water rushed inland up the mountain slope, bringing destruction to everything in its path. Where there had once been fire, there were now floods of water.

Johann and Sister Beatrice were speechless. They held hands and watched the water slowly retreat down the slopes of the mountain. The terrain had been transformed in an instant. The vegetation was now a hopeless jumble of uprooted plants, intermixed and intertwined, spread across the large area that had borne the brunt of the wave. After ten minutes most of the water was gone. The dimensions of the lake were again what they had been before the earthquake had begun, although some of the beaches were now littered with plants carried down the slopes by the retreating water.

Yasin's house had utterly vanished. "What we have just witnessed, Brother Johann," Sister Beatrice said emphatically, "was one of God's miracles."

The wave had decimated the lower elevations of the island between where Johann and Sister Beatrice had originally landed on the beach and the cave formations where Yasin had been living. From the mountain it was easy to ascertain the extent of the wave. Johann assured Sister Beatrice that Yasin would have survived if he had been inside his cave at the time of the impact.

"As long as he was sleeping, which is very likely, he would not have been in any danger," Johann said.

"But what if he was trying to fight the fire, or was around his house for some reason?" Sister Beatrice asked.

"We would have seen him," Johann said. "Besides, in that case, there's nothing we can possibly do for him anyway."

They were eating lunch. Beatrice had suggested at the beginning of the meal that they might carry a basket of food across the island to Yasin as a goodwill gesture, since the wave had destroyed virtually all the food supply in the vicinity of his cave. She also wanted to make certain that Yasin was okay.

Johann was opposed even to a humanitarian call upon Yasin. He reminded Sister Beatrice that the man was very resourceful and almost certainly did not need any help from them. That Yasin was all right, Johann said, he would personally verify the following morning from his mountain observation post.

"God has certainly blessed me in many ways," Sister Beatrice said then, abruptly changing the subject. "I remember hearing as a little girl the story of the parting of the Red Sea when Moses led the Jews out of Egypt. Our Bible-school teacher showed us a painting of the waters being parted while the people, tiny in comparison to the walls of water on either side of them, walked across the dry bottom of the sea. I remember yearning to have been there, to have seen one of God's miracles with my own eyes. . . . Now I know how Moses and the Jews must have felt. When I realized that God had sent that towering wave of water to save us from the fire, my body tingled all over with His presence. It was incredible."

Johann continued to eat his mixture of berries, cereal, and water. He made no comment.

"Brother Johann," she said after a minute, with just a hint of pique in her voice, "surely you are not going to sit there and *deny* that the hand of God was involved this morning? Even a doubter like Thomas would have had his faith restored after being confronted with such majestic power."

"Sister Beatrice," Johann replied, "I will readily admit to you that I have never seen a comparable sight. That wave was as tall as a fifty-story building when it crashed upon the island, and you were not the only one of us who was feeling tingles. . . . However, it is not only God who could have produced such a gigantic wave to put out the fire. Technologically advanced extraterrestrials, like the ones who built this island and the giant sphere in which we reside, could also use their knowledge of physics to maneuver the spacecraft in such a way—"

"But the wave was *perfect*, Brother Johann," Sister Beatrice interrupted. "It was just tall enough to put out the entire fire, and it hit the island at exactly the right spot. No unnecessary damage was done. Your aliens would have to be magicians. . . ."

"As they very obviously are," Johann countered. "Think about it, Sister Beatrice. Was the wave more fantastic than Hiroshima, or our excursion into the world of the Nazis?"

Beatrice was silent for a long time. Then she sighed. "It's at moments like this that I miss Sister Vivien the most," she said. "She had her skeptical side, and that kept me on my toes, but in the final analysis she was a dear comrade. We were united in our belief in God, and in our commitment to do His work. . . . You and I, Brother Johann, could never be that close. No matter how fond we become of each other, or how much we share, there will always be a gulf between us. Our different views of the purpose of life and the universe will always separate us."

She looked away from Johann. "Despite your care and affection, sometimes I feel so very alone. I know you love me, and that is comforting. But occasionally my heart aches for Sister Vivien, and everything she represents. She would have seen God's hand in the wave and we would have exulted about it for weeks. We would have talked about God and His miracles late into the night. . . ."

Sister Beatrice turned back to Johann. There were now tears in her eyes. "I'm sorry, Brother Johann," she said, trying to force a smile. "I have no right—"

"You are human, Sister Beatrice," he interrupted gently. "And loneliness is a very human emotion. . . . I'm sorry that I cannot fulfill more of your needs. Maybe in time . . ."

"Maybe in time, Brother Johann," she said. "God willing . . ."

Johann saw no signs of Yasin the following morning. He stayed at his observation post until midday and then went back to the cave to tell Sister Beatrice the news. He promised her that if he didn't see Yasin the next day, he would cross the island to find out what had happened to him.

Sister Beatrice climbed the mountain with Johann the next morning. Yasin did not appear. They continued to watch his cave until after their normal lunch hour.

"I have this strange feeling that Yasin is dead, Brother Johann," Beatrice said. "It makes no sense that we have not seen him at all."

"Maybe he moved to a higher elevation," Johann said without conviction. "Maybe he was afraid that there might be another earthquake, and another giant wave."

Johann knew that he had no choice except to honor his promise to Sister Beatrice. He packed some food, water, and medicine in a backpack. He grabbed his club and set out an hour later, taking the main path to the top of the mountain so that he would be able to keep Yasin's cave in view during his entire descent.

As he drew closer to the caves Johann spent several minutes at each vantage point, listening for telltale sounds as well as looking carefully for Yasin. There was no indication of any human presence in the cave area.

When he was only about a hundred meters away from the plaza with the perpetual fire, Johann veered toward the beach to make his final approach. This maneuver placed him directly opposite the front of the large cave in which the three of them had once lived. Johann noticed immediately that the large cave, which he had always favored because of its excellent view of the lake, had some kind of gate across its entrance. Puzzled, but remaining careful not to show himself or to make any sound, he crawled slowly toward the large cave.

At a distance of about twenty meters from the front of the cave, Johann peered around a rock. He saw a lattice of thin white poles with red markings wedged into the rock above and on both sides of the entrance. In the middle was a tall, skinny door, made of the same material as the lattice, that was presently open.

Someone, probably Yasin, Johann thought, *built this gate to control movement in and out of the large cave. He knew that the entrance could only be clearly seen from the lake. Was he protecting himself from us? From me? But if so, why was he still sleeping in the other cave?*

Johann did not have a chance to continue his thoughts or to examine the construction more closely. He felt a powerful blow strike the back of his head and an instant later he was unconscious.

15

It was dark outside when Johann awakened. He had a terrible head-ache. He touched the large knot on the back of his head and felt an excruciating pain.

Johann looked around. He could see reflected firelight on the far wall. He recognized that he was in the front room of the large cave where Sister Beatrice and he had tended Yasin. He sat up slowly, the painful pounding in his head increasing with his movement. He waited several seconds and then made a heroic effort to stand.

Johann somehow managed to walk the several meters over to the front of the cave. The door was now closed and locked. He tried unsuc-cessfully to push it open. Next he grabbed two of the bars that were part of the barrier and tried to bend them. They would not yield.

The exertion had made his headache worse. Johann walked slowly back into the cave, pulled one of the sleeping mats against the wall into the center of the room, and lay down upon it. He was asleep again in only a few minutes.

Johann was hungry and thirsty when he awakened the second time. It was daylight. The pain in his head had lessened considerably. He remembered his backpack and wondered what had happened to it.

He examined the construction across the entrance to the cave more closely. Each set of vertical bars was doubled, and tied together in a dozen places. The pairs of vertical bars were separated from the next pair by about fifteen centimeters, half the length of Johann's hand. Short horizontal bars scattered in no obvious pattern reinforced the strength of the barrier.

The narrow door to his cell was a meter or so taller than Johann, but only a meter wide. Two long rods on the other side of the bars ran from the floor to the ceiling and prevented the door from opening. At the bottom of the bars, over next to the rock wall on the left, there was a small square hole.

Johann's engineering mind began to look for weaknesses in the barrier. At each contact point where a horizontal or vertical bar touched the wall, floor, or ceiling of the cave, a small groove had been punched into the rock to increase the strength of the connection. All of the contacts Johann tested were absolutely rigid. Whoever had designed his prison had done a careful job.

Johann was sitting down on his mat again when Yasin appeared on the other side of the bars. He was carrying a long staff in one hand and a bowl of food in the other.

"Good morning, Ace," he said, pushing the bowl through the small opening at the bottom of the bars. "I trust you have slept well."

Johann approached the bars. "Let me out of here, Yasin," he said, trying to be as calm as possible.

"First explain to me what you were doing around here last evening," Yasin said. He was standing far enough away from the bars that Johann could not reach him with his long arms. "Your last words to me hardly suggested that our next meeting was going to be peaceful."

"Sister Beatrice and I were worried when we didn't see any sign of you after the wave. We were afraid you might have been killed or injured. I was bringing you food, water, and medicine. You have my backpack. You can verify—"

"Check, Ace," Yasin interrupted. "The contents of your backpack were an excellent example of contingency engineering. Perhaps you also have a good explanation for that club you were carrying as well. Are there now dangerous wild animals on our island that I don't know about?"

Johann was briefly silent. "I have no good explanation for the club, Yasin," he said finally.

"Did you need protection from me, Ace, a man only half your size whom you nearly killed with your bare hands?" Yasin's voice was laced with bitterness. "And for what reason would you have killed me, my German giant, if crazy Beatrice had not stopped you? Because I, unlike you, was not afraid to take her by force? In your screwed-up Christian mind, is that a legitimate reason to kill another man?"

Johann knew that Yasin was baiting him. He did not respond. "When we were working together at Valhalla," Yasin continued, "I thought you were an intelligent man. But I have had my doubts since we boarded that hatbox, and especially since I came to this island."

Yasin approached the bars. "Think about it, Siegfried," he said. "What is the only possible stable configuration of the three of us marooned forever on this island? You and I must share that crazy bitch Beatrice. If she is bonded to either one of us, sooner or later jealousy will explode. That's the nature of our species. Only if we are both screwing her can a stable equilibrium be reached."

Johann fought with his emotions. An inner voice reminded him that he was hardly in a position to argue with Yasin. Nevertheless, he couldn't hide his disgust.

"What is it with you, Ace?" Yasin said, probing Johann lightly in the midriff with his staff. "Has that woman cast some kind of a spell over you? You could have taken her whenever you wanted, and your passion for her is obvious, yet for over a hundred days . . . Are you gay, Ace? Is that your secret? Is it me you would rather screw?"

"I am not gay, you asshole," Johann said, no longer able to keep his mouth shut. "But I don't believe in taking women by force, especially not one who is trusting and compassionate and believes deeply that her chastity is part of her commitment to God."

Yasin began to laugh. "What a joke!" he said. "You must be as loony as she is. A woman priestess is a pathetic curiosity even on the earth, but here, in this place, it is absolutely insane. . . . Ace, we've discussed this before. Women have two purposes in life, having sex and bearing children. Everything else is nonsense. . . . But I've wandered away from the point I was trying to make. What bothers me the most about your nearly killing me is that your action indicates how warped your value system is. No reasonable man would ever try to kill another man for doing what is natural, namely trying to have sex with a woman. Not even if the woman in question was the man's wife, which was certainly not the case in this situation."

Johann was upset with himself for his earlier outburst. He forced himself to be silent and tried to shut out Yasin's voice. He picked up the bowl that Yasin had pushed through the hole and then returned to his mat.

Yasin was standing at the bars. "Okay, Ace." He grinned. "I guess you're telling me you've had enough for now. I assume from your reaction that you're not yet ready to apologize."

Johann looked up from his bowl. "Apologize?" he said.

"Yes," said Yasin. "I think an apology from you is in order. After all, you damn near killed me. An apology would be an excellent way to improve our relationship."

Johann stared at Yasin but said nothing. Yasin shrugged and then disappeared. He returned a few seconds later with another bowl of food and a water jug. "Here you are, Siegfried," he said. "This should be enough to hold you until Brunhild and I return."

"What are you going to do?" Johann said, not attempting to hide his alarm.

"I'm going to fetch the fair maiden," Yasin said. "I have been very lonely this past forty days and I have especially missed the company of a woman. I'm certain that Sister Beatrice will come gladly when I explain the situation to her."

Johann came forward to the bars. "Don't you harm her, Yasin," he said.

Yasin grinned. "Under the circumstances, Ace, you'll just have to trust me. . . . *Auf wiedersehen.*"

Yasin turned and walked away. He was wearing Johann's backpack and whistling one of the tunes from Wagner's *Gotterdämmerung.*

It was a day of agony for Johann. He made an effort not to think about Yasin, and Sister Beatrice, and what might be happening on the other side of the island, but he was unsuccessful. The image of Yasin astride her in this very cave repeatedly tortured him.

Johann attacked the bars with all his might. He pulled at them until his muscles were sore. He climbed one of the walls and yanked at one bar that did not seem to be firmly embedded in the ceiling. Desperate to escape, he searched through the back rooms of the cave, looking for a large rock that he might be able to hurl against the bars.

He found nothing. Johann was unable to bend the bars even one iota. The prison that Yasin had designed was secure.

Johann finished all the food and water soon after the middle of the day. He paced frantically about the cave for over an hour, and then, nearing exhaustion, he collapsed upon his mat. He awakened about half an hour before Yasin and Sister Beatrice returned.

"Are you all right?" Johann said, rushing to the bars when Sister Beatrice appeared.

"Yes, Brother Johann," she said. She touched his hands through the bars. "What about you? Yasin said that he hit you hard."

"My head is fine," Johann said. "But I've been worried sick about you. . . . Has he hurt you?"

Yasin was now within earshot, standing a meter or so behind Beatrice. He was still carrying his staff.

"Yasin has been a perfect gentleman," she said. "He asked me to come across so that the three of us could have a discussion about our future. I told him that I also thought it was time for all of us to talk."

"We're going to eat right here, in front of your cell, Ace, and share our food with you," Yasin said.

"Couldn't you let him out?" Sister Beatrice asked. "I give you my word that nothing untoward will occur."

"I don't think that's a very good idea, Sister," Yasin said. "Not even if Siegfried gave me *his* word. . . . My last encounter with him was not exactly pleasant. I don't want to expose myself to danger until we have all reached our understanding."

Sister Beatrice had brought Johann several slices of his favorite melon. Sitting in front of him, she mixed together fruit and berries laced with the sweet leaves of the plant that she called rosemary, because of its resemblance to the earthly herb. The talk during dinner was subdued. Yasin told them his story of the fire and the wave.

The fire had indeed been started by one of his torches. Yasin had been carrying some heavy wooden beams to his house and had inadvertently knocked one of the torches into the vegetation. He had thought that he had extinguished the fire, but it must have smoldered and then spread after he returned to his cave to sleep. Later he had been outside, not far from the edge of the fire, when he had first seen the huge wave approaching. He had scrambled up a slope out of its path with only a few minutes to spare.

It was dark by the time they finished dinner. Yasin ignited two torches and stuck them in torch holders on either side of the entrance to Johann's cell. Then he took Sister Beatrice aside and spoke to her in low tones.

When they returned Yasin ordered Johann to back away from the door. "I'm going to let her come in and visit you, Ace, but I'm not going to take a chance that you might try something. I want you against the back wall of the cave, but where I can still see you."

Johann moved back in the cave. Yasin opened the door cautiously, watching Johann the entire time, and Sister Beatrice entered. Yasin had the two locking rods in place again within seconds. Johann came forward and took Beatrice in his arms. Yasin stood at the bars watching them.

The torches provided good lighting in the front of the cave. When

Johann looked closely at Sister Beatrice, he could tell that she was deeply troubled. "What's the matter?" he said softly.

"Let's sit down and talk," she said. Johann pulled a second mat away from the wall and positioned it next to his. He waited for Sister Beatrice to sit first. She sat, cross-legged, and took off her headpiece. She pulled out the pins holding her blond hair against her head and it tumbled down her back.

"What's the matter?" Johann repeated.

"Yasin and I have agreed," Sister Beatrice said in a strained tone, "that the previous situation that existed on this island is untenable. We were not able to agree, however, on what to do about our problem. Toward the end of our conversation, we had an argument. That's when Yasin informed me that he intends to keep you prisoner unless his two conditions are met."

"What are his two conditions?" Johann said.

"Yasin wants you to apologize, in my presence, for nearly killing him when he was . . . forcing himself upon me."

"That little bastard," Johann muttered. "And the second condition, Sister Beatrice, what is it?"

Beatrice turned away suddenly. Her body was trembling. Johann reached over to her, but she shook him away. "It's all right, Brother Johann," she said. "I'll be okay in a minute."

She took two deep breaths and clasped her hands in front of her for a few seconds. Then Sister Beatrice faced Johann again. "Yasin believes," she said, "that all the potential for trouble among us would be removed if I were not a sexual prize that the two of you were competing for. If I become a wife to each of you, and you share me without competition or jealousy, then we can peacefully coexist."

"He explained his insane ideas to me this morning," Johann said. "But I'm lost. . . . I thought you were going to explain the second condition for my release."

"Yasin wants us to make love here, tonight, Brother Johann. He intends to watch. Then he will make love with me just outside the cell and you will watch. In his opinion that will defuse—"

"*Whaat?*" Johann interrupted with a shout. "I have never heard anything so ridiculous in my life. The man is absolutely crazy. Surely you told him that."

"He told me," Sister Beatrice said with difficulty, "that my opinion on this subject was of no importance, and that since I was the cause of all the tension in the first place, it was only proper that I should be the instrument of peace."

Johann jumped up from the mat and walked over to the bars. He shouted for Yasin. "You, al-Kharif," he said when Yasin responded to the call, "are a depraved animal. Are you out of your goddamned mind? What would make you think that either Sister Beatrice or I would agree to such a condition?"

"Careful with those insults, Ace," Yasin said. "Otherwise I'll start tallying them up and adding to your prison time, whether or not you meet the required conditions. And what's your problem with my suggestion anyway? I'm willing to let you have the first go at her and settle for sloppy seconds."

"You son of a bitch," Johann yelled, reaching vainly through the bars and trying to grab Yasin. Yasin whacked him twice on the arms with his staff. Johann pulled his arms back.

"It's not you, Siegfried, who is in control now," Yasin said sharply. "You had better be on your good behavior or you will never escape. Now, if you know what's good for you, you'll screw that bitch waiting for you on the mat. I may never give you another chance."

Sister Beatrice was crying softly when Johann returned to her side. "Brother Johann," she said, "I feel completely lost. I have prayed to God for guidance, and asked Him to forgive me for whatever I may have done. . . ."

"You have done nothing wrong," he said, taking her in his arms. "You are the best human being I have ever met."

She pulled away after several seconds. "I will do it, Brother Johann," she said in a low voice, "if that is what is necessary. I will make love to you, and to Yasin as well, if that will end this horrible nightmare."

"Don't be absurd," Johann said, pulling her to him again. "I would never let you demean yourself like that. I love and respect you too much."

"That's a good start," Yasin said from the bars. "But it's time for you two to stop dillydallying around. Tonight's the night, if you understand what I mean. There won't be another opportunity."

Johann lifted Sister Beatrice's face and kissed her on the forehead. "I love you," he said.

"And I love you," she replied through her tears.

16

Johann woke Sister Beatrice in the middle of the night. He whispered to her that they needed to formulate a plan. "This may be our only chance to talk," Johann said. "Yasin will probably never let you in here again."

Johann gently explained to Sister Beatrice that it was only a matter of time before Yasin would rape her. He might do it that day, or he might wait as long as ten or fifteen days, but sooner or later, Johann asserted, Yasin would force himself upon her sexually.

"Is there nothing I can do?" she asked. "Could I not beg him to leave me alone, and prostrate myself at his feet in an appeal for mercy?"

Johann's opinion was that Yasin would not be moved by any entreaties from Sister Beatrice. "It wouldn't work," he whispered to her. "In fact, I believe that any sign of fear from you will cause him to assault you earlier."

They concluded that the only possible way out of their predicament was to break Johann out of prison. Sister Beatrice wanted to wait a few days before trying an escape. "Yasin may soften up," she said, "or I may have a chance to unlock the door when he is not watching me."

Johann believed that the best opportunity to free him would come the following morning. "He will not expect *you* to do anything," he told Sister Beatrice. "If you push or hit Yasin just as you exit, before he has time to replace the rods and lock the door, that should give me enough time. And if I reach the bars before the door is locked, there's no way he will be able to keep me in here."

Sister Beatrice loathed the idea of committing an act of physical violence. Johann asked her which was "less unsatisfactory" to her, to push Yasin or to be raped by him. Terribly troubled, Sister Beatrice eventually agreed to Johann's plan. She spent the rest of the night praying and meditating.

Yasin did not appear at the bars until an hour after daylight. "Your time is running out, Ace," he said when he showed up. "The woman you adore is sitting right next to you, ripe for the plucking. Why don't you take off her clothes and see what she looks like naked? Then you'll know what you've been missing."

"Don't taunt me, Yasin," Johann said in a measured tone.

"And why shouldn't I?" Yasin replied. "After all, according to you, if I remember correctly, I'm an 'asshole,' a 'depraved animal,' and a 'son of a bitch.' Isn't it interesting, Ace, that I have never once called you an insulting name?"

"You have insulted Sister Beatrice and me in other ways," Johann said. "But I do agree with you that name-calling is useless."

"What's this?" Yasin said. "Is the German giant showing some humility after a night's sleep behind bars? Or is this some kind of ploy to cause me to drop my guard . . . ? While you're at it, Ace, how about that apology I asked for?"

Johann sighed wearily. "Please, Yasin, let's not fight now. Couldn't we just have a peaceful breakfast?"

"Sure, Ace," Yasin said, "if you're content to stay in that cell, I'm content not to discuss any of the issues that are open between us. But that apology would go a long way toward removing the locks on this door."

"In time I could live with the apology," Johann said. "It's the second condition for my release that is anathema to me. I would never humiliate Sister Beatrice or myself in that way."

"Isn't this a curious indication of just how different we are," Yasin said with a grin. "I would have no problem, even with you watching, jumping on the sister. I would do it in an instant, and I would thank you for letting me be first. An apology to you, however, that would stick in my craw."

"Could we have our breakfast now, please?" Sister Beatrice said, uncomfortable with the direction of the conversation.

"Good morning, Sister," Yasin said. "I was so involved in my discussion with Siegfried here, I had forgotten all about you. . . . Hmm, breakfast. What did I decide? Oh yes, now I remember. The two of you can have breakfast after you screw. Eating together is always great afterplay. On the other hand, if there's not going to be anything interesting for me to watch this morning, then I pronounce this visit over."

Johann and Sister Beatrice stared at each other in silence for almost a full minute. Then he opened his arms. She walked over to him for a farewell hug.

"I guess I'll be coming out now, Yasin," Sister Beatrice said, moving toward the bars.

"Just a minute, Sister," Yasin said, retrieving his staff from where it was resting beside the entrance to the cave. "We're not quite ready. . . . Ace, move all the way to the back of the room, and lie down facing the wall."

Sister Beatrice turned around and glanced at Johann. He could see the panic in her eyes. Johann smiled reassuringly. "Surely that is not necessary, Yasin," he said.

"Do as I say," Yasin said harshly. "I will decide what is necessary and what is not."

Johann nodded at Sister Beatrice and retreated to the back of the large room. He sat down first, then sprawled his huge body out on the floor.

"Now turn your eyes to the wall," Yasin ordered.

Johann complied. A second later, making only the slightest of sounds, Yasin slipped the locking rods out of position and gestured for Sister Beatrice to come through the door.

She hesitated a moment, and then walked outside. Yasin motioned for her to move away from the door. While he was turned slightly away from her she yelled, "Johann!" and threw herself against Yasin with all the force she could muster.

Sister Beatrice tried to tackle Yasin. Although she did not knock him to the ground, she did startle him and push him backward. He dropped one of the locking rods.

Yasin screamed, "You cunt!" and smashed Beatrice on the back with his staff. She let go of him and fell to the ground. Johann, meanwhile, was up and running toward the bars. He lost a valuable second when he tripped over one of the sleeping mats. Yasin saw him running forward and raced to the bars with his staff outstretched. Johann tried to dodge at the last moment, but the staff struck him a glancing blow to the chest, temporarily knocking him off his feet.

That was all the time Yasin needed to slide the first of the locking rods into place. Johann threw his body against the door only seconds later, but it withstood his charge.

"You failed, you stupid Christian fool," Yasin said contemptuously. "And now I'll *really* make you pay. You and that crazy bitch of yours."

At that moment Sister Beatrice leaped upon Yasin's back. He whirled around immediately, throwing her to the ground. For just a fraction of a second Yasin was close enough to the bars that Johann, leaning out of the cell, was able to grab him by the neck with his huge right hand. With his enormous strength Johann pulled Yasin toward the bars so that he could reach him with his other hand. Johann settled his hands around Yasin's throat and began to choke.

"Unlock the door," he shouted at Sister Beatrice, who was getting up slowly from the ground.

Terrible gasping, gurgling sounds were coming from Yasin. Johann did not let up.

"Don't kill him. . . . Please don't kill him," Sister Beatrice said, hurrying toward the door.

As he neared unconsciousness Yasin somehow found the strength to drive his staff directly behind him, striking Johann in the groin. Johann loosened his grip for only a moment, but it was enough for Yasin to slither out of his grasp. Yasin immediately pushed Sister Beatrice away from the door and then smacked her twice with his staff, once on the side of the head. She fell to the ground bleeding from a gash behind her left ear.

Yasin picked up the second locking rod at the same time that Johann threw the full force of his body against the door again. The door bent but did not open. Johann hovered near the door to prevent Yasin from inserting the second locking rod.

Yasin studied his adversary and clutched his throat. "That's twice, Ace, that you have tried to kill me. You will never have another chance. I promise I will kill you first."

Yasin retrieved one of the torches and approached the bars. When Johann would not back away, he suddenly thrust the torch between the bars, burning Johann's arm. "Come and get some more, Ace," he said. "There's nothing I'd rather do than fry your skin."

Johann pulled back and Yasin inserted the second locking rod. He replaced the torch in its holder. Then Yasin turned to Sister Beatrice, who was trying to use a corner of her robe to stop the blood flowing from her ear.

"As for you, cunt," Yasin said angrily, "I will now make you pay for your betrayal."

Yasin approached her brandishing his staff. Beatrice turned and tried to run. He hit her hard on the back, knocking her to the ground. She moaned at the impact and cowered in front of Yasin. "No, no, please don't," she pleaded.

Yasin grabbed her by the hair and dragged her roughly across the rocky surface until she was in front of Johann's cell. He leaned down and jerked on her robe, partially tearing it. When Sister Beatrice tried to defend herself, Yasin slapped her twice. She began to cry.

"Come over here closer, Ace," Yasin yelled at Johann, who was well back in the cave. "I'm going to show you how we treat women who misbehave."

Yasin bent down over Sister Beatrice and started tearing her clothes off. Each time she begged him to stop, he hit her hard in the face. At length, her spirit broken and blood pouring from her mouth, she stopped resisting.

She was lying on the ground, naked from the waist down, parts of her torn robe and underwear lying across her chest. With her right hand Sister Beatrice was clutching the amulet she had received during her ordination. She was trembling with fright. Yasin took off his pants.

"Please, Yasin," Johann said from between the bars, "don't hurt her anymore. She is innocent. I forced her to help me. Kill me, maim me, do whatever you want with me, but please leave her alone."

"It's too late for that, Ace," Yasin said. He was standing over Sister Beatrice, playing with himself. "The bitch must be punished," he said.

Johann could not watch. He tried to hide in the back of his cave. But even there he could hear Beatrice's pathetic cries and Yasin's shout of triumph. Johann buried his face in his hands and wept.

"Ace, come out here," he heard Yasin saying. "I have decided upon the sentences. . . . I thought you might like to hear them."

As Johann walked forward in his cave he was aware of his hunger. He had not eaten since the previous night.

"I tied the sister up in my cave—incidentally, she has quite a nice body, in case you've never noticed." Yasin grinned at Johann. "Then I took a long, refreshing swim in the lake. I always enjoy a good swim after sex."

Yasin yawned and stretched. "Since then I have been reflecting on our case, which I call *al-Kharif* v. *Eberhardt et al.*" Yasin laughed at his own wit. "That's in Western terms, of course, so that you can understand it. As you might expect, I approached the case from the point of view of Islamic justice."

He leaned forward toward Johann. "We're the ones, you may remember, Ace, who cut off the hands of convicted thieves. That tends to reduce their future thievery." Yasin chuckled.

"Will you cut the crap, Yasin," Johann said, "and just get on with it."

"By all means," Yasin said. "As I said, I have decided upon the sentences in our case. The 'et al' part of your team, namely the good sister, will receive a relatively light sentence. In fact, there would be those who would not consider it a punishment at all—I took into account your testimony that you 'forced' her into being your accomplice. . . . Anyway, Sister Beatrice will have intercourse with me right here in front of your cell, on a mat if she prefers, every day for the next thirty days, at a time of my choosing."

Yasin paused to wait for Johann's reaction. When there was none, he continued, "As for you, Johann Eberhardt, aka Ace, aka Siegfried, aka the German giant, you have been convicted of two counts of attempted murder. What possible punishment is terrible enough for someone who has *twice* tried to kill a man who has never harmed him at all? You can only die once. Therefore, that death should be slow and painful. Your sentence, Ace, is to starve to death in that cell. You have had the last food and water of your life."

As Johann listened to Yasin's gleeful pronouncement of their sentences, his thoughts were not of himself. All he could think about was Sister Beatrice. He felt that her sentence was much worse than his. *She will not survive this ordeal intact,* he thought. *That something bright and wonderful that makes her unique will be irrevocably destroyed.*

Johann was not afraid of dying, or even of starving to death. What he was afraid of were the daily self-recriminations. *Yasin would have raped her eventually,* he told himself. *But it would not have been so brutal. I am to blame for what has happened to her.*

The next three nights Yasin shouted and banged on the bars when he was preparing to have sex with Sister Beatrice. He wanted to make certain Johann didn't miss the event. Johann never showed himself. He would not give Yasin that satisfaction. While exploring among the maze of smaller tunnels at the back of his cave, he discovered a couple of locations, which he could reach with only a little crawling, where he could not hear any sound at all. On the second and third nights he stayed in those spots until he was sure that the activity outside his cell was over. On the first night he had heard Sister Beatrice cry out twice, and each cry had been like a knife cutting into his stomach.

Johann was feeling fairly weak on the fourth day. He began wondering how long it would take him to starve to death. To combat his constant despair, Johann promised himself that he would have nothing but happy thoughts until he died. He spent most of his time thinking about his childhood, remembering the good days before he became aware of his parents' financial problems. Unfortunately, Johann could not think about Sister Beatrice at all without being plunged into the darkness of depression.

The fourth night of his confinement Johann was astonished to hear Sister Beatrice singing. He came forward in his cell, curious, and saw her sitting on a mat just on the other side of the bars. She was facing the lake, so Johann could only see the back of her head. She was singing an old, traditional folk song.

"Hush little baby. . . . Don't you cry. . . . You know your mama . . . Was born to die. . . . All my trials, Lord . . . soon be over."

Her achingly beautiful voice pierced Johann's heart and caused tears to run from his eyes. A few seconds later he noticed that Yasin was watching him.

"Amazing voice, huh, Ace?" Yasin said, coming over closer to Johann. "The sister really has a talent."

Johann looked at him and wiped his eyes. "You're probably wondering how I got her to sing," Yasin said. "It was easy. I gave her a choice. She could sing for me or . . . I wasn't surprised at her decision. Even I have had enough sex in these last four days."

"The River Jordan is muddy and cold. . . . You know it chills the body . . . But not the soul. . . . All my trials, Lord . . . Soon be over."

"You can talk to her, Ace," Yasin said. "Go ahead. Judging from your condition, you may not have too many more opportunities."

Johann walked over to the bars beside Beatrice. He could almost reach out and touch her. "Sister Beatrice," he said in a strangely husky voice, "it's me, Johann."

She turned around slowly, continuing to sing. Johann immediately noticed the hopeless sadness in her blue eyes. Sister Beatrice forced a smile, but her eyes remained full of ineffable pain.

"Too late, my brothers," she sang. "Too late, but never mind. . . . All my trials, Lord . . . Soon be over."

Johann thought his heart was going to explode with sorrow. He could not look at her anymore. He stumbled back into his cell, picked up his mat, and carried it with him to the darkness at the very back of the cave.

There can be no hell worse than this, he thought. *I will not endure that pain again. I will stay back here, out of sight and beyond earshot, until I die.*

17

Johann felt certain that the eleventh day of his confinement would be his last. He lay on his mat in the darkness, too weak even to sit up. He wondered again what death would be like. Johann tried to imagine a God, and a heaven, and angels who would sing like Sister Beatrice. He could not. Even at this final moment his rational mind interceded and told him that any kind of an afterlife was unlikely.

Death will be like this, Johann told himself. *Darkness and nothingness forever. Only I will not be aware of it.*

For hours he lay without moving. Johann no longer knew if it was day or night outside his cell. He lapsed in and out of consciousness several times. The constant pain of his hunger no longer bothered him. He was slipping away.

Johann thought he was delirious and imagining things the first time he heard the scraping sound at the back of one of the side tunnels behind him. When the noise persisted, he shook himself and made a great effort to prop himself up on one elbow. He turned in the direction of the sound and watched and waited.

The noise continued for over an hour. Toward the end Johann thought it was growing louder. Then, suddenly, to his complete astonishment, the rocks at the back side of the tunnel were pushed to the side and he could see some light coming through a hole no larger than a soccer ball. Johann crawled into the tunnel as the light began to fade. In front of the new hole he found three food cylinders and a tiny container, white with red markings, which was filled with water.

Trembling with joy, Johann lifted the water to his lips. He had never tasted anything so delicious in his entire life. He swirled the water around in his dry mouth and then swallowed it very slowly. Next Johann bit off the end of one of the cylinders. The food felt strangely wonderful in his mouth. He ate the cylinders slowly, one by one, until they were all gone. Then he awkwardly clasped his hands in front of him.

"Thank you, whoever you are," he said softly. "Whether you are aliens or angels, I thank you with my entire being."

The food and water came twice a day, usually when Johann was asleep. Once, while he was lying awake on his mat, he saw a tiny light in the hole. He watched patiently as it grew into a glowing light, too bright for him to look at directly, and then swiftly disappeared. New food cylinders and water were beside the hole when he crawled to the back of the side tunnel.

Never once did Johann make an appearance in the large main room of the cave. He was also very careful not to make any noise. He had developed a plan. He expected that sooner or later Yasin would come into the cave to make certain he was dead. When he did, Johann was going to be ready.

Many days passed. Johann was surprised that Yasin had not yet come. His strength had returned. Between each sleep period, he did hundreds of sit-ups, push-ups, and other muscle exercises. He would be prepared when the final confrontation with Yasin finally occurred.

He saw the light reflecting off a distant cave wall before he heard the footsteps. Johann's heart began pumping furiously as he edged along the wall toward the corner. He stood still and listened carefully. The footsteps were soft and uncertain. Johann puzzled for a moment. Then he understood. *It's Sister Beatrice*, he thought. *Yasin has sent her first to see if I am dead.*

The footsteps grew more faint. Whoever was in the cave had obviously gone in the opposite direction off the large main room. Then Johann heard the footsteps again, coming toward him. He braced himself against the wall. When he was certain that Sister Beatrice was only a few meters away from him, and in a location that could not be seen from the entrance to the cave, he darted around the corner and grabbed her.

He put his hand immediately over her mouth and successfully muffled her scream. She dropped the torch on the cave floor. "Be calm," he whispered in her ear. "It's me, Johann. . . . Relax and do not say a word."

When he was convinced that she understood what was happening, Johann released her mouth and picked up the torch. He put his finger to his lips and led Sister Beatrice by the hand to the end of the corridor where his mat was lying.

"Sit down," he said in a low voice, surprised to find her wearing a blouse and pair of long pants. "We can talk back here if we aren't too loud. The cave walls attenuate the sound."

"Oh, Brother Johann," she said, joy apparent on her face, "you don't know how many times I have prayed that you were still alive. God has heard my prayers."

He told her about the hole in the side corridor, the lights, the food cylinders, and the water.

"It's a miracle," Sister Beatrice exclaimed, "an absolute miracle." She took his hand and kissed it. "I can't believe that you're alive."

They stared at each other for several seconds.

"So tell me," Johann said, "how are you?"

"Not so good," Sister Beatrice said, pain showing in her eyes. "But I guess it could be much worse. . . . God has helped me adjust to my hell, Brother Johann," she added. "Because I have been meek and submissive and have not caused Yasin any trouble, he has graciously allowed me time for my prayers and meditations, without which my soul would have died long ago. . . . I have learned again that you can endure anything if your faith is strong enough."

Johann took her hands in his. "I want you to tell Yasin that I have died, Sister Beatrice," he said. "Can you do this for me?"

She stared in his eyes, thinking. It did not take her long to make a decision. Sister Beatrice pulled a knife out of the pocket of her pants.

"He still doesn't trust me, Brother Johann," she said, "even though he calls me his wife. . . . Yasin told me that if you were dead, I was to cut off one of your fingers and bring it back to him as proof."

Johann didn't hesitate. He thrust his left hand forward. "I suggest the middle finger," he said. "I can do without it the easiest."

Sister Beatrice looked squeamish. "Would you like for me to do it for you?" he asked.

She nodded. "If you would, please . . . I'm not certain I could hurt you like that."

He handed her the torch. "There will be a lot of blood," he said. "We will need to cauterize the wound immediately."

Johann laid his left hand down on the floor of the cave. He asked Sister Beatrice to move the torch so he could better see what he was doing. Johann checked the knife. It was very sharp.

He cut off the middle finger of his left hand with one sure, strong stroke. Johann then held his stump against the fire, recoiling from the pain. He closed his eyes and took several quick breaths. When he looked at Sister Beatrice, he noticed the blood dripping from the gruesome finger remnant in her hand.

"What happens to your blood when you die?" Johann asked. "Doesn't it solidify when rigor mortis sets in?"

"I think so," Sister Beatrice said. "But I'm not certain."

"We don't want to take any chances," Johann said. "That might be something that Yasin would know."

Johann took the remnant, washed it off, and then burned it on the end where it was still bleeding. "Tell him you accidentally burned it with the torch," Johann said. "Now go, before he becomes suspicious."

Sister Beatrice reached over and kissed Johann lightly on the lips. "You have no idea . . ." she started to say.

"Yes, I do," Johann said with a smile. "Now go, please."

Johann anticipated that Yasin would come to examine his body in a few minutes. He was correct. Not long after Sister Beatrice had left, he heard two pairs of feet coming rapidly in his direction. Again he braced himself against the cave wall near the entrance to his corridor. Johann intended to jump Yasin the moment he was in view.

"Around that corner," he heard Sister Beatrice say. "His body is on a mat, at the end of a short tunnel."

"You lead the way, darling," Yasin said. "I will follow."

Beatrice made a wide arc around the turn and Johann pounced. Despite Yasin's surprise, he managed to elude Johann's first attempt to grab him. Yasin retreated several meters, holding his staff in his right hand.

Sister Beatrice stood to the side holding the torch. "Watch out," she called to Johann. "He has sharpened the end of his staff."

Johann circled around in the cave, cutting off all possibility of flight and protecting Sister Beatrice. Yasin surveyed the situation. "You have betrayed me again, cunt," he hissed. "You will die after I finish with him."

Yasin raised his staff above his shoulder like a spear and prepared to attack. "Allah, give me strength," he shouted as he rushed toward Johann.

Johann kept his eyes on the point of the staff, which was aimed directly at his heart. At the last moment of Yasin's run, he jumped to the side, grabbing the staff just in front of Yasin's hand and ripping it from the smaller man's grasp. In one swift, powerful, continuous motion, Johann thrust the staff completely through Yasin's gullet, the sharp point stopping several centimeters beyond the back of Yasin's neck.

Yasin's eyes bulged out of his head as he staggered around the cave. He reached up to his throat and pulled on the staff, but it was too late. Blood was already pouring from his mouth.

Sister Beatrice averted her eyes as Yasin dropped to his knees. He glanced up at Johann and tried to smile. "Well done, Ace," he gurgled. Then he toppled over and died.

Beatrice dropped the torch and ran over to Johann. She wept in his arms. "It's over now," he said. "It's all over."

They burned Yasin's body on a funeral pyre that same evening. Johann and Sister Beatrice slept next to each other, holding hands all night long, and in the morning he went for a long swim in the lake. She meditated on the beach and greeted him with a kiss when he returned.

They didn't talk much during breakfast. Neither of them wanted to discuss the killing or the horrors that they had each endured. Johann and Sister Beatrice spent the rest of the morning gathering up food and useful objects. At midday, just before they shouldered their backpacks for the trek across the island, Sister Beatrice said a prayer for Yasin's soul and thanked God for their deliverance.

18

Beatrice told Johann she thought she was pregnant the first night they were together in their home cave on the other side of the island. "I know my body very well, Brother Johann," she said, "and it already feels different. Besides, I'm seven days late for my period."

She suggested to him that they not become lovers until after they found out for certain whether or not she was pregnant. Beatrice added that she also wanted to wait for another reason, so that she could come to terms with her feelings of revulsion associated with sexual activity of any kind. "It's still difficult," she told Johann, "despite my love for you, to imagine being intimate. . . . The memories of Yasin are still too fresh, and too painful."

Johann understood. Although they had only alluded indirectly to becoming lovers, it had been obvious to him from her first kisses that Beatrice no longer felt bound to her vow of chastity that Yasin had forcibly broken.

The waiting was difficult. Each morning when they awakened, before Johann swam and Beatrice meditated, he would interrogate her with his eyes. Each morning she shook her head.

On the eleventh day after Yasin's death, Johann and Beatrice took a long walk on the beach. "You have been great about everything, Johann," Beatrice said, taking his hand, "kind, loving, so respectful of my feelings. I know that you have a million questions you have not asked. . . . I am not yet ready to talk about the time I spent with Yasin—God knows I would forget it completely if I could—but I do think it's time to assume that I'm pregnant. I am now eighteen days late. I have never been more than one week late in my entire life."

"What specifically do you want to discuss?" Johann said. "It's not as if we haven't talked about the subject."

"But you haven't told me how you really feel," she said. "And I haven't yet shared with you some of the private thoughts I have had during my many prayers about my pregnancy. . . . I have definitely had mixed emotions, and have changed my mind several times. In the beginning, I was horrified by the thought of bringing Yasin's child into our world. If I were going to have anyone's baby," she said, looking at Johann, "I would want it to be yours.

"However, the more I thought and prayed about it, the more I realized that my not wanting Yasin's child was both childish *and* inconsistent with my deepest beliefs. If God has allowed me to conceive Yasin's child, then He must have had some reason."

They stopped walking. Beatrice took Johann's other hand and looked fixedly into his eyes. "If I am pregnant, Johann," she said, "it is not just Yasin's child. It is my child, and God's, and yours as well. . . .

"I don't mean to imply that we would tell either Michael or Maria—those are the two names I have picked out, subject to your approval—that you are their biological father. We would tell the child the truth about his or her parentage. However, you would be the baby's 'true' father, if I can use that expression. The biological father supplies only the genes. In my opinion, and in yours, too, assuming I have understood what you have been telling me, the nurturing parents are the ones who really 'imprint' the child."

Beatrice waited patiently for Johann to say something. "I would be lying," he said at length, "if I told you that I am pleased with the idea that you might be carrying Yasin's child. I hope very much that you are not pregnant. But if you are . . ."

Johann kissed her on the forehead. "I love you, Beatrice," he said, "and I want to support you in every way. If you are pregnant, I will wrestle with the demons whispering in my ear, and eventually I will overcome them. It's as simple as that."

Her smile was full of love. "You are a wonderful man, Johann Eberhardt," she said.

The days passed. Life was good for Johann and Beatrice. They decided together that they would officially declare her to be pregnant on the thirtieth day after Yasin's death. There was some rationale for the date, but not much.

"I have heard of women," Beatrice had said while they were discussing the subject, "who sometimes skip a period altogether during times of acute stress. The time I spent with Yasin would certainly fit into that category."

On the appointed morning, Johann awakened unusually early. He lay on his mat and watched the firelight flickering on the wall of the cave. He tried to imagine what it would be like to share their world with an infant.

Beatrice was sleeping peacefully beside him. Johann glanced over at her and watched her take a couple of easy breaths. She was smiling. *She has looked exceptionally beautiful lately,* he thought. *Her cheeks have been full of color. I wonder if that old wives' tale about pregnant women being radiant is true.*

He waited until daylight to awaken her. Soon thereafter she checked herself. "Nothing," Beatrice said, smiling coyly as she shook her head.

"This is the thirtieth day," Johann said.

"I know," she said. "I guess I am officially pregnant."

Johann stood up and stretched. "Well," he said, "I don't know what to say."

"Don't say anything," Beatrice said. "Just come over here and kiss me."

He bent down beside her on the mat and kissed her on the lips. Beatrice put her hands behind his head and returned his kiss, softly at first, but then with increasing passion.

"Wow," Johann said with a smile when they broke the kiss. "That's a great way to start the morning."

Beatrice kept her arms around him. "I don't want you to leave this morning, Johann," she said. "I want you to make love to me."

Johann was deliberate and extremely gentle in his foreplay. He was worried that any kind of abrupt or forceful move would bring back painful memories for her. They kissed and touched until he was afraid that he was going to explode.

"I'm ready now, Johann," she whispered in his ear after tickling it lightly with her tongue. "Please come inside me."

For Johann, the next few minutes were pure ecstasy. Never in his life had he imagined that physical pleasure could be so intense. He surrendered completely to what he was feeling, surprising himself by emitting a long, plaintive cry when he climaxed.

"Goodness," said Beatrice moments later. "Are you all right?"

"All right?" Johann said, lifting his head from her neck and smiling. "No, sweet lady, I'm not all right. I'm absolutely, unbelievably, incredibly, *terrific*."

He jumped up quickly and began to dance around the cave. Beatrice laughed. "I have never, ever been better," he said. In a few seconds he was lying beside her again, kissing her wildly on the forehead, the neck, the lips, and the nipples of her breasts.

"And do you know *why* I'm terrific?" he asked.

Beatrice shook her head.

"Because I'm completely, madly in love with you," Johann said.

Sexual pleasure added an extra dimension to their relationship. Johann and Beatrice were already as close as good friends could possibly be, so the period during which they explored each other physically was a delight for both of them. Beatrice was the more creative of the pair, although Johann surprised her from time to time with an exciting suggestion that she had not considered. They made love in the lake, on the beach, in front of the fire, in the total darkness at the rear of their cave, and even in the grove, underneath the trees with the unusual brown nuts.

Johann's happiness amazed him. Often he would lie awake on his mat at night, chuckling to himself about his good fortune. *If I were a praying man*, he thought one night, *I would ask God to freeze time right here, right now. I want to feel like this forever.*

One night after a nude swim and some unusually athletic sex that left both of them exhausted and satisfied, Johann and Beatrice were lying side by side on the sand, staring idly at the dark ceiling above their heads.

"I don't see how heaven could possibly be any better than this," Johann said.

"Nor can I," said Beatrice. "But God's imagination is unlimited. And He knows us better than we know ourselves. I'm certain He'll have something wonderful—"

She stopped and glanced over at Johann. "What are we talking about?" she said with a look of mock seriousness. "You don't believe in heaven. . . . You just barely believe in God."

Johann reached over and kissed her. "If anything could cause me to become a believer," he said, "it's spending time with you. None of God's angels could possibly compare with you in bed."

"I'll accept that sacrilege as a compliment," Beatrice said with a laugh. "You are still in the grip of what we used to call 'neophyte aura' in the order. It's very flattering, but I know it will wear off in time. Then I'll just be your best friend Beatrice again."

"And that's a pretty wonderful thing too," Johann said.

Johann was in the midst of a dazzling dream. His dream screen was glowing with light and Beatrice was standing in the middle of a cloud, wearing a white dress. A deep, sonorous voice said, "She belongs to the universe."

He felt Beatrice's touch on his shoulder. "Wake up, Johann," she said insistently. "Wake up and give me your hand."

Johann stirred and reached his right hand in her direction. She took the fingers of his hand and placed them on her stomach. "The baby kicked me hard," she said excitedly, "not even a minute ago. Once before I felt two or three kicks before he stopped. . . . There, that was another one. Did you feel it?"

"I don't think so."

"Come on, baby," Beatrice said. "Kick once more for Uncle Johann."

Johann felt a tiny thrust against his fingers. He sat up. "Hey," he said. "I *did* feel it."

"That was the best one, Johann," Beatrice said. "And it was just for you." She was smiling broadly. "I wish you could know what it was like to feel a life growing inside you. . . . There's nothing like it. I could not possibly have imagined how exciting it is."

She adjusted the pillow behind her head and placed both her hands on her stomach. Johann lay back down on his mat and closed his eyes.

"Do you think it's unfair, Johann," she said, "that women can have babies and men can't?"

He opened his eyes again and smiled. "I don't know," he said. "I've never really thought about it."

"I had a friend named Ted at the University of Minnesota," Beatrice said, "who was studying music with me. He was terribly upset that he would never be able to be pregnant and have a baby. When one of the other students did become pregnant, Ted told all of us that he was jealous of her. . . . Are you jealous that I can feel this baby kick and you can't?"

Johann laughed. "Certainly not," he said.

"Would you be if it were *our* baby, I mean, yours and mine?"

Johann hesitated before answering. "I don't know," he said. "I might be a little jealous then."

"It still bothers you that this is Yasin's child, doesn't it?" Beatrice said after a brief silence.

Johann looked away. "Yes," he said. "But I wish it didn't. I keep hoping. . . ."

"Be patient with yourself, darling," she said. "You can't program your feelings from your brain. Maybe after she is born . . ."

"Oh, so it's a girl baby this week?" Johann said. "Last week you were so certain it was a boy that you insisted I refer to him as Michael." He laughed.

"Pregnant women change their minds about these things," Beatrice said. "It's their right."

Johann closed his eyes again. "When was the last time that I told you that I loved you?" Beatrice said.

"Sometime yesterday," Johann said. "I think it was right after dinner."

"I love you, Johann," she said.

"I love you, Beatrice," he said.

As the time for the birth grew near, Johann made certain that he was never gone from their cave area for more than thirty minutes at a time. Each time Johann left, Beatrice would talk to God, telling Him that she hoped it was not His will for the baby to come while Johann was away.

She spent most of her time inside the cave, lying or sitting on the mat beside the two basins of water and swatches of fresh soft material that Johann replaced each day. Whenever Beatrice tried to move about or do anything that required any effort, the baby pressed down painfully against her cervix. The extra weight also made her ungainly. Several times she stumbled on the rocks and nearly fell.

Johann had already built a cradle for the baby to sleep in, and Beatrice had sewn a couple of newborn outfits plus all the diapers the infant could possibly need. Together they designed and made a couple of backpacks to carry the baby after he or she was born. They were both ready. In her nightly prayers Beatrice told God that they had completed their preparations, and thanked Him for her good health throughout the pregnancy, but she stopped short of requesting outright an early birth.

When, according to her calculations, her due date had passed, Beatrice became impatient and anxious. "What are we going to do, Johann," she said one morning, "if the baby doesn't ever come? What if it just grows and grows and I never go into labor?"

"We certainly don't need to worry about that yet," he said. "If I remember correctly, first babies are often late."

She felt the first cramps of labor a few days later during breakfast. "What was that?" she said. Then her face brightened. "I think I felt my first contraction, Johann," Beatrice said excitedly. "I think it's beginning."

He helped her into the cave. Her labor proceeded slowly. Four hours later her water broke, but her contractions stayed more than five minutes apart until after it was dark.

As the hours passed Johann became concerned. Beatrice had been in continuous labor for thirteen hours. Each contraction was excruciatingly painful for her. Yet she didn't seem to be making much progress. The individual contractions remained separated by four minutes or more.

Her terrible cries at the peak of each contraction unnerved Johann. He did not know what to do to comfort her. It seemed that he had just mopped the sweat off her forehead and moistened her lips when another contraction would start.

"Oh, no, oh, Johann, here comes another one," Beatrice would say, tightening her grip on his hand. Her body would arch up, her face would contort, and she would take a few short breaths before the pain would overwhelm her. Then she would scream and Johann would fight against his own panic.

"I can't do it anymore. I just can't do it," Beatrice said several times between contractions.

"You can make it, darling," he reassured her. "Just a little more . . . The baby will be here soon."

Johann had positioned a torch just outside the entrance, but the light in the cave was still not very good. Every time Beatrice asked him to look at her and see if anything was different, Johann could not see well enough to tell her anything encouraging.

Several times during the long labor Beatrice prayed out loud. After one especially painful contraction, she again clasped her hands on her chest. "Dear God," she said, "please, please help me find the strength and courage to bring this baby into the world. I am afraid, dear God, and so very tired. Please let it be Thy will for my child to be born before too much longer."

The contractions became even more painful when the baby's head wedged its way into the birth canal. "I'm not big enough, Johann," Beatrice screamed desperately. "I can feel it. . . . I don't want to rip apart. You must cut me open."

"But how?" Johann said, becoming frantic. "I'm not a doctor. And I can't even see down there, it's too damn dark."

At her insistence he rushed out of the cave to the toolbox, over against a wall in the plaza, not far from the perpetual fire. Johann was so busy searching for the large knife, the needles, and the makeshift thread that he didn't see the burst of light behind him.

When he returned to the cave, the glowing light was hovering over Beatrice's body and another contraction was beginning. Johann did not have time to examine the ribbon. Rushing to follow Beatrice's instructions, he widened her opening by slitting the skin below the vagina. He wiped away the blood with the damp cloth in his other hand. The baby's head crowned immediately, filling the enlarged opening. With the next contraction, Maria spurted forward into Johann's hands. He wiped her off and cut through the umbilical cord.

"It's a girl," he said to Beatrice. "You have a beautiful baby girl." Maria began to cry.

"We have a baby girl," she said, correcting him. At the sound of the child's cry Beatrice's eyes filled up with tears of joy. "We have a baby girl," she repeated.

She took the newborn infant from Johann and laid her against her bare chest. "Thank you, oh thank you, God, for Maria," Beatrice said, looking up at the ribbon. Then she placed one of her nipples inside Maria's lips and rubbed it back and forth. After several seconds the child stopped crying and latched onto the nipple. At first she sucked intermittently, as if she wasn't certain that this was what she wanted to do. Beatrice remained calm. Each time that Maria let go of the nipple, she replaced it gently in the girl's mouth.

Once the child was nursing, and the placenta had been discharged, Johann tried to stitch Beatrice back together again. It was not an easy task —his hands were shaking and it was hard to see. Beatrice was also still bleeding heavily, making it difficult for him to concentrate on what he was doing.

At length, when he had only been able to complete four painful stitches in several minutes, Beatrice suggested that he make a large absorbent pad that could be tied around her hips and thighs. "Try to press the two sides of the incision together before you apply the pad," she said. "That should help it to heal."

When Johann was finished, he washed his hands in a fresh basin of water. Without warning, the ribbon abruptly flew out of the entrance to the cave and disappeared into the night. "Thank you," Beatrice shouted as it departed.

"Thank you," echoed Johann, who sat down wearily next to the new mother. Maria was now asleep on her chest.

"I'm sorry," Johann said, "that I wasn't better with the stitching business. . . . I didn't mean to hurt you."

"Don't be silly," Beatrice said with a radiant smile. "You were wonderful with everything. I couldn't have done it without you."

Johann smiled and took her hand. "Are you happy?" he said.

She looked down at Maria. "Supremely, divinely happy," she said.

19

Maria cried most of the night. The only time she was quiet was when she was nursing or taking a short nap. Johann was more tired when daylight came than he had been after the birth.

His first look at Beatrice frightened him. Her face was exceedingly pale, and her eyes were bloodshot. She told him that she assumed her weakness was normal, since it had been a long and arduous birth.

Johann held Maria in his arms several times and examined her carefully. She had a small patch of dark hair near the front of her head. Her skin color was dark like her father's, but her face and eyes reminded Johann of Beatrice.

"I think her eyes are going to be blue, like yours," Johann said.

Beatrice forced a wan smile. "When you have a chance," she then said, "will you make me a new pad? I feel as if this one's already completely soaked."

Johann put the crying Maria in his backpack and strapped it over his shoulders. He bent down next to Beatrice's mat and lifted the long robe she was wearing. What Johann saw sent chills through his body. Blood was everywhere—on the pad, on the robe, even all over the new mat to which he had moved her after the birth. Johann had made the pad extra thick, with many layers of material, thinking that he would not need to change it for a day or two. He had been wrong.

Being careful not to alarm Beatrice, he excused himself quietly and went to the storehouse cave. He was back with a new pad and a large tub of water within minutes.

"Are you sore?" Johann said to Beatrice as he gingerly unfastened the old pad.

"A little," she said.

Johann saw the problem as soon as he removed the pad. He wiped off the area around the incision, but it became bloody again within seconds. Rivulets of blood were still running out of Beatrice. He touched the area lightly with his fingers, trying fruitlessly to locate the sources of the blood. She winced with pain when he touched her.

"I'm sorry," Johann said, his mind struggling to absorb what he was seeing. *What should I tell her?* he thought next. *I don't want to scare her.*

"You're still bleeding," Johann said in a measured tone. "Do you know if that's normal, or what we should do to stop it?"

"I don't know, Johann," she said. "My crash course in childbirth during my training didn't go that far."

He cleaned Beatrice thoroughly and applied the new pad. She continued to bleed the entire time.

"I'm really tired, darling," she said when he was finished. "Do you mind if I take a nap after I feed Maria? Can you take care of her for an hour or two?"

"Gladly," Johann said, suppressing his fears.

With Maria sleeping in the pack on his back, Johann walked down to the beach next to their cave. He waded into the water up to his knees, just below the bottom of his shorts, and gazed out across the lake.

"And how will we explain all this to you, little Maria?" he said out loud. "Will you ever be able to comprehend fully that you, your mother, and your uncle Johann live on an island in the middle of a giant spherical spaceship, both of which were created by extraterrestrials, or God and His angels, for purposes completely unknown?"

He tried to look over his shoulder at the sleeping child. Johann laughed to himself. "You probably won't even care about all these mysteries for many years. Your world will be your mother, your uncle, the caves, the lake, the mountain—and it will be more than enough. You will have love and companionship. You will not need to know the answers to the infinite questions. . . . Not soon anyway."

Johann walked slowly down the beach. Maria stirred and began to cry softly. "You were conceived in pain and anger, my little Maria," he said. "But I promise you that your life will be altogether different."

He carefully unstrapped the backpack and placed it on the sand. Johann lifted Maria out of it and held her over his head, her legs dangling in the air. "I love you, Maria," he said, "and not just because I love your mother so much." He kissed her on the forehead. "I love you because you are a human being, a very special, unique creature in this universe, with unlimited potential for intellectual, emotional, and spiritual growth. . . . I also love you because I know that I will learn from you what it means to be unselfish."

Beatrice was still sleeping on her back when they returned to the cave. Johann could tell that she was dreaming; her eyelids were fluttering rapidly. Maria had fallen asleep again on the walk home. Being careful not to jostle the backpack too much, Johann sat down on his mat.

"Yes, I understand," Beatrice said in her sleep. "God's will be done." Tears formed in her eyes. "Thank you, thank you, Michael," she said. "Yes, I will tell him."

She was silent for no more than a minute before she opened her eyes. "Johann?" Beatrice said immediately.

"We are here, beside you," he said. "Maria is sleeping."

"Come over here, please," she said, a strange tone in her voice. "I have had a vision."

Balancing the child in the backpack, Johann crawled over next to Beatrice. She reached out and grabbed his hand. "St. Michael came to me in a dream, Johann," she said with a faraway look in her eyes. "He told me that God has called for me. . . . I am going to die."

Johann felt a sharp pain in his heart and then a weird tingle spread throughout his body. He tried to speak but could not. He barely managed to catch his breath.

Beatrice did not take her eyes off him. "Michael looked exactly as he did the last time I saw him in Italy," she continued, "before I went home for my father's funeral. Michael was smiling, Johann. Such a beautiful smile . . . He did not tell me exactly when I will die, but I know it will be very soon."

"*No!*" Johann said, shaking his head in protest. "You are not going to die. It cannot—"

Beatrice put her finger to his lips. "Please listen to me, Johann," she said. "I have a lot to tell you and there's not much time left."

She struggled to sit up. Johann hurriedly grabbed some pillows and put them behind her back. When he looked at her again, a trickle of blood was flowing out of her left nostril. The blood was pale red, like the rivulets Johann had seen earlier in the morning, not the deep, dark red blood that had accompanied the birth of Maria. He shuddered involuntarily and daubed at her face with a piece of moist material.

She thanked him softly and squeezed his hand. The blood continued to flow from her nose. "I know you will love Maria, Johann," she said. "I'm not in the least worried about that. And I'm certain you will raise her in a way that demonstrates to God, or your aliens, if you prefer, that we humans are capable of transcending our darker feelings. To be able and willing to love and care for the child of an enemy is a tribute to the best qualities in our species.

"But there are two things I want you to promise me now, Johann. First, that you will tell Maria the truth—about her mother, about her real father, and about how she came to be. How much of the truth you tell her at what point in her life, I leave that to your judgment. But, Johann, Maria deserves the truth."

Beatrice reached over with her other hand and wiped the tears off Johann's cheek. "Dear, dear Johann," she said with a weary smile. Then she took a deep breath and spoke again.

"I want you also to promise to tell Maria about God. That will be more difficult for you. I don't expect you to change what you believe, but I beg you to try to tell her as much as you can about her mother's religion, how it affected the way I lived, and what an integral part of my life it was. Teach her about prayer also, Johann." Beatrice leaned toward him with a great effort, her eyes full of passion. "Please, please, tell her what I felt and believed about Christ and St. Michael, and how important they were to me."

She put her head back against the pillows and closed her eyes for several seconds. She had started to bleed from the other nostril now. Johann wiped away the blood mechanically. He was speechless, overpowered by the intensity of his feelings.

Beatrice pulled herself up again and then lifted the necklace with the carved amulet over her head. "One more thing," she said, handing the necklace to Johann. "Please put this around Maria's neck now," she said. "When she is old enough, explain to her what it means."

She fell asleep immediately. Johann continued to sit beside her, his silent suffering unabated. He absentmindedly shifted the amulet from hand to hand. Occasionally he mopped her brow and cleaned up the blood on her face. He regularly checked her breathing and her pulse.

He noticed again how pale and gaunt she was. Suddenly, from deep inside him, a terrible cry burst forth. Tears flooded his eyes. *"No, no, no,"*

Johann heard himself say. He put his head against Beatrice's chest. "I promise," he said in a low voice.

Johann stayed beside Beatrice as long as he could bear it. There was no change in her condition. When he finally rose, he picked up the knife that he had used the night before. He walked outside the cave and sat on one of the large rocks in front of the fire.

He looked at the amulet. Carved on the wooden front was an image of a young man with curly hair, his arms raised to the heavens, standing on steps in front of a gigantic fire. Johann turned the amulet over. The back was empty. He took the knife and cut the word "Maria" into the wood.

The infant girl awakened a few minutes later and began to cry. Johann lifted her out of the confining backpack and tried to give her some water. She spat it out. Johann laid her down gently on a nearby mat and slid the necklace with the amulet over her head. The wooden carving rested against the front of her diaper.

"It's too big right now, Maria," he said. "But someday it will fit you perfectly."

Johann changed Maria's diaper while her wailing increased. He knew that she was hungry. He carried Maria into the cave where Beatrice was sleeping. Fluid was still flowing from both nostrils. This blood was even lighter in color than before.

"Darling," he said, touching her softly on the shoulder. "I'm sorry to bother you, but Maria's hungry."

Beatrice awakened quickly. Although she was paler than ever, she managed to smile. "I have seen angels, Johann," she said while she cradled the nursing Maria against her breasts. "And I have heard them sing. . . . Their voices are so beautiful, Johann, you would not believe it."

"I have heard an angel sing," Johann replied. "And I have seen one as well."

Beatrice cocked her head slightly sideways and gave Johann a curious look. Then a smile spread across her face. "Please kiss me, Johann," she said softly. "I would like to feel your lips upon mine one last time."

He leaned down and kissed her, being careful not to disturb Maria. While they were kissing, grief overpowered Johann. His body shook and he began to sob uncontrollably. The baby began to cry also. Beatrice tried to console them both. "There, there," she said. "Everything is going to be all right."

Johann stood up. He dried his eyes and blew his nose. Beatrice coughed twice, a light red fluid coming out of her mouth with the second cough. Johann sat down to wipe up the new blood on the front of her robe. *She is going to die*, he thought. He felt a hollow emptiness that was beyond sorrow.

20

B eatrice died before the daylight
was gone. Johann was beside her,
holding her hand. When he was
certain she was dead, he wrapped three large pieces of material completely around her body. Then he covered her face. He could not bear to
look at her, it caused him too much pain.

Johann did not have time to dwell on his grief. There was an infant
to care for. Maria cried throughout the last moments of her mother's life.
She was clearly hungry and Johann was already terrified that he would
not be able to figure out how to feed her.

Johann hurriedly squeezed juice out of three different kinds of fruit.
He tried to think of some way he could make a nipple that would allow
her to obtain the juice by sucking, but there were no materials similar to
rubber in the storehouse cave.

At first Johann held Maria in his arms and patiently let each kind of
juice fall, drop by drop, upon her lips. She wouldn't take the juice into
her mouth. Sometimes Maria would open her mouth wide enough that a
drop would actually fall inside, but always she would push it out with her
tongue and cry more heartily.

For over an hour he tried unsuccessfully to coax the infant girl to swallow some juice. He stopped for a few minutes, to settle his nerves, and then tried using a tiny spoon, as well as a little more force, to get Maria to drink the liquid. She fought him frantically, eventually falling asleep exhausted and still hungry.

Johann was beside himself with both frustration and grief. He left Maria sleeping peacefully on a mat and raced down to the beach. The moment his feet touched the sand, he began to yell. He shouted as loud as he possibly could, yelling nothing but noise with as much energy as he could manage, for almost a full minute. Then, after pausing to draw a few breaths, Johann gazed at the dark ceiling above his head.

"Can you hear me up there, aliens, or God, or whoever is in charge of this place?" he said. "I hope so, because I have a few things to say. And you'd damn well better listen.

"I promised Beatrice, my angel whom you stole from me, that I would care for her daughter, Maria. I intend to fulfill my promise. But there's one serious problem, one insurmountable obstacle that I can't overcome. Infant humans need breast milk, provided by their mothers. The males of our species, like me, are not supplied with any of this milk that can nurture an infant. . . . Are you following this? Do you understand what I'm saying?"

Johann stopped a moment to gather his thoughts. He was shaking. "I have nothing to feed her," he yelled. "I have no way of making anything that is like breast milk. If Maria does not eat, then she, too, will die.

"So what am I supposed to do? Watch her die a painful death from starvation? I will not do it. I know how terrible it is to be starving, and I will not subject an innocent infant to that horror. If you want us to keep living, then you must help us now. Otherwise, I will have no choice except to kill us both. I will not let Maria starve to death."

Nothing changed in the dark ceiling above him. Nevertheless, Johann had the distinct feeling that someone or something was listening to him.

"And one more thing, while I have your attention," he shouted. "Just what the hell is going on here anyway? What is this place all about? If there is some grand plan or purpose in all this, why can't I know something about it?"

Johann remained on the beach, still staring at the ceiling, for five minutes. Then he heard Maria crying. He dashed back to the cave area, arriving just as the ribbon of light departed. He picked up Maria and tried to comfort her.

"Did that ribbon scare you?" he said in a soft voice. "Don't worry, Uncle Johann is here to protect you."

He walked completely around the plaza, trying to determine if anything had changed. Then Johann went into the storehouse cave. There was nothing new there either.

Johann's excitement at seeing the ribbon had begun to fade when he returned to the front of the cave he had shared with Beatrice. He debated about whether or not he should go in; he knew even seeing the outline of Beatrice's body would trigger another bout of grief. Nevertheless, he cautiously entered the cave.

Over against the far wall, illuminated by the flickering firelight, was an object Johann had never seen before. As he drew closer he saw that it looked like a woman's brassiere, white in color with two red circles surrounding tiny nipples at the end of the breast cups. Johann picked it up. The object was surprisingly heavy. He shook it. There was something inside the breast cups.

Johann temporarily placed the crying Maria on a mat beside her dead mother and pulled the strange red-and-white object over his head. It fit perfectly. He crossed the cave and picked up Maria. Rubbing one of the little nipples against her lips, as he had seen Beatrice do soon after Maria's birth, Johann induced the baby girl to put her mouth around it. A few seconds later she was sucking contentedly.

"Well, I'll be damned," he said, smiling at the bizarre scene taking place in his hands. He took his eyes off Maria and glanced at the top of the cave. "Thanks again," Johann said, "whoever you are."

When Maria fell asleep after her meal, Johann went to the storehouse cave and retrieved a large shovel. Out in the flat area where Beatrice and he had farmed their grains, he began to dig a deep hole. It was already very late in the night, but Johann wanted to bury Beatrice before daylight.

Once the grave was large enough, he returned to the cave and hoisted Beatrice's body, still completely wrapped in material, over his shoulder. He noticed that two more of the red-and-white, brassiere-shaped objects were now lying against the cave wall. Johann smiled to himself briefly and then carried Beatrice's body to the grave site.

Johann thought it was important for Maria to be present at her mother's burial, even though he knew that she would never remember it. He set Beatrice's body down beside the hole and returned for the child. When he awakened Maria, she began to cry from hunger. He picked up one of the new nursing brassieres and carried it with him to the grave site.

He sat down on the ground, leaning against the trunk of a small nearby tree, and fed Maria. While she was eating, Johann held her tiny hand and she uttered her first soft coos.

Before Maria was finished, two ribbons of light came over the mountain on Johann's right, stopping to hover five meters or so above the empty grave. They frightened the little girl. She temporarily stopped nursing, but Johann was able to reassure her with his voice while he changed her from one nipple to the other. Soon Maria was busily suckling again, oblivious to the bright ribbons of light in the sky above them.

She fell asleep while she was nursing on the second breast. Johann laid her down gently on the ground and stood up. For a long time he stared at the pair of ribbons, following individual, dancing particles as they sparkled inside the illuminated structure. As they had years before in the Tiergarten in Berlin, the particles floated until they reached the side of the formation, where some unseen force inverted their momentum and sent them back toward the center of the structure.

Johann's heart grew heavy as he approached Beatrice's body. He felt the waves of grief beginning again. He fell to the ground beside her.

"I loved you so much, Beatrice," he said out loud. "I don't know how I'm going to live without you."

Johann put his head down against the material surrounding her body and began to cry. He had been in that position no more than fifteen seconds when he heard a sound that caused his hair to stand on end and goose bumps to form immediately on both arms.

"No more talk of darkness . . . Forget these wide-eyed fears. . . . I'm here, nothing can harm you. . . . My love will warm and calm you."

It was her voice! There was no question about it. Johann bolted upright, terrified, and started looking around him. He glanced up in the air, where the song seemed to be originating, and saw that the two ribbons had coalesced and changed their shape. They had formed into a perfect image of Beatrice's face, and it was her mouth that was singing the song.

"Say you'll love me, every waking moment. . . ."

Johann listened, dazzled and transfixed, tears streaming down his face. The sound was perfect, unbelievable, miraculous.

"Love me, that's all I ask of you," the vision of Beatrice sang the final words of the song. A few seconds later her face was gone and the two ribbons were again hovering over the grave site.

"Thank you," Johann said, waving at the ribbons. "That was wonderful."

He picked up Beatrice's body and dropped it into the grave. Johann shoveled in a little dirt, then some more. Soon her body was completely covered. At that point he turned around and noticed that Maria was awake. The child wasn't crying. She was simply staring at the ribbons.

Johann remembered his promise to Beatrice and realized that he had not said a prayer over her body. He picked up Maria and held her up closer to the ribbons.

"Some people believe," he said to Maria, "that if you've been a good person in this life, then when you die you join God and all the other good people in a place called heaven. Your mother believed that. And she was a very, very good person, so she may be in heaven with God right now.

"It's customary, when someone dies who is a Christian like your mother, for a prayer to be said at the time of their burial. This prayer usually asks God to receive into heaven the soul of the person who has just died. Now your uncle Johann is not very experienced at this prayer business, but I'm going to give it a try."

Johann took a deep breath and kissed Maria, who was still staring at the ribbons, on the forehead. "Dear God," he began. Then he stopped. He didn't know what to say, and he was certain that as soon as he mentioned Beatrice's name, he was going to burst into tears again.

At that moment the two bright ribbons suddenly merged, rapidly forming themselves into a huge sphere. The sphere was white everywhere except for a pair of shaded bands around the equator, two shaded circles that looked like eyes in the northern hemisphere, and a shaded hood on the top. The sparkling particles had become an unmistakable representation of the spacecraft in which Johann and Maria were living.

While the sphere was forming, a dozen more long, bright ribbons zoomed into view, coming from all directions and filling the sky with light. They temporarily arranged themselves in two neat rows just to the right of the sphere.

Johann and Maria both squinted, protecting their eyes from the profusion of light. What was surprising was that the child did not cry. She seemed fascinated by the light show above her.

The new ribbons broke their array after a minute or so and changed into a set of concentric circles, like a target, with a large bright light at the center, and tiny, twinkling lights moving in orbits around the circles. The sphere that resembled their spacecraft shrank rapidly, becoming a tiny twinkling light itself before moving into the target and occupying a position very close to the light fourth in distance from the center.

The formation remained static for over a minute. The twinkling lights moved slowly in their orbits. Awestruck, Johann suddenly recognized what he was seeing.

The tiny twinkle representing their spacecraft moved slowly away from Mars. It drifted out past the orbits of Jupiter and Saturn. Then, suddenly, its velocity away from the central source increased markedly. The entire target pattern in the sky above Johann and Maria shrank until it was only a pinpoint of light. Other stars showed up in the sky above them as their tiny twinkle left the solar system behind.

Johann glanced at Maria in his arms. "I might not be understanding this properly," he said to her, "but I think we're being told that we're going to be interstellar explorers." His mind was already asking a thousand questions. Johann turned his eyes back to the display above him just as their tiny twinkle approached a new light source, one rapidly growing larger and brighter.

The target pattern around this second star contained fourteen orbiting planets. The twinkle representing their spherical spaceship headed directly for the light fourth nearest to the new sun. This special planet grew in size until it was by far the most dominant object in the sky above Johann and Maria. When their twinkle appeared to land on its surface, the sparkling particles created a huge new panoramic scene out of light and shade. Among the patterns Johann thought he could see the waves of an ocean crashing on a beach, a forest of trees whose leaves were being blown by a strong wind, and tall, snowcapped mountains. Two majestic full moons shone in the planet's dark sky.

"That must be where we are going," the amazed Johann said to the child in his arms.

Her face reflected the changing lights in the sky. When he turned around, all the particles and ribbons had again formed into a sphere that resembled their spacecraft, except this time the brilliant sphere was enormous, and looked as if it were solid. It filled almost the entire sky above the island. As the sphere moved slowly closer to Johann and Maria, its equatorial bands parted and a long, white, helical ramp descended, touching the ground only a few meters from where they were. At the top of the ramp, in the dark gap between the hemispheres, a glowing white figure stood. Johann nearly fainted when he recognized Beatrice in her robe and headpiece.

"A-ve Ma-ri-i-a," the vision of Beatrice sang. The magnificent voice was unquestionably hers. It was joined after a few bars by a chorus of other, equally astonishing voices, coming from everywhere in the sky. The sound was beautiful, divine. Johann was enraptured.

When the song was over, Beatrice took three steps down the ramp. "Come with us, Brother Johann," he heard her voice say. "We will help you take care of Maria."

Johann was trembling so much he was afraid he would drop the child. Every part of his body was experiencing an extraordinary, intense tingle.

"Come up the ramp, Brother Johann," the voice said. "We are waiting for you."

Johann looked up at the vision of Beatrice, standing above him with a radiant smile and outstretched arms, and felt a peace unlike any he had ever known. He walked over to the bottom of the ramp. Maria cried softly, and he comforted her.

After one cautious step, Johann raced up the helical ramp. "I'm coming," he said excitedly, his face reflecting the light from above.

Here ends *Bright Messengers.*
This story will conclude in *Double Full Moon Night.*

ABOUT THE AUTHOR

Gentry Lee has been chief engineer on Project Galileo, director of science planning for NASA's Viking mission to Mars, and partner with Carl Sagan in the design, development and implementation of the television series *Cosmos*. He is co-author of *Rama II, The Garden of Rama* and *Rama Revealed*. He is currently at work on a novel that will conclude the story begun in *Bright Messengers*, entitled *Double Full Moon Night*, to be published by Bantam Books in 1996.